Where Seagulls Soar

By the same author

The Stonecutter's Daughter
A Handful of Ashes
Beyond the Plough
A Dorset Girl

Born and brought up in Parkstone in Dorset, Janet Woods now lives in Perth, Western Australia, although she returns to her English roots on a regular basis to visit family and friends.

Where Seagulls Soar

Janet Woods

POCKET
BOOKS

LONDON • SYDNEY • NEW YORK • TORONTO

First published in Great Britain by Simon & Schuster, 2006
This edition first published by Pocket Books, 2006
An imprint of Simon & Schuster UK
A CBS COMPANY

1 3 5 7 9 10 8 6 4 2

Simon & Schuster UK Ltd
1st Floor
222 Gray's Inn Road
London WC1X 8HB

www.simonandschuster.co.uk

Simon & Schuster Australia
Sydney

A CIP catalogue record for this book
is available from the British Library

ISBN 9781471150968

Typeset in Monotype Baskerville by M Rules
Printed and bound in Great Britain
by CPI Group (UK) Ltd, Croydon, CR0 4YY

For my granddaughters
Abbie Woods
and
Kate Larsen,
with love.

*

The author is happy to receive feedback from readers via her website
http://members.iinet.net.au/~woods
or by post
PO Box 2099
Kardinya 6163
Western Australia

My thanks to historian Stuart Morris for his wonderful book,
PORTLAND
An Illustrated History
first published by The Dovecote Press in 1985.

An invaluable source of information for this, and my previous novel,
The Stonecutter's Daughter

1

'With this ring I thee wed, with my body I thee worship, and with all my worldly goods I thee endow. In the name of the Father and of the Son, and of the Holy Ghost. Amen.'

The ring Alexander Morcant slipped on to Joanna Darsham's finger was fashioned from a nugget of gold unearthed from the Victorian gold fields by a convict jeweller.

'Those whom God hath joined together may no man put asunder.'

Thaddeus Scott, master of the clipper *Joanna Rose* – en route from Australia to England with a cargo of wool, 65,000 ounces of gold, seventy-three passengers and mail destined for families left behind in Great Britain – closed his Bible and smiled at the couple standing before him, both of them dear to his heart.

'Best you tie the knot properly in a church when we go ashore, just to make sure it's legal.'

Later, Thaddeus wrote an entry in the ship's log:

Thursday 15th April 1858. Weather fair with following winds. Progress 203 miles. Able Seaman Philip Divers charged with falling asleep when on watch. First offence.

Reprimanded and docked two days' pay. Joanna Darsham and Alexander Morcant exchanged marriage vows before several of the ship's passengers and some of the crew. The marriage conducted by Thaddeus Scott, Master of the Joanna Rose. *Solemnized over the King James Bible and entered therein. May God bless their union.*

It had been a fast voyage so far. The anchor having been hove up eight weeks previously, the *Joanna Rose* had been towed by steamer to open water, where a wind from the north west had filled her sails and seen 260 nautical miles pass under her keel and turn into wake by the following midday.

The shores of England were now only three weeks away, the equator crossing having been celebrated just the day before. Alex had proposed to Joanna during the revelries, and in front of everyone. He had suggested this unorthodox and romantic ceremony himself, knowing it would appeal to her adventurous nature.

Joanna couldn't stop smiling, and Alex couldn't prevent himself from smiling back at her. 'Now I've made an honest woman of you I can claim spousal rights without the damned passengers gazing upon my overtures towards you with disapproval,' he whispered against her ear.

She'd noticed that Alex was getting used to the ship's motion now, though compared to her master, Thaddeus Scott, who'd spent his entire life at sea, he was a beginner, for he still had to cling to whatever was handy each time the ship canted, and he wove from side to side when walking, as if he'd imbibed too much liquor.

The nimble-footed Joanna was much better at adjusting to the ship's movement, but even she could be taken unawares. Alex laughed when a jolt pitched her forward into his arms and she said, 'I swear, the sea's got lumps in it today.'

'You'd think that a ship which had been named after you would treat you more gently,' Alex said.

Blue eyes blazing with happiness she gazed up at him. 'Ah, but she threw me in the right direction, for this is exactly where I want to be.'

'Is it now?'

Just then young Toby began to kick up a ruckus. Alex released her and stooped to pluck their son from the arms of the Chinaman, Chin Lee, who'd been holding him during the ceremony.

Toby had been born three months earlier in Melbourne, on the eighth day of January. Named Tobias Alexander, he'd quickly become Toby.

Father and son were alike with their dark hair and liquid dark eyes. For that reason alone, nobody would ever be able to dispute the relationship of the pair, though they might speculate about the boy's sudden appearance.

Joanna would never forget the look on Alex's face when he'd first set eyes on his son, and, although Alex hadn't said so at the time, Joanna knew the existence of the boy had given him someone to provide a future for. It would be a close relationship, a far cry from the lonely childhood Alex himself had experienced, which had been reinforced by the shock disclosure that he was the son of his mother's affair, and not the absent father he'd always looked up to.

'I must take Toby below and feed him,' she said, refusing the celebratory tot of rum Thaddeus Scott laughingly offered her. It was a brew that was reputed to strip varnish from the mast.

Alex declined it too, saying casually, 'I'll come with you and collect your luggage, for you'll both be with me in the stateroom tonight.'

Later, when they were alone in their luxurious cabin together, Alex said, 'Do you realize you've kept me waiting eight weeks?'

'But we'd agreed to wait until we reached England before we wed.'

'Damn it, Joanna, you never needed a ring on your finger before. We've already produced a son between us to prove it.'

'I wanted the second one I conceived to be legitimate. Besides, it's not my fault you were sick for the first few weeks at sea.'

Alex shuddered. 'Don't remind me. Thaddeus had no sympathy at all. He said I'd get over it, and as head of the Darsham and Morcant Shipping Company I should have gone to sea earlier with my brother Oliver, to learn the ropes.' He brushed a finger gently down the side of her face. 'So why did you change your mind about waiting until we got back to England?'

'Why?' She grinned. 'How could I reject such a romantic proposal. And if you kiss me again, you will know exactly why. I just cannot resist you, Alex

Morcant. We'll cause a scandal as it is when the existence of Toby is made known. And it will be me who's whispered about, not you.'

He smiled at that. 'I'll tell them we were secretly married at Gretna Green.'

'No more falsehoods, Alex. They're too hard to maintain. Will you change the name of the shipping company now?'

Her blue eyes drowned in the darkness of his gaze. 'Is that what *you* want, Joanna Rose?'

'Yes. I talked it over with my father, and that's what he wants too. He said that the less people who are reminded of the Darsham name, the more comfortable he'll feel.'

'But when you married him neither of you knew of the blood tie between you.'

'All the same, I can't help feeling that I ruined his life. If he and I hadn't accidentally met he'd still be running the company. He gave up everything he loved to save my reputation.'

'And his own, and the future of the company.' Alex kissed the sadness from her lips. 'You needn't feel guilty, Joanna. Despite the problems it caused, finding you brought Tobias Darsham great joy. It was just a pity that you wed. Luckily, he realized the mistake before any harm was done. Your father knows what he's doing, he always has. He's enjoying the challenge of his new life.'

'And he and Jane are expecting their first child.' A smile spread across her face at the thought of having a brother or sister after a lifetime of being an only child. 'He deserves to be happy, Alex.'

'Aye, he does. He told me that learning of your survival was something he'd treasure for the rest of his life. One day we'll make this trip again, I promise. I can't turn my back on Tobias, or Gabriel Tremayne, as he now calls himself. He was always there for me as a child. I love the man as much as I love his daughter.'

'Do you truly love me, Alex?'

'What a thing to ask me on our wedding day,' he said, his voice gruff. 'Would I have wed you otherwise?'

She wondered. If circumstances had been different, with their different backgrounds, would he have considered her a suitable wife for a successful businessman?

She dismissed the lingering doubt that she'd manoeuvred Alex into following her to Australia, and the thought that the existence of Toby had tightened the noose around him. 'I'll be a good wife to you, Alex. I promise.'

She was sitting on the bunk, which was fitted against the wall. He traced a fingertip across the breasts so recently exploited by their son. One by one he opened the buttons on her bodice to expose the camisole beneath. She quivered when his lips grazed over the material, seeking the swollen nubs where their son had recently suckled.

He gazed down at her, unsure. 'Are you positive you're fully recovered from Toby's birth?'

Her arms snaked around his neck and she gave an exasperated snort. 'Are you going to talk all night, Alex Morcant?'

His eyes met hers for a moment, his lips twitched and his hands slid under her buttocks. Lifting her from the bunk he held her against him. Her long legs wound around his waist. How enticing she was. He surged up to connect with her warmth, his need for her making him as eager as a youth as he pressed against the front of his linens. 'I imagine not.'

She was laughing now, covering his face with kisses. He had a job lowering his trousers, and they were trapped around his ankles, so he teetered backwards on to the bunk with her on top of him, his head in an awkward position against the bulkhead.

She stood up to pull his ankles free, throwing aside his shoes at the same time, then she bent forward and gently kissed him where it ached the most.

'Oh, God,' he groaned, feeling his control falter as she slipped from her skirt and tossed her bodice and camisole aside.

'Do you like what you see?' she cooed, parading in a red satin corselette, frothy petticoat and high buttoned boots.

'You're exquisite.'

She turned her back on him, looked over her shoulder and demanded, 'Loosen my laces, then.'

He grinned at her tease. 'Damn it, Joanna. I'm going to have you wearing them, first.'

'Feeling frisky, are you?' she whispered. 'Lay down then, else you'll break your neck.'

He was surprised by the request, but complied, sliding down on to the pillows. Under her flaming petticoat she wore nothing.

Kneeling across his lap she gently lowered herself on to him, covering him in red taffeta. Her thighs trapped his hips, her hands were planted either side of his head and her glorious dark hair tumbled in a fragrant curtain about their heads. Bare buttocks cushioned themselves on his thighs, her leather boots grazed against his knees.

Joanna's sleepy blue eyes were an inch from his, her mouth a curve of desire. 'I adore you, Alex Morcant.'

He liked her uninhibited ways and found himself sinking into the mesmerizing depth of those eyes – losing himself in her, in the intimate togetherness of them.

Reaching up he took her face between his palms and, bringing her mouth down to his, he drowned in the sea of her sensuality as she gently tightened her muscles around him.

As they neared England the weather worsened and they sailed into a series of squalls.

To Alex, the ship became a highly unstable creature. Her stern rose and fell like a whore's backside. Her prow cut into the water and scooped it up. It rolled along her deck at knee height to pour over the legs of the unsuspecting, then it cascaded out of the scuppers. Spray was thrown sky high, to run off the snapping sails in every direction, usually the one he was standing in. To make matters worse, the horizon canted this way and that, so his perspective was constantly shifting.

Her master, thinking nothing of this ungainly behaviour from his elegant ship, calmly smoked his smelly tobacco and threw incomprehensible orders to the crew, who swarmed over the rigging, seemingly with complete disregard for their safety.

Sails were run down lines, others just as quickly run up, so there was a constant kaleidoscope of movement.

Although Alex had determined not to succumb to seasickness again, the *Joanna Rose* had other ideas. Much to his chagrin, he was overtaken by the misery of it. Even though he wasn't actually sick, he was constantly queasy and was forced to remain in his cabin. As he hugged his stomach, Alex swore he'd never go to sea again unless desperation drove him to it, whatever he'd promised Joanna.

Thankfully, Toby had inherited Joanna's stomach, for he was affected not at all. He bawled loudly and forcefully when he was hungry or uncomfortable, but otherwise was sunny natured.

At least he had Joanna to care for him now, Alex told himself, and he wouldn't have to live in that big house, alone with his own thoughts. But he envied the fact that his wife seemed to thrive on, even enjoy, the uneven motion of the ocean, as if she were a piece of seaweed floating on the currents.

She looked after him, washing the sweat from his pallid face, or coaxing him to eat a little. She tempted him with morsels of food, soft words and sympathy in her eyes. When they made love she was passionate and innovative, and he couldn't get enough of her.

But when Joanna came to the cabin one day, her eyes sparkling and raindrops glistening in her hair, to bring the news, 'England is on the horizon, come and see,' Alex instantly began to feel better.

'Thank God,' he croaked. 'I hate living on this damned ship, even though I now own the company. I worked hard enough to get it, though, and thanks to you it's now mine. And I've got myself a wife into the bargain.' The pride and arrogance in his words suddenly vanished as he said pathetically, 'I'll be so pleased to have solid ground under my feet again.'

She giggled and held his head against her breasts. 'My poor darling man, I know you will. But you'll change your mind about the ship when we go ashore, and you'll look on the voyage as an adventure.'

'I shouldn't be at all surprised.' He felt quite comfortable being held like this and wondered if his own mother had put him to her breast to feed, as Joanna did with Toby.

A shudder ran through him at the thought. But no, Clara Nash hadn't been a motherly type. He'd spent most of his childhood with Tobias Darsham and his mother, unless his late father had been home from sea. Despite their mother and son relationship, Alex had never felt close to Clara, and neither did he hold any respect for her. Surprise filled him, for he realized that he didn't even like his mother.

He turned his head to kiss the pert little bud that had suddenly ripened against his ear.

Joanna laughed and combed her fingers through his hair, relaxing his scalp. 'You're beginning to feel better, aren't you?'

'By the second.' His mouth moved a little further up. 'How do you feel?'

In the cradle next to the bunk, Toby woke. His legs

rose in the air, taking the blanket with them. They quivered in a stretch for a moment, then the blanket fell off and covered his face.

'In demand,' she said, grinning as Toby's head turned from one side to the other, as if wondering where the light had gone. He began to punch at the air and voice his annoyance at the event.

Alex gave a rueful smile and rolled off the bunk.

Toby's indignant squawk became a chuckle when his father uncovered him. Smothered in Alex's kisses and convulsed in paroxysms of giggles, the beautiful and robust little boy who so resembled Alex was brought to the bunk and placed in Joanna's arms. Alex was going to be a good father to him.

She frowned when Alex paled and an expression of pain appeared on his his face.

'Do you feel unwell again?'

'It's nothing much. It comes now and again. I'll be all right once I get ashore.'

And that was only a day away.

Up on deck with the rest of the passengers, who were beginning to disembark, Alex glanced towards the building where the company's offices were situated.

Joanna grinned. 'I suppose you're going straight there.'

'I'll see you and Toby home first.'

They said farewell to Thaddeus, who had completed his last voyage and was about to retire from the company.

'Who's taking my place as master?' he said gruffly.

'Edward Staines. He'll be the senior master.'

'She should have gone to your brother. One thing's for sure, though, we'd never make a seaman out of you however hard you try.'

Alex grinned and the pair shook hands. 'I know. As for Oliver, it's not my fault he went haring off to America after a woman's skirt. Come to the office in the morning. I'll hand over your severance pay and bonuses.' Alex also intended to present the company's senior captain with a gold watch. He just hoped that his manager, Henry Wetherall, had remembered to order it, for Thaddeus would be off down to Poole as soon as he could, to visit Charlotte Darsham, the woman he intended to wed.

Joanna hugged the captain. 'You'll let me know when the wedding is, won't you, Thaddeus?'

'Maybe, but maybe not. The pair of us are too old for fuss, so don't be surprised if your grandmother has become Mrs Scott the next time you see her, for I expect she'll have things all arranged.'

'You know, I'll never forgive the pair of you if you marry without me there.'

'I reckon you will, lass,' he said calmly, 'for you're not a fussing woman yourself. Now, stop hugging me and go off home with your husband. He's tapping his foot, which means he's impatient to get started. I'll send your luggage up on a cart.'

After six months' absence, Joanna and Alex's house at Southwark had a neglected look to it. The garden was overgrown, though threaded through with May flowers. The windows were dusty, but the blackthorn was in bloom and the heavenly scent of the massed cream blossoms was heady to the senses.

Their housekeeper came scurrying through from the back when they entered the dusty hall.

'Where are the servants, Mrs Bates?' Alex asked her, frowning as he glanced around.

'Your mother . . . Mrs Nash dismissed them. She said they weren't needed.'

'Did she now.' Alex's mouth tightened. 'And your husband. Where's he?'

'Bates up and died a month or so ago. He caught the cholera, he did, and it took him off real quick.' A tear or two tracked down her cheeks. 'I'm glad you're home, sir, and you, Mrs Darsham.'

Toby was looking around his new surroundings with interest. Mrs Bates eyed him uncertainly, then gazed from one to the other, as if not quite knowing what to say.

'I'm Mrs Morcant now,' Joanna told her gently. 'And this is our son, Tobias Alexander, though we call him Toby. I'm so sorry to hear about your husband.'

Mrs Bates gave a deep sigh as she dried her eyes on the corner of her apron. 'Bates was older than me, but a good man for all that. I'm going to miss him. It will be nice to have a child running around the house, though.'

She looked gratified when Toby decided to bestow his best smile on her, revealing the pair of sharp teeth he'd grown in his bottom jaw on the journey. 'He's a dear little lad,' she said, her mouth stretching into a smile. 'And so like you, Mr Morcant. Shall I fetch some refreshment to the drawing room?'

Alex shook his head. 'Not for me, Mrs Bates, thank you. I'm going to the office. We'll do something about the servant problem tomorrow.'

'And I must sort out a nursery for Toby. He needs a sleep.'

'Use the room next to mine . . . *ours*.' He grinned and kissed her cheek in a slightly perfunctory manner, as if he were impatient to be off. 'I'll be going then. I'll leave you ladies to sort things out and will see you at dinner, I expect.'

'Don't work too hard, Alex. You look tired.'

'I can't promise that, my love. I'm sure I'll be fine in a day or two.'

'Right,' Joanna said, turning to Mrs Bates after the door had shut behind him 'Where does my husband sleep?'

'In the room next to the one you used to occupy.' A faraway expression filled her eyes. 'It's the room Mr Darsham used to use when he was still alive, poor man. Such a nice gentleman, he was, even though he wouldn't take any nonsense from anybody. Still, you'd know that, you being his widow.'

Mr Darsham's widow, once his wife! It was odd imagining herself as ever being his wife, when Joanna now knew the man was her father. That ill-fated yet innocent liaison seemed a long time ago now – as did her upbringing on the isle of Portland as another couple's daughter.

Mr Darsham is still alive, did you but know it, Joanna thought, saddened because her father had been obliged to abandon his home and identity for her sake.

Only he lives in Australia and is calling himself Gabriel Tremayne, these days.

It was lunchtime. The offices of the Darsham and Morcant Shipping Company were almost deserted except for one or two familiar faces – clerks who greeted Alex with welcoming smiles.

He nodded pleasantly to them as he walked through. It smelled familiar, and he felt at home here, in charge of himself.

Alex hadn't expected to find his mother waiting for him in his office.

The arrangement of the lines on Clara Nash's face made her look dissatisfied and unpleasant, a true reflection of her meddlesome nature.

As the door closed, he gazed at her, saying sharply, 'Why are you here?'

Clara was wearing a powder-blue gown that matched her eyes, a colour too young and fresh for a woman of her mature years. Her skin had a yellowish tone to it.

'Is that any way to greet me? Come, Alexander, give your mother a kiss.'

His mouth stretched into a thin line. 'I'd sooner kiss a viper, Mother. I believe you've been interfering with my household staff.'

'Actually, I've saved you considerable money in wages. Servants are easy to come by, you can hire others.'

'It's my money, not yours. Now, why are you here?'

She turned and walked towards the window. 'I saw

the ship come in, and I wondered if you'd be on it. I heard you went running after that girl?'

'*That girl* is called Joanna. What of it?'

'What of it?' She turned, her eyes blazing. 'Don't be a fool, Alexander. The girl is an opportunist. First it was Tobias Darsham, now it's you. I hope you've left her in Australia.'

'Why would I do that when I went all that way to bring her home?' he said. 'Joanna and I were married on the ship on the way home.' Swallowing the urge to strangle his mother, Alex smiled. 'You might as well know. Joanna has borne me a son. His name is Toby. Now let me see, doesn't that make you a grandmother?'

'You fool,' she scorned. 'You could have done much better than marry some stupid island girl. She didn't even have the sense to hang on to what she inherited from Tobias. Instead, she used it to buy you with.'

He didn't allow her to see how badly that stung, but crossed to the door and opened it. 'I've got work to do . . . goodbye, Mother.'

She didn't budge, just stared at him. 'Aren't you going to ask after your sisters?'

He'd forgotten the twins in his rush of anger, and sighed. 'Of course. How are Irene and Lydia?'

'Tiresome. They're resisting my efforts to find them husbands. They said you told them they didn't have to marry the men I chose for them.'

He smiled at the thought that his half-sisters had found the guts to resist his formidable mother. 'For God's sake, they don't have to wed yet. The pair are only sixteen. Allow them to grow up first.'

'They need to be found husbands of means.'

His eyes sharpened. 'Has something happened to the inheritance from their father, then?'

She shrugged. 'Entertaining in London is costly, especially for three of us.'

And his mother was excessive in every way. 'I'll invite them to stay when Joanna and I are settled back in. Have you heard from Oliver recently?'

'He wrote to you saying his marriage is in trouble. The fool invested his money in some get-rich-quick scheme, and that girl he married, along with her father, has absconded with it, leaving him to shoulder the blame. I took out a private loan to bail him out of trouble and repay the sum owing. The bank has since dropped the fraud charges against him. You can read about it for yourself. Oliver's letter is on the drawing-room table at your house.'

Alex frowned as he stated the obvious. 'You opened my letter and read it?'

She shrugged. 'Oliver is my son, why shouldn't I read it?'

'Because it was addressed to me.'

'If I hadn't read it, he'd be in a prison cell now.'

Alex hated complimenting her, but swallowed his pride to say stiffly, 'It was good of you to raise the money.'

'All it took was a signature. I used the *Charlotte May* and the *Clara Jane* as security. Lord Durrington witnessed it and Henry Wetherall endorsed it.'

Anger surged, then ebbed, leaving him drained. He paled as the pain in his side came back to nag at him and was hard pushed not to double over and retch. Sweat coated his forehead. 'You signed over half of the company ships? To whom?'

'Barnard Charsford.'

'That usurer! Are you insane? You didn't have the authority to do that. How much was the loan, for God's sake?'

'Considerable. But it didn't take long to persuade Henry Wetherall that the signature I had was genuine. Your signature is easy to copy and, after all, it was all for the company's good.'

'Like hell! There were other ways of raising the money than compound a fraud with another fraud. I could have you and Durrington arrested.'

'Don't be tiresome, Alexander. It would simply be your word against ours. Lord Durrington is a peer. He witnessed your signature and backdated it. And Barnard Charsford is a friend of ours, who will swear on oath that you lodged the document yourself, before you went gallivanting off after that girl.'

'Joanna is my wife, and I'd have you talk of her with more respect.'

'We will never have respect for each other, since we are sworn enemies.' She gave a small, tight smile and her eyes suddenly became as cold and as hard as ice. 'May I remind you that Oliver used to own half of this company before your *wife* persuaded him to sell it cheaply to her. Do you ever wonder how she managed that? Perhaps she spread her legs for him, in the same way she did for you.'

Clara gave a light laugh when his fists clenched. 'You

didn't imagine I'd bailed Oliver out with my own money, did you? I haven't got that much left. The cards have proved unlucky, of late.'

'I did think for a moment that he might have roused some motherly spark in you. I should have known better. And you can only apply your own low standards to the situation, since I never knew who my father was until recently. Certainly not the man you were married to at the time. But don't imagine Joanna is the same. She has more love and compassion in her little finger than you have in your entire body. Now, get out.'

And his voice was so hard that Clara left rather quickly.

Later, Alex heard Henry Wetherall come in. His manager came straight to his office, a wry smile on his face.

'I'm sorry, Mr Morcant. I wanted to be here when you arrived. There's something I need to discuss urgently with you, regarding a loan taken out against the company assets.'

'I've already talked to my mother, Henry. She forged my signature on the document.'

Henry looked shocked. 'Mrs Nash said the loan was authorized by you. I'm sorry. If I'd known I'd have never endorsed it, for the interest rate was extremely high. However, I was led to understand it was an emergency.'

Alex shrugged. 'I believe it was. Don't feel bad about it, Henry, it's not your fault. But I'd be obliged if you kept what I've told you to yourself, for there were extenuating circumstances. I'd have done something similar under the circumstances, I expect, though I'd probably have sold the *Nightingale* rather than take on such a loan.'

'I did suggest that, but the guarantor wouldn't consider it, because of her age. It was the clipper ships, or nothing. They threatened to impound them, otherwise. At least the *Joanna Rose* is free of debt. I insisted that the ships were insured for the sum required, and was able to prove it, so *Joanna Rose* wasn't included as collateral.'

'Aye, there's that, but you can be sure they'll seize her too if the need arises. We'll have to try and keep her at sea, with a quick turnaround every time she's in port, Henry. Fetch the books. It looks as though there's going to be some hard work in front of me before the company's solvent again.'

'You could take in a partner, sir, cut your losses. I know Lord Durrington is interested in purchasing a share of the company.'

Alex tried to keep a sour look from appearing on his face. Durrington was the man who'd fathered him, but Alex detested him, and knew he'd never publicly acknowledge him as his father.

'I could, except for one thing.' He smiled broadly at his manager. 'I married Joanna Darsham, and my wife has recently presented me with a healthy son. So, you see, I have his future to prepare for. That future doesn't include Lord Durrington, believe me.'

2

May had ticked over into a flawless June when Joanna threw the door wide to allow Tilda Lind inside the house.

She stared hard at her childhood companion and friend, amazed by the change in her over the previous year or so. The last time they'd met, Tilda had still been building up her strength after being reduced to the point of starvation and degradation by her family. Joanna could hardly believe this was the same woman.

Tilda had always been considered plain, with her brown, heavy-lidded eyes and angular face. Now she was glowing. Apart from her trim figure, Tilda's other claim to beauty was a glossy sweep of brown hair, now almost hidden under her dark blue bonnet.

'Oh, Tilda, you look wonderful.' Joanna took her in a crushing hug. 'I'm so happy to see you again.'

The pair clung to each other, their eyes moist, Joanna remembering a time when they'd only had each other to rely on.

Eventually, Tilda pushed her to arm's length and looked at her severely. 'I should be angry with you for going off to Melbourne without a word. The continent of Australia is so far away and you missed my wedding.'

'There was a good reason for it, Tilda, one I couldn't tell you about at the time.' And she still couldn't tell Tilda all of the story, for the fewer the people who knew the truth, the better. 'Alex told me all about your wedding. Being married to the Reverend David Lind obviously agrees with you.'

Tilda's smile was the most spontaneous and engaging that Joanna had ever seen from her friend.

She gazed from her to the grave-faced child clinging to Tilda's skirt. The girl was named Grace and was a child born to Tilda's elder sister. Mary Rushmore had died from a disease brought about by plying her trade as a prostitute on the streets, when Grace was about four years of age. It was Grace's good luck that Tilda had been in a position to offer the girl a home.

Joanna shuddered at the thought of being forced to live such a life. She was thankful she'd had someone to turn to when she'd been in trouble. Neither she nor Tilda would have survived without help.

'Hello, Gracie,' she said. Smiling at the little girl, Joanna held out the rag doll she'd made for her on the ship. She'd just been stitching the eyes when she'd seen her visitors come up the path. 'I don't think you'll remember me. You look very pretty.' Grace *was* pretty, with her dark curls and glowing brown eyes.

Smoothing her hands down over her smock, the girl gazed up at Tilda.

'It's all right, dear,' Tilda said. 'This is my best friend, Joanna. Remember, I told you all about her?'

Grace gave her a shy smile as she took the doll and held it tight against her. 'Joanna went away on a ship,' she whispered and hid her face in Tilda's skirt.

'Now I'm back home again, and we'll soon become reacquainted. Come through to the drawing room and I'll fetch some refreshment for us, since Mrs Bates has gone to the market. I've got a surprise for you.'

The most pressing, of course, being the existence of Toby, who had managed to roll off his rug, and who looked pleased with himself as he sucked noisily on his fist.

'You renegade,' she scolded, 'You'll get dirty on the floorboards.'

Tilda sucked in a slightly shocked breath. 'A baby! Joanna, is he yours?'

'Of course he's mine. Because you married a clergyman, don't you dare go all prissy on me, Tilda. Toby is Alex Morcant's son. We were married on board ship by Thaddeus Scott on the way home.' She picked Toby up, cuddling him close, enjoying his milky baby smell and falling in love with him a little bit more. 'Isn't he the most beautiful baby in the world?'

Grace detached herself from Tilda's side and came to inspect him. Toby stared solemnly at her for a moment or two, then he grinned at her.

'The baby likes me,' Grace exclaimed, smiling at Tilda.

'Of course he likes you, and so do I.' Joanna was unable to hide her smile as she stooped to kiss the little girl's cheek. Handing her son to Tilda to mind, Joanna took Grace by the hand. 'Come through to the kitchen with me while I make some tea. You can carry the napkins, then open the door for me while I bring the tray through. I hope you like muffins, because my housekeeper has made some. And there's some gooseberry conserve to spread on them.'

While they were gone, Tilda gazed at Joanna's son, wondering why her initial reaction had been disapproval. She couldn't help but smile at him, though. 'Your mama is full of surprises, young Toby, but I imagine you've learned that already. And how handsome you are, the very image of your papa. I have a surprise for Joanna, too, but not one as great as you are to me.'

When the pair came back, Tilda noted that Joanna had drawn Grace out in the short time they'd spent in the kitchen. Grace was usually cautious of strangers, but she was chattering away about anything that came into her head. Joanna listened intently to her, any comment she made complimentary to Grace. Joanna had always possessed a knack of making people feel better about themselves.

'David and I are going back to Portland to live,' Tilda said when they'd settled down to having tea.

'But why?'

'The Reverend Prosper Quinby has died, and the parish has been offered to David. Besides, we're tired of living in two small rooms when we could live in the house David's uncle left him. We're not impoverished, so why should we choose to live amongst the poor and act as if we are? That's no way to earn respect. I don't want to spend my life serving the poor, and giving away everything I own. David is so gentle, and they take advantage of his good nature.'

Tilda sounded a trifle disenchanted with playing the role of good samaritan.

'What about . . . *your family*?'

Tilda drew in a deep breath. 'David and I have talked the situation over. I think I can cope with them. They can't hurt me now, since my position will place me above them. I certainly wouldn't socialize with them after what they did to me.'

'I do wish you wouldn't go, Tilda. I know I'm being selfish, but you're the only friend I have in London. Oh, I know I've neglected you over the past few weeks, but it wasn't deliberate. I've been trying to get the house and garden back in order, and time has just flown by.'

'I meant to contact you sooner, too, but David expects me to help him carry out his duties. Both of us are married now and have to consider our husbands' wishes first.'

'Mine always makes sure I do that,' Joanna said darkly. 'Alex is as arrogant as ever and does as he pleases. I'll miss you.'

'No doubt we'll visit each other from time to time.'

'Well, on my first visit we'd better arrange for Alex and I to wed properly. Thaddeus Scott wasn't sure whether a ship's marriage was legal or not.'

'Joanna!' Tilda cried out. 'Why are you always so headstrong? You should have waited until you'd stepped ashore, and then arranged things properly.'

'I had Toby to consider. Alex and I became lovers long before I came to London. Remember in Poole when he took me out for the day and caused an argument between my . . . self and Charlotte Darsham. We were caught in the rain, and made love in a barn in the straw. It was so exciting.'

Tilda couldn't stop a scandalized expression from spreading across her normally placid features. 'It's not polite to talk about matters which should be kept private.'

'Oh, will you stop that, Tilda. Have you forgotten we were brought up on an island where it's natural to lie with a man and prove your fertility before marriage?'

'We're not in Portland now. David told me the custom was passed down by the pagans. Did you deliberately become pregnant so Alex would marry you?'

'Indeed not, since I didn't know I was with child until a few weeks after the ship sailed. But I needed to find out whether Alex wanted me for the company, or whether he truly loved me. So I put everything I owned in his name and sailed away.'

Trust Joanna to come up with a plan so outrageous, thought Tilda. She had to admit, though, it was a romantic notion. 'What if Alex hadn't gone after you?'

Joanna shrugged. 'As you know, Alex was raised with the expectation that he'd inherit the company. Tobias Darsham had made that clear to him. Alex had worked towards that end all his life. He deserved to have the company, Tilda. I wanted him to have it.'

'Knowing pride would bring him running after you, and knowing a man with any honour would have had no option.'

When Joanna's cheeks flamed, Tilda knew it was

caused by anger rather than shame. 'That thought didn't enter my head, Tilda Lind. I was hoping he would, I admit, but only because I was in love with him.'

'But what if he hadn't followed you?'

'I would have made a life for myself and Toby in Australia. I liked it there. It's not as primitive as people would have you believe. Melbourne is a fine city. The air is clean and there's room to move. Believe it or not, I didn't know about Toby when I left England.' Her mouth pulled into a smile and her voice softened. 'You should have seen Alex's face when he set eyes on his son for the first time. He looked so proud I nearly cried. He adores Toby.'

'You would have stayed there all by yourself . . . for ever?'

'Oh I wasn't by myself. Tob—' Joanna bit down on her lip. 'Toby apart, there was someone there I'd known before.'

'Someone you'd known before? Is it a man?'

Joanna gave a small, secretive grin. 'It is a man, but before you give me another lecture allow me to tell you about him. His name is Gabriel Tremayne, and I would trust him with my life, and the life of my son. He and his wife have a hardware and ironmongery establishment. I could have worked there and lived in their house. They're a respectable couple. Jane helped deliver Toby when he was born, and she's expecting a baby herself now.'

A little knot of jealousy formed in Tilda's chest. 'I see. I've never heard you mention Gabriel Tremayne before. Where did you meet him?'

Joanna's smile faded as she said gently. 'You're turning this visit into an inquisition. Be happy for me, Tilda? I love Alex. That's all that matters.'

Tilda's heart melted. If it hadn't been for Joanna, with her indomitable spirit and her courage, Tilda would have starved to death by now. 'Of course I'm happy for you. I must be turning into a shrew.'

'You'd better not, else I'll cut off your tail. Bring David over for dinner with us before you leave for Portland. I'm sure Alex will want to see you both.'

Toby began to fret and Joanna picked him up. 'I'll have to put him to the breast. You won't mind, will you?'

'I'm not quite as prissy as that, yet.' But Tilda was forced to swallow her envy as the child was suckled, for she longed for an infant of her own.

Alex had been working too hard – now he was greeting his brother, who'd unexpectedly turned up. Oliver had just stepped ashore from a ship he'd worked his passage on, and had come straight to the office.

Oliver Morcant was not the same man who'd gone to America to marry his sweetheart, Susannah. He was shabby and downtrodden and his face was seamed. With a growth of unkempt grey beard on his chin, he looked older than his forty years.

The two men hugged each other. Alex said, 'You'll come and stay with me, won't you?'

'I promised to spend time with our mother when I arrived, since she raised the money to bail me out.'

Alex raised an eyebrow. 'You can't go to see her

looking like a tramp. There's some clothing at home that used to belonged to Tobias. I was supposed to get rid of it, but I didn't have the heart. You can have it if you like. And you can take a bath and have a shave, at least.'

Oliver nodded, shamefaced. 'I never thought I'd come to this. God knows how I'll ever pay mother back. All I have is what I stand up in.'

'You might as well know, Oliver. That wasn't mother's money. She raised a loan by forging my signature and using company ships as security while I was absent.' Alex tried to prevent the worry he felt from creeping into his voice. 'The Morcant Shipping Company is struggling to stay afloat at the moment. Our cargo will be servicing the loan for years to come, and I'm working round the clock to keep on top of it. As it is, I've had to lay men off, and put the *Nightingale* up for sale. I'll be surprised if we get a decent offer, though. We're in a bit of a slump, and the banks are being tight-fisted.'

Pouring himself a small brandy, Oliver turned to gaze out of the window into the dying afternoon light. The ships' masts cast long pointing shadows across a river of pleated pewter. He said sadly, 'I was going to ask you for a job.'

'I can't afford to take you on,' Alex said bluntly.

There was desperation in Oliver's eyes when he turned. 'I'll work for nothing to start paying the loan back. I'll do anything, even crew.'

'Stop it, Oliver. You're too highly qualified for that.'

'How do you think I got home from America?'

Oliver said bitterly. 'The tub I was on leaked like a sieve, the rigging was rotten and the captain was a whisky-soaked, foul-mouthed scab. He spent the entire crossing humiliating me. When a man needs a meal in his stomach, he can't afford to indulge in pride.'

Alex flung an arm around Oliver's shoulder in a sympathetic squeeze. 'Aye, you're right, but you're my brother, and everything I have is yours to share. You'll feel more human when you've had a bath and dinner. Come home with me and meet my son. Mother won't know you're home yet, so you can stay the night. Tomorrow, I'll ask around and see what there is going in the way of employment.'

'You have a wife and son now?' Oliver smiled for the first time. 'No, don't tell me. I'll wager it's the Darsham widow. Anyone could see that she'd grabbed you by the balls.'

'And hung on to them, for that hasn't changed. First, though, she got it into her head to take off for Melbourne, and left me dangling on a string. I had to go after her on the *Joanna Rose*.

'You actually went to sea, and on the Australia run?' The laugh Oliver gave was laced with incredulity. 'How did Thaddeus take it, having you on board?'

'He loved every moment of it, especially when it got rough. I'm not ashamed to admit that I turned out to be as lousy a sailor as I thought I'd be. Thaddeus has retired from the company now. The *Joanna Rose* has been offered to Edward Staines, else you could have had command of her. *Charlotte May* is on the Australia run as well, now. At the moment she's heading southward with the former first mate at the helm. When she returns, we'll see how she's placed for officers.'

Oliver tried to hide his disappointment as he nodded, making light of Alex's news. 'You weren't tempted to return to naval school and earn your ticket after the Australian run, then?'

'Hell no! Joanna would make a better seaman then me. I wasn't born with saltwater instead of blood in my veins, like you. I puked my guts up most of the way to Australia and most of the way back. To be honest, I still haven't settled back to normal, and I've been on dry land for over a week. My stomach still hurts, and sometimes I suffer from queasiness.'

'It'll pass.'

The brothers smiled fondly at each other and a lump formed in Alex's throat as he said gruffly, 'It's damned good to see you again, Oliver. I'm sorry your marriage didn't turn out to be what you expected.'

'I was a fool to trust Susannah, or her father. I sincerely hope you fare better.'

'If nothing else, I have a feeling my life with Joanna will be damned interesting.'

With that said, the pair of them headed for the door, jostling each other like young boys, to cover the emotion of the moment.

Joanna flew from the drawing room into the hall, and threw herself into Alex's arms. 'You're home early! How wonderful.' She soundly kissed him, then gazed up at him, her eyes sparkling, to scold, 'How tired you look, my love. You're working much too hard . . . Oh! There's somebody with you.'

Flustered, Joanna smoothed her skirts and, trying not to grin at being observed by a stranger in a moment of intimacy with her husband, straightened up. But then he moved out of the shadows. She'd met this man on occasion before, even though he looked ill-used at the moment with his shabby clothes and beard. 'It's Captain Morcant, isn't it?'

He gave a rather self-effacing smile. 'Nobody's addressed me that formally for quite a while. Please call me Oliver.'

'I'm surprised you recognized him,' Alex drawled. 'He needs a bath and some clean clothing. I thought he could have those suits and shirts Tobias left behind.'

'You make it sound as though Tobias went off on an adventure instead of—' Oliver suddenly looked awkward. 'I'm sorry, Joanna, I'd forgotten you were once married to Tobias. I hope I didn't distress you.'

Alex exchanged a glance with her. She said, 'You don't have to apologize, Oliver. You knew Tobias Darsham much longer than I did, so it's natural that you'd talk about him with Alex. I don't mind, since it helps me know him a little better, too. And perhaps his departure from our midst *was* an adventure for him.'

'Of course.'

'Now, I'll go and sort out those clothes. They're stored in the closet of one of the spare bedrooms. I'll put some kettles and buckets of water on to boil. You can help me carry them up when they're hot enough, Alex.'

'I'll do that,' Oliver said, 'I can't have you waiting on me.'

'Nonsense.' Halfway across the hall she remembered her brother-in-law's troubles and turned back to give him a hug. 'I'm so pleased you've come to us, Oliver. You must stay for a while. It won't take me long to prepare a room.'

'That's kind of you, Joanna. I'll stay tonight, at least. Thank you.'

Alex said, 'Where's Toby?'

'In the kitchen with Mrs Bates. He fell asleep in his carriage, but I imagine he's awake by now, and probably being a pest.'

'I'll get him. You go into the drawing room and help yourself to a drink, Oliver. I'll be with you in a moment to show off my son.'

Our son, thought Joanna.

Following after her, Alex slipped his arm around her waist and turned her round to face him when they reached the privacy of a shadowy little passage to the kitchen. There, he kissed her. 'Thanks for not minding about Oliver.'

'Why should I mind? I like him.' She touched her finger against his cheek. 'How bad is the situation with the company?'

'It's a nightmare. Some of our oldest clients have got wind of what's been going on, and are wary about shipping with us. I can't afford to lower the rates, this time, and our rivals are beginning to move in.'

'We could sell the house, buy something smaller.'

'It wouldn't be enough.'

'Well, I have my mother's jewellery to sell. It's in the safe keeping of my grandmother.'

'That's yours, Joanna. I'd never dream of asking you to sell it. And we must remember to guard our tongues in front of Oliver, for he knows nothing about your true identity, nor that your father is still alive.'

'Can't you trust him, then?'

'I think so, but he might let it slip out, and the fewer people who know about former events, the better. I wouldn't like my mother to find out.'

'Neither would I.' Joanna refrained from making further comment but her mouth tightened. Previous encounters had left Joanna despising Clara Nash, and the feeling was reciprocated. She hoped they would never have to meet again.

At dinner Oliver Morcant seemed more like the man Joanna remembered. Although still pleasant, however, there was a general air of disillusionment about him now. She was sorry he'd been taken advantage of, since he was a kind man who didn't deserve it.

When the men began to discuss the London sewerage system over dinner, Joanna grinned, recalling being chastised by her grandmother for doing the very same thing.

The men had forgotten her presence, she thought, and she enjoyed watching the brotherly interaction between them and listening to them talk.

'If they hadn't ruled that houses had to be drained

into sewers, the river wouldn't be in the state it's in now,' Alex said. 'From the sewer pipes, the effluent is conveyed straight into it.'

'Are you saying the cesspits were a better method of disposal?' Oliver answered.

'Certainly not. When the river backed up, they flooded into the houses.'

Joanna transferred her gaze from the apple pie she was serving to the two men. 'That's because the streets are below the level of the river at high tide. The problem will no longer exist when Joseph Bazalgette's new pumping system is completed. Would you like custard on your pie, Oliver?'

When both men stared at her in astonishment, Joanna shrugged. 'I read it in an engineering journal, somewhere.' Exasperated she gazed from one brother to the other. 'Custard anyone?'

'Thank you.' Oliver exchanged a grin with Alexander. 'Perhaps we should change the conversation.'

Her eyes widened in consternation. 'Forgive me, I found it interesting, and didn't intend to interrupt.'

'It isn't a subject for the dinner table, anyway,' Alex said casually. 'And women certainly shouldn't concern themselves with such things.'

'Pish! Why shouldn't they be concerned when their children die from diseases that could be prevented by better hygiene?'

'Like Oliver said, we should change the conversation. What have you been up to, today, Joanna?'

She bit down on her retort. 'Tilda visited. We went for a walk with the children. She and David will be leaving in a few days time, going back to Portland. I'll miss her.'

'No doubt you'll make other friends.'

Joanna doubted it. She didn't really fit into London's merchant class, and resented the loss of freedom that came with it. Being caged in crinoline hoops was a stupid fashion, and she didn't like having to watch every word she uttered, lest she offend. There was a false gentility about the women she'd met here. Although they might disapprove or complain about the dirt, they wouldn't roll up their sleeves and help clean it up, preferring to tread daintily through it, their noses in the air, pretending it didn't exist.

Joanna had thought she'd never want to go back to Portland, but a twinge of envy surfaced for Tilda. At least the air was clean there. Life on the island had been uncomplicated on the whole, and distance had made her regard it with a certain nostalgia. Here in London she had no place to stand and stare, to dream.

If she'd been given the choice she would have stayed in Melbourne, for there was a sense of adventure and purpose there that she'd never come across anywhere else. However, once Alex had made his intentions clear there had been no choice for herself or her son but to return. Toby needed to grow up knowing his father, and Alex's life was here, in this dirty city, doing what he'd been brought up to do. As if he'd never had a choice, her husband lived and breathed the Morcant Shipping Company. It was his heart and his soul. Sometimes, Joanna feared his intensity and sense of purpose, for it excluded her.

Oliver's voice jerked her out of her reverie. 'You have a beautiful son, Joanna.'

'He favours Alex,' she said, and her husband turned his dark eyes her way, to smile in a manner that melted her heart and banished her small moment of melancholy.

'I'm taking Oliver along to my club this evening,' he said.

'You look as though you need to rest.'

Alex had eaten very little and there were lines of strain about his mouth. Brushing away her concerns he kissed the top of her head as he rose from the table, saying a trifle curtly, 'Stop fussing, Joanna, and don't bother waiting up for us.'

An arrow of hurt drove into her heart.

The club was crowded with engineers. The talk was mostly about the virtues of steam power, with the same arguments being batted back and forth. Normally, Alex would have joined in, but he had Oliver in tow, and there was only one ship owner there.

'You're a wind-ship sailor,' the ship owner said to Oliver. 'Get yourself an engineering degree and I might have something for you. If I hear of an opening anywhere I'll let Alex know.' His eyes shifted. 'It might serve you better to try another port.'

Oliver looked disappointed.

Alexander shrugged. He was feeling restless and needed to release some tension after a week behind his desk poring over figures and trying to make sense of them. 'It's early days yet. Let's go to the theatre. There's a new revue being touted at the *Pantheon*. I wouldn't mind seeing it.'

'I can't afford theatres.'

Alex took some money from his pocket book and stuffed it in Oliver's pocket. 'Now you can.'

They were late for the start, but managed to get a table near the stage, and bought an overpriced bottle of wine. The night was balmy, and the room so filled with noise and smoke it was a wonder the actresses could be heard, or the dancers find the breath needed to fuel their energetic efforts.

In the interval the roof was wound back to loud cheers. Debris showered the patrons, but the night was filled with stars. There were several catcalls until a row of dancers trooped on to the stage, holding huge fans made of feathers.

In the mood to unwind, Alex put his fingers to his lips and gave a strident whistle. Sally O'Leary was in the line-up, a woman whose favours he'd enjoyed in the past. Sally peeled off her glove, came to the front of the stage and dropped it into his lap. 'Who's your friend, Alex?'

'My brother, Captain Oliver Morcant.'

She dropped the other glove in the grinning Oliver's lap and blew him a kiss. 'Get Alex to bring you backstage afterwards, sailor. We're having a party.'

She'd hardly got back in line when the orchestra began to play. In unison, the girls slowly brought their fans up their bodies, exposing a length of naked thigh.

A roar of approval went through the audience. As

the dancers began to twist and turn, feathers floated through the air.

Alex hadn't intended to be unfaithful to Joanna. He'd drunk too much over the course of the show, and he consumed more at the backstage party.

Oliver had disappeared into the dim recesses of the theatre with Sally O'Leary and Alex had been led to one of the private boxes with a pert piece of goods called Bridie Johnson.

Dressed in nothing but a flimsy robe over a spangled but grubby corset and chemise, Bridie gave him a wide and inviting smile, then proceeded to divest him of his coat and trousers. She threw his garments over the chair. Her hands cupped him. 'There's a nice big boy,' she cooed, and leaned forward to kiss him.

Her robe fell open, her body smelled of sweat and musk.

'I'm married,' he said defensively and rather ineffectually, for the pertinent part of him responded to her attention and surged into her hands. Even so, he didn't find the woman particularly attractive.

Placing a finger over his lips she said, 'Shush . . . I won't tell anybody.'

She was an expert at arousing a man, and was willing to be used. Her price was modest. Alex thought of Joanna, clean smelling, willing and responsive, of the way her teasing kisses turned into passion. Fuelled by the image of her, he used Bridie with reckless abandon, but fell short at the end. He felt none of the ecstasy he enjoyed with Joanna, just the relief of releasing his immediate need. He felt disgust when she bucked and squealed noisily in faked delight.

He paid the girl what she asked and, feeling soiled, declined a second ride.

'I have a baby at home to support,' she told him as she went in search of a better prospect.

The pain in his guts began to gnaw at him. 'So have I,' he muttered guiltily.

He dressed and waited for Oliver in the foyer, where several posters advertised coming attractions. Zanders Cavara, the mesmerist from Cuba, with his wild eyes and even wilder hair, seemed to display a tendency towards lunacy. There was an Indian maiden called Little Lone Star, with her famous dancing stallion, Cherokee. Straight from the American West.

Turning his head to one side, Alex examined the underside of the horse more closely. When Oliver turned up, looking happy and relaxed, Alex asked for a second opinion. 'You've been to America. Does that horse look like a stallion to you?'

'Not yet.' Oliver took the stump of a pencil from his pocket, licked the end and industriously added the required appendage. 'There, that's better.'

'Very realistic, if rather on the large side.'

'I used myself as a model,' Oliver said with studied modesty.

Alex punched him on the arm and grinned. 'Let's go home.' He was beginning to wonder how he'd face Joanna in the morning.

The brothers made their way home unsteadily, their footsteps lit by a white moon riding high in the sky. Alex was obliged to heave into the gutter a couple of times.

'Cheap booze and loose women,' Oliver said sympathetically, thumping him on the back as if trying to empty him out. 'There's nothing worse for a man, but if you'd gone to sea at an early age you'd have learned how to handle both.'

The pain in Alex's stomach grew worse. As his hands clutched over the site of it, he promised himself he'd do what Joanna had told him to do – visit a doctor in the morning.

When they arrived home the house was in darkness, except for an oil lamp, which had been left burning low in the hall. He gave it to Oliver to hold.

Somehow, they managed to make it upstairs without making an unholy noise.

Entering Toby's room, Alex gazed down at his son. The boy's sweet, innocent face was washed by moonlight. Such a beautiful gift Joanna had given him. For some reason he felt like crying, but his mouth trembled into a smile.

Joanna was asleep in the room next door. Her hair was spread all about her on the pillow. Gently, he touched her cheek, wishing there had been no tonight.

He felt ashamed of himself. If he got in beside her she would turn into his arms. He would make love to her gently, so her body was unresisting and open to him, and she wouldn't wake until they reached the moment of climax.

When the pain clawed savagely at him, he was hard pushed not to gasp. Perspiration soaked through him. He could smell the cheap scent of the dancer on his body, and knew he wouldn't touch Joanna again until he'd bathed.

Not that he could have touched her, with the severe pain he was suffering at that moment. Leaving the bedroom he crept into the room across the hall, the one Charlotte Darsham always used when she visited the Southwark house. The bed had a mattress, but no sheets.

There was a blanket in a cupboard. Divesting himself of his clothes, he pulled it over himself and lay down. Drawing up his knees he hugged his aching stomach.

On the river, a steam tug hooted.

Alex was nearly asleep when he thought he heard someone groan.

He opened his eyes. A charcoal dawn was creeping through the gap between the curtains. He lay in the dampness of his own sweat, in so much pain that the intensity of it scared him. His body was on fire.

'Joanna,' he whispered, because that was all he could do, even though his body was screaming.

There was another groan, louder this time. It was coming from his own mouth. He began to sink into unconsciousness, yet could still feel the agony of it. He didn't know how long it went on, the agony and the groaning.

There came the patter of bare feet.

'Alex! Oh, my dearest. How long have you been like this! Oliver, come quickly. Help me!'

Oliver's voice. 'What's wrong with him?'

'I don't know.' A cool hand was laid against his brow.

'He's burning up. Mrs Bates, fetch me a bowl of water and a flannel. Oliver, go and tell the doctor to come as fast as he's able.'

She sat there, bathing his face, his beautiful Joanna, her blue eyes filled with anxiety. Nobody had ever loved him before, and he'd let her down.

'I'm sorry, Joanna,' he muttered. 'You won't stop loving me, will you?'

'Hush, Alex. How could I ever stop loving you? Sleep if you can. I'll look after you until you're better.'

He heard Toby rattling the bars on his cot. Soon, his son would roar for his breakfast.

Alex sensed rather than saw Joanna leave. The initial demanding roar turned into chuckles. After a moment came the reassuring rustle of her skirt. He opened his eyes. Seated in a chair next to the bed, she suckled their child at her breast.

Her blue gaze was fixed on him, though. Tears trembled on her dark lashes. She looked beautiful with their son's head held against her breast. Joanna and Toby were the best thing that had ever happened in his life.

'I love you, Joanna,' he whispered, and tried to smile.

3

The doctor had purged Alex with a dose of laxative, and had given him a generous amount of laudanum to ease his pain.

That had been the night before. He'd slept a little during the night, but the effects of the treatment had exhausted him. Grey faced, he lay in his own sweat, too tired to do anything but whimper.

Worried almost to the point of sickness herself, Joanna fed Toby and gave him to Mrs Bates to mind. As she bathed her husband's heated body with lukewarm water to cool him, she noticed his stomach was swollen and rigid. His teeth suddenly began to chatter, his body to shiver violently.

She abandoned the task of bathing him, instead tucking the blanket back up under his chin. Soon he broke out in a sweat again and began to mutter.

'I've sent Oliver to fetch the doctor again, my love,' she told him, but Alex didn't respond to her voice.

The doctor was a long time coming.

Her observation on his tardiness was treated sternly. 'A man can't work on an empty stomach. I was eating

my breakfast,' he said in an entirely disapproving manner. He looked comfortably full with his stomach bulging under his frock coat. A streak of grease smeared his collar.

'Damn your breakfast,' she said under her breath as he got on with his examination.

'As I feared, peritonitis,' the doctor informed her a few moments later. 'His appendix has probably ruptured.'

'Will my husband be all right?'

He avoided her eyes and rocked back and forth on his heels. For some reason he consulted his watch, sliding the heavy gold timepiece from his waistcoat pocket and flicking open the cover with his thumb. He closed it with a click. 'I've done all I can for him.'

Which was exactly nothing, she thought.

'He needs a surgeon now, I'm afraid.'

He was afraid. A thrill of fear ran through her as she exchanged a glance with Oliver. 'He's in so much pain already. Is it necessary? I don't want him to be hurt.'

The doctor said loftily, 'My dear woman, he will be under anaesthesia. I assure you, your husband won't feel any pain during the procedure, for he'll be in a deep sleep. Come to the hospital tomorrow. It should be over by then.'

Joanna was vaguely aware that anaesthesia was a state of unconsciousness brought about by the inhalation of poisonous vapours. If it would ease Alex's pain during the operation she was thankful.

A horse-drawn ambulance came an hour later. Two men carried Alex down the stairs on a stretcher. He groaned at even the slightest jolt. Stooping to kiss his

cheek, she wondered if he could hear her when she said, 'I'll be praying for you, my love.'

Oliver put a comforting arm around her shoulder, pulling her to one side as the door closed behind the men. 'I'll go to the hospital after I've told my mother the news. I'll stay with him.'

'Would you also tell the company lawyer and Henry Wetherall?' she asked him.

He nodded. 'Try not to worry too much, Joanna. Alex is strong. I'll let you know how he is.'

'Thank you. I'd appreciate it.'

As the vehicle trundled off, Joanna burst into tears. An uneasy and frightening thought had surfaced that Alex had disappeared from her life for ever.

It was a long day. Toby picked up on her edginess and became fractious. Outside, the weather turned gloomy, the sky was low with clouds, the day damp and drizzly.

Joanna tried to keep herself busy. She cleaned the drawing room and hall, scrubbing with a stiff brush, so her hands became red and blistered, her knees sore. As she wandered through the house that had once belonged to her father, cleaning the dull mirrors and removing the dust, she remembered to pray for Alex. But there was resentment in her that somebody with his strength could suddenly become so weak.

'What sort of God makes people suffer for no reason?' she shouted out in frustration, and her voice woke Toby from his nap. She snuggled her son against her, wondering if Alex was being punished for the sin of conceiving their beloved son out of wedlock.

Oliver hadn't returned by evening. Joanna had forgotten she'd invited Tilda and David Lind to dinner. When she opened the door to their knock later in the day, her face crumpled as she said, 'Oh, it's you.'

'Whatever is the matter, Joanna?' Tilda said immediately.

'It's Alex. He's ill. They took him to the hospital this morning and I'm worried sick. The doctor said he's suffering from something called peritonitis. He told me to visit the hospital in the morning, but it's so hard waiting. I forgot you were coming to dinner. What must you think of me?'

Tilda took her in her arms. 'Hush, Joanna. I'll think of you as I always have, that you're my friend and I love you. I'll talk to Mrs Bates, see what's in the larder, for you need to eat something yourself. Where's Toby?'

'I've fed him and put him to bed. There's a pot of soup in the kitchen, I think. Oh, I can't think of food. I'm too worried about Alex.'

David's smile had faded. 'I'll go to the hospital and see what I can find out, if that will help.'

He was back within an hour, his face so grave that Joanna knew that her worst nightmare had come true.

'Alex is dead, isn't he?' she said dully.

'I'm afraid so, my dear. I'm so sorry to be the bearer of bad news.'

The world seemed to retreat from her. The tick of the clock sounded loud, like Alex's heartbeat against her ear after they made love. *Dead! Dead!* She couldn't believe it.'

She sank into the nearest chair, stunned. 'Are you sure, David?'

'I met Captain Morcant coming from the hospital. He was about to come to break the news to you. He said his brother didn't wake up after the operation. Alex passed away peacefully in his sleep with the captain at his side.'

'Alex wouldn't have gone peacefully, he had too much to live for,' she said fiercely. 'He would have fought death every inch of the way. It was that damned anaesthesia the doctor talked about. They must have given him too much.'

'My dear, something like that would be hard to prove given the circumstances.'

Joanna felt suddenly defeated. A tremor started in her hands as her mind told her to accept the truth. Soon, she was trembling all over. Tears filled her eyes and poured over her face. Her throat felt swollen and thick, as if she were drowning in her own tears.

The clock ticked, louder and louder. '*Stop it! Stop it!*' Picking up the nearest object she hurled it at the mantelpiece. The face glass smashed into pieces and the noise ceased. 'It shouldn't tick. It reminds me I'm still alive, and right at this moment I wish I wasn't,' she said irrationally.

Tilda stood up when Toby began to cry, his voice coming from a great distance. 'I'll fetch him. David, give Joanna a brandy to help calm her.'

David Lind went to the sideboard, coming back with a small amount in the glass. 'Here, Joanna, drink this. It will help. Try not to feel too bitter. It was God's will.'

'What sort of God takes a husband from his loving

wife, a father from his son?' She took the brandy and gazed at it, thinking, was this anaesthesia to stop her becoming hysterical? She swallowed it in one gulp, then began to cough, for it tasted like poison.

David looked embarrassed as he handed her his handkerchief. 'I'm so sorry, my dear, I should have warned you. We'll stay in London for the funeral, of course,' he said.

'Of course. Thank you for your support, David. I appreciate it.'

All went quiet, since they'd ran out of things to say to each other.

Tilda appeared with Toby, his face streaked with tears. Toby held out his arms to her, and gave her Alex's smile, a mixture of confidence and mischief. Alex was in the depths of his eyes, looking out at her. There was never a son so like his father. Joanna took the boy in her arms, hugging him protectively. Thank goodness he was too young to know anything untoward had occurred. He fell asleep on her shoulder. She must remember that Alex lived on in her son.

She gazed over him at David. 'I want to see Alex. Will you take me?'

'Is it wise, Joanna?'

She shrugged. 'Wise or not, I need to see him. Besides, arrangements will have to be made.'

David nodded. 'The morning might be best.'

There was an urgency in her, a note of anger in her voice. 'I want to go *now*.'

Tilda exchanged a glance with her husband and nodded. 'I'll look after Toby while you're gone.'

'I'll put him to bed first, he should sleep until morning.'

Joanna kissed her son's downy cheek as she lowered him into his cot. 'We only have each other now, my darling boy, but your papa will be watching over us and we'll survive.'

Ten minutes later she set off through the darkening streets with David. Now and again a stench rose from the river, like the mouth of a dog gusting a foul breath. Mist thickened on the surface of the water.

The rain had stopped, but the air was damp. The hem of Joanna's skirt dragged forlornly through the puddles.

'The air in Portland will smell fresh after London, I expect,' she said suddenly, attacked by a strong sense of nostalgia as she remembered the wind flattening the grass in the churchyard and the seagulls soaring in the air currents. Funny how she'd recalled the good and ignored the hardship.

David smiled in a humouring sort of way. 'I never imagined myself as a country parson, but rather as a teacher or a missionary.'

'Then that's what you should do, David. You won't have a large congregation in Portland. Most of the islanders are methodists, you know. They enjoy the preaching.'

'It's too late to change my mind now. Tilda is looking forward to going home.'

Home? It seemed strange to think of Portland as home, now. It wasn't that long ago since she'd left the island, though, barely three years. But it had been an eventful three years, in which Joanna had discovered her true identity, had sailed to Australia and back on the *Joanna Rose* and had given birth to Toby. She'd married Alex and now . . . she was widowed.

She gazed up at David, troubled. 'You'll look after Tilda, won't you? She wants to please you, but she might become melancholy in Portland.'

'Because of her ill-treatment at the hands of her family? She's my wife, of course I'll look after her. And, Joanna, if you need any help in the future, we'll always be there for you.'

'You're a kind man, David Lind, just like your uncle. He was always a good friend to me.'

'Richard enjoyed your friendship. He said you brought meaning to his life, and I know his last year was the happiest he'd ever known.'

'How sad it is when good men die. What will I do without Alex to love?'

He took her hand in his and gently squeezed it. 'You'll go on living, Joanna, for you have no choice. You'll love and care for his son, and raise the boy to love and respect his father's memory, as God intends you to do.'

'Yes, I'll do all of that, but because I'm his mother and I love him, not for any other reason.'

They fell silent for the rest of the way to the hospital morgue, where a further shock awaited them.

'Alexander Morcant's body was claimed by Mrs Clara Nash, not more than half an hour ago,' the orderly on duty told them. 'She came to sign for the body accompanied by an undertaker's cart. I understood her to be the patient's mother.'

Joanna's face blanched. 'I'm Alexander Morcant's wife.'

The man shrugged. 'Sorry, missus. You'll have to take it up with his mother, then.'

'And right now,' Joanna said when they were outside.

'Shouldn't we wait?' David cautioned, for the mist had thickened considerably and was taking on the appearance of a fog.

'You needn't come,' she said gently. 'There will probably be an unpleasant scene, since Clara Nash and I despise each other.'

He placed a hand on her arm. 'Remember, Clara Nash is Alex's mother. She will be suffering too, Joanna.'

'Hah! It's obvious you've never met her,' Joanna told him, wishing that David wouldn't assume that everyone was as gentle and generous natured as he was. 'The woman hasn't got a motherly bone in her body.'

'A few more hours won't make any difference,' David urged. 'I'll accompany you there in the morning, when you're refreshed by sleep and your mind is more accepting of the situation. As it is, we'd better get you home before this mist gets any thicker.'

She bowed to his greater wisdom, and they trudged back to her home, where Tilda waited with a pot of hot soup to warm them.

Joanna forced her food down, at the same time trying to comfort the weeping Mrs Bates, who kept saying, 'What will become of us now the master has gone?'

'Don't worry, Mrs Bates. Whatever happens, I'll

look after you,' she said with more confidence than she felt.

The company lawyer, James Stark, arrived after dinner, his face hollowed with shock. 'I've just heard about Alex. This bodes very badly for the future of the company. Oh, my dear . . . I'm so sorry. How can I be of service?'

'I don't know, James. What's likely to happen?'

'The company assets could be seized and sold to cover the loan.'

'But only two of the ships are affected.'

'There's more to it than that, Joanna. Alex's death will send company business into chaos. The clients will go elsewhere to secure cargo space. Without cargoes and passengers you won't be able to cover the interest payments. The loan guarantor will take everything and sell it off cheap to cover what's owed, plus interest.'

'That's not fair.'

'Business is hardly ever fair.' He gazed at Tilda and David, who promptly excused themselves and went to help Mrs Bates in the kitchen. 'If you've got anything valuable in the house I'll take it with me. And you might as well know, while you were in Australia, before you were wed, Alex began to pay back the money you withdrew from the company account. There is a large amount still outstanding.'

'I thought that money was mine. I gave it to my father when I was in Melbourne.'

'My dear, I can't give away a large chunk of company money without it being accounted for, not even to the owner. You signed a receipt to keep the account books legal, and there have been regular amounts paid in, as if to repay a loan.'

'Are you saying the house will be seized?'

'Unless you can reimburse the money it's bound to be questioned, since it's an asset. The creditors might demand payment.'

'Oh Lord! Of course I can't repay such a large amount. What a mess everything is. What if somebody asks me what I did with the money? I can hardly tell them I gave it to a man who supposedly died two years ago, a man with whom I entered into an incestuous marriage.'

Alarm filled James's eyes. 'That you can't, else we'll all end up in prison. Charlotte Darsham and Thaddeus Scott included. If asked, you might have to tell them the money was stolen.'

She nodded. 'Who would have thought so many problems would arise from discovering my true identity. If Charlotte hadn't noticed the resemblance between her son, her former daughter-in-law and myself, I might have lived happily with Tobias Darsham as his wife.'

'If that marriage to Tobias hadn't taken place, all would have been well. If the timing had been more fortuitous you could simply have lived with him in your proper place, as his daughter. Everyone would have rejoiced at the reunion. What has happened is nobody's fault, it was just a chain of well-intentioned events that seems to have suddenly grown a will of its own.'

'Trying to keep the company afloat, knowing it could destroy the people involved in this deception, just doesn't seem worth the risk. Alex could never grasp that. He lived and breathed the company. Why couldn't he just let it go, like my father did?'

'Because your father was the only person Alex respected and loved. He felt he needed to prove himself to him, and earn his respect.'

'Alex didn't have to do that. He already had my father's love and respect. I often wondered if he loved me for myself, or because he wanted to please my father.'

'Alex was never in any doubt. The reason he went after you was because he loved you, even though he was terrified of going to sea.'

'Thank you, James. You don't know how relieved I am to hear you say that.'

'Is Alex's body in the morning room? I'd like to say goodbye to him before the funeral.'

Bitterness welled up in her. 'Alex died in the hospital. Clara Nash claimed his body and has already handed it over to a funeral home. You know about the signature Clara forged to get funds to have Oliver released from prison, don't you?' When he nodded, she said, 'Oliver has been staying here as our guest. He went with Alex to the hospital, and he promised to come back. But he never did. I feel so betrayed by him. David Lind is taking me to see Clara Nash in the morning. I intend to discuss the situation with her. The meeting will not be pleasant, I imagine.'

'Oliver is an honest man of good intention. He's not as strong minded as Alex was, but he wouldn't deliberately let you down. Clara would have done this to provoke you. Too much can be said in the heat of anger. I advise you to let it go, Joanna.'

'I can't, James. I loved Alex. I want to see his face again and I need to say goodbye, too.'

'Then allow me to accompany you to the house of Clara Nash, and act as your spokesman.'

Joanna nodded, tears thickening her throat. 'I have borne a son who's the image of Alex. His name is Toby.'

A brief smile flitted across the lawyer's face. 'I'll make his acquaintance tomorrow, I hope. I'll be here at ten sharp, and we'll sort things out between us. In the meantime, pick out anything you want me to hide.' A slight bow of his head and he was gone, striding off into the layers of the fog that was beginning to blanket the city.

Joanna sent her friends home, saying, 'The fog is becoming thicker. I'll be all right now. And, David, James Stark has offered to take me to see Clara Nash tomorrow. He will act as my spokesman. You were right, I must sleep on it, for I'm often headstrong, and I'm exhausted at the moment.'

'Then you must go to bed at once,' Tilda said, and the pair exchanged hugs.

Joanna was relieved after they left. She went through to the kitchen, where Mrs Bates sat in the rocking chair in front of the stove, tears streaming down her face. The kettle was singing on the hob. Steam puffed from its spout and rattled its lid.

Taking up the china teapot they always used, Joanna made a strong brew and poured them both a cup. She took up the chair on the other side of the stove.

The women gazed at each other.

'It's hard when someone you love dies,' Joanna said, remembering that Mrs Bates had lost her own husband just a few weeks before.

'Especially somebody as young and strong as Mr Morcant was. He'd hardly lived.'

They fell silent for a moment, united in the common misfortune of their widowhood. Then Mrs Bates said, 'Mr Morcant adored his son.'

'Toby will forget him in the years to come, I expect. Perhaps that will be a blessing. I don't know what will happen in the future, Mrs Bates. Mr Stark thinks the house and company will be seized, and sold to pay off the creditors. If that happens I'll probably leave London and move back to Dorset. Do you have anywhere else to go?'

'Without Bates I'm all alone in the world.'

'You have me. I doubt if I'll be able to pay you, but we can share what I have, and I can find work, even if it's only farm labouring.'

Mrs Bates managed a smile. 'It's a nice girl you are for thinking of me. We'll manage, I'm sure, and I can be of help with young Toby.'

Joanna lit a candle from the embers. 'I'm going upstairs, Mrs Bates. I have the feeling tomorrow will be a long day.'

It was hard going into the room Alex had used on that last night. The bed was still tumbled where he'd tossed and turned in his pain. She should hang his clothing in the wardrobe, she thought. Taken aback by the smell of stale sweat and sickness, she murmured,

'When I feel stronger, I'll scrub the room clean.'

Alex's clothes had been thrown on a chair in the corner. As she grabbed them up, a whiff of perfume cloyed her nostrils and a woman's glove fell to the floor. Joanna picked it up and stared at it. It was grubby and the seam between thumb and finger was ripped.

Had Alex been with another woman? Something inside her head screamed out in anguish at the thought. She couldn't bear thinking about it, not on top of his death. Going back to their room, she took a pair of scissors and cut the glove into pieces. She threw them into the small black fireplace and soaked the fabric with spirit from the lamp on the dressing table. Lighting a taper from the candle, she set the pieces on fire.

When the last spark had died, she went to bed and cried all night.

At the age of fifty-eight, Clara Nash was dried up and thin. Her blue eyes were devoid of warmth, her mouth drooped with dissatisfaction. Upon her head she wore a black wig, the harshness of which made her face appear haggard.

She sat upon her chair like a queen on her throne, flanked by her two flawless daughters, who were almost seventeen years old. Lydia was the one with the slightly lighter hair, Joanna remembered. She and Irene looked uncomfortable, their faces tear-stained and sullen.

'Stop snivelling,' Clara said when Irene sniffed back her tears. 'It's about time the pair of you got some backbone.'

A tear tracked silently down Lydia's cheek, which was badly bruised. The pair looked quite desperate. Joanna felt sorry for them, for they'd adored Alex. He'd always protected them from the worst excesses of their mother as she ruthlessly pursued wealthy husbands for her two innocent and reluctant daughters.

Clara's fingers glittered with rings, her thin arms jangled with bracelets, her ears were stretched with the weight of the earrings she wore. Odd how wearing so many jewels could make a woman look so cheap, Joanna thought.

'Mrs Morcant wants to know where her husband's body is,' James told Clara.

'My son isn't her husband. I've been assured that a marriage aboard a ship has no legality ashore unless it's been registered.'

Joanna bit her tongue, for she knew that to be the truth.

'Joanna and Alexander had a son together. They had every intention of making the marriage a legal one.'

Clara's smile was almost a sneer. 'I doubt if she knows who fathered the child.'

Joanna stepped forward. 'Oh, I'm quite sure who fathered him, and so was Alex. You'd know the truth of that, too, if you saw him. He's the image of Alex. Now, I haven't come here to argue about the paternity of my son. I want to see my husband's body. Where is he?'

Clara examined her fingernails. 'Why should I tell you?'

'If you don't, I'll go to the law and tell them you

forged Alex's signature on a company document to raise a loan for your own use. And I'll tell them that Lord Durrington witnessed that signature.'

'They won't believe a fortune-hunting little slut like you.' Clara laughed. 'You won't get anything now, since the company will be bankrupt. Without Alex, you won't be able to run it.'

Lydia sucked in a deep breath as she gazed defiantly at her mother. 'You don't care that Alex is dead, do you? And the authorities *will* believe Joanna if she tells them the truth, because I'll go to them too, to back her up. And I'll tell them what goes on in this house, the opium parties, and the men you—'

Both girls screamed when Clara casually back-handed Lydia across the face and blood spurted from a cut to her mouth.'

'Leave Lydia alone!' Springing from her chair, Irene came between them, taking the next blow on her chest. 'My brother is in the funeral parlour just around the corner,' she sobbed, sending a glance Joanna's way. 'Alex is to be buried the day after tomorrow.'

'You ungrateful pair, get out of my sight,' Clara shouted.

'I wish I could,' Lydia spat at her, her eyes blazing. 'I loathe you as much as Alex did. You're wicked, and I wish you weren't my mother. And neither of us will ever marry the old men you pick for us. We'd rather die, like Alex.'

'That will be a fine day for me,' Clara said. 'If you're not careful, I'll throw you out in the street. We'll see how you fare then. You'll soon come crawling back, begging for someone to offer you the respectability of marriage.'

'As long as I have a roof over my head, so have you,' Joanna told the girls.

Her words elicited a smile from Clara. 'Then we must make sure you don't have one.'

The door opened and Oliver came in. He appeared harassed as he looked from one to the other. When the girls went to him, he took them, one in each arm, so they nestled against his shoulders.

'Mother?' he said. 'What's going on?'

'These people are being tedious. This slut your brother lived with came here with her lawyer to make trouble.'

'On the contrary, Oliver,' James told him. 'Joanna is simply trying to discover the whereabouts of Alex's body.'

Oliver gave his sister-in-law an apologetic look. 'I've just come from your house. I was going to take you to see him.'

Clara rose to her feet. 'Get rid of her, Oliver. I don't want her or her bastard to set foot in my house again. She's just accused me of stealing company money, and threatened me with the authorities. Don't you dare believe her, Oliver. She's a liar.'

'Alex had already told me how you raised the money to secure my release. I see no reason to disbelieve him.' Oliver gave Clara a pleading look before turning Joanna's way. 'Let me try and sort this out please, Joanna. Perhaps my mother can sell this house to help pay back the loan.'

Clara gave a thin smile. 'It's mortgaged.'

'Then perhaps you could sell the jewellery you're wearing.'

Clara flung a vindictive smile at her. 'It's not real.'

'We have only your word for that.' Taking a grip on her anger, Joanna nodded towards Oliver, knowing there were too many skeletons in her own closet to risk rattling those of Clara's. She wasn't going down without a fight, though, and tried a bluff. 'Perhaps I should alert the authorities, after all. Let them sort it out.'

Clara rose and headed for the door. 'Go ahead. Much good it will do you,' she spat out before she slammed it behind her.

'I think my mother's bankrupt,' Oliver said miserably.

'She's spent our inheritance,' Lydia said. 'Now she's trying to marry us off to old men. I hate her. I wish we didn't live with her, and I wish Alex hadn't died. He was the only person who was really kind to us, except you, Oliver. But you were always at sea, or were too busy to have time for us. What will happen to us?'

'There's Joanna,' Irene said, and the pair gazed at her.

Lydia smiled. 'Mother would be incensed.'

Oliver stepped in. 'It's out of the question, of course.'

'Why is it?' Joanna said.

The two sisters exchanged a significant glance.

Alex was lying in an ebony coffin, his head on a white pillow. Dressed in his linen shroud and with his arms tucked neatly under the sheet, he looked like a soldier at attention. Joanna gave a small, watery smile and ruffled his hair with her fingers. Alex had never slept on his back so tidily, he'd always sprawled.

James had said his farewell and had withdrawn, leaving her to snatch a few private moments. They knew she would never set eyes on her husband's beloved face again.

All the tension had gone from him. But when she bent to kiss his cheek, his skin felt cold and waxy, as if he were a beautiful marble statue. She sensed he was hollow inside, remote from her, as if all that had made him a man had been withdrawn from her.

'Oh, Alex,' she murmured, a tear falling on to his cheek. 'Toby and I loved you so much. Why did you leave us?' Gently, she wiped away the tear with her handkerchief, knowing it was wasted on him. He'd gone.

Two days later they buried Alex's body. There was quite a crowd attending. Men she didn't know. To Joanna's relief, Clara Nash was absent. Oliver looked harassed and his twin sisters clung to one another, weeping. Joanna held her son in her arms. As if aware that the occasion was a solemn one, Toby behaved himself.

When Toby smiled at someone standing behind her, Joanna fought the urge to turn. She had a fancy that perhaps Alex's spirit had joined them, and Toby could see his father, watching them both. The skin at the back of her neck prickled.

When the service was over, she turned. Lord Durrington stood behind her, grey whiskered, stooped and distinguished. There was something about him that repelled her, however – something she couldn't identify. His dark eyes glowed in the pouched and wrinkled skin of his eye sockets, his gaze was intimate and assessing.

How great the resemblance of this man to Alex, who was his bastard son. Alex had loathed the man. But he was Toby's grandfather, Joanna suddenly thought.

'My commiserations, Mrs Morcant,' he said, and he tickled Toby under the chin, making him chuckle. Lord Durrington smiled. 'A charming child, with a strong resemblance to his father. Has he a name?'

Feeling a sudden urge to protect her child from the old man, Joanna's arms tightened around her son. 'Tobias Alexander.'

'Ah, of course,' he said.

The undertaker sidled over to her and cleared his throat. 'May I talk to you for a moment, Mrs Morcant?'

Lord Durrington turned politely aside, but stayed within earshot.

'What is it?' Joanna said, lowering her voice.

'A question has arisen over who is to pay for the funeral. Although Mrs Nash made the arrangements, I understand she has now gone abroad. The account totals over one hundred pounds. If I cannot be assured that the bill will be paid, I must make other arrangements for the body to be buried. You do understand what I'm saying?'

A pauper's grave, he meant. Joanna couldn't bear

the thought, and she offered the only thing of value she had on her. 'Perhaps my wedding ring will cover the cost.'

Lord Durrington turned to say quietly. 'You will not worry Mrs Morcant with such a trivial issue in her time of grief. You may send the account to me.'

'Yes, sir.' The undertaker bowed and moved away. A signal with his finger and the gravediggers began to shovel earth on to the expensive coffin Clara had chosen.

'Thank you,' Joanna said as the mourners began to wander away. 'That was kind.'

'*Noblesse oblige*. It was the least I could do for my son. Do call on me if you need anything else.' A cruelly derisive smile touched his mouth. Then it was gone. Doffing his hat, he walked off towards his carriage, leaving her with a feeling of unease.

Escorted by James and the Lind family, Joanna and Mrs Bates walked home, not talking much, Toby riding astride Joanna's hip. As they turned into the gate they heard the sound of hammering. A man was boarding up the windows.

Another burly-looking man, stepped from the porch and handed Joanna a paper. 'I can't let you in, I'm afraid. Court order. We've taken possession.'

Joanna appealed to James. 'Can they do this?'

James perused the paper, and nodded.

David Lind appealed to the man. 'Would you allow the ladies ten minutes to fetch personal clothing for themselves and the child?'

The man's eyes sharpened. 'It could be arranged.'

Money changed hands.

'I'm going off to have a pipe, then. Be back in ten minutes,' the bailiff said.

Inside, the house wore an air of mourning with half the windows boarded up and keeping out the light.

Luckily, James had taken anything of portable value the day before. Joanna swiftly packed a bag for herself and a basket for Toby. As an afterthought, she tied the rolled painting of her mother to the strap, and took the baby carriage from the hall.

They stood in the road outside, looking at each other, uncertain. Mrs Bates, her change of clothing in a small basket, was quietly weeping.

'I wish we could take you in,' Tilda said, her eyes full of worry, 'but we'll be gone tomorrow. We're staying the night at the inn, and I've left Grace with the landlady.'

'Clara Nash has fled,' Joanna told them with some satisfaction. 'This is her fault, so let's go and stay in her house. Oliver and the girls won't mind.'

'Don't be surprised if the same thing happens there,' James said.

'But not for a day or two, surely. That will give us time to decide what we're going to do. Mrs Bates and I will probably go to Dorset and throw ourselves on the mercy of my—' She caught James's warning glance in time. 'Mrs Charlotte Darsham.'

She exchanged a farewell hug with the Linds. 'Tilda, you'll tell Mrs Darsham what's happened, won't you? Give her my love and tell her I'll be in touch as soon as possible.'

After they'd gone, Toby was placed in his carriage,

the basket laid across the bottom. James picked up her bag.

Joanna looked at Mrs Bates. 'Dry your eyes, Mrs Bates, crying won't help. Let's go, before Toby decides he's hungry and kicks up a fuss.'

Joanna was the only one who didn't look back.

4

Tilda finished unpacking her few possessions, then tied an apron over her skirt and rolled up her sleeves.

Not that the stone house they now resided in was dirty, but the windows were dulled from salt borne on the sea air, and a film of pale grey dust had settled on the furniture.

It was one of the finer houses in Portland, built for one of the quarry owners, and sold to David's uncle, Richard Lind, when the quarry had changed hands. Pride in having her own home to care for had filled Tilda with the urge to see the place gleam, and she wanted to stamp her own mark on it.

She would sew some new curtains and cushion covers, she thought happily. And she'd sit by her own fireside on winter evenings and make a patchwork quilt for Grace's bed, as she had once sat and sewn with Anna Rushmore and Joanna all those years ago.

'Grace, you can dust the furniture and windowsill in your own little room. I'll help you make the bed when you've finished.'

Tilda had given Grace the room Joanna had slept in

when she'd worked as a housemaid for David's late uncle. It was a small room, so Grace would feel safe in it. The ceiling sloped to a window set under the eaves, which, in turn, led the eyes to a view down through Fortuneswell to the glittering sea beyond.

From here, Tilda could see the roof of the cottage in which Joanna had grown up, a place where Tilda had spent the happiest years of her childhood. She pointed to it. 'See that orange chimney pot over there. It belongs to the house your Aunt Joanna grew up in.'

Grace picked up the calico doll Joanna had given her when they'd first met, the doll Joanna had made for her on the voyage home from Australia. Now the girl cuddled it against her and Tilda smiled at the sight. The doll's face was unintentionally cross-looking, with frowning eyebrows, spidery eyelashes, a red pout and black woolly curls. Grace adored it.

Tilda's smile faded as she thought of Alex. How sad his death was, coming so soon after that of Joanna's first husband. Her friend deserved some lasting happiness. Perhaps she would come home when she discovered the Rushmore family no longer lived on the island.

Tilda's father had died in her absence. Gin had addled his widow Fanny Rushmore's brain. Partially crippled from a beating inflicted on her by her husband, her mind failing her from time to time, Tilda's mother lingered on in the local infirmary, where the doctor had sent her. 'A baffling case,' the man had said. 'She has long periods of lucidity, then just as I think she'll be able to manage for herself, she relapses.'

Her mother was as sly as a fox, Tilda thought uncharitably. She wouldn't do anything to help herself unless she was forced to.

Of Tilda's three brothers, Peter had been shot trying to escape the revenue men. Brian was in prison, serving a life sentence after viciously raping a young girl. He would never set foot on the island again. But if by some chance he did, the girl's brothers had vowed to hunt him down.

Tilda shuddered, for she'd suffered badly at Brian's hands herself. If Joanna hadn't rescued her and nursed her back to health . . . But she didn't want to think about that. She didn't feel the slightest bit of remorse over her family's demise, even if it wasn't as Christian an attitude as David would expect from her. She had flatly refused to take her mother in and personally care for her. Now David was talking about installing her mother with a carer, in a church-owned cottage over at Southwell. Tilda wished he'd leave well alone.

Only her eldest brother was left behind. Leonard lived in Poole with his wife and two children, where he worked on a paddle steamer. Her eldest brother had changed since she'd last seen him. He'd become more confident and he'd smiled at her when she'd greeted him, something she'd never seen him do before.

Grace tugged at her skirt. 'Can we visit Aunt Joanna and Toby, Mama?'

'The house is empty now, my angel. But when we've made this place our home, we'll go and look inside Joanna's cottage and tidy it up, in case she comes to visit.' Tilda was reluctant, though. Now she was back on the island the memories of her abuse had become sharper, and more painful – something she hadn't expected.

She suspected Joanna's cottage would have been left as it was when Brian Rushmore had been arrested. Knowing how her brother had lived, it was probably filthy. But the islanders had always been honest with their neighbours, so she had no doubt that the contents would have remained untouched.

She stroked the child's silky hair. 'Just look at the big garden we've got for you to play in, Grace. And you can have a little patch of your own to grow things in, though you'll be going to school during the day.' Her hands went to her hips as she surveyed the vegetable patch. 'That's going to take some digging over to prepare for a winter crop, I can tell you.'

'I'm sure we can manage without you growing our food,' David said from the doorway.

She turned to him with a smile. 'You'll never take the island girl out of me. I'm not too proud to get my hands dirty, and it won't hurt Grace to learn how to use the soil to her advantage, since you never know when your fortunes are going to change. Look what has happened to poor Joanna. Best to have something put aside for a rainy day, even if it's only the skill to survive.'

David nodded. 'You'd better find me a hoe then. At least I can lend some muscle to the enterprise. From what I can observe, the church here doesn't have much of a congregation, so digging will keep me gainfully employed.'

'You can build me a chicken coop if you've a mind to.'

He chuckled. 'I rather thought you might sleep in the house with Grace and myself.'

She laughed and threw a pillow at him. 'Don't give me any cheek, David Lind. Why are you home so early?'

'A letter came from that greeting-card company you sell your work to.'

The letter contained a bank draft, and there was a request for some more designs. Tilda beamed her husband a smile as she handed the letter to him.

He gazed at her, his eyes full of pride because her gift for painting was finally bearing fruit. 'Does this mean I can hire an architect to build the chicken coop?'

'Certainly not. You're quite capable of doing it.'

'As long as you understand that I'm not the carpenter Jesus was.'

'The hens won't mind what it looks like as long as they're warm and dry in the winter and have some clean straw to lay their eggs in.'

'Hmm.' David's forehead wrinkled. 'Perhaps I should build them a little church with a Norman tower, and a bell they can ring when they've laid an egg.'

'They kick up enough fuss without a bell,' she called after him as he walked away.

Because they had a baby and luggage to handle, and she didn't want to change trains, Joanna decided to book a passage on a coastal boat. There was a brisk wind to push them along and, although Mrs Bates looked a little pale from time to time, Joanna found the voyage along the coast to Poole an invigorating experience.

Stepping ashore, their luggage was loaded on to a donkey cart and they followed the lad and his beast of burden up the hill, where it was placed on Charlotte Darsham's doorstep while they waited for their knock to be answered.

'Good gracious! I wasn't expecting you so soon. Joanna . . . and Mrs Bates is with you.'

'We had nowhere else to go. You won't mind, will you? Mrs Bates and I will find work as soon as we can, and I'll rent a place.'

'You're both welcome.' Charlotte's expression sobered, as if she'd suddenly remembered the reason why they were here. Taking Joanna and Toby in her arms she hugged them tight. 'Poor Alex, and poor you, my dearest ones. The news came as such a shock. Thaddeus is so terribly upset.'

Toby patted his great-grandmother on the head with a dribbly hand. Charlotte couldn't help but smile and, taking a handkerchief from her sleeve, dried it. 'I've never seen a boy so like his father, young man, but don't think you're going to rule the roost around here.' Her glance went to Mrs Bates. 'Perhaps you'd like to take your things and go through to the kitchen. Stevens will show you to your quarters, and you can help her with the household chores while you're here.'

'Yes, ma'am,' Mrs Bates said humbly. Picking up her bag she trudged off towards the door Charlotte pointed out to her.

'Mrs Bates was going to help me with Toby,' Joanna said in her defence.

Charlotte gave her a long, assessing look. 'It doesn't pay to become too familiar with servants, dear, and she still can help with Toby.'

'You don't understand. I can't afford to pay Mrs Bates. I have nothing myself now so we're on an equal footing.'

'Nonsense. Class comes from family connection, not from the size of one's bank account. Anyone who thinks differently has no class, at all.' She sniffed. 'Clara Morcant is a perfect example of that.' Her voice dropped to a whisper. 'Clara was an actress in a travelling show when she met Lucian Morcant. He was a nice man, but a fool who was easily taken in, and she had her eye on the main chance. Oliver is just like his father. Take my word for it. Mrs Bates will be happy to work for bed and board if necessary.'

Joanna chuckled. 'You're an awful snob sometimes, Grandmother Darsham.'

'I know. And I'm now Grandmother Scott, since Thaddeus and I were wed just a few days ago; though where my husband is at this moment, I'm not at all sure. Probably at the quay, watching the ships come in and go out. I think he's going to find retirement hard.'

Joanna kissed Charlotte's cheek. 'I hope you'll be very happy.'

'I am very happy.' A slightly smug smile touched Charlotte's mouth and her pale blue eyes began to sparkle. 'Thaddeus Scott has turned out to be a surprising man. I wish I'd married him years ago instead of mourning John Darsham for all those years in so noble a manner. Such a waste of time, since dead is dead, and no amount of wishing will bring them back.' Her eyes engaged Joanna's. 'You're young, Joanna. Don't allow your love for Alex to blind you to the good qualities of other men.'

'My feelings are too raw to contemplate another man in my life yet, and I have Toby to raise.'

'Grieve then, but don't make a virtue of your widowhood, as I did.' Charlotte gazed at Toby, who'd begun to wriggle in his mother's arms and voice a protest at being ignored. 'He looks as if he needs a nap. You know where your rooms are, don't you? Come down to the drawing room when you're ready, my dear, and we'll have some tea.'

Joanna fed Toby and placed him in the cradle that had once been hers, rocking it with her foot, as Joseph Rushmore had once done with her. Joseph hadn't been her real pa, though. A man with a wife but no children of his own, the stonecutter had found her secured in the cradle as it was tossed in the stormy waves off the Portland coast, twenty years before.

''Twas guided by the spirit of a dead sailor whose soul had entered a seagull,' her beloved pa had said, and Joanna had since come to believe that the gull had been the spirit of the master of the ship she'd been travelling on, Captain Lucian Morcant.

Joseph Rushmore had taken her home to his wife, to be loved and cared for. He was a man Joanna remembered with affection for the warmth and security of his love, though he'd died when she was young. Although he'd been in the wrong to keep her, Joanna couldn't think ill of him.

Then there was the father who'd lovingly carved the cradle for the daughter he'd thought he'd lost. Circumstance had eventually joined them, but it had been the wrong circumstance, leading to a hasty marriage of convenience. That had forced them apart once again, and had set in motion a chain of events that had been the downfall of the Darsham and Morcant Shipping Company. Gabriel Tremayne, as her father was now called, was a tough, unselfish man – a man she'd grown to love and respect in the short time she'd known him.

Toby's eyes began to droop as she rocked him back and forth. He only just fitted in the cradle. 'Sleep, little man, you've had two busy days,' she whispered. 'May your pa come to guide you in your dreams.'

Thaddeus had come home, Joanna could hear the rumble of his voice as she went downstairs.

His smile was sympathetic as she went into the drawing room, his voice brusque with the emotion he was trying to hold back. 'How are you bearing up, girl?'

'I keep thinking it's all been a mistake, that Alex will go back to the house alive and well, find it boarded up and think we've left him. I don't want to believe he's gone. It happened too quickly.'

'Aye, it did, but maybe that was a blessing. You'll get used to living without him.'

She crossed the room and kissed him. 'I shall have to. You and Charlotte married without telling me, I understand.'

'We did at that. I reckoned I'd waited long enough and had better get the vows said before she changed her mind.' Thaddeus aimed a smile at Charlotte, who promptly blushed.

Joanna's numbness soon wore off. The pit of despair she then plunged into was made all the more unbearable by Charlotte's happiness. Joanna tried not to show her grief during the day.

But at night her body betrayed her when she thought of Alex, and she was appalled by the thought that she could feel the need for the flesh to be satisfied when she had no husband to share that particular intimacy with. She lost her appetite, but forced herself to eat so her milk didn't dry up. The tears she shed at night bit into her sleep. Soon her tiredness took a toll on her and she began to look as strained as she felt.

Only Toby kept her sane over the following two months. His frustration in his attempts to crawl brought a smile to her face as he rocked back and forth on his hands and knees. He soon outgrew the cradle. Now he was sleeping in a cast-iron cot Charlotte had found in the attic. It rattled and clanged when he grasped two of the bars and shook them, which he did as often as possible.

Sometimes his progress was watched intently by Albert, the tabby cat Alex had given her. The pair talked to each other, Albert with perfectly modulated meows, and Toby with shrieks and chuckles.

Joanna spent most of her time closeted in the private sitting room attached to her bedroom, or sometimes in the garden, where her active son could enjoy some freedom of expression without annoying anyone. After a while she began to feel penned in. She hadn't been raised to live a life of idleness.

One fine day in August she placed Toby in his carriage, with the intention of setting off for town. On the way out she passed a man who was writing down something in a small notebook. He was tall and well-dressed, and doffed his hat politely when he saw her.

It was a good walk. Joanna enjoyed the sun against her face, though her dark gown seemed to draw the heat and perspiration trickled between her breasts. The air had a slight humidity to it and was heavy with the scent of roses, flowers which seemed to bloom in every garden she passed. How intense the perfume was.

She walked slowly through the park and along the busy quay, dotted with vendors of cockles and whelks, and a brazier over which eels were being smoked. The smell of eels seemed particularly unpleasant today, and as she passed the stall she averted her eyes from the long black creatures with their sharp teeth and staring eyes.

'Smoked eel, missus?' someone said hopefully, and the oily smell grew stronger, so it cloyed her throat.

Charlotte didn't like her coming to the quay. But to Joanna the dockers busy unloading the ships with their roughly shouted jokes and laughter were just an interesting part of the landscape. When they cheekily doffed their caps, or shouted, 'It's a grand day, my lovely,' to her as she passed, she smiled at their greetings.

Headed for a café in the High Street, not far away,

Joanna intended to rest and refresh herself before returning home.

Heat was being thrown up from the ground and the water had taken on a white glare. She could taste the greasy eel smoke on her tongue. Overcome by a slight nausea and dizziness, she looked for somewhere shady to sit and rest, but the quay was devoid of shade. Good grief, was she going to faint? She was.

Although she tried desperately to hold on to her fading senses, she sank to her knees, automatically releasing the baby carriage so it wouldn't tip over. To her horror, the carriage slowly rolled off towards the edge of the quay. She could see Toby gazing at her, laughing through Alex's face, as if she were playing a game with him.

'No! Oh my God, don't let our son be taken from me, Alex,' she whispered irrationally as the light faded around her.

The shriek of a seagull brought Joanna round. She opened her eyes to the sight of one perched on a bollard a little way off. How clean it looked with its grey and white jacket, jaunty red boots and bright yellow bill.

'Lucian Morcant,' she murmured, feeling oddly comforted by the bird's presence.

'Seth Adams,' someone said.

Its head cocked to one side, the bird observed her for a moment, then rose gracefully into the air and glided away.

Joanna was puzzled when she discovered her head

was resting on someone's lap. In this upside-down position she didn't recognize his face or the steady grey eyes, so filled with concern.

Her eyes widened and she struggled to get up as she remembered, her son's name bursting from her lips. '*Toby!*'

'Your child is safe,' he soothed, and, rising, he helped her regain her feet.

Joanna clung to his arms for a dizzying moment. When her head cleared she saw her child in the arms of another man. The pram was on its side, right near the edge of the quay.

There was no mistaking Tilda's brother, with his long face, muddy eyes and taut mouth. Leonard never usually found much to smile about, but he smiled now, mainly because Toby was gazing at him with a pouting lower lip, deciding whether to laugh or cry after his spill. 'Leonard?' she said wonderingly.

Joanna hurried to take Toby in her arms when that pout began to tremble, holding him tightly against her. 'Shush, my love. You're safe.'

'I heard a shout from that gent there, saw the carriage coming and managed to catch a wheel with a boat hook before it went into the water. It was a close thing.'

'Thank you, Leonard, I'm in your debt.' Joanna shuddered as she thought of what might have happened. She turned to the stranger. 'And you, sir. My thanks.'

'You still look pale. Are you sure you're all right?'

'It was a silly faint, brought on by the heat, I expect.'

The man wore an expensive looking frock coat, but his grey trousers were soiled from kneeling on the ground. Brown wavy hair streaked with gold gleamed in the sunshine. He gazed at her, in a frankly assessing way that made her conscious of herself. Inanely, she said, 'I'm afraid your trouser legs have become dusty. Mr . . . um?'

A faintly cynical expression flitted across his face as he slapped the grime off with his immaculate leather gloves. He bowed slightly. 'Seth Adams is my name.'

'Ah yes, of course. Didn't I see you outside Mrs Scott's residence on Constitution Hill?'

'You may have, since I've just walked down from there. There's a fine view from the top. Will you introduce yourself?'

'Joanna Morcant . . . Mrs,' she hastened to add. 'And this is my cousin, Leonard Rushmore.'

When his glance seemed to sharpen in on her she gained an impression that he didn't miss much. He aimed a casual nod in Leonard's direction. 'That was a quick reaction, Mr Rushmore.'

'It was down to you, sir. If you hadn't shouted I wouldn't have seen what was going on, since I had my back turned.'

The stranger bent to pick up her reticule while Joanna watched Leonard go to the baby carriage, right it and bring it back to her, clearly embarrassed.

Leonard wasn't used to praise and he shuffled awkwardly from one foot to the other. 'It's nice to see you again, Joanna. But I'd better get back on board before the boss comes after me. I'm going to visit Tilda on

Wednesday, if you're interested. She'll be pleased to see you, I know.'

Unsure, Joanna gazed at him. 'I'm not sure if I should.'

'You needn't worry. Except for Tilda, none of the Rushmores live on Portland now. Be here at nine, we'll surprise her.'

'Len, where the hell are you?' somebody shouted from the depths of the steamer.

Joanna smiled and said, 'It's nice to see you too, Leonard.'

He stared at her for a moment, colour mottling his cheeks, then said abruptly, 'I was sorry to hear about the death of Alex Morcant. He was a good man.' With that, he strode on to the paddle steamer and, with a wave of his hand, disappeared below deck.

Seth Adams handed over her reticule and placed his tall and stylish hat back on his head. The man was a bit of a dandy, but there was a shrewd look to him. 'You're recently widowed, Mrs Morcant?'

She nodded.

'I'm sorry. You still look pale. I'd feel easier if you'd allow me to escort you and your son home. I imagine you live with the Mrs Scott you mentioned?'

She inclined her head. 'That's kind of you. But first I must find a workshop where Toby's carriage can be repaired. The wheel has buckled.'

'Allow me to wheel the carriage, then. I'll try and keep the damaged wheel off the ground. There's a blacksmith's shop just around the corner, and a tea room not far away. The carriage can be repaired while we have some refreshment, if you'll permit it. Take my arm for support in case you feel faint again.'

'Thank you, I do still feel a little shaky.' They strolled along the quay like a married couple. Toby giggled every time the damaged wheel accidentally touched the ground, and he was jiggled up and down.

Seth Adams smiled at him. 'Your son has a happy nature.'

'He has, but he can be demanding when he feels like it.' Feeling stronger now, Joanna wanted to withdraw her arm but couldn't quite bring herself to do so, in case she appeared ungrateful. 'Do you have children, Mr Adams?'

He gave her a sideways glance, saying briefly, 'I'm not married.'

He didn't look the type to invite further questioning from a stranger, so she accepted his answer without comment.

Soon they were settled in the tea rooms. It was hard handling the tea things as well as holding a wriggling child, who appeared to have suddenly sprouted as many arms as an octopus.

'Why don't you hand him to me while you drink your tea?' Seth said, spreading a napkin on his lap to receive the child when she nodded. 'Now, young fellow, you behave yourself.'

Toby gazed up at this person with the authoritative voice for several long assessing seconds, then he smiled and blew a bubble.

Taking a silver watch from his pocket, Seth hung it from his lapel. Toby's eyes were drawn immediately to it and he reached out, his hand closing possessively around the shiny object.

'You have a way with children.'

'I have a niece. How long have you been widowed, Mrs Morcant?'

She hadn't expected such a question. 'Just a few weeks.'

'Ah . . . I see, and how long were you married?'

About to give the same answer, she caught herself just in time. 'Not long enough.' She suddenly remembered Alex bringing her to this tea room once, and the small posy of flowers he'd presented her with. Her voice caught in her throat as she added curtly, 'I'd prefer not talk about it.'

'Perhaps you should have given yourself more time to recover before venturing abroad.'

She drew in a deep, steadying breath, suspecting that the reason for her sickness might be more than a mere faint. She softened towards her companion. He was being perfectly decent towards her, and it wasn't his fault she'd become a widow.

'I'm sorry I was so sharp. You weren't to know. But hiding myself away won't bring my husband back.'

'No, of course it won't.' Toby was becoming restless again. Picking up a teaspoon, Seth smeared the back of the bowl with plum jam and handed it to the boy to suck on. 'I apologize if my questioning was too direct.'

'There's no need to apologize. I didn't mind.' When the watch casing sprang open Toby gazed at it in astonishment, then screeched in delight and banged the spoon on it. Seth Adams chuckled, even though his lapel was now smeared with jam and dribble.

Joanna leaned forward and dabbed at the sticky patch with her napkin. The timepiece said it was past Toby's feed time. She glimpsed a likeness of a young woman inside the lid of the watch before her companion snapped it shut, just as Joanna said, 'I didn't intend to stay out this long. My son is getting hungry.'

Making sure she'd finished her tea, Seth placed the child in her arms, then beckoned to the waitress and paid the bill. 'Wait here,' he said. 'I'll go and see if the baby carriage is ready.'

He was back within five minutes. 'I've hired a carriage to take you home. It will be quicker.'

'Thank you, Mr Adams.' She fumbled with the drawstring of her reticule. 'You've been most kind. You must tell me the cost of the repairs, so I can reimburse you.'

A hand over hers prevented her retrieving her coin purse. 'I won't hear of it.'

When the carriage came he helped her in, lifted Toby's carriage in after her and slipped some money into the driver's hand. 'The lady will tell you her destination. Perhaps we shall meet again sometime, Mrs Morcant.'

'I think that might be nice, Mr Adams.'

'It might, at that.' His sudden smile took her unawares, and invited one from her as he took a step back and waved the carriage on.

She saved her own smile until he was out of sight.

*

Seth Adams watched the carriage grow smaller, then he smiled and turned, his long legs carrying him rapidly back towards the quay.

Boarding the paddle steamer, he leaned down the stairway and called out Leonard's name.

The man came up on deck, rubbing his oily hands on a piece of grey rag.

If Seth had thought their recently shared experience was going to make this man his ally, he learned differently.

'You wanted something, mister?'

'Tell me about Joanna Morcant.'

Leonard shrugged, said flatly, 'Why?'

'She dropped something. I want to return it.'

'You can give it to me. I'll return it to her the next time I see her.'

'I'd rather give it to her myself.'

'No doubt you would.' Hands on hips, Leonard stared at him. 'Leave Joanna alone, she's had enough strife in her life of late. She's just been widowed, and doesn't need another man chasing her skirts.'

'I rather think that's up to her.'

'Mebbe it is and mebbe it isn't, but you'll not get her address out of me.'

Seth sighed. 'I know her address. I just want some information about her.'

'Such as?'

Their eyes narrowed in on each other, then Seth said, 'Anything. Where was she born? Who are her parents?'

Leonard Rushmore scratched his head, then gave a

faint shrug. 'Give me your card. I'll makes sure she gets it. I daresay my cousin can answer those questions herself if she's of a mind.' He held out his hand. 'Now, if you don't mind giving me the property you've found at the same time, I'll make sure she gets it.'

Seth had already inspected the purse he'd palmed from Joanna Morcant's bag. It contained almost four shillings, and a ring set with a blue, heart-shaped stone. She would have had difficulty paying for the repairs to the baby carriage so he'd dropped a few extra coins in.

'You're wasting my time, mister.'

Frustrated, Seth frowned at the man as he handed the purse over. Leonard Rushmore wasn't as stupid as he looked.

A grin slowly tightened the man's mouth and he jerked his thumb towards the quay. 'The gangplank's there, if you're leaving.'

The pair exchanged a hard stare. When Seth took his calling card from his waistcoat pocket and handed it over, Leonard grunted, 'Thanks.'

'Make sure she gets it.'

Placing it in his pocket, Leonard walked away without another glance, whistling a tune.

5

'Oh, Tilda, what an awful smell!' Joanna held a handkerchief to her nose as she glanced around the main room of the comfortable cottage she'd been raised in. 'I don't know what my ma would say if she could see the place now.'

'I wish I'd come here earlier.' Crossing to the mattress on the floor, Tilda picked up the ragged patchwork quilt. 'Remember all those winter hours we spent stitching this together. I wonder if it can be repaired.'

'I don't want anything Brian Rushmore touched with his filthy hands,' Joanna said fiercely, rolling up her sleeves. 'I'm going to make a bonfire with this rubbish.'

She began to bustle about, carrying out mouldy food, empty gin bottles, dirty clothes and bedding, anything she could move. Rats and spiders scattered before her onslaught. She heaped the rubbish in the middle of the overgrown garden, then, running out of energy, threw herself on the bottom of the stairs and burst into angry tears. 'This place doesn't look as if it's been cleaned in years,' she muttered.

Tilda wrapped her arms around her in a hug. 'Hush, Joanna. We'll do it together. Next week you'll come over again and we'll clean the place. Bring Mrs Bates with you, she can look after the children. Now, hand over that quilt and the bedding. We spent too many hours making it not to attempt to rescue it. I'll soak everything, and repair the rips.'

Joanna looked around her, sighing. 'I can't bear to see the place like this when my ma took so much pride in it.'

'Why don't you come back to the island to live, then we can see each other often. After all, it's your cottage, and you could make a comfortable home for your son here.'

It wasn't the life Joanna had expected to give Alex's son, but it was a decent life, for all that. Better than some had. Joanna smiled through her tears. 'Is it my cottage? Your family didn't think I was a Rushmore, and neither did many of the locals.'

'Who cares what they think, and who cares if you're not blood kin? Joseph and Anna Rushmore brought you up as their own. None would have argued any different, except behind their back and in private. Most of the islanders will keep their counsel with strangers, as they always have done. Except for old Hiram, and who listens to him, anyway?

'What about Leonard?'

'He's never wanted what can't be earned with his own two hands.' Tilda drew her out through the door and closed it behind them. Bundles in hand they made their way up the hill towards Tilda's house.

Leonard was waiting to get back to the paddle steamer.

'Joanna's going to move back home next week,' Tilda said, taking Toby in her arms and planting a kiss on his cheek.

Leonard nodded. 'I'll give you some help with moving your things, then. Our Brian was none too fussy, so I daresay you'll need to scrub the place clean. Could be my Kirsty will give you a hand. And I'll dig over a vegetable patch for you on my day off. It's likely I can manage a couple of laying hens, too.'

Twelve days later the cottage walls were gleaming with fresh whitewash, the windows shone, and the glowing patina on the heavy wooden furniture had been exposed by the application of a slathering of beeswax and plenty of elbow grease.

Joanna's helpers had now gone back to their own homes, including Mrs Bates, who'd been offered paid employment by Charlotte's next-door neighbour. It was peaceful being on her own with her blessed son, and they sat together and watched twilight fill the spaces until Toby became fractious.

Joanna fed her son some mash, then put him to the breast before laying him in his cot to sleep. She stooped to kiss his downy cheek, then unfurled his plump little hand and placed a kiss in that, too, whispering, 'Sleep well, my angel.'

Charlotte had objected to Joanna moving back to the island. 'I'll miss you both so much. How will you manage, my dear? Stay a little longer.'

'You forget that I was raised to be self-sufficient. I

need to go now, so I can establish myself and prepare the vegetable plot before the ground hardens.' Joanna also needed to be alone for a while, but she didn't want to hurt Charlotte's feelings by saying so.

'Do you have money?'

'Enough to see me through if I'm careful.'

'You mustn't be afraid to ask if you need anything, Joanna.'

Joanna had hugged her then. 'I know. Thank you. We're not too far away to visit.'

Downstairs, she placed Toby's soiled linens into a metal bucket and set it to boil on the stove. When they'd cooled sufficiently, she carried the bucket out into the yard to rinse the squares in cold water from the pump, wringing them between her bare hands, because the winding mechanism on the mangle had rusted solid. Tomorrow she'd slather the cogs with grease, in the hope that they could be worked loose.

There was a pain in the pit of her stomach, as if her muscles were reacting to the days of manual work. She was unused to it now.

Leonard had strung her a washing line from the shed to the corner of the house. The rope was stiff, pale and untested, but it was strong, and hung where a line had always hung. It had an air of permanence when she finished her task and the linens dripped water into the weeds.

It was late. The sun sent a path of rippling flames across the sea, so Joanna could almost fancy she heard it hiss as it slid into the water. Shadows were elongated. Dusk deepened from amaranth into violet and filled the clamouring spaces inside her with peace. An owl landed on the roof and quietly hooted.

She went inside, seating herself on the shabby couch, now covered by the refurbished quilt. She felt glad Tilda had saved it as she ran her hand gently over it and said, 'I'm home, Ma.'

But it didn't feel like home, for her spirit had moved on from the island life and was no longer content. She must be thankful and make the best of it, she told herself sternly. They had a strong roof over their heads to shelter them from the weather, and she'd been raised to be practical, which was more than many people had.

Joanna sat there as darkness surrounded her, thinking of nothing in particular. She couldn't shake off a feeling she'd never been away, that her life in between childhood and the present had been nothing but a dream – a dream that had become a nightmare.

After a while she rose, locked the doors and went upstairs to bed. Through the window she saw that the moon had risen. It embroidered silvery patterns across the water and shone through the window on to her bed – the bed of her childhood.

She remembered the events of earlier that day. How, to her surprise, Leonard had handed over the purse she'd thought she'd lost. Ten shillings had been added to the small amount of change that it had already contained.

'Seth Adams found it and asked me to return it to you,' Leonard told her.

She'd glanced at him then, puzzled. 'There seems to

be more money in it than I thought I had. Have you lost any from your pocket? It might have slipped inside.'

Leonard had scratched his head and shrugged. 'It hasn't been in my pocket. I only opened the purse to slip his card inside, otherwise it's as Seth Adams handed it to me. You must have forgotten the amount you had, it's easy done.'

Joanna hadn't forgotten, since she didn't have enough money now to overlook a farthing of it. Seth Adams must have placed it in there. Her face burned at the thought. How dare he be so presumptuous on so slim an acquaintance.

Seth Adams. Agent of Enquiry, his card stated. The man had an office near the Old Bailey law courts in London. She must remember to write and thank him for returning the purse, and try to find a way to return the extra ten shillings.

'I'll never sleep,' she whispered as her body sank into the soft feathers, now smelling of fresh air and sunshine.

But she did. When she woke it was to find that the tender new life she thought she'd been carrying inside her had slipped away. She should have felt sorrow, but her reaction was only one of relief that she didn't have an extra mouth to feed.

Dear Mr Adams,

I'm grateful for your assistance during and after my collapse in Poole, in August.

On your behalf, Mr Leonard Rushmore has returned my coin purse. I'm indebted to you, and in more ways than one, I suspect. However, for me to take offence at your generosity would be churlish since, although I considered it a presumption, I believe your charitable gesture was kindly meant.

I will keep the sum of ten shillings to one side in case you find yourself in a position to collect it, and should I visit London in the future I'll certainly deposit the amount at your office for collection.

Your integrity in this matter is appreciated.

Yours sincerely,

Joanna Rose Morcant (Mrs)

Seth finished reading the letter and crossed to the window of his offices, which occupied a corner situation and looked down into a street jostling with people on one side, and on to a laneway full of the same – but less prosperous looking – on the other.

The two rooms were adequate for his needs. The larger one, on the lane side, was occupied by his clerk, who doubled as a detective since his ability to snoop equalled Seth's own. It also served as a waiting room. Seth always kept his door locked from the inside, his clients having to go through Mr Geevers first.

Seth's enquiry business was hard to find, since he didn't have his name on the door and the building itself was something of a rabbit warren. But it was deliberately so. Seth didn't need the money his profession brought him. Along with the interest from a healthy inheritance he'd invested, his main income came from the rest of the tenants in this building, and the tenants of one or two others.

Seth only took on cases that interested him, whether they paid a fee or not. And he never involved himself with more than one at a time. He read the letter again and grinned, for he knew that his honesty in any matter was ambiguous and, in this case, a means to an end.

'The widow has taken the bait,' he said, and chuckled as he folded the paper and tucked it into his pocket. Rising to his feet, he placed a tall hat on his head, picked up his cane and sauntered into the other office. 'I'm going out, Mr Geevers.'

'Will you be long, Mr Adams?'

'I shouldn't be at all surprised. Look after things while I'm away.'

'Certainly, Mr Adams. Don't I always?'

Outside, the air was still and slightly oppressive, and the whiff of cat's piss rose sharp and feral from every corner. Rubbish and horse dung embraced in fevered heat in the gutters while clouds of flies danced in busy attendance.

Seth strode out, his long legs carrying him over the ground at a fast pace.

He reached the home of his client, leaving his hat and cane with the servant when he was announced. Waved to a seat, Seth accepted the proffered brandy. The pair savoured their drinks for a few moments, then Seth said, 'I've made some progress. The girl is living in Portland with her son.'

'She's gone to earth back to where she came from, then.'

'Has she? I didn't realize she was from those parts. What exactly did you want with her?'

'I want her background investigated. Who her parents were, the details of her first marriage—'

'First marriage?'

'To Tobias Darsham. He drowned a couple of weeks after they were wed, and left her the Darsham and Morcant Shipping Company. It was several months before the body turned up and he was buried in Southampton. I heard that she put everything in Alexander Morcant's name, then married him. Now *he*'s dead.'

'You think she killed him? She'd have had nothing to gain by doing that.'

'Of course she wouldn't, which is why it needs investigating. Something very odd went on there.'

'Such as?'

'The two husbands were friends long before Joanna arrived on the scene. Alexander Morcant was Tobias Darsham's heir. But when Darsham died and his will was read, everything was left to the widow. Not long after, everything was transferred to Alexander's name and she shipped herself off to Australia. Alexander went after her. They came back as a family, the girl with their son at her breast. They'd been married on board ship. Alexander died not long after they got home.'

'Was there anything suspicious about his death?'

'Not according to the doctor. He said it was a straight out case of peritonitis brought about by a burst appendix. I've got no reason to disbelieve him. Joanna Morcant was visibly upset when Alex died.

'One scenario presents itself immediately. She may

have conspired with her second husband to kill the first. Did any money go missing?'

'I understand that the widow withdrew a large amount of money from the company account before she transferred it into Alexander's name. The transaction was quite legal, since she was the sole owner of the company at the time, and was entitled to draw down a director's salary and expenses. Odd, though, that she couldn't afford to pay for his funeral. I settled the account.'

Seth's grey eyes settled on Lord Durrington. 'Why would you do that?'

Durrington shrugged. 'Alexander Morcant was my son, though he refused to acknowledge me as his blood.'

Seth began to like Alexander Morcant. 'I see. And your motive in this case?'

'It's too late to beget myself a legitimate heir now, but that girl is the mother of my grandson. I want to have legal guardianship of the boy and raise him as my own. If I have to discredit his mother to do it, I will.'

Seth only just stopped his lip from curling. 'Have you asked Joanna Morcant if you can have legal guardianship?'

'I intend to. But I need something to tip the scales in my favour.' Rising to his feet, the old man clapped Seth on the shoulder. 'I'm relying on you, lad. Your brother recommended you.'

The affair was beginning to stink like a foxhole. 'Which one of my two half-brothers do I have to thank for this? Surely not the earl himself, since we've not spoken in years.'

'Barnard.'

'Ah, the *banker*.' Though usurer would be a better name for Barnard's profession. 'Good friends, are you?'

'We have mutually beneficial dealings from time to time. Barnard said you would be discreet over this matter, and would welcome the fee, for you have a child to raise.'

A threat, if ever he'd heard one. 'And raise her, I shall. I never discuss money with clients. They can either afford to pay, or they can't. Those who can will be billed by my clerk in due course.'

'Of course.'

Seth smiled gently. 'I heard that Barnard drew in his loan on the company, then seized the assets of the Morcant Shipping Company. You bought it cheaply from him, I understand.'

Durrington shrugged. 'Clara Nash's dislike for the girl overrode her good sense and she played right into my hands. My only sorrow is that Alex died before I could carry through my plans for us to jointly own the shipping company and expand into steam. You know Clara is ill, don't you? Serves her right, she should never have meddled with opiates.

Seth had never met Clara Nash, knowing her only by reputation. He'd long been aware of her excesses and appetite for the exotic and unusual. 'Didn't the lady have young daughters. What happened to them?'

Lord Durrington smiled. 'The sweetest pair of

innocent doves I ever set eyes on. Clara guarded them with her life, since it's all she had left to bargain with. I had intended to wed one of them so I could get myself an heir on her. But Alexander got in her ear and the girls dug their heels in. I could have had the pair at a price, the second as my mistress. But it meant forcing the issue, and Clara wanted too much for allowing me that little pleasure.'

Although the breath hissed between his teeth, Seth's smile was pleasant. 'No man wants to dance to the tune of a greedy woman.'

'Greed is built into Clara Nash, but a lot of good it will do her now, since she won't live much longer. At the moment the girls are living with their brother in Clara's house, but the lot of them will be out on the street shortly, when Barnard forecloses. I thought to buy the house myself, but it would stretch me too thin at the moment. I've just signed a contract to build a steamship, and have plans to erect a warehouse on the site of Alex Morcant's former home.'

Seth's grey eyes gave nothing of his thoughts away. He stood up, shook hands with the man and nodded. 'You've told me all I need to know. I'll be in touch in due course. Good day, my lord.'

When he got outside Seth drew in a deep breath. Even the streets of London smelled fresh after the stench of decadence in that drawing room.

He headed for his home, one in a row of houses exactly alike in design and situated not far from Hyde Park. It was a convenient location for Seth, since he liked to ride every morning when he was in residence.

Handing his hat and cane to the butler, he said, 'Where's Miss Kate?'

'In the garden with her governess, sir.'

Strolling through the house, Seth paused at the French windows, smiling at the sight of his niece, who was lying on her stomach under the copper beech tree, drawing something in an exercise book.

She looked pretty in a blue flowered dress with a frilly white smock over it. Nearby, Kate's governess was nodding off in a wicker chair. As Seth watched, Kate picked up a long blade of grass, got to her hands and knees and tickled the end of the governess's nose.

By the time the governess came awake, flapping a hand in front of her face and saying crossly, 'Bothersome insects,' Kate was back where she'd started from, drawing industriously in her book.

When Kate looked up and smiled, her eyes wide and innocent, the governess smiled back at her and said, 'All right, my turtle dove?' Kate nodded, and the woman's chin gradually sunk on to her chest again and she began to snore gently.

Seth chuckled as Kate picked up the blade of grass again. She was more the magpie than the dove. Catching sight of him, she scrambled to her feet and dashed across the garden, hurling herself into his outstretched arms. 'You're home, Uncle Seth. It's been so boring without you.'

'I saw what you did to Miss Tanner.'

'You're not going to be vexed, are you?' Her grey eyes alight with mischief, the five-year-old giggled in a manner which reminded Seth very much of his sister.

Sixteen-year-old Sarah Adams had died giving birth to Kate. Too shamed to tell anyone she'd been violated by a guest in her eldest brother's home, she'd run away from the row that had ensued when her secret had been detected, and had ended up in a poorhouse.

He and Sarah had only shared a mother with their aristocratic elder brothers. Their own father had been of more lowly birth, but had been a learned and gentle man, philosopher and teacher. His heart had failed him when he'd learned of his beloved daughter's fate. The two had been buried together, their mother having been laid to rest some two years previously, in the family tomb of the peer who'd been her first husband.

There had been no choice for Seth but to take the child in and make himself responsible for her. But he hadn't considered how strong the emotional attachment would become. Advised by his brothers to get rid of the unfortunate by-blow, he ignored them. As a result, he was now a family outcast, and so was Kate. Not that it mattered to Seth, for he'd never got on with his brothers, who had always considered it rather vulgar of the widowed countess to wed a commoner and produce more offspring so late in life.

However, wealth had arrived in an unexpected legacy from a renegade aunt of his father's family, who'd run off with a West Indian sugar planter of mixed blood – and that wealth was something his brothers remained in ignorance of.

Kate's future bothered him a little, for he was the only family she had in life. At the moment the girl was too young to understand, but he knew she'd be slighted in later years, when people learned of her background.

So he hugged Kate tight and laughed, because he couldn't be cross with her, however hard he tried. 'I just came in to say hello.'

The smile left her face as she accused, 'You're going away again, aren't you?'

'Yes. For a short time.'

'Can I come this time? You said I could when I'd grown up.'

'And you think you're grown up now?'

Scenting success, Kate emphasized her good points. 'I'll be good. I promise I won't fidget or talk too much. I can do up my own buttons now and brush the knots from my hair, though you'll have to tie the ribbons. And Miss Tanner said I have lovely manners when I put my mind to it.'

Seth's thoughts went to Joanna Morcant. He smiled as he remembered her wide blue eyes – he couldn't help himself. Towing Kate along might break the ice between them, help her to trust him a little more.

Kate squashed his face between her palms and produced her most winning smile, obviously keeping the best for last as she wheedled, 'You're the best Uncle Seth in the world, and I love you.'

How could he resist such a blatant example of female strategy? He said, chuckling as he set her down on her feet, 'I'll ask Miss Tanner to pack you a bag. We'll leave in the morning and take the railway train to Southampton, where we'll stay the night in a boarding house, for I have some business to conduct there.' That business being to satisfy himself that the death of

Tobias Darsham had been above board. 'Then we'll go on to Dorchester. There, we'll hire a carriage to take us to Portland.' Seth intended to bypass Poole, in case he ran into the uncooperative Leonard Rushmore again.

'A railway train?' A blissful smile split her face and she went skipping off down the garden, her skirts flaring up behind her, calling out excitedly, 'Wake up, Miss Tanner. I'm going with my uncle on a real railway train . . .'

Toby had learned to crawl and could now haul himself up on the furniture.

Outside, Joanna had been obliged to make a pen from a length of fishing net wound around four poles, and secured by stonecutter's pegs hammered into the ground. Inside it she'd placed the quilt, so Toby wouldn't be encouraged to devour any hapless insect that wandered into his inquisitive gaze or within the clutch of his fingers. It would also provide something soft for him to sleep on, if the urge took him.

Even though it was mid-September, the warm weather had lingered on, so to give her son some shade she'd hung a crinoline hoop covered in a silk petticoat from the washing line. The clucking hens outside his prison kept Toby entertained as Joanna bent her back to her task. She could hear him chuckling to himself, above his chatter, the raucous squawk of gulls and the slow clip clop of a horse making its way up the hill. It was probably the coal supplier.

With the colder weather coming, Joanna had two priorities in life, firstly to sow seeds for winter crops –

cabbages, beans, carrots and potatoes. Her other priority was winter fuel. The bunker was almost empty and she had no money to buy more unless she sold some of her mother's jewellery. That would mean a visit to the *Lugger Inn*, at Easton, where, no doubt, the wily Barnes brothers, who dealt in anything they could sell, and without asking questions, would pay her far less than its full value.

There was a soft breeze blowing and the seagulls were gliding high on it against a blue sky as she placed her hands against her aching back and straightened up to ease it. Perhaps the coal man would accept her mother's ring instead of payment, she thought, though she was loath to part with any of her jewellery.

The islanders had been generous so far, but she couldn't rely on their charity for ever. She'd hardly moved in when she'd discovered various items left on her doorstep overnight. A basket of vegetables, a jug of milk or a loaf of bread now and again. Then there was the sack of flour and a flitch of smoked bacon, a generous gift indeed.

She supplemented her diet with the snalters she trapped, the little birds making a tasty, though not a very substantial, dish. The wheatears would leave the island for warmer parts of the world soon. Then she'd have to rely on the fish she could catch and eggs from the hens. Her time was fully occupied with trying to survive. But she would.

Thinking of winter made her remember the ten shillings Seth Adams had placed in her purse. The money now resided in the brown jug, waiting for its owner to claim it. That would buy her some coal, she thought, bending back to her task. Seth Adams would hardly go to the expense of coming all the way from London to collect it and she could always replace it later.

Behind her, Toby had quieted. He'd probably fallen asleep. Then she heard him begin to babble and chatter, in the way he always did when he was excited. A child giggled.

Grace, most likely. Though Joanna had thought Tilda was going off to market today.

She turned, her eyes widening when she saw Seth Adams leaning against the wall, almost as though she'd conjured him up just by thinking about him. How had he got here? He hadn't come through the gate, because the squeaking hinges would have alerted her. A child was perched on the wall, one arm around Seth's neck, her head resting on his shoulder.

Pulling himself up the fishing net, Toby fell forward and somersaulted over it. He landed on his back, quickly turned on to his hands and knees and headed for the visitors at as fast a crawl as he could go.

'Now look what you've done,' Joanna scolded. 'He'll escape all the time now he's learned how to go about it.'

As she grabbed her son up, Joanna suddenly became aware of her dishevelled appearance, of the perspiration on her body, her bare feet, calloused and dirty hands and the untidy appearance of her braided hair. She quickly fastened the top button on her bodice. 'I'm not in a condition to receive visitors.'

He slid her a teasing grin. 'I noticed you're not wearing your hoop and petticoat today.'

Damn him, he'd made her blush. She turned her face away, her eyes going to the girl, who'd jumped down from the wall to stare at the hens. When the girl looked up at her they smiled at each other.

'Do the chickens have names?' she said.

'I haven't thought of names for them yet.'

'My hen at home is called Victoria, after the queen. She lays brown eggs and I have them for breakfast. My name is Kate Sarah Adams.'

'That's a pretty name. Mine is Joanna Rose Morcant.'

'That's a nice name, too. I came here in a railway train. It was exciting but I got some soot in my eye and it made me cry.' She gave Joanna a sideways look, then lowered her voice to an urgent whisper. 'Do you have a chamber pot? I badly need to go.'

Joanna nodded, and taking the girl by the hand began to lead her towards the house.

'Aren't you going to invite me in, as well?' Seth said.

'Eventually, but Kate is *uncomfortable*, and I need to tidy myself up and feed my son. I'd be obliged if you would give me a half an hour of privacy first.'

Seth began to remove his coat. 'I'll do a bit of digging for you while I'm waiting.'

She gave a slight smile and nodded, sure he'd quickly tire of it.

Kate was soon made comfortable. Joanna poured some water into a bowl and washed her face and upper body, then she gave Toby a quick feed. The girl watched the proceedings with great interest. Afterwards, Joanna slipped into a clean bodice, then vigorously brushed out her hair, tying it into a knot at the nape of her neck.

Toby had fallen asleep on the bed. Carrying him downstairs she laid him on the battered settee. He wouldn't sleep for long.

Through the window she saw that Seth was attacking the garden bed with ease. His muscles moved smoothly in unison under his shirt, and he seemed to be enjoying the exercise.

Putting the kettle on to boil, Joanna placed cups on a tray, all odd ones. Brian Rushmore hadn't left much in the cottage intact. Thank goodness she had some milk, though.

'Is there any cake?' Kate asked her. 'I'm hungry.'

'I haven't got any cake, but I have a piece of bread and some apple and strawberry jam to spread on it.'

'Why haven't you got cake? Don't you like it?'

'I'm too poor to buy anything but essentials, so I have to live without cake,' Joanna told her, cutting a slice from the remainder of the loaf.

A pair of bright eyes remarkably like Seth's came up to engage hers, and Joanna wondered what the relationship between them was. Sister and brother perhaps? 'Bread and jam is nice too.' Thanking her politely, Kate waited for the bread to be spread with jam, then began to eat it.

'You can go and tell Mr Adams he may come into the house now if he wishes,' Joanna told her.

Seth came in a few minutes later. He must have held

his head under the pump, because water dripped from his hair and arms.

Joanna handed him a threadbare towel. 'Why have you come, Mr Adams?'

'To collect my ten shillings, of course,' he said, and smiled.

Joanna's heart sank.

6

Seth Adams didn't as much as flicker an eyelid when Joanna handed him the mismatched cup and saucer. Murmuring his thanks, he took a seat on the threadbare chair, crossed one elegantly shod leg over the other and sipped at it.

There was a catlike smugness to the smile he gave her as she seated herself next to the sleeping Toby and prepared to engage in polite conversation.

'You were not very well the last time I saw you, Mrs Morcant? I do hope your condition has improved.'

Had there been a slight emphasis on the word condition? His astute eyes told her he'd guessed exactly what that condition had been. She returned his smile. 'Thank you for enquiring. I'm in perfect health now.'

'And your son?'

'None the worse for his mishap.' Her glance went to the little girl, and her eyes questioned him.

'My niece,' he said.

'There's a remarkable resemblance between you. Is Kate your brother's child, perhaps?'

Seth's eyes hooded and he put the cup to his lips and murmured something indistinct.

Kate came to gaze down at Toby and her fingers gently stroked his dark silky curls. 'He's nice. Are you his mother?'

'Yes, I am.'

'I wish I had a mother. Mine is in heaven. Her name was Sarah and she was uncle Seth's sister.'

Seth's next breath flattened into a hiss of annoyance.

Amused by the girl's innocent candour, Joanna's glance slid over Kate's head to meet the level gaze of her visitor. An ironic twist of his lips met her spare smile. 'You were lucky to have a kind uncle to look after you.'

Kate tugged at her skirt for attention. 'I haven't got a father, either. Has Toby got one?'

'His father is in heaven, too,' she said, feeling a rush of guilt for entertaining another man in her house. Not that Alex had ever been here in this snug cottage she'd grown up in. If he had been, he would surely have scorned it.

'It's not polite to ask Mrs Morcant so many questions,' Seth reminded his niece.

Joanna grinned at that. 'Nor for me to ask Kate questions, I take it. You may ask your own if you wish. It doesn't seem fair to use an innocent child for our own ends.'

Placing the cup down he laughed, as if her observation had caught him unawares. 'Are you always so straightforward?'

'No, but it does tend to dispense with the social

preamble and cut through to the point. Why are you here, Mr Adams? I can't believe it's to collect ten shillings.'

'It's not. I was utterly captivated by your blue eyes and wanted to see you again.'

Joanna was overcome by a vague sense of disappointment as she gazed at him. 'I'd formed an opinion that you were an exceptionally intelligent man. Must I revise that?'

His shrug contained an embarrassed awkwardness. 'The truth is, I liked you when we first met and wanted to learn a little more about you. Is that so hard for you to accept?'

Now it was her turn to feel awkward. 'Then I'll tell you about me. I was brought up in this cottage, the only child of Anna and Joseph Rushmore. The cottage was built by my pa, a stonecutter by trade. He died in the quarry when I was about Kate's age. Ma and I tended the fields, and worked as housemaids to earn our living. My ma was a good, hardworking woman and I never went without food . . . or love.'

'So you've always lived here?'

'Not always. I left the island when I married. Now I'm widowed and have come back with my son. As you can see, we're living in relative poverty. My immediate concern is to grow enough vegetables so we can survive the coming winter, and to scrape together some money to buy the fuel to keep us warm.' She spread her hands. 'This is what I am, and always have been.'

Joanna stood. Crossing to the shelf, she took out the velvet pouch that contained her mother's jewellery and tipped the glittering contents on to the table. 'Perhaps you'd like to buy something for your niece while you're here. Take your pick. It will save me going to the Lugger's Inn and trying to sell it to the Barnes brothers, who will cheat me.'

Seth stared at the array of jewels with some shock, but he had a slightly speculative look in his eyes.

She realized she'd made a mistake and couldn't meet his eyes as she whispered, 'It's not stolen. This belonged to my mother. See, I have no pride left. I'll sell everything I own to keep myself and my son alive this winter, for there's a turnip in every precious stone, at least.'

'Everything you own?'

She gave a slightly bitter laugh and looked him straight in the eye. 'Only a man would speculate on that. Who knows, I might even consider that, too, if it buys me a couple of sheep.'

'I didn't imagine you to be the type of woman who would indulge in amateur dramatics,' he drawled, words which hit her like a douse of cold water in the face, so she gave a spluttering gasp.

Her dismay brought a taut smile to his lips. 'However, if the latter profession takes your fancy I'd be quite willing to pay a good price to be your first client.'

She coloured as she spat at him, 'I'd see you in hell first.'

'I'm quite sure you wouldn't.' His smile faltered as he leaned forward and swept the jewels to one side. 'I'm sorry, that was unforgivable of me.'

'You're obviously expecting me to succumb to such

a suggestion. Don't you think that's a little arrogant of you?'

'Damn you, woman, can't we behave like civilized people? I didn't come here to negotiate a rate for the use of your body.'

She tossed her head. 'Damn you, too, Seth Adams. I didn't ask you to come here at all.'

Kate picked up a pendant with a diamond in it and held it up, watching it glitter in the light. Toby woke with a start, his face flushed with sleep. When he set eyes on Kate with the pendant he began to chuckle. Joanna lifted him to the floor and the two children went off behind the couch to play with the stone.

The adults stared at each other like a pair of bristling dogs, then Seth took out his wallet and threw a wad of notes on to the table.

'What's that for?' she asked him suspiciously.

'The rose brooch. Kate has a birthday soon.'

She shook her head. 'Anything but that. I've had the brooch since I was a baby. It was a gift from my ma.'

'A kiss then.'

'For Kate?'

He chuckled. 'I'll pass it on in a modified form.'

Joanna only just managed to hang on to her sudden urge to laugh. 'You follow your instincts too easily.'

His eyes filled with amusement. 'A kiss in exchange for a couple of sheep. Surely that's a bargain.'

'For whom, Mr Adams?'

'That remains to be discovered. I can't bear to think of you and your child going hungry this winter. Is a kiss such a high price to pay?'

The chance to say no was lost to her when he moved to where she sat and took her face gently between his palms. Up close, his eyes displayed a dark edge around the wintery grey, so they resembled those of a hawk. His mouth was a strong curve, but his lips were delicately soft as they touched against hers.

Joanna had never considered a kiss to be a work of art, but Seth Adams kissed with such finesse that the subtleties of his caress reached into the very depths of her soul. She closed her eyes, responding to this stranger's intimacy, trying to ignore the warning clamour of her body.

When he drew away, her eyes remained closed for a few seconds. His smile was tender when she opened them. 'Definitely a bargain for me, I'd say, Mrs Morcant.'

She didn't want to flirt with this man. There was something ruthless about him. 'Not for me. I feel . . . *soiled.*'

'Nothing about that kiss soiled you, my dear Joanna. What you're feeling is guilt, since your response told us both how much you enjoyed being kissed. Despite being a grieving widow, your nature is sensuous.'

She stiffened. 'You're no gentleman.'

He chuckled. 'I've never pretended to be.'

She drew in a deep breath, trying to keep a check on her temper, rising from the settee so she could put some distance between them. Fetching the brown jug, she emptied the coins it contained on top of the notes. 'Here is your ten shillings. Take it with you when you leave. The kiss was free of charge.'

Picking up Toby, who gave a cry of displeasure at being parted from his new playmate, Joanna stomped off upstairs, leaving her guests to their own devices.

After a short while footsteps pattered up the stairs and Kate's voice whispered against the door panel, 'Are you cross with us, Joanna?'

She shouldn't vent her temper on the child. 'Not with you, Kate.' Opening the door, she gave the girl a hug. 'Goodbye, my dear. It was lovely to meet you.'

Seth appeared at the bottom of the stairs, hat and cane in hand. He looked contrite. 'Thank you for the tea.'

She offered him the hand of friendship with, 'I was too churlish.'

'I goaded you.'

'Yes, you did.' Against her better judgement Joanna took two steps down the stairs towards him. 'Deliberately, I think.'

His smile was slightly enigmatic. 'You could be right, at that. Can we still be friends?'

Seth had helped save her son's life. Descending a few more stairs she allowed her expression to soften. 'I don't want us to part thinking badly of one another. Thank you for the hard labour. I appreciate the help.'

'I enjoyed it.' He held out a hand to her. 'Will you see me out, then?'

There was a moment of hesitation before she took his hand to close the gap between them, for she was reluctant to let him go now. His palm was firm against hers, as he turned it up to inspect the calluses. 'These were hard earned.'

'I'll get used to manual work again.'

'You shouldn't have to,' he said almost angrily.

'But I will, for I have my son to raise.'

'May I call on you again the next time I visit the island?'

She nodded, even though Portland was not a place one passed through to reach anywhere else.

They parted on the doorstep and she watched him walk off, not down the hill as she'd expected, but up towards Reforne. She supposed he was staying the night at one of the inns, for travelling with a child wasn't easy, and Kate would tire quickly. Both of them turned to wave before she closed the door.

Thinking the money was gone, Joanna's heart sank a little at having nothing set aside to fall back on. She noticed that the brown jug was back on the shelf as she scooped the jewellery back into its bag. Later that evening, she discovered the money was tucked inside the jug. There was a note, written in pencil, the letters scrawling across both sides of two small pieces of notepaper.

Joanna, my dear,

I can easily afford this. Forget pride, which, although satisfying, will not keep you warm. Accept the money as a gift and embrace the thought that it came to me through legacy, so it wasn't hard earned.

I cannot bear the thought of you or your son being deprived of food and warmth this winter.

Until we meet again, yours in all sincerity,

Seth Adams

As Joanna finished reading the note for a second time, she murmured, 'So, he does intend us to meet again.' Her smile held an element of relief. On that basis, she decided it would be stupid not to keep the money.

Touching her mouth with her finger she grinned as she admitted to herself that Seth had been right. That kiss certainly had been a bargain.

From Joanna Morcant's cottage, Seth went straight to the church, where an old man with dimming eyes and a white beard was sleeping in the sun, his back against a gravestone.

When Seth stirred him with a foot the old man came awake. 'Hiram is my name. How can I help you, sir?'

'Is the Reverend Lind around?'

'The reverend who inherited the scholar's house over yonder? Richard Lind the scholar's name was, and it was said he had devils plaguing him so he fell to the ground and jerked about to fight them off. For all that, a kinder man you could never wish to meet, indeed you couldn't. 'Tis the nephew who's the reverend.'

'That's the one.'

Hiram lifted his cap and scratched his head. 'The reverend, he be gone to market with his missus just now, her who used to be Tilda Rushmore whose father was George. If it's praying you're after, the back door of the church allus be open for sinners who need to have their souls cleansed.'

Seth smiled. He doubted if praying would wash his sins away. 'Thank you.' He hesitated before asking, 'Have you worked here a long time?'

'Since I was a boy. Never been off the island,' the old man said proudly, 'and I've outlasted two wives and four of my children.'

'You must have a strong constitution, Hiram.'

'Nothing wrong with my memory, either. I saw you come from Joanna Rushmore's house. A sprightly girl with a mind of her own, though fallen on hard times now. I didn't expect to see her come back here after she married that London fellow.'

'Tobias Darsham,' Seth prompted.

'That's the one, him who drowned not two weeks later.' He jerked his thumb. 'Darsham's first wife be over yonder. She and their daughter lost their lives in the storms of thirty-eight. Off the *Cormorant*, they were. A bad year for wrecks, indeed it was. Her master, Captain Lucian Morcant, is buried nearby. One of his sons used to come and visit his pa, but not recently. I heard he'd married Joanna Rose.'

'He's dead.'

'Do that be so? That accounts for her coming back then, and her with a son of her own, I hear. The girl has a shape to her a man could enjoy, and nice titties, like a pair of plump white doves nestling in her bodice. I do like a lass with a nice pair. Not that I'd be much good to a woman now, no good at all. Fact is, 'tis a wonder I can still draw air.' The old man grinned toothlessly at him, then fell silent.

'Tell me about Joanna's parents,' Seth prompted.

'There were none better than Joseph and Anna, though the Lord didn't bless them with any children until late in life, when Joanna Rose came along.'

Glancing around him, Hiram lowered his voice. 'There's some who say Joanna Rose is an outsider who was brought in from a wreck by the storm. Her cradle sailed safely to shore, guided by the soul of Captain Lucian Morcant hisself, who entered the body of a seagull. 'Tis said, and no secret hereabouts, that Joseph Rushmore found her on the beach and took her home to his Anna. And I knows for certain there's a boy child buried with Honor Darsham, since I saw him before the box was closed.'

Hiram's chin settled gently back on his chest and his eyelids closed as he mumbled into his beard, ''Tis probably true, since Fanny Rushmore herself told me, her who's in the infirmary at Poole and dying from the scourge of the gin. Though I wouldn't tell another living soul, indeed not, and the dead allus keep their counsel.'

Not always, Seth thought, and, smiling a little, he dropped a couple of shillings into the old man's pocket. He called out to Kate, who was inspecting the statue of an angel.

Indignantly, she said, 'The angel has got hardly any clothes on. Isn't that rude?'

'Not if you're an angel. Luckily, you're not, in any shape or form.'

He thought Kate had begun to look a little wilted, though she hadn't complained. 'As soon as I've been into the church we'll go to Mrs Henry's boarding house. I'll carry you up the hill on my back if you're tired. Tomorrow we'll go home.'

'Can't we sleep in Joanna and Toby's house? I like it there.'

Titties like plump white doves nestling in her bodice, Hiram had said. Seth grinned. He'd only snatched a glimpse of those particular birds before she'd swiftly buttoned her bodice. But Joanna Morcant certainly wasn't in the market for a man yet. And from a professional point of view he couldn't afford to get involved.

'Sorry, it will have to be Mrs Henry,' he said firmly.

It didn't take Seth long to find what he was looking for in the church, since there was nothing to find. Oddly, there was a complete absence of records for Joanna Morcant. There was an entry of birth, marriage and death for her parents, though. A little digging revealed a whole heap of cousins, including Leonard. And if Joanna had been married to Tobias Darsham in this church, as Lord Durrington had suggested, it also hadn't been recorded.

Joanna herself had never mentioned her first marriage, which struck him as rather odd. She'd been cautious, not giving much away. Her ability to out think him had not only surprised him, but had gained his respect.

So whose daughter was she? Seth didn't attach much credence to gossip, but he didn't like the way this was beginning to look.

Joanna was hanging out the washing the following week when Oliver Morcant and his two sisters arrived unexpectedly.

Joanna's heart went out to him, for he looked so gaunt. 'My mother's dying and we've lost our home,' he said bleakly. 'I wondered if you'd take my sisters in, since I need to get to America and sort her affairs out. I was hoping to pick up a ship in Poole and work my passage. I was going to throw myself on the mercy of Charlotte. But my sisters said you'd offered, and . . .' He spread his hands with a helpless gesture that tugged at her heart. 'Here they are.'

'When I said they could come any time, I meant it.' She smiled at the girls, who looked travel stained and weary. 'You've had a hard time of it, haven't you? Of course you're welcome to stay.'

'It's horrible being poor,' Lydia said. 'We had to walk all the way from London, except when people gave us rides. And we got so hungry.'

'I quite enjoyed it, except I got blisters on my heels and the luggage was heavy,' Irene remarked. She gazed dubiously at Joanna's cottage. 'This is rather a small house.'

'It's quite large for an island cottage, and is fairly roomy inside. But I haven't got much, and you'll have to help, for we'll need to earn the money to feed ourselves.'

Lydia said offhandedly, 'Oh, we won't mind, since Oliver told us you were not well off, and neither are we now. It will probably be fun learning how to manage, and we'll help in any way we can, won't we, Irene?'

The pair exchanged identical but slightly dubious smiles.

Irene suddenly seemed to brighten. 'When we came up the hill we saw a ladies' clothing store, though it looked dreadfully old fashioned. We know a lot about fashion, so we thought we might apply for a job there and earn some money. Let's go and unpack our bags, Lydia.'

It wouldn't be that easy to find work, as they'd learn, but at least they were willing and optimistic. Smiling, Joanna nodded towards the house. 'Upstairs there are two small rooms under the eaves you can use. If you'd prefer to share, there's a larger room downstairs.'

And the big bed Fanny Rushmore had used was still in there. Tilda had brought a new mattress cover made from ticking for it, and they'd filled it with fresh feathers bought from a market stall.

'It was my mother who ruined the mattress in the first place,' Tilda had said when Joanna had protested, for the original one, disgustingly stained with several years of spilled food, and liquids of a dubious nature, had clearly been beyond redemption. Joanna had shuddered at the sight of it, and had thrown it on top of the bonfire.

'The downstairs room is a sitting room really, but it's never been used as one. You'd have to share a bed, but it's a large one and the mattress is new. Try not to wake Toby up when you go in. He's having his nap.'

The twins carried in the luggage, struggling a little under the weight of the bags and coming back for the boxes Oliver had been carrying.

'What have they brought with them?' she said with a smile.

'Anything they could lay their hands on, I think. It weighed a ton.' Oliver picked up his own modest travelling bag and shuffled his feet. 'I've got a long way to go, so I'll be off. I'm sorry I can't offer you anything for the girls' keep, Joanna. But we have nothing left, and I was at my wits' end.'

'We'll manage, and they'll learn to survive, I promise you.' As he turned to go, she said, 'Wait a minute, would you?' Going into the house Joanna took ten shillings from her precious hoard then, when she returned, slid the thick gold wedding ring from her finger and pressed it into his hand. There was no room for sentiment when hunger was an issue.

'The money should buy you a meal or two and a bed for the night if you need one. Alex gave me the ring when we exchanged our vows on board the *Joanna Rose*. It's solid gold. Wear it, and sell it if you need something to fall back on. God speed, Oliver. Come back to us.'

'Aye, I will. Who would have thought the Morcant family would ever have been brought so low?' Tears came into his eyes. Hugging her tight, he said thickly, 'I can't thank you enough, Joanna.' Then he was gone, striding briskly off down the hill, though his shoulders were slumped with tiredness. Joanna wished he would have stayed for the night.

She finished hanging the washing out and went indoors. The twins were settling themselves in the downstairs room. Clothes covered the couch.

'There's nowhere to put anything,' one of them wailed.

'You can use one of the small bedrooms for clothing, but, goodness, you won't need all those fancy things here, and if the wind gets under those crinoline hoops it'll lift you off your feet and blow you away. What's in these boxes?'

'Silver candlesticks in that one. We thought they might come in handy if we had to sleep in a barn, or something. But we forgot to pack candles. There's our crystal dressing table stands, mirrors and hair brushes, and some figurines from our bedrooms that we liked. I don't know how we'll manage without a maid to do our hair, though.'

'Joanna manages,' Irene pointed out.

Gazing at Joanna's windswept braid, Lydia gave a bit of a giggle that sounded close to tears. 'Mama would have a fit.'

Irene shrugged. 'Since our mother will soon be dead, I doubt it. Besides, we said we wouldn't mention her name again after she cast us aside.'

The girls were certainly impractical, if enterprising. 'Well, just keep those figurines out of Toby's way,' Joanna said, hearing her son begin to rattle the bars of his cot. 'Perhaps it would be better if you left them packed for now.'

The visitors were a distraction for Toby, who pulled on a charming smile at the sight of his aunties.

Tears came to Irene's eyes, and Lydia choked back a sob as she whispered, 'Toby is so much like Alex. Our brother was always so nice to us, and he often took our side against Mother. We loved him so much.'

'So did I,' Joanna murmured, unable to keep a brave façade in the face of this unrestrained demonstration of female grief. Soon, the three of them were sobbing in each other's arms.

Pulling himself up against his mother's knee, Toby laid his head on her lap and joined in with distressed howls.

Lydia and Irene learned the hard way.

Joanna had to teach the girls the basics. How to structure their day, so every minute was gainfully employed. How to eke out the food they had, so they ate what they needed without waste. How to bake bread, kill and dress a chicken, and make a stew.

October came in with a roar and some of the worst storms the island had experienced in years. Ships were lost, and Joanna prayed that Oliver was safe.

They all lost some weight, except Toby, who gained some. But the girls never complained when food was scarce, and they laughed at each other's mistakes, regarding the whole thing as an adventure. They adored Toby and spoiled him constantly.

Christmas came and went, celebrated with a feast at Tilda's table after the church service. Toby celebrated his first birthday early in January, and a month later found his feet, and some new adventures because of it. Towards the end of a cold and hard winter, when Joanna's money jug was almost empty, she was offered a cleaning job at one of the quarry owners' houses.

Her new mistress, Mrs Abernathy, was a thin, unhappy woman, who complained bitterly about her lot in life. Her daughter, Harriet, was rather cowed, and Joanna felt sorry for her.

'I don't see why we should have to live on the island,' Mrs Abernathy said one day. 'Harriet is missing out on so much and I want her to marry well. She's reached the age when they need to be taught certain refinements, and I can't keep taking her to Weymouth.'

'I think I can help you, Mrs Abernathy. My sisters-in-law are well versed in social matters, even though they've fallen on hard times.'

Mrs Abernathy gazed down her nose. 'I've seen the young ladies about. Can they play the piano, dance and sing?'

Joanna crossed her fingers. 'Most certainly.'

The woman sighed, but her eyes had sharpened. 'I'm not well off. I can only pay them a small amount.'

The Abernathy family were as wealthy as lords, and as pinchpenny as misers. 'That's unfortunate, since I have no intention of allowing them to work for subsistence wages. I thought to give you the first chance of employing one of them, but others are interested.'

'I shall interview them,' Mrs Abernathy said hastily. 'If they suit, I'll talk to my husband. You may bring them up this afternoon and if I like them I shall choose one. Now, get on with folding that washing up. The windows needs cleaning and you haven't got all day.'

When they learned of their fate, the pair smiled ironically at each other. Irene then said lightly, 'What fun. We shall go to the interview, and we'll share the job and home chores between us. As for payment, Mama used to pay our music tutor and dancing master a vast amount of money. We shall charge the same.'

'I doubt if Mrs Abernathy will pay a professional fee.'

'We shall see.'

As expected, Mrs Abernathy balked at the fee they intended to charge.

'We were taught dancing at the Germaine St Claire academy for young ladies,' Lydia cried out in faked affront. 'My sister was awarded first prize in the piano recital contest at the Boston music conservatory, and we won't be condescended to.'

Irene promptly seated herself at the piano to play several sweeping and elaborate trills, which seemed to impress the woman. Toby clapped his hands and jiggled up and down on Joanna's lap.

Mrs Abernathy gazed from one to the other, looking surprised and slightly overawed, making it obvious she had very few social graces herself. 'How will I tell you apart?'

They exchanged a glance. The slight difference in their hair colour was rarely noticed and it amused them when people couldn't tell them apart. 'Goodness, you'll have no need to, since we'll both answer to Miss Nash.' Lydia drew forth the daughter of the house. 'Come, seat yourself beside Miss Nash, young lady. We shall decide if you have any talent.'

With Mrs Abernathy having been placed on the defensive, the twins decided to put Harriet through her paces. At the end of five minutes the girl could manage a clumsy scale. Irene and Lydia exchanged a long and meaningful glance.

'Well?' Mrs Abernathy said.

Lydia hummed doubtfully in her throat and Irene reluctantly nodded. 'Miss Abernathy will have to work hard, but she has a modicum of talent.' She pulled on her gloves, fussing with the fingers as she said in a superior way, 'My sister and I are agreed then, we shall take your daughter under our wing.'

'Thank you, Miss Nash.'

'Good. Then I shall be here at ten a.m. sharp, and Harriet shall receive a two-hour music and singing lesson. In the afternoon, my sister will teach her dancing steps, followed by a painting lesson. At the end of each week, you may pay to Mrs Morcant the sum we agreed upon for our services. Good day Mrs Abernathy.' The pair swept off.

Nodding at her employer, Joanna followed after them, trying not to grin. They'd picked up some useful airs from their mother, she thought.

As for Lydia and Irene, arms around each other's waists, they chatted and laughed all the way home, pleased by the thought that they'd be able to contribute to the household expenses. They were a bright pair. Joanna was grateful for their company, since she hadn't had time to be lonely, and they had taken her mind from the loss of Alex.

There was a hire carriage waiting outside the house. The horse fidgeted and its foreleg dug at the road. The driver chaffed his hands together, nodding when the quartet stopped and stared, and jerking his thumb at the house. 'The gentleman has gone inside.'

'Perhaps it's Oliver. He should be back by now,' Lydia said, gazing hopefully at her sister.

But it wasn't.

Once inside the house they all fell quiet, staring with disbelief at the figure seated on the couch. A dark-skinned woman occupied the chair by the wall. She had an odd, exotic look to her.

Beside Joanna, one of the twins gasped and clutched at her hand. She was trembling.

Lord Durrington gazed from one to the other, his glance settling on Joanna. He said, 'I have some private business to discuss with you, Mrs Morcant.'

7

Lord Durrington came straight to the point.

'I want to raise my grandson as my heir. I'll pay you handsomely and give you a one tenth per cent share of the shipping company profits, so you'll have an income.'

'Don't be ridiculous. I have no intention of selling my son to you.'

He held up a hand. 'Just listen. Tobias will be well looked after, and you'll be allowed to see him once a year.' A set of papers were placed on the table between them. 'I'll wait while you examine them.'

The woman with him picked Toby up. Tall and wiry, she wore a long cowled cloak over a red military jacket and skirt. Petting the boy, she seemed to be edging towards the door at the same time.

Sensing danger, Joanna twisted to her feet and snatched Toby from the woman's arms. 'Leave my son alone and get out of my house.' Opening the door to the twins' room, she handed Toby over to them. 'Lock the door and don't come out until I call you.'

Up close, the woman's face was angular, her dark eyes sly. She had a flat, broad nose, dark olive skin, and she smelled strongly of perspiration and liquorice. When the woman tensed, but didn't back away, Joanna groped behind her back, her hand closing around one of the silver candlesticks on the dresser.

The woman gazed at the earl, saying in a low voice, 'My Lord?'

Lord Durrington jerked his head and the woman turned and headed for the door. 'Bisley would have cracked your neck with one hand if I'd snapped my fingers.'

Joanna's grip on the candlestick relaxed. 'I'd have brained her first.'

'I doubt it. Apart from his other duties, Bisley is my valet and bodyguard.

She felt her eyes widen. 'Bisley's a man?'

'Since he's a creature of many parts, it really depends on how he feels at the time.' The condescending smile Durrington gave made her feel sick. 'Your lack of education about such matters is rather refreshing, my dear.'

Her cheeks warmed. 'I must ask you to leave too, Lord Durrington. I won't sell you my son.'

His glance slid to her breasts and the pink tip of his tongue slid along his lip. 'Come, come, Joanna. I can do a lot for the boy. I'm sure it's what Alexander would have wanted.'

Dragging her shawl from the chair Joanna draped it round her, holding it tightly at the front as she tried not to shudder. 'You may think you're sure, but I know you're wrong. My husband despised you, and everything you stood for.'

His mouth tightened. 'Only because he learned of our relationship too late. I was unable to acknowledge him while I was still able to father a legitimate child of my own. That time has passed. Won't you even read the papers? I'm offering you a large amount of money.'

'Money you stole from us in the first place.'

'It's not my fault the business was mismanaged. Think of young Tobias's future. He'll get the best education and inherit my title. He'll never go without.'

'And will grow up despising the very person who loves him the most, his mother. Never, for I won't hand him over willingly.'

'I admit, I'd not considered such a notion. But then, I never knew my own mother, so she wasn't really important to me.' He smiled at her. 'There's a solution, of course.'

'Which is?'

'You could move into my house, become my . . . *companion.* For a man of my age, a young and desirable female is a sop to his vanity, and it makes him a source of envy amongst his peers.'

Joanna's response fell between a gasp and a disbelieving laugh.

Lord Durrington shrugged. 'You're almost presentable when you're properly gowned, and your manners and speech are not too shocking. It wouldn't take much to improve you further and it would please me to have a young woman on my arm.'

'I'd sooner move into hell and live with the devil.'

'When living in my house would give you access to the boy all the time? I think not. You'd have your own rooms, of course.' He shrugged. 'And I'd turn a blind eye to any extracurricular enjoyment you wished to indulge in, though I might want to witness it from time to time. A man of my age can't stand the excitement of having a young woman constantly in his bed.'

How disgusting a creature he was. 'I have access to my son all the time now, so no thank you.'

His eyes hardened. 'My dear, it would be simple to arrange matters so you had no access to your son at all. Your romantic shipboard marriage to Alexander Morcant was not legal and binding, as could easily be proved in court. Pretending to be a widow for gain carries some penalty, I should imagine. As does withdrawing a large amount of capital from the company.'

Her heart thumped painfully in her chest. 'What do you mean by that?'

'A thousand guineas, wasn't it?'

'The company belonged to me, then.'

'Ah yes, a legacy from your first husband. One can't help but wonder what further investigation of the unfortunate demise of Tobias Darsham might uncover. As a matter of interest, what did you do with the money?'

She couldn't tell him she'd given it to that first husband – a man who was supposed to be dead. Hoping she wasn't as pale as she felt, she said, 'What has it got to do with you?'

'I'm just curious. You might as well know that I'm now the owner of the Morcant Shipping Company – though it's now known as the Durrington Line.'

'Since you are old and have no heirs, why do you need a shipping company?'

'Tobias will inherit it, of course, as his father had intended him to, I imagine.'

'As long as you have control of him, you mean. Go to hell.'

His mouth tightened. 'Let's return to the one thousand guineas. If fraud were to be proved it might mean a spell in prison – or transportation to the western region of Australia, a particularly hot and isolated part of that continent, I believe. What would happen to your son then?'

'The only fraud was committed by you –' Joanna suddenly remembered James Stark's advice – 'and the thief who robbed me of the money when I stepped ashore in Melbourne, of course. It was you who conspired with Clara Nash to ruin us all, though. Much joy may it bring you. You're not getting my son.'

The door to the twins' room was flung open. 'And since we're Toby's aunts, we would look after him if anything happened to Joanna,' Irene cried out with great passion. 'And we'd tell the court what a vile and depraved person you are if you try to steal him.'

'Your reputations are already beyond redemption. Several witnesses would testify that the pair of you are exactly like your mother – sluts. As for you, Joanna, others might testify that I'd actually fathered the boy. I might even be able to present evidence of a marriage between us, and a birth certificate with my name on to the court.'

This time Joanna did shudder. Lord Durrington smiled when the three of them fell silent and gazed at him with horror in their eyes.

'I can see you need to think this over,' he said, his voice so gentle it contained a menace all of its own. 'I'll leave the papers for your perusal, but my verbal offer still stands. Let me know your decision as soon as possible. I advise you to be sensible, for I won't let the matter lie indefinitely. In fact, I might take it into my head to remove the boy from your care by force, and take him to London to live with me.'

Toby must have instinctively sensed the family resemblance to Alex in the peer, for he suddenly smiled at his grandfather and shouted out, 'Papa!'

Lord Durrington smiled back. 'I'm so glad you think so, young man.'

After Lord Durrington had gone there was silence, except for Toby, who now he'd found a word had decided to practise it. Beaming a proud smile around at everyone, he said, 'Pa, pa papa papa pa pa.'

'Do we have a cork to stick in his mouth, or shall I use needle and thread?' Irene said. Lydia stood up, shaking out her skirt and saying brightly, 'I think we need a cup of tea. I'll put the kettle on, shall I?'

Filled with dread, Joanna put her head in her hands. 'I don't know what to do.'

The girls' arms came around her in a hug. 'Oliver will be back soon. We'll ask him.'

But Oliver had been at the end of his tether when he'd departed. Joanna was beginning to doubt if he'd come back at all, since there had been no news from him. It was an added worry.

She drew in a deep breath to hold back her tears.

What type of man would remove a son from his mother's care? Toby was part of Alex, a child born of their love. Lust, really, she amended, her sudden objectivity shocking her all the more because of its easy admission. She'd deliberately seduced Alex at the time of Toby's conception, then had sailed off on the *Joanna Rose* hoping he would prove his love for her by chasing after her – which he had, for when she'd signed over the company to him she'd given him no choice.

Handing her precious son over to a stranger to raise was a last resort. Joanna had always been practical, though. If the only way to ensure Toby's survival was to become Durrington's companion, she'd do it, no matter how distasteful such a liaison would be.

At least she wouldn't have to accept him as her lover, for he'd stated he'd be unable to father a child of his own now.

It seemed as though the air in the room had closed in on her with cloying intensity, as if the presence of Lord Durrington had somehow soiled it.

She needed to be alone, to think. 'I'm going out for a walk before dusk falls.'

'We'll look after Toby.'

'Lock the doors in case Lord Durrington comes back.'

She found a quiet spot sheltered by a wall, where she could gaze out over the sea. Just in front of and beneath her, the cliff face was a pale gouge of tumbled spoil from the quarries. Quarrying uncovered the fossils of the ancient sea creatures that had created the rock from which the island was formed. The moulds of ancient gastropods kept many a cottage door propped open to the breezes in the summer, and there was a profitable trade for children who sold the Portland fossils to visitors.

Evening was lengthening the shadows. The March wind had lost its bluster and low grey clouds banded across the sky, releasing fine drizzle to drift in undulating curtains.

To Joanna's left, the fishing lerrets were being escorted home on a pewter sea by a noisy, low-flying crowd of wheeling seagulls.

Soon the clouds would drift lower to release the mist, which would pour over the hill to engulf her inside its clinging wetness. Joanna was suddenly overcome by a strong sense of nostalgia for the simplicity of her childhood. Here she'd grown up, part of the island and its ways. The stone she sat upon could have been cut by her pa before it had so cruelly crushed him into the earth.

But Joanna realized there had been a subtle shift inside her. She was not like Tilda, who, now she was home and living with a husband she loved and respected, seemed to have settled happily into her allotted place once again. Contented with her life, and pleased with the elevation her marriage had provided, Joanna had the feeling that it wouldn't bother Tilda if she never left the island again. But she still refused to visit her mother, who'd been moved into a cottage at Southwell with a carer to look after her. Tilda was finding excuses not to visit, and Joanna didn't blame her for not yielding to the pressure her husband's act of kindness had placed on her.

But she was pleased that her friend had found happiness here. Tilda knew exactly where and to whom she belonged. She'd fitted back into the island like a piece of lost dissection puzzle that had suddenly turned up. Joanna had not.

A seagull drifted up from the cliff to float on ghostly white wings within the gloaming light. It made soft noises in its throat, as if it were trying to communicate.

'Somebody pulled up my roots and I'm drifting on the wind like you,' she told it, wishing she could fly – like the clipper ship *Joanna Rose*, her sails joyously pouched with wind and slicing through an ocean of dark blue sky.

When had Portland changed for her? When had she become an outsider, or a Kimberlin as strangers were called by the islanders? Inside her was a strong feeling that she'd been brought here to rest and to heal, before moving on to some other destiny.

The island had once been a Saxon settlement, from which attacks on mainland Britain were launched. It had been the Saxons who'd named the place as one of the ancient Royal Manors, whose court governed local affairs. They had also established the methods of agriculture that were still used by their descendants.

Portland was the first entry in the Doomsday Book and Joanna had grown up with its long, and sometimes bloody, history all around her. But although the blood of the original inhabitants didn't flow in her veins, she sensed the place would strengthen her spirit before it sent her on her way.

She rose to her feet, brushing dust from her skirt and

drawing that strength into her body as she set off back to the cottage with tendrils of mist clutching at her heels.

The light in the window was a welcome sight, as was the sleepy and rather demanding welcome from her son.

As Joanna hugged him tight and his mouth sought the comfort of her breast, Jane Tremayne came into her mind. She hoped Jane's infant had been safely delivered, and wondered if the child had been a boy or a girl.

Gabriel Tremayne doubted if he'd ever get used to being a shopkeeper, though the business was proving to be lucrative. He was now looking for premises in which to open a ladies' fashion emporium.

He'd already bought another small shipping agency to merge with his own, and had moved into larger offices near the harbour. This had caused much satisfaction to his head clerk. Samuel Stitch would no longer have to share his office with bucket, brooms, shovels and the other implements needing storage space. Indeed, Samuel Stitch had developed an altogether superior manner of late, and was well respected by the clients. Gabriel had recently raised his salary in appreciation.

Grinning to himself, he gazed up at the new sign going up over the door. Gold on olive green. *Gabriel Tremayne & Son. Melbourne. Established 1857.*

Jane joined him, laughing as she teased, 'What if the next one is a boy?'

He gazed at the slight swell of her stomach and took

Christopher from her arms. The boy had inherited his own grey eyes and looks, he thought with smug satisfaction. 'I'll add an S to make a plural.'

Add an S. His grin faded as a memory came of a windswept cemetery on the island of Portland, where the body of his first wife lay under the tough coastal grasses. They had mistakenly buried a boy baby with her – named him Ross. He had asked the stonemason to rename the infant Rose. Not that Gabriel begrudged the boy child his place in Honor's arms. But for twenty years he'd thought his daughter had perished with Honor, and he'd needed mother and daughter to be together. It had been a shock to discover that Joanna Rose was very much alive.

Honor Darsham didn't come into his mind very often now, but the daughter they'd produced and the miracle of her survival did. More so now the news of Alexander Morcant's death had reached him, an event that had signalled the end of the shipping company Gabriel had spent his life building up. He'd grieved for the young man, for he'd mentored and loved Alex Morcant since boyhood. How would Joanna and his grandson manage now?'

Jane laid a hand on his arm. 'You're thinking of Joanna, aren't you?'

'Aye.'

'I only knew her for a short time, but I formed the impression of an enterprising young lady with a lot of inner strength. I'm sure she'll be all right. In her letter, your mother said Joanna had gone back to Portland to live.'

He nodded. 'There's that. Joanna has a roof over her head, and she'll be able to survive there, for that's the way she was raised. No doubt my mother will help her out, if need be.'

'Then you're worrying unnecessarily. Are you going to the shipping agency today?'

'Not until the *Joanna Rose* has sailed, I don't want to run into her master. After that I've got an appointment with William Barnes, to see if he'll rent me some shop premises.'

'Do you know the captain of the *Joanna Rose* then?'

'Aye. James Stark's letter said Edward Staines has taken over her command and, although I'd dearly love to see Edward, I can't take the risk. James wrote to say that Barnard Charsford had seized the *Joanna Rose* even though she wasn't used as collateral. She was sold to Durrington as part of the company stock.'

'But isn't that illegal?'

'It's piracy, but there's none who can prove it. Durrington kept Staines on as master, though. He couldn't have hired a better man, except Oliver Morcant, perhaps. But word's out about Oliver being arrested in America, and he'll be blacklisted. He'll take it hard. Although Oliver is no businessman, he's the most honest man I've ever known. I wish I could do something to help, but Oliver doesn't even know I'm still alive.'

'We might think of something.'

'I can't see what. Oliver's two sisters are living with Joanna, I understand. She has a big heart.' He fell silent, then gazed at his son and murmured, 'You and your mother are the only good things to come out of this mess I started.'

'Nonsense,' Jane said quietly. 'What about Joanna and your grandson? Why don't you write and ask them to join us? We have enough room now the house extensions are complete. The shop and agency are doing well and Joanna could work in the fashion emporium.'

'Do you think she'd come?'

'She liked it here. She told me she was only going back to England because she loved Alex, and he regarded his purpose in life as being to run the shipping company.'

'Aye, he did. That's something I brought him up to do. But Joanna might not want to leave Clara's girls behind.'

'Goodness, Gabe, do stop finding obstacles. There's nothing to stop those young women from coming with her, is there? You said you only met them once, as children. They probably won't remember you.'

Gabriel gazed at this intelligent women he'd married. Her eyes were brown and honest, her looks indifferent and her voice so quiet that she tended to be overlooked when in company. He felt very tender towards her. Giving one of his rare smiles, he said, 'Have I ever told you that I love you?'

He adored the blush that crept under her skin and the pleasure contained in the smile she gave. 'No, Gabe, you never have.'

Jane looked all dewy eyed and emotional now he'd declared himself. If they hadn't been standing in the street he'd have kissed her. He pulled her handkerchief from her sleeve and handed it to her with a gruff, 'Well, now I have. You don't have to weep over it, do you?'

She slid her hand into his and gently squeezed it. 'I love you too, Gabe.'

Gabriel smiled for the second time that day, for he'd never thought he'd be offered this second chance at happiness. 'Dammit, woman, d'you think I don't know it?'

The *Joanna Rose* was due to sail at seventeen hundred hours. At nineteen hundred Gabriel made his way from the shipping agency office to the crowded hotel bar where he was to meet William Barnes.

A couple of drinks secured him the offer of the shop premises he wanted. They sealed the deal with a handshake, and a promise of a formal lease to follow.

Barnes had a dinner party to attend, so left shortly afterwards. Gabriel stayed on, nursing a whisky and enjoying the noise in the smoky atmosphere. As he sipped his drink his gaze went along the polished curve of the bar and met the probing scrutiny of another man. His eyes widened, his hand jerked and whisky slopped down the side of the glass.

What the hell! It was Edward Staines!

Edward half rose, shock and recognition coming to his eyes, though there was uncertainty too.

Gabriel didn't bother finishing his drink. Rising to his feet, he strode rapidly from the bar and out through the double glass doors. Instinctively, he headed in the direction of the shop.

Edward came after him. When Gabe reached the

corner he heard him shout, 'Tobias . . . Tobias Darsham.'

Gabriel hadn't been called that name in a long while, and the pull of it was hard to resist. Steeling himself not to look back, he turned the corner and began to run, letting himself into the shop before Edward could catch him up.

But the master of the *Joanna Rose* was not far behind. Edward turned the corner and footsteps pounded along the road as Gabe latched the door. He flattened himself against a set of shelves, without having time to shoot the bolts.

Edward Staines stopped right outside the shop, so close Gabe could have touched him, had there not been a thin sheet of glass between them. Dear God, how he'd like to have shaken his former employee's hand. Gabriel was breathing so heavily it was a wonder to him that Edward couldn't hear him.

Staines cursed in a heartfelt fashion as he turned his head this way and that, searching the shadowy doorways. Then he shaded his eyes and peered through the glass door into the interior of the shop. If Edward had shortened his vision he might have seen Gabe, but he didn't.

Gabriel had the feeling that the man could sense him, though, and he held his breath as Edward carefully turned the handle and exerted pressure. The door moved until it met the resistance of the latch, and held. A solid thud with the heel of his palm would have seen Staines through it.

Ten minutes passed before Edward seemed to satisfy

himself that he'd been mistaken, and he moved away, shaking his head in a perplexed manner.

Breathing a sigh of relief, Gabriel shot the bolts and let himself out through the back of the shop, to where his horse was tethered.

'The damned girl refused,' Durrington said, thumping a fist on Seth's desk. 'Haven't you found anything I can use yet?'

'You have my report, My Lord. Joanna Morcant is an intelligent woman, who has recently been bereaved. If I question her relatives or go too fast I'll lose her trust completely.'

The peer leaned forward. 'I'm not asking you to gain her trust. I'm telling you to find something I can use as a lever to get custody of my grandson. I've already threatened Joanna Morcant with court action over her shipboard marriage, and suggested that the money she took from the company was fraud.'

'You'd have a job proving it, since the cash was properly receipted, and the company was hers at the time.'

'I know that, you damned fool. I just thought to scare her a little. I even offered her a home with me if she'd sign over young Toby.'

Seth jerked upright. 'The hell you did! What did she say to that?'

'That she'd rather move in with the devil.' Durrington cackled. 'I should have told her I was the devil.'

Seth matched Durrington's grin, conceding that the peer had a sense of humour, of sorts.

'The girl doesn't scare easily, I tell you. She was about to brain Bisley with a silver candlestick. She got some stupid idea in her head that he was trying to make off with her son.'

Seated by the door, Bisley's half-hooded eyes, broad nose and petulant mouth were set in a finely boned face. He smelled of lavender oil. Seth tried not to shudder when Bisley sent him a seductive smile that had something coquettish about it.

Durrington chuckled. 'Bisley would have broken her neck before she'd had time to lift the candlestick from the sideboard.'

Seth looked Durrington straight in the eye, his senses prickling with uneasiness at the threat implied by the earl's words. His voice sounded calm enough, though. 'Joanna Morcant is a small woman. She'd lack the strength to damage a fully grown man.' *But she was loaded with pluck.* 'It would be easy to disarm her without causing her damage. Anything else would have been excessive use of force.'

There was a moment of silence, then Bisley gave a high-pitched giggle. 'It would have been self-defence.'

Seth's tongue salted and the juices in his mouth seemed to dry up as alarm speared through his mind. 'You do understand that my agency operates strictly within the laws of the land.'

'Yes, yes.' The earl's eyes narrowed in on Seth as he stood up. 'I simply want something I can use as a lever. D'you understand?'

Tempted to tell him to go to hell, Seth only just stopped himself. He hadn't told Lord Durrington everything, and neither did he intend to. With just the right amount of deference in his stance, he opened the door to the corridor for his visitors to depart. 'I'll certainly do my best, My Lord. There's no hurry, however, since the child has yet to be weaned.'

Crossing to the window, Seth concealed himself behind a screen. Through a gap in the fabric he watched the peer disappear into his carriage and the vehicle move away. Durrington's man had entered a bookshop opposite. Using a small telescope Seth gazed into the interior of the shop, where the man lounged in the shadows, book open in hands. He was pretending to read while he kept his eye on the main entrance to the building Seth occupied.

Obviously, the earl didn't trust him. Neither of them knew where Seth lived. He had made sure of that. Not even his brothers knew.

Leaving through the outer office Seth smiled at Mr Geevers. 'We're under surveillance so I'm going out the back way.'

'I understand, Mr Adams.'

Seth went up two flights of stairs to the roof. Once there, he walked along a narrow gutter where grey slate roofs formed a valley. The gutter was the width of his foot. Jumping across a span a yard wide, he landed lightly on the roof of a neighbouring building. Seth took a left turn, strolled along another gutter and up a short, metal ladder to a skylight. Sliding the catch open with the blade of his knife, he stepped down a wooden ladder into the attic rooms he rented.

This was an accommodation address, which he'd

furnished comfortably. Seth rarely stayed in the rooms, though he sometimes enjoyed the company of women here. On occasion, they had also served as a place for others to lie low. Kept clean by his landlady, who asked no questions and ventured no opinions, Seth knew he could never find a better hiding hole

From the attic it was easy to gain the street that ran behind the building backing on to his office. Making sure Bisley was not amongst the thronging crowds below, Seth slipped downstairs and out of the door to join them.

He must visit Joanna Morcant again, he thought as he strode off in the opposite direction from which he'd come. But this time, he intended to go to Portland alone.

Oliver Morcant was back in London. He'd received short shift from the Nash family, for most of them had disliked his mother intensely. Nor did the Nashes want anything to do with their impoverished female relatives.

'Your mother was immoral, a parasite who spent our cousin's fortune and drove him to an early grave,' one of them declared, leaving him with the suspicion that they mourned the loss of the fortune rather than the wealthy cousin.

Not that they were without funds, since the Nash bank remained in business under their directorship. Oliver tried to salvage something for his sisters, but on enquiring about his mother's share he learned that she'd sold her interest in it some time ago.

Clara had not been allowed to set foot in the marble

halls of the Nash mansions since she'd returned to Boston. Only Agatha Nash had taken pity on her, paying her rent on a room in a poor part of town. There, the sale of Clara's jewellery funded her need for opium, an expensive habit which had eventually killed her.

His mother had lasted several months after Oliver had arrived, drifting in and out of a narcotic cloud, pathetically happy to see him, her dependency keeping him there. But not once had she mentioned the daughters she'd left behind to fend for themselves. He'd worked in a bar at night, cleaning the place after the clients had left, emptying the spittoons, polishing the tables and washing the vomit and piss from the floor and back alley. It had kept him in food, while his mother, growing thinner by the hour, seemed able to live without it, as long as she had her medicine.

Clara had been buried in a pauper's grave. Nobody had turned up to mourn her passing except Oliver, and the elderly woman who'd paid the boarding-house rent.

Agatha Nash had stepped forward afterwards, handing over a leather satchel. 'Take very good care of it, Captain Morcant. The money is for my great nieces, and is unreceipted. It's all they'll get from the Nash family.'

'Why have you supported my mother?' he'd asked the woman.

'Because Clara was cheated out of her share of the bank and my nieces are impoverished as a result.

Clara's share was worth five times what they paid her for it. But they discovered her weakness and exploited it.'

'Thank you for telling me. I'm glad somebody cares.'

'You misunderstand me, Captain Morcant. I've never cared for the woman. She was a reckless and despicable person of dubious breeding, one who selfishly pandered to her own needs and desires. But it's different with Lydia and Irene. I have no children of my own. Indeed, I never married. The family will never support or acknowledge Clara's girls. They've convinced themselves that the twins have no Nash blood in their veins.'

Oliver hadn't been surprised at the revelation, for his mother had been shameless. 'And you?'

'I have no opinion. But my cousin loved those girls, and I loved my cousin. We were engaged to be married once. Lydia and Irene provided him with much happiness while he was alive.'

'You trust me with this, knowing I was once arrested for fraud?'

'I had you investigated, Captain Morcant. I know about your past. You were exonerated. Have you been informed that your former wife has died?'

He jerked with the shock of hearing it. But this was followed by a sense of relief that he was no longer tied to Susannah. 'No . . . I haven't. How?'

'She tried to escape arrest from a Pinkerton agent by jumping from a locomotive. She fell under the wheels and was cut in half, I believe.'

Ignoring his shudder, Agatha held out a hand. 'I doubt if we'll meet again, Captain Morcant. Goodbye.'

A brief shake and she was gone, walking rapidly towards a waiting carriage, an upright figure dressed in dark grey.

When he was alone, Oliver opened the satchel. It contained a steerage ticket back to England and a large amount of cash.

Oliver had not allowed the satchel out of his sight on the uncomfortable voyage back to England. Almost as soon as he stepped ashore he placed the money in a trust fund. He marvelled that Agatha Nash had brought herself to trust him with it after his mother's excesses. Not that he'd proved to be much of a businessman himself, but he wouldn't steal.

Oliver didn't intend to allow his sisters to squander the windfall, for there wasn't enough of it to indulge in the luxury they'd been brought up with. They had their futures to consider, and he hoped they didn't have ideas that were too grand.

He stroked his finger over the ring Joanna had placed in his care. Her gesture had humbled him, and the fact that he could return it to her was a cause of pride. He silently blessed Agatha Nash, too. There were some good women in the world to compensate for poor, dead Susannah and his self-serving mother. He must remember that.

8

It was a lovely June day. Joanna was just about to bathe Toby when a knock came at the door. The breath caught in her throat in alarm.

Tucking Toby's naked body in the crook of her elbow she peered cautiously out through a chink in the curtain. Seth Adams was in the process of polishing the toes of his dusty shoes on the back of his immaculate grey trousers. First one leg, then the other, nearly losing his balance in the process.

As if the soft chuckle she gave attracted his attention, he turned and saw her before she could duck out of sight. Her chuckle became a laugh when he grinned and moved to the window to peer through it. 'May I come in?'

He had the cheek of the devil to come back here. She shouldn't allow him inside, but she needed to know for certain who he was working for, and the urge to know more about him was irresistible. She pulled back the bolts. He gave a slight frown when she bolted the door after him, and set the package he carried on the dresser. 'Judging by the precautions, someone's been bothering you. Or are you just frightened I'll escape?'

She smiled at the teasing arrogance of the latter query, ignored the rest. 'I was about to bathe Toby before putting him down for a nap. I'd better get on with it before the water cools. Come through to the kitchen, if you like.'

'I take it that Toby is the source of that peculiar ripe smell.'

'He got into the hen house when my back was turned.'

Toby offered Seth a beatific smile. 'Papa.'

'Unfortunately, no, but I'll take it as a compliment?'

'I'd rather you didn't. He uses the word indiscriminately.'

'A rather crushing reply. Do I detect disapproval?'

Joanna wouldn't be drawn as she lowered Toby into the metal tub and lathered his hair. Quickly rinsing off the suds, she rubbed the excess water from his hair and started on his body, smiling when Toby began to giggle. She dropped a kiss on his damp curls. 'Stop showing off.'

But Toby would have none of it. He slapped both hands hard on the surface of his bath water so it splashed all over them.

'I'm so sorry. I should have warned you,' she said as Seth brushed the water from his coat.

Standing her dripping son up, Joanna kept a good grasp on him with one hand while she tipped a jug of fresh water over him with the other. While he spluttered and gasped, she plucked him from the bath, wrapped him tightly in a towel and set about drying him.

Glancing at Seth over Toby's head, Joanna spied laughter in his eyes when he said, 'You stand no nonsense from the male of the species, I see.'

She gave a light laugh. 'When they're dependant on you like this, you wonder why boys grow up to be such strutting, arrogant creatures who imagine women are fools.'

'I do hope I'm not included in that cruel assessment.'

She slid him a sideways glance and smiled. 'Am I to take it you think I'm a fool, then?'

'On the contrary,' Seth said smoothly. 'I think you're a rare combination of beauty and brains. And you blush delightfully when I compliment you.'

'It's the steam.'

The grin he tossed her made her blush even more. As much as Joanna tried not to, she rather liked Seth Adams.

He took Toby's garments up from the chair, handing them over to her as they were needed. Afterwards, he carried the bath into the garden to empty the contents on to the vegetable patch, as if it were a domestic task he performed every day of his life. Joanna's cynicism asserted itself, telling her it was an action designed to disarm her.

When he returned, she headed up the stairs with her son. 'I won't be long.'

Joanna rocked Toby protectively against her breast, her mouth a kiss away from his sweet head, so her breath stirred the fine strands of his dark hair. Soon,

Toby's eyes began to droop and he fell asleep, his lashes a dark sweep against his translucent skin. Love for him almost overwhelmed her as she kissed his flushed cheek and laid him gently in his cot. With luck, he would sleep for a couple of hours while she got on with the washing.

But first she must give her guest some refreshment before she sent him on his way – for send him away she must.

The sound of hammering came to her ears as she drew a curtain across the window. Seth was in the garden, repairing the hole in the hen house that Toby had pushed himself through. The hens were huddled in a tight bunch at the far end of the run, their necks bobbing up and down as they watched him through nervous eyes and clucked amongst themselves.

Joanna knew how threatened they felt. They assumed the same nervous stance each time she selected one for the pot. But this time her attention was not fixed on the hens, but on the cockerel.

Seth was in a crouching position, the material of his trousers pulled tightly across his buttocks. Tossed by the breeze, his hair seemed spun through with sunshine and the muscles under his shirt sleeves moved easily with his every exertion. He had removed his jacket, revealing a pearl-grey waistcoat. Her glance followed the sinuous line of him.

Desire pulled at the very core of her. With an effort she tore her eyes away from the temptation. But it was harder to control her thoughts, though she told herself it was too soon after Alex. Then she remembered the woman's glove she'd found amongst Alex's clothes, the smell of perfume on him. Racked by a strong sense of betrayal, her next intake of breath was almost a sob of anguish. She gazed at Seth again. It had been over a year since she'd felt a man's arms around her. But it couldn't be this man – this *Judas*.

He turned, his glance coming up to the window, giving a lazy sort of smile. He unfolded to his feet, arching his back into his hands to ease it. His body displayed a tensile strength and grace with the movement.

Joanna closed her eyes for a moment, giving in to the excitement of the craving to touch him. When she opened them it was to look away and she despised her lack of control as she went down to the kitchen.

The package he'd brought had been moved to the kitchen table. It smelled delicious as she unwrapped it. She placed a small portion of the dark fruity cake it contained in her mouth. A decay of autumn fruits was released against her tongue, an aroma of brandy exploded into her brain. It was a cake of great riches, made for lovers to sample.

Only he wasn't her lover, Joanna thought crossly as she made the tea and cut a couple of slices of the cake. She called Seth in when the hammering ceased. He was still shrugging into his coat when he entered.

She would allow him the opportunity to explain, she thought.

Automatically folding down his collar for him, she found herself gazing into his astute grey eyes. She took a hasty step backwards, picking up the tray to create a barrier between them. 'Thank you for bringing the cake.'

'Kate helped our cook make it. She insisted that I deliver it personally to you.'

'How is your niece?'

'Perfectly well, though rather disgruntled at being left behind. She sends her best wishes.'

'You should have brought her with you. Children are so delightfully honest.' Joanna handed him the best cup and led the conversation to where she wanted it to go. 'It was good of you to come all this way just to deliver a cake.'

The smile he offered was charmingly wry. 'You know perfectly well I didn't do that. I came to see you again, Joanna.'

Deep down where it mattered, she was disappointed by the smooth delivery of his answer. Quietly, she told him, 'I don't believe you.'

His laughter rang out, slightly nonplussed, but deep and pleasurable, nevertheless. 'Are you always so blunt?'

'Not always, Seth, and don't try to convince me that you are, either.' She drew his card from her pocket and threw it on the table. 'What are you trying to find out this time?'

He sobered as his eyes came up to hers, wary now. 'I don't understand.'

'Of course you do, Seth.' How clever he was, and how revealing the tiny expression of shame growing in those eyes when she placed before him the dreaded name, 'Lord Durrington?'

Heart pounding, Joanna stared at him, hoping he'd deny it, for she was acting only on her instinct that the two visits were connected.

He didn't deny it. After a while he leaned forward to gently kiss her cheek, saying before he rose to his feet, 'Forgive me for not telling you.'

Forgive him, when her beloved son's future was at stake? Her mind flooding with fury, she said, 'I came here with my son to recover from the death of a man who I loved. Now the future of his child has been threatened by the actions of someone I'd begun to trust.' She gave a bitter laugh. 'Do you really expect me to forgive you?'

'Allow me to explain—'

'No! Allow me to explain why my doors were locked. Lord Durrington and his servant Bisley paid me a visit. You knew that, though, didn't you?'

He inclined his head.

'They threatened me. Now I spend my days and nights in fear, in case Toby is stolen from me, or harmed in some way. What if it was Kate they were after?'

His face paled. 'I intended to tell you about this, that's why I came here.'

She took a step towards him, keeping her voice low so as not to rouse Toby. 'That's not what you just indicated, you conniving snake. You thought you could flatter me, so I would lower my guard.' Throwing caution to the winds she lashed out at him, whipping her hand across his face. 'Get out!'

Joanna couldn't believe she'd hit him, nor the feeling of satisfaction the act had brought to her. Tears came into her eyes as she stared at the crimson patches beginning to burn on his cheeks. 'I was beginning to like you,

Seth, but you've turned out to be hollow. Have you no conscience?'

'You're angry now, Joanna.' When he placed his hand in caress against her face, her instinct was to nestle against his palm. Instead, she jerked away from his touch.

He drew in a deep breath at that, shrugged, then said, 'I'll never do anything to harm you or your son, Joanna, I promise. Please believe it. I can't leave you like this. I'll be back when you've had time to calm down.'

Picking up his hat, gloves and cane he was gone, closing the door gently behind him and leaving her shaking.

Seth climbed the steep hills of Portland up a winding path along the cliff edge, striding out so his thighs and calf muscles protested when he reached the top.

His face still felt roasted from Joanna's slap. The shameful indignity of being treated that way by a woman made his cheeks glow even more. But he conceded that he'd deserved the treatment she'd meted out. He'd underestimated her intelligence to start with. She'd lulled him into a false sense of security before showing her hand today. Nothing but complete honesty would redeem him in her eyes now.

The inn he chose to purchase his lunch from was filled with smoke and noise, which temporarily faded into astonished silence when he entered. A well-dressed stranger in their midst was a rare event. Leather-faced quarrymen, most of them were, dressed in shirtsleeves, cloth caps and braces. There was a strong smell of sweat about them, suggestive of the honest toil they engaged in.

Not that Seth could understand much of the talk, for the locals' voices were gravelly from inhaling years of stone dust, and they constantly cleared their throats with a rattling sound.

Seth placed some money on the bar then carried his meal of a large, crusty pork pie and a glass of beer outside. There he seated himself on a rickety rustic bench, which allowed him a view over the sea. He attacked the pie with some gusto, for he hadn't eaten that morning, and was hungry.

When his appetite was satisfied, he looked beyond the pitted and scarred immediacy of his surrounds to the delightful vista that was spread out below him. A beach of pebbles scimitared towards the haze that surrounded Weymouth. A train chugged along a breakwater, still under construction and slicing into the sea after several years of toil. Behind the steam engine, trucks piled high with stone were dragged, their destination the next section of the breakwater. There were sightseers walking along the line – marvelling at this fine feat of engineering, no doubt.

Beyond, sailing boats and steamers plied busily back and forth on a sea of shifting blue glass. A steam yacht with side paddles patrolled the length of the breakwater. He could just make out the figures on her deck.

Soon, Seth was surrounded by an arc of seagulls, who'd sailed in on the breeze to salvage the crumbs from his feet. Around him the island was a constant hive of industry, making his own profession seem insignificant by comparison.

Although Seth had always like to pit his mind against a puzzle, there was something grubby about the contemplation of aiding a powerful man to part a mother from her child. Listening to his conscience was something Joanna had forcibly reminded him of today.

Joanna Rushmore's pa had been a quarryman who, by all accounts, had been a decent and hardworking man. He'd built the cottage Joanna and her son lived in with his own two hands, a monument to his skill that would withstand centuries of storms.

Seth had no such practical skills himself. He lived on his wits, and he craved adventure. The arrival of Kate had kept him grounded, something he'd regretted at first, although he wouldn't be without her now.

What if it were Kate? she'd said, and he knew he'd kill to defend his niece, if he had to. Thus, Joanna Morcant would defend her own to her last breath. She deserved more than consideration. She demanded it.

A little while later Seth set off down the hill, hoping Joanna's anger had abated enough for her to accept his apology.

He went in through the back way. On her washing line several undergarments danced in the breeze. A petticoat flicked a miniature rainstorm over him from a frilly hem.

The back door was open to the sunshine. Joanna was in the kitchen, up to her elbows in washing. Strands of dark hair lay damply against her face as she expended her energy on a garment applied to the washboard. She didn't look up as his body blocked the sunshine in the doorway.

He knocked gently on the door jamb. 'Joanna, it's me. Seth.'

'I saw you coming down the hill.' The anguish he'd caused her was an accusation in her voice. Lifting the skirt of her apron, she dabbed her face before gazing at him through eyes the colour of crushed bluebells.

Guilt filled him to the brim. 'You've been crying.'

'A soapsud went in my eye.'

'Liar!' he said softly.

The corner of her mouth quirked. 'Say what you have to, Seth Adams. I'm busy.'

'I'm sorry, and yes, I do have a conscience, which is why I'd decided not to work for Lord Durrington. It was a decision I made before I came here today. Rest assured, I've told him nothing he didn't already know.'

Head slanted to one side, her eyes sharpened as she regarded him. 'What's the nothing you didn't tell him?'

He was beyond being surprised by her. 'Conjecture.'

'Such as?'

'Why there's no birth recorded for Joanna Rose Rushmore.'

She shrugged and her eyes momentarily flickered away from him. 'Perhaps my ma and pa forgot.'

Her ma? Instinct told Seth something didn't ring true here, and Seth always went with his instincts. He sifted through the information and conversations he'd stored in his brain, remembering when Joanna had tried to sell him some jewellery. She'd said it had belonged to her mother. But not the mother of this humble home she'd been raised in, surely.

The old man at the cemetery had said she'd washed ashore in a cradle. The graves from the wreck told their own tale. There was only one conclusion he could reach, the same one he'd examined, then discarded as too improbable. Her mother was Honor Darsham and her father Tobias Darsham. He wondered if she knew that.

'Not many parents would forget to register the birth of an only child when it was born. What about your marriage to Tobias Darsham?'

Despite her casual voice, her face closed up and her eyes were wary. 'What about it?'

'You've never once talked about him.'

'Tobias Darsham was a good man. We were wed for only a couple of weeks when he drowned. His body was washed ashore many months later, and is buried at Southampton.'

Seth already knew that, and also that Alex Morcant and a lawyer called James Stark, who'd once handled the legal business for the Darsham and Morcant Shipping Company, had identified his body. 'You called your child after Tobias. Didn't Alex mind?'

Her head slanted to one side. 'Toby bears both their names. Tobias had always been a father figure to Alex while he was growing up. Alex was pleased I'd named him after Tobias. It was like a tribute to the man who had loved and mentored him.'

'Alex would have regarded Tobias as a grandfather to your son, then.'

Joanna shifted from one foot to the other and tried to make light of the suggestion, though it clearly disturbed her. 'You're quite ruthless in your interrogation, Seth. Are you sure you're not still working for Lord Durrington?'

She was clever in shifting the focus of the conversation, but he intended to shift it back. 'Durrington is not the type to let the matter rest, or to allow any stone to remain unturned. If he can gain control of your son by discrediting you, he will – and he'll hire someone more ruthless and less discreet than me. Did you love Tobias Darsham?'

'Not when we first married, though we were drawn to each other. He helped me when I was attacked. Tobias was looking for a wife and I had nowhere to go, so he offered me his protection and a home.' Her smile came then and her face was transformed from sadness to joy. 'I grew to love him later.'

A strange statement when she'd only been married to the man for two weeks. Oddments such as this, when pieced together with other oddments, often made sense out of nonsense. Envy stabbed at him that a dead man could evoke such a smile in her, though, father or not.

Anxiety came to the fore. 'Why does Lord Durrington want to investigate my first marriage?'

She knew why, but he wanted her to tell him. The anxiety in her eyes was replaced with awareness, then resignation. Her shoulders drooped a little as she sought for a convincing lie, so he felt sorry for her and helped her out. 'You needn't say anything, Joanna, I've already worked things out.'

The anguished little cry she gave touched his heart. When he took her in his arms she laid her head against his chest and whispered, 'What are you going to do about it?'

'Nothing. There's one thing I'd like to know, though. It's a rather delicate matter and I risk—'

'My first marriage was in name only if that's what you're asking me, Seth,' she said.

Seth admitted to himself he was relieved beyond measure. 'Only an honourable man would take his own life in such a situation.'

She started, then gazed up at him and smiled. 'Yes, you're right . . . Tobias Darsham was honourable.'

Her breasts were soft against his chest, her mouth a delicious curve. In the position they were in it was natural for him to incline his head and take advantage of what those soft lips had to offer, and it seemed natural for her to respond to his overture. The intimate and entirely distracting embrace was quickly terminated when there came the sound of voices and laughter, of footsteps running down the path.

Guiltily, they sprang apart.

'Joanna, Mrs Abernathy said we had a visitor. Has Oliver arrived home?' They bustled into the kitchen, two young women who looked delightfully alike. The laughter in their faces faded to disappointment as they gazed from Seth to Joanna. A few seconds later the expression was replaced by curiosity.

'May I present my sisters-in-law, Lydia and Irene Morcant,' she said. 'They are living here until their brother returns from America.'

So this was the pair Lord Durrington had intended to debauch, the two girls whom the peer had evicted from their home without a moment's remorse when his desire had been thwarted. Seth stifled a grin. No wonder there were so many petticoats drying on the line! He wondered how Joanna would explain him.

The glance she gave him was slightly flustered, but when he grinned encouragingly at her, she recovered quickly. 'This is Mr Seth Adams, a friend of mine from London. He had business in Weymouth and dropped in to see how I was getting on.'

'Then you must stay for tea, Mr Adams. Oh look, Irene. Fruit cake. How absolutely wonderful. I haven't seen anything so delicious for months. You look flushed, Joanna. Allow me to take over your task while you tidy yourself up. If Mr Adams has come all this way to see you, you can't entertain him in the kitchen, can she, Irene?'

'Indeed not, Lydia. I despair of you, Joanna. Go and tidy your hair this minute, you cannot entertain a gentleman looking like a washerwoman.'

The pair grinned at each other and shooed them gently but firmly into the sitting room

'You must forgive the twins,' Joanna said laughingly. 'They're good girls who are trying hard to get used to their poverty and be useful. Now and again they become a little . . . *imperious*.'

'They're a spirited pair. It was kind of you to take them under your roof.'

'Oh, I love them completely. They're such good company for me.' Her smile came and went uncertainly, and, flustered, she fiddled with her disarrayed hair, tucking a bit in here and there. It was a losing battle, for it freed from its style and fell gloriously about her. 'I must look completely untidy.'

Seth took a seat on the battered old settee and chuckled. 'You look wonderfully rumpled, as if we'd made love all night and you'd just just woken from sleep.'

She gave an involuntary and rather regretful sigh. Upstairs, Toby began to rattle the bars of his cot. The mouth Seth had just tasted rearranged into a trembling oval, making him want to kiss her all over again. 'You're being much too personal.'

'And you're trying too hard to be prim. It's not as if I took advantage of something you didn't encourage. You enjoyed the experience as much as I did, even though it was an attempt to distract me from my line of questioning. Admit it.'

Amusement struggled with annoyance in her eyes. She made a small exasperated sound in her throat, then turned and scurried up the stairs.

When she reached the top she turned, giving a soft, provocative laugh. 'I'll admit to no such thing.'

Seth grinned. 'Then I'll have to be more convincing next time.

Oliver had spent several weeks in London trying to get a berth on a ship.

The spare key to Joanna and Alex's former home in Southwark had always been kept behind a loose brick. It was still there. As the place was boarded up, at night he sneaked in after dark and slept there.

The personal items had been removed, but some furniture was still in place and he found a mattress to sleep on. The house had become an empty, echoing, black cavern, for hardly a chink of light showed through the shutters, and he didn't dare risk lighting a candle, because the place was patrolled by a night-watchman.

Oliver and the river rats were the only inhabitants of the house. Over the next month his beard grew long and his clothes ragged. He began to beg on the streets for enough money to eat. Always slim, now he was gaunt – and he began to dislike himself.

The ring Joanna had entrusted to him was tied around his neck on a piece of string, and it was that which kept him from giving up altogether.

Use it if you have to, she'd told him.

So far he'd avoided doing so. But returning to his hiding place one night he discovered that the remaining furniture had been removed, the doors and window frames were missing and some of the floorboards had been prised up. Any attachment to its former owners now seemed to be gone. Durrington was probably demolishing the place to make room for warehouses.

The only course Oliver could now think of to take was his last resort. Ask for charity from the lawyer, James Stark. He spent his last night at the house, cold and draughty now, curled in a corner. Dawn brought a foot thudding against his thigh, as a rough voice yelled, 'Get out of here and don't come back, else you'll be charged with trespass.'

Oliver stumbled away, heading towards the city.

James Stark's clerk didn't recognize him. 'What business would someone like you have with Mr Stark?'

'It's me, Mr Potter. Oliver Morcant.'

'Good gracious, so it is!' Potter slid his glasses to the end of his nose and peered doubtfully through them at him. 'My, you do look down on your luck, Captain Morcant. We thought you'd gone to America. I'll ask Mr Stark if he can see you. He's a very busy man, you know.'

But James wasn't too busy to see him. After shaking hands he ordered some coffee and muffins, and watched as Oliver wolfed them down.

'It's obvious you're in trouble. Christ, Oliver, why the devil didn't you contact me sooner?'

Oliver spread his hands. 'Looking like this? I've been trying to find work for months. I've been too ashamed even to go and see my sisters. They could be dead, for all I know.'

'They're not. Joanna Morcant wrote to me. She said they're well. The girls are working as private tutors, giving piano lessons and such. They're still living with Joanna and I understand they get on very well with each other. They're worried about you, though, and asked me to make enquiries about your whereabouts.'

Relief filled him. 'I must let them know I'm safe. I need a favour, James.'

'Of course. How much do you need?'

'It's employment I need. I've tried every shipping line in London and nobody will employ me.'

'You're blacklisted, my friend. That's why.'

Oliver's midriff tightened. 'For what reason?'

'Who can fathom Durrington's mind. He has many friends and a long reach. The Morcant family are finished in this city. You might have to try the other ports.' He leaned forward, taking a longer look at him. 'By God, Oliver. You do look hard done by. Come, I'll take you home. We'll clean you up and trim those whiskers on the way so you feel more human. And I'll buy you a ticket to Portland, so you can visit your sisters.'

'Why should you do that?'

'Because Tobias Darsham is my friend and he'd expect me to.'

'You make it sound as if Tobias is still alive.'

James shrugged and dug the blade of a paper knife into his blotter. 'Do I? I was thinking of him earlier, that could account for it. Alex helped me identify Tobias, you know.'

Oliver gave a faintly ironic smile, for the family fortunes had plummeted swiftly after Tobias had died, making him recall, with a stab of guilt, that his own gullibility had played a major part in the demise of the company. He'd realized how particularly inept he was at business that day. 'Alex told me he lost his dinner at the sight of the corpse.'

'Yes, he did, but the state it was in was enough to make anyone sick. Alex always had a weak stomach, as you know. It killed the poor sod in the end, and Durrington couldn't wait to pick up the scraps from Barnard Charsford.'

'I thought Durrington had bought the company from the bank.'

'From the banker. A private deal. Charsford is the

brother of the Earl of Alsonbury, and a friend of Durrington's. There's a half-brother, too. Goes by the name of Seth Adams.'

They fell silent for a few minutes, then James stood up. 'Come on, Oliver, let's make you presentable before I send you back to your sisters. Will you stay the night?'

'No, but I'll accept a loan and you can take this as collateral. Joanna offered it to me to use in an emergency, and I know you won't sell it on before I can redeem it.' He jerked the string from his neck and held out the gold ring she'd given him.

James smiled, turning it over in his fingers before handing it back. 'Alex gave this to Joanna. It represents her marriage to him, and, although it wasn't a legal one in the strictest sense of the word, it's all she has left of Alex except for Toby. Take it back to her. Its return will push you up in her estimation.'

'You like her, don't you?'

'I do. She's a rare creature who can adapt to her situation, and is loyal to those who she loves and trusts.'

Remembering the night he'd spent with his brother at the theatre, Oliver said, 'Did Alex really love Joanna, or did he marry her for the company, as Tobias requested?'

James shrugged. 'I guess we'll never know that now.'

9

The *Joanna Rose* had cleared her cargo and Edward Staines had reported to the offices of the Durrington Line to complete the necessary paperwork.

There, he was shocked to discover that the company would dispense with his services after the next voyage, since the clippers were to be auctioned off.

'I'm so sorry, Captain,' the company manager, Henry Wetherall, told him, looking extremely unhappy about the situation he found himself in. Henry had worked for the company since it had first become the Darsham and Morcant Shipping Company, and he knew all the officers well. 'Lord Durrington has purchased the Green Star Steamship Company, and the clippers are to be auctioned off in the new year, after your return from the next run.'

'And what about my severance pay, as per contract, which still has a year to run.'

Henry hummed dubiously in his throat. 'That I'm unable to answer, since your contract was with the former owners of the company and the present owner has his lawyer examining the contracts. I'll make enquiries on your behalf.' He gazed nervously around him and lowered his voice. 'My own position is in doubt too, Captain Staines. The company is financially overextended, and the new owner doesn't know the shipping business. If any one of the clippers doesn't make it back to port with a full cargo, God forbid, then Durrington will be plunged into debt . . . and he still has progress payments to make on the new steamer.'

Swallowing the bad news, Edward strode through the streets to the office of James Stark, before the lawyer finished work for the day.

The sky overhead was a dismal grey. A light drizzle began to fall, turning the streets into a sticky stew of unsavoury origin.

Potter lifted his head from his ledger, snapped it shut and sighed. His large, beaky nose pointed directly at Edward and a frown puckered his eyebrows, so they resembled a pair of dark wings outstretched over the bridge. 'I thought I'd locked the street door.'

'It was unlatched. I have an urgent matter to discuss with Mr Stark.'

'You're lucky to find him in the office at this time.' Potter consulted his watch and made a tut-tutting sound as he straightened up on long, thin legs. 'I'll announce you.'

Edward was a sturdy, sensible man of middle years, whose looks could be described as pleasant but unremarkable. Tucking his hat under his arm in a no-nonsense manner he followed the man in without waiting to be invited.

James rose to his feet, a hand extended in welcome. 'Captain Staines, to what do I owe this pleasure,' and he nodded to Potter. 'You can go if you wish. I'll lock up.'

Pouring them a brandy apiece James handed one to Edward as he indicated the client chair. 'I take it you're aware that I don't handle the legal affairs of the company now Durrington has taken it over. I hear he's selling the clippers. A mistake to put all his eggs in one basket, to my mind.'

'I was informed I'd no longer be needed after the next return run to Australia. Durrington's going into steam kettles with Green Star.' This last snippet being said with all the scorn a true sailing man could muster.

'And you're wondering about your contract, perhaps?'

Edward took a measured sip of the brandy, gazing appreciatively into his glass. 'No. It's nothing to do with my contract, since I learned how to make some money on the side under the tutelage of Thaddeus Scott, and have put a bit by for a rainy day. Besides, once she has cargo *Joanna Rose* won't move from her berth under my command until I say so. And that's when my officers are guaranteed payment.'

'You're every bit as feisty as Thaddeus Scott.' James grinned. 'A pity Oliver isn't. He's in dire straights at the moment.'

'Oliver can hold his own, he just goes about things differently. The man hasn't got a mean bone in his body. He was always generous and I'm sorry he's down on his luck. I'd trust myself to his seamanship any time.' Edward lifted his gaze to look the lawyer straight in the eye. 'I must warn you, James, I have the greatest respect for my former shipmates, as friends and employers.'

'No criticism was implied.'

'Good, because there's something you need to know.' Edward drew in a deep breath. 'I saw Tobias Darsham in Melbourne.'

Interesting how the lawyer's hand jerked, but he recovered quickly and said with studied calm, 'You're mistaken, Captain. Tobias Darsham has been dead for the past three years. I identified his body myself. So did Alex.'

Edward smiled slightly. 'Do you expect me to swallow such bilge? You know as well as I do that the body would have decomposed beyond recognition after all that time, despite the coldness of the water. There's nothing wrong with my eyesight, James, and neither am I a fool. I *know* it was Tobias I saw.'

Giving a chuckle, James said, 'This is a rather a preposterous tale you bring me. Nobody would believe such a thing.'

If James thought the captain would be pushed off course, he was mistaken. Edward knew exactly who he'd seen. Tobias had taken off so quickly when he knew he'd been recognized, he'd dispelled any doubts Edward might have harboured. He'd puzzled over the problem on the homeward voyage, wondering why his former employer would want to fake his own death. He'd been unable to reach a credible answer. Now he gave James a level stare, intending to have an answer, even if he had to force the lawyer to part with it. 'You won't mind if I tell others of my suspicions, then.'

James tried to stare him down. 'To what end? Do you want to break his mother's heart?'

'You know I don't. If Tobias chose to disappear it would have been for a perfectly good reason, something beyond his control for him to sacrifice all he held dear. Somebody would have had to conspire with him to bring it about. As his closest friend I'd guess that someone would be you, James, or Thaddeus or Oliver. All three, perhaps?'

James shrugged.

'Could be it's none of my business, but I don't like mysteries. When I observe what's happened to the company I worked for, and learn of the downfall of the men I admired, I need to know the reason behind it. It's no good approaching Thaddeus, who's as close lipped as an oyster. But if you won't tell me, perhaps Oliver will. I'd be obliged if you'd furnish me with his address, and be warned, James, if you don't tell me I'll shake the information out of you.'

James sighed. 'Oliver isn't in London, and he doesn't know anything.'

Edward now felt he was getting somewhere. 'But you do?'

Reluctantly, James nodded. 'Since you're forcing me to break a confidence and a bond of trust, I need to consult with others over this. Have you the time to accompany me to Poole?'

'Aye, I reckon I do. Durrington has cut down on the lay days, but I understand he's finding cargo hard to come by. As my skills are to be dispensed with, the provisioning of the ship can wait, since he can't dismiss me twice.'

'After the weekend, then. We'll take the train and I'll tell you the whole story on the way down.'

Satisfied, Edward nodded. He could hold on to his curiosity for a few days longer.

'We're going to open an academy for young ladies,' Irene announced towards the end of September. 'On Saturday mornings we shall show the girls deportment, how to conduct themselves and embroidery. In the afternoon we will teach them how to dance, and provide them with drawing and painting lessons.'

Joanna stared at the twins, trying not to laugh. 'You're the most enterprising pair I've ever set eyes on. But where are you to conduct this academy? There isn't room in the cottage.'

'Reverend Lind has allowed us the use of the church hall for a small fee. And Mrs Lind has offered to help with the art classes. We shall teach Grace to play the piano in return.'

'But what about your other pupils?'

'We can manage the private piano students during the week. We'll charge by the lesson at the academy.' Lydia smiled broadly. 'It will be such fun, and we'll still be able to help with the work about the house, and look after Toby while you scrub and polish for Mrs Abernathy. Mrs Lind has promised to design some display posters for us to put in shop windows as an advertisement. What do you think?'

'I'm proud of you. I wish your brother was here to see this.'

'Oh, Oliver seems to have abandoned us.'

It was sad that this pair could embrace such a concept so easily, but their bravado hid a deep-seated hurt at the way their mother had treated them, she thought. 'I'm sure he hasn't. Perhaps he's taken up employment and is presently at sea.'

'He could have written to us before he left.' The pair gazed wryly at her and Irene said, 'Poor Joanna, having us foisted on to you. Mother always told us we were useless creatures, so I'm sure we must be the most awful nuisances.'

'Stop it,' she said fiercely. 'You're not useless and I love you being here. I know it's been hard for you to adapt. I admire your spirit. I love you as if you were my sisters, and I don't know what I would have done without your company and help. So shut up and give me a hug before I clout you.'

When the pair of them hugged her tight, Joanna choked back a sob, for these lovely girls badly needed to feel wanted. 'Oliver will come one day, I promise.'

And just as if wishing had made it happen, he did, the very next day. The three women were enjoying the golden evening as they worked together in the garden for an hour before dinner. But despite the lingering sunshine there was a definite nip in the air. Joanna knew it wouldn't be long before a fire was needed in the grate and the wind roared around the chimney.

Since she'd heard no more from Lord Durrington, Joanna had reached the conclusion that he'd thought better of the idea of bringing up Toby as his own. Having relaxed her guard a little, when the gate squeaked noisily on its hinges, her mouth suddenly dried. Her gaze flew to Toby, standing between her and the gate.

Her heart leaped in fear just as Lydia suddenly shouted out, 'Oliver! It's Oliver!'

The pair dropped their tools and went running across the garden at full tilt to fall upon their brother and hug him tightly as they scolded, 'We thought you'd abandoned us, too. Lordy, look how thin you've become, Ollie. Like a bean pole. We shall have to feed you up.'

Toby had gone running after them, laughing because he'd sensed the excitement of the moment and wanted to be part of it. He fell flat on his face as he tripped over his feet. He'd just scrambled upright again and taken a step when he tripped over the next tussock.

Irene scooped him up and they all held each other tight, the sight causing tears to form in Joanna's eyes, making her feel like an outsider. Then Oliver smiled at her over their heads. 'I'd forgotten how much like Alex my nephew is. Will you spare a hug for your brother-in-law, too, Joanna?'

Oliver's ribs were a bony spread under his jacket, his face was gaunt in a way that spoke of hunger and hardship. She said, feeling sorry for him as they drew apart, 'Welcome back, Oliver. You're just in time for dinner.'

His smile contained a twist of wryness. 'There's not enough meat left on me for a cannibal to enjoy, I'm afraid.'

At least he could still joke about it.

Irene hooked her arm through his. 'We'll soon fatten you up, dearest Ollie. Will you settle for mutton stew and dumplings? I made it myself.'

He gazed at her with a mixture of amazement and admiration. '*You* made it? I didn't know you could cook. It smells delicious.'

'Joanna taught us to cook. I can make bread, as well.'

'I made the apple pie,' Lydia said proudly, competing for his attention.

'Better and better, since apple pie is my favourite. The pair of you look wonderful . . . just wonderful.' He gazed at them, his eyes moist, and had to clear his throat before he could speak. 'There are several things I must discuss with you, and not all of it is pleasant.'

'Any news you have can wait until after dinner,' Joanna said firmly. 'We must sort out somewhere for you to sleep.'

Irene smiled at her sister. 'He can have our room, and we'll move upstairs. Otherwise, he won't be able to stand upright without thumping his head on the ceiling. Just keep things out of Toby's reach, Ollie, since he's developed a light-fingered trait recently.'

To prove her point, Toby snatched at a tarnished button on Oliver's coat.

Oliver shrugged when the material tore. 'Aren't you rather taking things for granted? You are both guests here yourself.'

There was a short silence after the reminder, in which the girls turned to gaze at Joanna.

She said firmly, 'Your sisters are part of the household and are at liberty to invite you to join us, Oliver. You're welcome to stay. We share the work at home, and we pool most of the money we earn, so an extra pair of hands will be welcome.'

'I haven't got a job to go to.'

'But you can catch a fish, or dig over the garden patch, which will ease the workload for us, so don't think you've got nothing to contribute. Now, let's go and eat. Then I'll put Toby to bed and go and visit Tilda while you talk things over with your sisters.'

An hour later, Joanna wrapped a shawl around her shoulders and slipped from the house. Taking a quick, precautionary look around, she headed up towards the church, and the fine house Tilda's husband had inherited.

Although it was almost dark she stopped at the graves of Anna and Joseph Rushmore, the couple who'd raised her with so much love. Even though the lie had been proved, she couldn't find it in her heart to blame them for taking her under their roof and bringing her up as their own. As her fingers ran over the rough, weathered stone of the markers she thought she could hear their voices sighing in the wind that flattened the tough grass.

My princess, her pa had always called her when a glass of contraband brandy had warmed the cockles of his heart and loosened his tongue. *Your cradle came floating in on the storm-tossed sea. A seagull had swallowed the spirit of a drowned seaman and perched on the prow of your little craft, guiding you safely to shore. 'Twas the Master of the*

Cormorant, *I reckon . . . him who was named Lucian Morcant.*

'And you were probably right, Pa, for my link to the Morcant and Darsham families is now indisputable,' she whispered. 'But knowing how many ships were wrecked off the Portland coast in the storms of thirty-eight and how many good men died while my own insignificant life was spared is of no comfort to me at all. Everything I sought to claim turned to ashes in my hands. You should have named me Jonah, not Joanna.'

And she seemed to hear her ma's scornful snort, as if she'd been alive and standing right next to her. 'I taught you better than that, Joanna Rose. Life's not going to stop still for the likes of you. Don't mope about what's past. Live with the present and put a bit aside for the future, for a body never knows what surprises it holds.'

Joanna's snort rivalled the late Anna Rushmore's as Seth Adams came into her mind. But the womanly core of her responded with a favourable warmth. 'How could I ever trust a man as devious as him?' she said out loud.

There was a sudden burst of laughter as the door to an inn in the street below opened. Light spilled out as a man went inside, followed by his dog. It would be nice having a man in the house, Joanna thought, but the mild-mannered Oliver would be no match for someone like Bisley.

The thought of Lord Durrington's valet made her shudder. Tension filled her. The wind became a sinister whisper and shadows shifted furtively within shadows, as if Bisley were watching her, waiting for his chance to strike. Pulling her shawl closer, she shivered and hurried towards the welcoming light of the Lind house.

She could see Tilda through the window, her head bent over a child's gown she was stitching, her needle drawing cotton through the fabric as she joined hem to skirt. She looked up and smiled when Joanna tapped on the window pane, rising to open the door.

Tilda was gaining a little weight, Joanna thought, but her face had a drawn look to it, as if she wasn't sleeping well.

They exchanged a hug.

Apart from a few female touches such as embroidered cushions, the house was exactly the same as it had been when Joanna had worked there as housekeeper for David's uncle.

Of David there was no sign. 'He has a meeting with the church wardens,' Tilda told her. 'They're concerned because they're losing congregation to the methodists.'

'Why should that be of concern? It's the same God they worship. The methodists have some fine preachers, I believe.'

'David's a fine preacher too. People always say so.'

'Especially his wife,' Joanna teased.

Unexpectedly, Tilda went on the defensive. 'You should come to church and listen to him preach. He could do with your support, and we need the money that the collection brings in.'

'Then I shall. I'll make sure the girls come with me, and Oliver, as well.

'Oliver?'

'Oliver Morcant. He's back from overseas. The poor man is so dreadfully thin, Tilda. He's been looking for work in London, and it's obvious he hasn't had enough to eat for weeks. It will be nice to have a man about the house.'

Tilda gave her a sharp look. 'He's staying in the cottage with you?'

'Of course. He has nowhere else to go.'

'Are you sure it's wise?'

Exasperated, Joanna said, 'Tilda Lind, I'm going to box your ears for you if you don't stop being so prim. The girls are moving upstairs into the rooms you and I used to sleep in, and Oliver will have the downstairs sitting room. Why do you insist on thinking so ill of me?'

Tilda looked slightly ashamed of herself. 'I don't. It's just . . . people comment.'

'Gossip, you mean. Who's saying this, David's parents and brother?'

She didn't answer. 'All the same, it doesn't seem right, you giving a home to a man. He's not even from these parts.'

'For goodness sake, he's my brother-in-law, and Toby's uncle. I'm a widow with a young son to raise.'

'David told me that marriage vows said before a ship's master aren't legal unless the marriage is registered in a church.'

In the silence that followed, Joanna sucked in a deep,

slow breath. Then she rose to her feet. 'You seem to have something on your mind, Tilda. Let's get it out in the open.'

Tilda stood up too, her face flushing, her arms folded over her chest. 'You weren't married to that first man either, were you?'

'Of course I was. I stood in the church and exchanged my vows in front of Reverend Quinby, his wife, Richard Lind and Doctor Scutts.'

'All of whom are no longer around to confirm it.'

Tilda, her mouth pursed and a disbelieving look in her eyes, had never resembled her mother more.

'Oh, Tilda, don't look at me like that, as if you think I'm lying.'

'Aren't you? I was helping Mrs Abernathy to sort out the church records last week. There's no record of a marriage to Tobias Darsham.'

Hurt jolted through Joanna like a bolt of lightning. 'You must have overlooked it.'

'No, I didn't. Admit it, it was a tale you made up, and it fooled everyone.'

'Tobias Darsham was good to you,' she reminded Tilda. 'If it hadn't been for him you'd be—'

'Dead. I know. You don't have to remind me. All my life I walked in your shadow and lived for a kind word from you and your folks.' Her face suddenly suffused with colour and her voice dropped to a whisper. 'Poor Tilda Rushmore, they said.'

Joanna wasn't about to let Tilda sink into self pity. 'I never thought to hear you say such awful things, Tilda. I loved you like a sister. I still do.'

'But I wasn't your sister.' Tilda bit back a sob. 'Did you think I enjoyed living off your charity?'

Joanna stared at her, shocked rigid, for Tilda seemed hell bent on getting it all out of her.

'*My charity?* Good God, I was just a child.'

'What sort of person are you, Joanna? You've lived in sin with two men, given birth to an illegitimate child and have men coming and going from your house at all hours. People like Lord Durrington, with his vile reputation, and some other man from London. You should be ashamed of yourself.'

'Don't go on, Tilda, I beg you.'

'Do you deny you've been entertaining men?'

Taking Tilda by the elbows Joanna stared at her in perplexity, wondering what had brought this sudden outburst on. 'Lord Durrington entered my home with his servant while I was out. He's Toby's grandfather. He wants my son and he threatened me.'

'Oh!'

'The other man is called Seth Adams. He's an agent of enquiry who was working for Durrington at the time. But now he's not, and that's what he came to tell me the last time he was here.'

'I didn't know,' Tilda said, her eyes filling with tears. 'You never seem to confide in me any more.'

'I didn't tell you about Durrington because I didn't want to worry you. The girls and I are doing the best we can to survive. Have you forgotten how hard it is to earn your bread here? I can't get up on a pulpit, preach, then pass the hat around like a street performer.'

'It's not a hat, it's a plate.' Tilda gave a small giggle at the image Joanna had conjured up, then she sighed. 'I've hardly seen anything of you since those girls moved in.'

Joanna hadn't considered that Tilda might be jealous. 'You mustn't envy them, Tilda. They're wonderful girls, who are learning to cope in the best way they can. They're so grateful you're going to teach painting to their pupils, and their offhand manner simply disguises the hurt they feel at being abandoned by their relatives. Surely you can understand that.'

'And your marriages? Tell me they were not lies.'

'You've already made up your mind that they were,' Joanna said quietly. 'It's not up to me to try and persuade you otherwise. If the records are missing, that's not my fault. You know how absent-minded Reverend Quinby was, perhaps he never recorded the marriage. To be honest, I never thought you'd listen to island gossip, or seek to pry into my private life. I'm surprised David can't find more charity in his soul. At the moment, I'm beginning to think the pair of you are a better match for each other than I first thought. His uncle Richard Lind certainly wouldn't have approved of this from either of you. Goodnight, Tilda. I don't want to hear any more.'

A stricken look came to Tilda's face as she whispered, 'Don't go. I didn't mean it. I'm sorry. And it wasn't David who was gossiping. He hasn't got a bad word to say about anyone. It was Mrs Abernathy. She heads the church ladies' committee. She said there were no records of anything concerning you, as if you don't exist . . . and as if she wasn't a damned Kimberlin herself.'

'And you believed her.' Close to tears and sick at heart, Joanna turned away from her childhood friend.

Tilda's voice sounded forlorn. 'Please don't leave, Joanna. I don't want us to squabble.'

'We already have squabbled.'

'I've said I'm sorry. I think I'm ill and I'm scared. I've been feeling wretched, lately.'

Joanna turned, her voice a whiplash. 'What ails you, apart from a nasty disposition? You're acting as though you've swallowed a nest of wasps.'

'I just feel out of sorts,' Tilda said, biting back a sob. 'I'm tired and I'm often sick.'

So this was what all the bitterness had stemmed from. 'What about your menses?'

'I haven't bled much for several mon—'

The two women stared at each other for a moment, then Tilda burst into tears. 'It can't be that. It's not possible.'

'If you're having normal relations with your husband it's entirely possible.'

'But we've been married for three years and David and I thought it was unlikely because of . . . well, you know. My brothers' sins against me. And now David wants me to visit my mother. He said that because she is my mother it's my duty. He just can't understand how awful she was. I shan't visit her. I told him he was too gullible and he got upset and went out without eating his dinner.'

'For pity's sake stop allowing what happened in the

past to govern your life, Tilda. You have to learn to live with what can't be changed. Mop up those damned tears of yours and try to smile.'

There was a tentative stretch of the lips, then Tilda gave a trembling smile. 'It would be so wonderful if it were true. Oh, Joanna, I hate myself for what I said to you, since you've never been anything but kind to me.'

'That's probably because I love you, you ninny.' Joanna gave a reluctant laugh. 'Well, normally I'm fond of you, but at the moment I feel angry enough to rip your hair out by the roots if you just look at me the wrong way again.'

Tilda gave a nervous giggle.

Closing the gap between them Joanna gave her friend a brief hug. 'Go and put the kettle on, we'll have a gossip over a cup of tea and pretend this didn't happen, though you can tell me what that cat Mrs Abernathy said. And don't let her bully you on that committee either. She's got no right to go poking about in other people's business. You're the rector's wife. If I was you I'd have a lock put on those records, and let her know why. For all we know she might have destroyed the records herself, just to make mischief.'

Tilda's eyes widened. 'I'll talk to David about it.'

'If you can stand up to me, you can do the same to her. And don't tell her anything private, like Grace's background, else she'll be making her life a misery next with her slanderous gossip. And tomorrow you'd better get yourself to the doctor. Now I've said that I'll stop being bossy.'

There was a smile edging across Tilda's face now. 'What if it's not what you think?'

'Then you'll have to learn to live with it, the same as everyone else.' Joanna grinned. 'But I bet you the loan of my cradle that you're carrying an infant inside you.'

Eyes widening, Tilda gazed at her. 'Your cradle? But it's so precious to you.'

'So are you, Tilda dear, and don't you ever forget it.'

Oliver couldn't believe the change in his sisters. Gone were the slightly hysterical and pretentious creatures he'd always known. Two lovely and capable girls had emerged. 'Joanna has wrought miracles with you,' he told them, at which Lydia laughed.

'It was a question of survival.'

Irene shook her head. 'We were so useless to begin with, Joanna must have thought we were a couple of idiots. We've learned so much from her, and it's been such fun, except . . .'

The twins exchanged a glance, then Lydia took over the conversation with, 'Lord Durrington came here with his horrible servant, Bisley. He demanded that he be given custody of Toby.'

'Toby? What for?'

'He needs an heir, and Toby is his grandchild on account of Alex having been his son.'

Shock registered in Oliver's brain. 'I didn't realize you knew about that particular family secret.'

'Oh, we've always known about it. Remember that dinner in London when Alex threw something in Elijah Morcant's soup and stormed off. Then the old man went blue in the face and died? That's when we found out.'

'Yes, I remember. You were just children.'

'Alex was so brave,' Irene said wistfully. 'He was the only one who stood up to mother on our behalf. We miss him so much. And Lord Durrington will have to kill us all before he can have Toby. We keep a good watch out for them and we never leave Toby alone, just in case.

Oliver was wondering how he should break the news to them about their mother's death when Lydia said, 'Did our mother die peacefully?'

'Yes. She had her medicine.'

'Opium, I expect. She was addicted to it. We used to make it for her. Two ounces of opium, one of saffron and a finely ground clove, dissolved in wine. She used to sip at it all day.'

Oliver gazed from one to the other, surprised by their calm acceptance of the event.

Lydia said, 'I expect the Nash family were pleased. They despised her. They didn't like us much, either. Aunt Agatha was the only one who was civil to us.'

'Agatha Nash has settled some money on you. Not a great deal, you understand, just something for the future, in case you need it. I've placed it in a trust account, and it will provide you with a modest income once it starts earning interest.'

'Don't worry, Ollie, dear, we've learned to economize. You should have spent some of that money on food for yourself. You're so dreadfully thin.'

'I thought that you might be able to rent a little

cottage for yourselves. At least you'd have a roof over your heads.'

Lydia's forehead wrinkled into a frown. 'Irene and I have discussed it and we're not leaving Joanna unless she marries again. We love Joanna and Toby and, except for Alex, she's the only person who's ever made us feel as if we have any worth. She needs us, too, for company and support.'

Oliver hadn't realized things had been that bad for his sisters, but he'd barely known them, and knew Joanna even less. 'Is it likely that Joanna will marry in the near future, then?'

'There was a gentleman caller once. Seth Adams. He's handsome and elegant, has beautiful manners and the most wonderful silver eyes.'

Irene sighed. 'I do wish he'd called on me instead, but he only had eyes for Joanna.'

'And to think she sent him away,' Lydia continued. 'But I heard that gentlemen prefer women who resist their overtures, because they regard them as a challenge, so he'll probably visit her again.'

Grinning at their prattle, Oliver leaned back on the battered couch with his legs stretched out towards the fire. His stomach was full to bursting and his hand surrounded a glass, warming a generous tot of excellent brandy.

Irene had hastened to inform him it wasn't contraband, since they'd found it on the beach after a high tide had washed the pebbles from around it.

'Joanna said it was good for medicinal purposes, so we removed a couple of bottles and filled in the hole, in case it was washed out to sea and wasted.'

And that *would* have been waste. As Oliver watched the flames leap and dance he was feeling more contented than he'd felt in several months.

But, still, something nagged at his mind. Where had he heard the name Seth Adams before?

10

Thaddeus Scott was giving the window frames a coat of paint when Edward Staines and James Stark came in through the gate.

Edward, dressed in standard navy blue, wore his company cap. Thaddeus's rush of pleasure at seeing his former first officer was dampened by a twinge of envy that Edward was still young enough to ply his profession. He took Edward's outstretched hand in a firm grip and in a voice warmed by the emotion he felt, growled, ''Tis nice to see you, Edward. How the hell are you?'

'Fine, Thaddeus.' Edward smiled broadly at him. 'In fact, I feel better than I have in a while.'

James shrugged when Thaddeus gave him a questioning look. 'Edward knows, Thaddeus. He saw Tobias in Melbourne.'

'Aye,' said Edward, 'and he ran like a horse with ginger up its arse before I could grab him by the scruff of the neck, but the bugger won't escape me next time. I'll turn Melbourne upside down to find him, by heck I will.'

Thaddeus offered James a hard stare, and said, 'What have you told him?'

'Not quite everything, but he'd already worked most of it out for himself before he came to see me. This is a very worrying situation, Thaddeus. It will affect us all if there's speculation and it gets back to the authorities.'

'Rest assured, I've no intention of letting this out,' Edward stated.

'I know, Edward, but you're not the first person to realize what happened. Joanna and Charlotte were. Why do you think Joanna sailed off to Australia on the spur of the moment? Shortly afterwards, young Alex put two and two together and followed on after her.'

'So many things make sense now. The company hasn't been the same since Alex died, though,' Edward said. 'I understand Oliver is having a run of bad luck, too.'

'Oliver's gone to Portland to be with his sisters, he's living in Joanna's house,' James told them, causing Thaddeus to gaze sharply at him.

'Oliver didn't want you to know, Thaddeus. Durrington has blacklisted him and he couldn't find work. He's ashamed of his poverty. He had to beg for food on the streets for a while and has lost some weight. That Durrington is a bastard who soils everything he touches.'

'We'll see Oliver tomorrow, then. Charlotte and I are going to Portland. We thought we'd take a look over the *Great Eastern*. I understand you can have a tour for half a crown.

Choking out a laugh, Edward scoffed, 'I never

thought to see Thaddeus Scott aboard a steam kettle. I thought she was about to leave for her cable-laying contract.'

'Aye, she was, but an explosion blew her forward funnel apart. Several crew members were killed and she's laid up for repairs.'

Edward muttered, 'You can't trust steam, and what will happen to the sailing men when it takes over, as it eventually will. Alex was convinced of it.'

The three men gazed soberly at one another at the mention of Alex.

Charlotte said lightly, as she came around the corner of the house, a velvet shawl wrapped around her, 'Why such long faces? It's Captain Staines, isn't it? And you, James. What a lovely surprise. What are you thinking of, Thaddeus, keeping our guests standing outside in the cold? And where's your scarf. Wear it round your neck, unless you wish to catch cold.'

Thaddeus grinned at her. 'Wear my scarf! Are you barmy, woman? 'Tis as balmy a day as you can get, isn't it, gentlemen?'

The men nodded agreement, managing to keep a straight face until Charlotte said with some asperity, 'Don't you be fool enough to try and twit me, Thaddeus Scott. Wasn't it just yesterday you decided it was cold enough to don your longjohns. Wear your scarf, I didn't spend all those hours making it just for it to be ignored.' From a nearby chair she plucked a woollen object and hung it around his neck, where it dangled like a couple of long red tongues over his shoulders. 'There, that's better.'

'Very pretty, Thaddeus,' James drawled. 'I bet the colour matches your longjohns.'

When Edward roared with laughter Thaddeus glared at him. 'If my longjohns become common knowledge I'll have your liver sliced and fried with bacon for breakfast.'

'I can't believe that this is a purely social visit. Is somebody going to tell me what this gathering is about?' Charlotte said, her eyes as bright and inquisitive as a bird's as she gazed from one man to the other.

Putting an arm around Charlotte's waist, Thaddeus pulled her against him and planted a kiss on her cheek. 'My dear, Edward ran into Tobias while he was in Melbourne town.'

Charlotte's eyes widened, but she said calmly, 'How is my son, Edward?'

'We didn't speak, but Tobias looked well. We were about to discuss the situation.'

'His name is Gabe Tremayne now, you know.' Charlotte smiled as she said softly, 'I would so love to see him and meet my daughter-in-law, Jane, who is shortly to give birth to their second infant.'

Edward nodded in a satisfied manner. 'There was a store named Gabriel Tremayne and Son. So, Tobias has married again and has a son? I don't understand. What about Joanna?'

Thaddeus placed a finger over Charlotte's lips. 'We'd best go and see Joanna tomorrow, let her know what's happened. No doubt she'll enjoy having visitors.'

Charlotte smiled and gazed round at them all. 'You will all come, won't you? We can take the steamer. I'll tell Stevens and Mrs Bates to pack a hamper or two. Joanna has enough mouths to feed as it is. Are you gentlemen staying the night? We have room. I'll just caution you not to discuss the situation in front of the servants, though.'

Before they could answer Charlotte bustled off, saying happily, 'Good, I'll go and make sure the sheets are aired, then.'

Seth Adams faced his half-brother over the highly polished oak table in his study.

Fifteen years his senior, the corpulent Barnard Charsford lived in a house in Hanover Square. It was richly furnished in predominately dark red velvet and mahogany, and was stuffy and dark.

Mrs Charsford had shown him in without saying a word, though her eyes had momentarily met his, and he was shocked by the despair in them. Barnard's wife was comfortably cushioned, her trunk sturdily supported by whalebone. Sallow face lined into a map of discontent, she'd long ago lost any attraction for her husband, who, since he'd been provided with four sons from her, preferred the delights to be sampled at Lord Durrington's house.

As far as Barnard Charsford was concerned, duty lay in the woman's domain. Any opinion his wife might have held had long ago been browbeaten out of her. Seth couldn't even remember her name, and he doubted if Barnard could, for he'd always referred to his wife as Mrs Charsford.

'You were a damned fool to put Durrington out of

countenance. I was doing you a favour, for he can put a lot of work your way.'

'I don't like the type of work he wants me to do. And I advise you to sever your connection to him, Barnard. People in the city are beginning to talk about the methods you and he employed to relieve the Morcant widow of her living and home.'

Barnard's eyebrow arched. 'Sever my connection, when he owes me a fortune? That transaction was entirely legitimate, since the loan had been defaulted on.'

'Couldn't you have waited until the body grew cold?'

'Business is business, and I'd thank you not to try and advise your elders and betters.' Barnard's whole body jiggled when he laughed. 'Don't be such a fool, Seth. The Morcant widow had her eyes on the main chance right from the beginning. She just wasn't smart enough to hang on to it. At least she has a roof over her head, I understand.'

'She's back on Portland, living in the house she was raised in, forced to grow her own food and to work as a maid to make ends meet.'

'Then she's doing what she was brought up to do. There's many worse off. The streets are full of the starving. Forget her, she's nothing.'

'Lord Durrington is after her son.'

'He simply wants an heir. You can understand that, can't you? The boy is the bastard son of a bastard. The mother should be grateful he's been offered a good start in life, since only a fool would turn their nose up at the chance of a title. Not that I approve of giving a home to some mongrel by-blow, myself. You mark my words . . . blood will out. That girl you took in will come to no good in the end, too, just like her mother. You should put her in an orphanage, forget her.'

'My sister was abused in the house of her half-brother, and the perpetrator of that abuse was never brought to justice.'

'Matters such as this should not be aired, for they offend the sensibilities of the public. It was bad enough that our mother married beneath her station. If this other affair ever comes out it will ruin the reputation of the family. People are bound to ask questions, which is why the child will never be acknowledged. Be advised. It's best to sweep such things under the carpet and forget them.'

Seth felt a pulse of anger begin to beat in his skull, but it was no use trying to change Barnard's mind. As far as his two elder brothers were concerned, Kate was beneath contempt. He'd nearly come to blows with his elder brother over her future. Hard things had been said, all irredeemable, and they hadn't spoken since. Seth decided not to push the issue, for Barnard was useful, in that he was indiscreet at times, as he proved to be now.

'I shouldn't be surprised if Bisley isn't jealous over the whole affair. He's been with Durrington since he was a child, and thought he was set to inherit the estate, if not the title. But Bisley is of mixed blood, and although Durrington looks after his by-blows, he's not about to allow the son of an African slave to inherit. Durrington will have to keep an eye on Bisley when the boy comes to London to live with him.' Barnard's eyes washed critically over him. 'You're looking rather down at heel. Work drying up, is it?'

As if Barnard didn't know Durrington had put the word out. Not that it mattered to Seth, for he had contacts in the law courts, and also at number four Whitehall Place, otherwise known as Scotland Yard. Both sources kept himself and Geevers supplied with investigative work.

Seth shrugged, flicking a piece of lint from the lapel of the respectable but slightly shabby suit of clothes he usually wore when visiting his brother. 'Oh, it comes and goes. How are your sons?'

Barnard's chest swelled at the mention of his offspring. 'Chips off the old block, all of them. They're all at Rugby now. The discipline will do them a world of good. Mrs Charsford spoiled them in the nursery. As far as I'm concerned, the less a mother has to do with a man's sons, the better. It makes them soft. That was my father's policy and, by damnation, he was right!'

Pity rippled through Seth, for their mutual mother had borne great love for her children, just as Joanna Morcant loved her son. The bond of maternal love was something joyous and natural that Barnard had not been allowed to enjoy in infancy, for his father had been a strict disciplinarian, by all accounts.

Now Barnard had delivered his message, Seth was dismissed in a rather perfunctory manner.

As he was leaving, Mrs Charsford came to help him into his overcoat. She gazed nervously towards the study door and whispered, 'I overheard them talk of abducting the boy from his mother.'

'Who?'

'Lord Durrington and Mr Charsford. It's not right, separating a mother from her children.'

'Did they say when?'

'No, but I believe it will be soon.'

He nodded and handed her his card. 'Thank you, Mrs Charsford. If you ever need my help, this is where my office is situated. You may speak freely to Mr Geevers if I'm absent. In an emergency you can go to my home.' Seth whispered his home address in her ear, then added, 'For your own sake be careful, I beg of you. And please, if you know the history of my niece, you will understand why I ask that you be discreet and not allow my brothers to learn of my residential address.'

'You don't have to tell me that.'

'What's your first name?'

'Constance.' The card was slid swiftly into her sleeve as the door to the study opened and Barnard looked out.

'Not gone yet, Seth?'

'As you see. I'm just about to depart.'

Barnard's eyes darted to his wife, who immediately lowered hers to the floor in a submissive manner when he asked her, 'Where's the footman?'

'I sent him to find one of the housemaids.'

'I see. May I remind you that your place isn't to linger in the hall and gossip with the visitors. Mr Adams can see himself out. Go about your business now, Mrs Charsford. You can wait for the maid in the morning room.'

Before she had a chance to move Seth took her hand in his and brushed his lips across her knuckles. 'It's nice to see you looking so well, Constance.'

'Thank you, Mr Adams, you're most kind.' As their eyes met for a second she coloured slightly, then she darted a nervous glance at her husband and scuttled away towards the stairs.

Seth let himself out when the study door closed again. As he stood on the pavement he realized he'd been given a legitimate excuse to go and see Joanna Morcant again, for she had to be warned.

Catching sight of the procession coming up the hill, Joanna swiftly changed into a clean bodice, tied a freshly ironed apron around her waist, then tidied her hair. She pulled a clean smock over Toby's head, gave his face a lick and a promise with her handkerchief, then brushed his dark, unruly curls into a semblance of submission.

Going downstairs when a knock came at the door, she couldn't stop smiling when she set eyes on her visitors, and she didn't know who to hug first. She settled for Charlotte. 'It's so good to see you, do come in.'

The cottage suddenly seemed crowded, the men blocking out the light from the window. Toby went to stand amongst them, craning his head upwards, not at all awed by their height, as if trying to recognize the one who belonged to him.

Charlotte stooped to pick her great-grandson up.

Toby bestowed his Alex smile on her and plucked at the pearl brooch on her bodice. 'No you don't, young Toby,' she said, and in the next breath, 'My, how you've grown; you look more like your father every time I see you.'

Joanna gazed from one man to the other, Thaddeus, James Stark and . . .?' She remembered meeting the third, but only once before for a few moments. She smiled as his name came to her. 'Captain Staines, I believe.'

'I'm surprised you remember me.' His voice was gruff as he gazed at Toby. 'The boy's like his father. Alex would have been proud of him, I reckon.'

'Yes, he was.' Her glance settled on James. 'Is something wrong, James?'

'Not exactly.' He looked around him. 'Are we alone?'

She laughed. 'Hardly, but if you're asking if Oliver and his sisters are around – no, they're not. Oliver is fishing for our dinner, and Irene and Lydia are at their places of employment, teaching piano. What do you need to tell me?'

James offered Edward a sly glance. 'Edward saw your father in Melbourne.'

'So that's the reason for this visit. That's wonderful. Is he well? What about Jane?' Her voice tailed off when she saw Edward's confused expression.

He opened his mouth to speak but nothing came out except a strangled snort and a muffled 'Well, I'll be beggared.'

'Are you all right, Captain Staines?'

'Tobias is your father? The devil he is. How can he

be when you were married to him?' Edward said, choking out an incredulous laugh.

'We didn't know about our relationship when we wed. Luckily, my grandmother saw my resemblance to my mother before . . . well, before any harm was done. He then removed himself from my life . . . from all our lives.'

Edward shook his head and chuckled. 'Now I see it all. What a schemer.'

Joanna gave him a big smile. 'Captain Staines, I apologize for giving you such a shock, but I daresay you can understand why it was kept quiet.'

'It doesn't take much imagination to figure out the reason for his disappearance, now. And that smile of yours is unmistakably Tobias Darsham.'

'I hope you don't mind. But you haven't told me how they are.'

'Your father avoided me, he ducked out of sight into a shop when he saw me. Gabriel Tremayne and Son was painted on the sign over the door. Tobias Darsham a shopkeeper?' He shook his head.

'He's opened a shipping agency as well.' Alarm overcame her happiness and she gazed back to James. 'I've had trouble with Lord Durrington snooping around.'

'Lord Durrington? What did he want?'

'As Toby's grandfather, he wants Toby to live with him and become his heir. He's gone so far as to threaten to abduct Toby and take him back to London to live with him. He said my shipboard marriage to Alex wasn't legal and has set an investigator on to me, who's also guessed the truth about my relationship with Tobias – though it seems that the marriage doesn't appear in the church records. What if he learns the truth about my father's supposed death, too?'

Charlotte gazed from one to the other. 'I have a confession to make. I told Richard Lind of my fears regarding your marriage, Joanna. I told him I thought you were my long lost granddaughter. Although he laughed, after Tobias disappeared at sea Richard removed the marriage entry from the parish records. He hid the page in his journal. With his dying breath he asked me to burn it. So I did.'

James groaned. 'A felonious marriage will probably bring twelve months with hard labour. But more charges can be brought against us. Tampering with parish records. And conspiracy carries a heavier penalty. Although he's not liked, Durrington has a lot of influence. If he wants the child, all he'd need to do is prove you're an unfit mother, Joanna.'

'The investigator said that under the circumstances he wouldn't work for Durrington. He's promised not to tell him anything. He doesn't know that my father's still alive, though.'

Thaddeus shook his head. 'You can't trust anyone, Joanna Rose.'

'I *have* to trust him; I have no choice.' She brightened. 'Lord Durrington only came here once, so perhaps he's changed his mind. Having Oliver here is reassuring, though. James, this affects us all. We must tell Oliver and his sisters. Then I must think of what to do.'

'I have a solution,' Edward said calmly, and they all gazed at him. 'Mrs Morcant and her son can sail with me on the *Joanna Rose*. She'll be out of Durrington's reach in Melbourne.'

'Smuggle her out as a passenger on one of Durrington's own ships?' Thaddeus began to chuckle. 'Damn it, Edward, you're a devious so and so. I didn't think you had it in you.'

'I had a good teacher, Thaddeus.'

'I have another idea,' Charlotte said a trifle breathlessly, her casual manner not quite hiding her excitement at the daring of it. 'Why don't we all go to Melbourne? Not on the *Joanna Rose*, since Thaddeus and I would need to sell the house and settle up here. We could follow on later – make an entirely fresh start.'

They fell silent for a few moments, then Thaddeus grinned. 'You know, that's something worth considering.'

'Aye,' said, Edward. 'I'd be happy to join you, and so will my woman and my sons, since we've already discussed the possibility.'

James grunted. 'I don't know what my wife will say to such a scheme.'

'Imagine what she'd say if you went to prison.'

'There's that.'

Joanna couldn't leave Oliver and the girls to fend for themselves, she just couldn't. 'We'll have to tell Oliver and the girls the truth, since I can't just go and leave them behind.'

'Of course you can't. What truth, and where are we going?' Oliver said from the kitchen doorway, a broad smile lighting his features at the sight of Thaddeus and Edward.

James began, 'We were discussing whether or not to go to live in Australia, and Joanna said—'

'I heard what Joanna said. Is there a reason for this migration of the families – or must I guess?'

Those present gazed from one to the other.

'Could it be something to do with Tobias perhaps?'

'How long have you known?' Joanna said, so indignantly that everyone laughed, relieving the tension in the room.

'I've suspected for some time. There was the way you and Alex used to exchange glances and carefully change the subject whenever Tobias was mentioned. You referred to Charlotte as great-grandmama once when you were playing with Toby. And you sometimes wear Honor Darsham's brooch and ring. But the biggest clue is in the way you carefully tend Honor's grave, as if she means something to you.'

'I also tend your father's grave, Oliver. Why didn't you say something?'

'I figured that if you thought it was my business, you'd have told me. As for tending my father's grave, you feel you have a connection with him. Thaddeus told me the tale of your cradle coming ashore in the storm with the seagull guiding it.'

'It was just an old tale my pa told me.'

'Didn't he also tell you that Lucian Morcant, the master of the *Cormorant*, was the spirit of that seagull?'

A smile touched her lips at the reminder of the tale. 'Yes, he did, and although you might think it fanciful,

I believe it. I like to think of Lucian as my protector, since my pa told me that only a true seaman could have rigged my cradle to bring me safely ashore in such a sea. I first met Tobias right next to Lucian's grave, too, as if he'd meant to bring us together.'

Oliver grinned. 'I don't think it at all fanciful. Seafarers are a superstitious lot and set a lot of stock in the lore of the sea.'

'Especially when they've had a skinful,' Edward muttered.

Charlotte murmured, 'Lucian would have been so pleased to have heard Joanna say that, wouldn't he, Thaddeus?' And she nudged him in the ribs with her elbow.

Clearing his throat, Thaddeus announced, as he tried to hide his grin, 'Aye, I reckon he would at that. Lucian always fancied being a seagull. Remind me not to look up at the sky when he's flying overhead, though.'

Joanna joined in the general laughter. 'What was Lucian like?'

'You don't have to look far. Oliver has the same look and the way of him.'

'Then he must have been a nice man, and now he's the nicest seagull in the sky.'

Leaving Oliver looking abashed by the compliment, which served him right for teasing her, Joanna went off to make some tea. In the kitchen a medium-sized cod lay on the table. Already gutted, it was big enough for a meal, and the head and bones would make a delicious soup stock. Having Oliver living here had certainly eased the workload on herself.

There was a sudden commotion as Irene and Lydia arrived home. Not at all shy, they greeted the visitors with cries of delight and an animated conversation began, as if they'd been starved of social contact.

They probably had been. The life they were living was a far cry from what they'd been used to and, although they never complained, they must be bored with such a simple and relentlessly hard existence, as she was herself. Joanna sighed. Now everything would have to be explained all over again, for the simple lie her father had set in motion seemed to be growing out of all proportion.

But as she set the kettle on the hob and began to unpack the hamper Charlotte had brought, the thought of a new life in far off Melbourne sent a thrill of delight running through her. How wonderful it was that she had accidentally uncovered a family and friends who would support her through thick and thin.

Then she remembered Tilda and felt uneasy. Should she trust her friend with the secret of her first marriage, she wondered?

Her thoughts were interrupted when the girls came through, expressions of enquiry on their faces. 'Oliver said there's something important you must tell us.'

'Yes,' she said quietly. 'I rather think I must. It's about Tobias Darsham . . .?'

The pair weren't as shocked as she'd thought they'd be.

'How wonderful,' Irene cried. 'I wonder if Australia is anything like America.'

'It will be better,' Lydia said caustically, 'for the Nash family doesn't live there.'

In Melbourne, Gabriel gazed at his second son and shook his head. 'Jonathan is the image of Christopher.'

'Both of them look like you, Gabe.' Her smile came spontaneously as she gazed at her husband. 'Thank you for my sons.'

'And thank you for mine, Jane my dear. You've made my life worth living.' He stooped to tenderly kiss her cheek. 'You look tired.'

'It won't be long before he sleeps all night.'

Rising to his feet, Gabriel stretched. 'I'm going into the agency to see if there's any mail arrived from home.'

'It's too soon to receive an answer to your letter.'

'I know, but I thought James might have written to tell me the latest news. The last time I heard from him he said the two smaller clippers had been sold and the *Joanna Rose* would be going on the market shortly. If I had the money, I'd buy her myself.'

He gazed around at the house, which was a far cry from the large residence he'd once owned in England. However, thanks to Joanna's foresight in drawing money from the company for him to use, their home had progressed from the little wooden shack it had first been to a comfortable size. Two large bedrooms had been added to supplement the smaller ones.

He'd had the back of the house extended, too, using ballast blocks, which were easy to obtain. A decent sized kitchen for Jane to cook in had replaced the lean-to, and a new drawing room had doors that opened out on to the veranda for summer. He'd hung curtains on Jane's instructions, blue velvet that tied back and lace at the windows for privacy.

Gabriel grinned. Not that anyone could overlook them, for his house was set back from its neighbours and surrounded by a high wall. On the river side, he'd erected a sturdy fence of wrought iron to keep his sons within the confines of the garden.

In winter Melbourne was cold and wet. He'd had a fireplace built with a stone chimney. There was also a still room, where he'd once kept his home-made wine, though his first attempt had been a disaster, with corks popping off at odd times of the day and night, like bullets. Now he sold his grapes to a vintner, who paid him well and supplied him with a crate of the finished product. There was also a room to bathe in, with a cast-iron bath coated in enamel.

Generally, they lived a simple life, now and again socializing with a few of his business acquaintances and their wives. Most of the business was conducted at his club.

After discussions with an architect, Gabriel had every intention of dividing the block and building a splendid two-storey house for his family in the years to come. But not yet. He wanted money put behind them, so Jane wouldn't have to worry if anything happened to him.

He'd discussed with his wife the possibility of moving after his encounter with Edward Staines, for seeing his old employee and friend had driven home to him how very much he missed his family and former acquaintances. It had also made him aware of the precarious position he'd placed his daughter and friends in.

Edward was bound to mention the incident to someone, for he had a dogged nature. And he'd probably come looking for him the next time the *Joanna Rose* docked in Melbourne, so Gabriel would have to make himself scarce.

If he hadn't been so stupid as to panic over his ill-fated and outwardly incestuous marriage to Joanna, then the Darsham and Morcant Shipping Company would still be solvent, and he'd still be running it, he thought.

But then, he wouldn't have met Jane, and his life wouldn't have been given a new meaning. Having Jane and two fine sons to care for was a blessing he'd never thought to experience.

Jane had talked him out of moving. 'You've worked hard to establish yourself here,' she'd said. 'If the *Joanna Rose* is up for sale, Captain Staines is unlikely to come here again. Besides, didn't you have plans to buy a paddle steamer and ply your trade upriver?'

It had been an idea that had appealed to him at the time, a symptom of his restlessness. For he knew nothing about steamboats, and had enough work to occupy his time with. He missed his former life and friends, that was all. He'd get over it. He'd have to! And if Joanna and his grandson decided to join them, all the better.

*

Brian Rushmore didn't know who'd helped him escape from Newgate. In the dead of night, he was freed from his fetters and was bundled along the filthy corridors, to be shoved unceremoniously outside a wall. The door was locked behind him.

There was a chill wind blowing and grit swirled around his ankles. Brian dragged his ragged clothes close to his body and crossed his arms on his chest, wondering which direction to go in, for he couldn't stay here. The law would be after him by morning.

A darker shadow detached itself from the shadows.

Toughened by several years of incarceration, where survival of the fittest was an unwritten rule, Brian spun round, his only weapons his large, meaty hands. But before he could react further, an arm came round his neck and a cold blade pricked against the throbbing pulse just under his jaw.

'At the end of the road is a carriage. Get inside it,' a voice said quietly against his ear.

'And if I don't?'

'I'll kill you.'

The voice was so unemotional it chilled Brian to the bone. 'What do you want of me?'

'We want a job doing.'

'And after it's done?'

'You'll be given a ticket to go abroad.'

'What about money.'

'That too.'

'I want the money first.'

'I'll take you to a place where you can clean yourself up, give you a new suit of clothes and an advance for your immediate needs. Do you accept, Rushmore?'

'What about a woman?'

'Don't take me for a fool,' the man snarled. 'I can always arrange for you to go back inside, though I wouldn't go to the bother. Life can be very short when the need arises. Would you like me to demonstrate how quickly it can be snuffed?'

A chill ran through Brian. 'Like hell, I would. What do I have to do?'

The man's laugh sent goosebumps racing up Brian's back. 'It'll be as easy as taking a child from its mother.'

11

The crowds visiting Portland to see the *Great Eastern* seemed endless, the harbour was crowded with boats coming and going, the narrow streets were bustling with sightseers. Local children took advantage of the rush of visitors by selling fossils. Oliver couldn't stop laughing when Joanna sold her doorstop. 'We'll be leaving in a few days and I can't take it with me,' she said.

Uneasily, she thought of Tilda. She'd put off telling her friend she was leaving, but knew she must tell her by the end of the week. She intended to give Tilda the cottage, too. Being a genuine Rushmore, Tilda had more claim to it, anyway. It would bring in rent to supplement David's modest income.

Joanna looked round the cottage with very little regret. 'I'll be off on my travels again, Ma and Pa, and this time I won't be coming back.' The sense of connection inside her had lessened, as if her emotional ties to the cottage were unravelling. It seemed to be telling her that she didn't really belong any more. The island was letting her go.

Joanna knew she'd need to sell her mother's jewellery to give herself a stake in her new country – something she'd managed to avoid doing so far. Even though she'd never known her real mother the jewellery held some sentimental value for her, especially the rose brooch and the ring her father had slid on to her finger. Oliver had pleased her by handing back her wedding ring, which she intended to keep.

She wasn't going to the Barnes brothers, though, for they'd cheat her. Instead, she intended to go to Poole, where there was a proper jewellery shop. She'd ask Thaddeus to negotiate a price for it on her behalf.

She set off down the hill in a blustery wind with Toby strapped into his carriage, hoping Leonard would be there to help her to board the ferry.

Because of the crowds she didn't notice the man who fell into step behind her. As they were passing the open gate of a dingy net-maker's yard, a hand grasped her arm and she was steered swiftly through it.

Joanna hardly had time to gasp when she was pushed forward. As she tried to scramble to her feet she was hit from behind.

'No,' she whispered, fighting desperately to hold on to her fading senses as her knees buckled under her.

As she fell forward to the floor, something heavy was thrown on top of her, pinning her down. The light began to darken. Fighting the weight just tangled her up, like a fly in a spider's web. After a moment or two, she was too weak to move. Her wedding ring was wrenched from her finger.

'Bitch,' somebody grunted against her ear. 'I'd give

you the length of me if I had the time, just to teach you a lesson. You can have this instead.'

An unexpected kick to the stomach robbed her of breath and she began to retch. 'Toby,' she gasped out as she heard her son begin to cry.

Hands closed around her throat, squeezing relentlessly.

The last sound Joanna heard before her world went black was the steamship whistle.

Joanna had been unable to hang on to the consciousness she'd drifted in and out of. When she fully regained her wits it was to the soft charcoal light of evening.

Pain hammered in her head. Her ears were assailed with a clunk followed by a swishing noise, as if somebody was using a pump nearby.

She groaned as she tried to move, felt her bonds tighten. Cautiously, she moved her hands to see if she could loosen them, her fingers encountering many knots. She was caught in a fishing net, so she must still be in the yard of the net-maker. There was a weight on top of her body, pinning her down.

The thought of Toby brought her to full awareness, and she began to struggle and shout. The swishing noise stopped as there was an alarmed screech. 'Get yourself out here, our Ernie! Something be caught in the nets.'

'It'll be Tommy Snodgrass's auld tomcat. I'll slice its balls off this time, just see if I don't.'

'It's me. Joanna Morcant.'

'Well, I never did. 'Tis the devil's magic. *Ernie!*' she shrieked, 'The cat says his name be Joanna.'

Ernie's voice came closer, along with the glow of a lamp. 'The methodists' fire and brimstone be making you mazed, woman, a bleddy cat can't speak.'

'Well, this one does, I heard it with my own two ears, you daft auld bugger,' she muttered under her breath.

A hysterical giggle exploded from Joanna's mouth. 'I'm not a cat. I'm under the fishing nets.'

'See. I told you it could speak. A real fright it give un, too.'

'Get away with you, Gertie. 'Tis a woman's voice. Here, make yourself useful and hold the bleddy lamp.' Hands felt carefully round Joanna's body and she groaned when one of them touched against her bruised side. 'You lie quiet, missus, while I get you out of there. I'll try not to hurt you.'

The bulk of the net was lifted from her and the net-maker started on her arms, his nimble fingers quickly untangling her bonds. As he helped her to her feet, she clung to him, fighting off dizziness.

'What happened to you, missus?' Ernie said.

'Somebody hit me, and they took my son and stole my wedding ring.'

'There's some right wicked folk around these days,' Gertie said with a sniff. 'Weymouth folk come over the bridge to cause mischief all the time. And all those comings and goings to see that damned great eyesore of a ship in the harbour. What if it blows up again? Like as not it will take the island with it. It shouldn't be allowed. Do you be from these parts, then?'

'Just up the hill. Fortuneswell. I'm Joanna Morcant.'

'The only Joanna I heard of was Joseph Rushmore's

daughter. A right saucy piece, she was. She was washed ashore in a storm, I heard, though don't you go tellin' anyone that because it be a secret that Fanny Rushmore told me. A real comfort to her ma, the girl was, though. Anna set great store by her, and she was the apple of Joseph's eye.'

A lump rose to Joanna's throat. 'I'm Joanna Rushmore, though Morcant is my married name.'

'I'll be blessed. You don't look like no Rushmore to me. Those boys of Fanny Rushmore's were a ratty looking lot. Funny that. I thought I saw that younger son of hers today, not Peter, though, since he be dead. Brian, his name be. He must have got out of the jail. Came off the boat, he did.'

Joanna shuddered at the very thought of running into Brian Rushmore, the man who'd nearly raped her and had succeeded in doing the same to his own sister, Tilda. But the old woman must be mistaken. She deliberately put Brian from her mind, for Tilda had said he'd been sentenced to life imprisonment.

'That would have been Leonard you saw.' Joanna couldn't stand here chatting any longer. 'Can you see my bag anywhere? I've got to get on.'

At least her jewellery hadn't been stolen, she thought as her bag was discovered nearby. 'Would you do me a favour?' she asked the couple, because she didn't want to have to go back and explain everything when she was frantic to go after her son. 'Go up to Fortuneswell, to the Rushmore house. Tell the people living there that Toby has been abducted, and Joanna has gone to London to find him.'

'Who be Toby, then?' Ernie asked.

Desperation filled her and she shouted, 'He's my son . . . will you tell them?'

'Aye, missus. There's no need to take on so.'

'Thank you.' She was gone, running headlong down the hill, for she had to get to London as soon as possible. That's where Lord Durrington had threatened to take Toby, and nobody else would have taken her son.

Behind her, rain suddenly splattered on to the couple, who stood with their mouths gaping open, watching her go.

Gertie eventually said, 'Well I never. It weren't a devil tomcat, after all.'

'Course not, you ought to wash your lugholes out with soap if you can't tell the difference between a human voice and the caterwauling of a tomcat. Fetch my coat, would you,' her husband said with a sigh.

Gertie's hands went to her hips. 'You don't want to go walking up the hill in this rain, it'll give you rheumatism. You leave it till morning, since the girl won't reach London afore then. 'Tis too far away, I hear.'

Seth crossed to Portland at midday. The water was choppy, making his stomach uneasy. The lash of the wind was nearly strong enough to blow his head off.

Leonard came up on deck as they neared the shore, giving him an assessing look. 'I reckon Joanna must like you, at that.'

Something leaped inside Seth's heart. 'Why, what has she said about me?'

The man grinned. 'Not one word, either for or against. Odd that.'

Seth drew in a deep breath. It was time he made friends with this man. 'Are you married?'

He was rewarded with a slim smile. 'Aye. I've got two children.'

'Didn't you used to fish?'

Leonard hunched into his collar and shrugged. 'Had my own boat and crew, once. My brothers burned it and robbed me of my living. Joanna's husband put a word in for me and I was offered this job.' Leonard's glance brushed over him. 'Alex Morcant was a good man.'

And it was obvious to Seth that he'd never measure up to Alex Morcant in this man's eyes. Not that he was interested in Joanna as a suitor, he told himself. Just trying to unravel an intriguing mystery to his own satisfaction. A thought arrowed sharply into his denial and it had one word etched on it. Liar!

He smiled and casually asked Leonard, 'Which of Joanna's husbands was that?'

The crewman gave him a flat stare. 'I reckon you're too damned nosy. I've told you enough.'

'If you're trying to warn me off, it won't work. I've decided to wed Joanna. I'd be obliged if you'd keep that to yourself, though. It's best she doesn't know yet.'

'There's something you should know then.' The grin Leonard gave was measured, but laced with amusement. 'I hear tell Joanna's got a man living in her home now.'

Dismay yawned inside him. 'The devil she has. Who?'

'He's a master mariner by profession, I believe.' Leonard didn't satisfy his curiosity any further, but leaped ashore to secure the boat fore and aft. He waved to the man at the wheel. When the engines cut out, he ran a small gangplank across and helped the passengers on to the pier. 'If you want to wait, I'll walk up the hill with you. I'm paying my sister a visit.'

But his sister had come down to see him. She came running to the boat, her face agitated. Leonard took her by the arms as she stooped to catch her breath. 'Nay, Tilda, you shouldn't be running like that. It's bad for a woman in your condition. What would David say if you fell flat on your face?'

She gasped out, 'Ernie Brown came up this morning with a message. Toby's been abducted and Joanna's gone haring off to London by herself to get him back. You know how headstrong she is. Oliver is going into Poole to tell Mrs Scott and her husband. We're all frantic with worry.'

As if that would help get the child back, Seth thought, trying to hide his own alarm as he snapped, 'How long ago did Joanna leave?'

The woman stared at him, her mouth tightening slightly as she said with aggravating slowness, 'And who might you be?'

'It's all right, Tilda. This is Seth Adams. He's a friend of Joanna's.'

'Is he, indeed?' Seth found her thorough scrutiny rather disconcerting, then after a few seconds, she relaxed. 'Well, I doubt you had anything to do with it, else you wouldn't be here visiting her today.'

'And I'll be heading straight back to London after her. I might be able to help get the boy back, since I know where he's likely to be. Tell me what happened.'

'Ernie Brown said Joanna left just as it got dark. He found her in his yard. Somebody had hidden her under his fishing nets. Ernie said she was right mazed. She must have been lying there for most of the day, because she said she was on her way to catch the earlier steamer. You knew she was going to Poole yesterday, Leonard. Didn't you wonder why she wasn't on board?'

'It was my day off.'

Seth sighed with impatience. 'Will the skipper take me to Southampton? I can catch the train from there and overtake Joanna, perhaps.'

'Not in the paddler. She plies a regular run between Poole and Portland and the passengers rely on her. Jack and Robbie Dunn have a fishing cutter they use for hire, and for other activities. There's a bit of weather on the way by the look of it, but you'd be in safe hands. The boat's over yonder. Tell them Leonard sent you.' He threw Seth a set of oilskins before he could move off, and grinned broadly. 'Here. Most likely you'll need them.'

Most likely became a definite when they left the shelter of the harbour. Before too long the boat was wallowing up and down in the swell and spray was being thrown at him from all sides, causing him to hang miserably over the side and lose the contents of his stomach. Immediately he felt better, though he was frozen to the bone from the wind and his feet were wet and cold.

The Dunn brothers, weather-beaten men old enough to be his grandfathers, attended to their task of keeping the boat on course with a singular unconcern that was reassuring, especially when the sky seemed to come down and touch the water.

They grinned toothlessly at him when he shrugged and gave them a shamefaced smile. 'It happens to us all, lad.'

Lad? Seth grinned, for he was twenty-seven, and there was something exhilarating about being tossed about at the mercy of the waves and wind, though it was a bloody cold occupation, even with the oilskins on.

Above him, the faded red sails whipped and snapped in the wind, and the ropes slapped tirelessly against the mast. They were being escorted by seagulls, who dived into their wake to snatch up anything that was turned up.

One of the brothers jerked a thumb towards a hatch that led to a dark hole under the deck. 'It'll get worse before it gets better, so best you go below for a while. Wedge the hatch open a bit so you've got some light. Get a drop of brandy inside you, and mayhap you'll find some dry socks and boots for when you come out. Watch your head, though.'

The small, dark space that doubled as a cabin smelled strongly of fish, tobacco smoke and stale sweat. There was a keg of brandy hanging in a rope cradle from a hook. Seth helped himself to a tot, whispering as it warmed him through, 'By God, this is fine enough for the palate of a king.' The brothers were involved in other activities, Leonard had said. Smuggling perhaps?

He took his thin hose off, hanging them over a line slung from two hooks, then pulled on a pair of thick socks knitted from greasy wool. They smelled as though they'd come straight off the sheep's back and were none too clean, but Seth was past being fussy.

Another tot relaxed him enough to lay down on a wooden plank that served as a seat, his arms triangled under his head to act as a cushion.

He applied his mind to where Durrington might take young Toby. Probably his London house to start with, as Barnard had indicated in the conversation Seth had had with him. Though the man had property in Ireland, as well. Seth didn't think the boy would come to any harm, since that would defeat the object of the abduction. Durrington would have the nursery all ready for Toby, and would have hired a nursemaid to look after him. Most likely, it would be at the top of the house and well guarded.

Joanna would be beside herself with anxiety. He hoped he could get there before her and could intercept her before she went banging on Durrington's door – even though she had several hours' start. Joanna acted on impulse instead of thinking things through in a rational manner. Still, she was an intriguing woman.

He smiled. And a magnificent woman with those blue eyes and her graceful, well-proportioned body, though he'd like to put her across his knee for placing herself in danger. He calculated his odds of getting the boy back as slim. Walking into Durrington's house undetected would be virtually impossible.

His eyes drifted shut and he was almost asleep when

the boat canted sideways and he rolled off the bunk. He scrambled to his feet and was propelled back in the other direction. When he straightened he forgot to stoop, and hit his head on the deck above. 'Sod it!' he muttered.

Pulling on the boots and oilskin he went up on deck. The Dunn brothers nodded approvingly when he closed the hatch behind him. Standing with their legs braced apart, neither of them moved an inch as the boat rolled from side to side, while Seth was forced to clutch at the nearest rope to balance himself.

'Don't 'ee pull on that too hard else you'll have the sail down on top of us, lad.'

They'd made good progress. Portland was a dot on the horizon behind them.

Jack Dunn aimed his pipe stem at the streamers of clouds racing across the sky. 'Wind is a bit fresh, but she's pushing us along at a goodly gallop.'

The gallop all seemed to be in Seth's stomach as the horizon kept changing direction. No wonder Leonard Rushmore had grinned when he'd seen him off. He gulped and headed for the side, changing direction when Jack shouted out, 'Not upwind, lad.'

Later, Robbie was on hand to catch Seth by the collar as he nearly lost his footing. 'If you be staying on deck, best you hold on tight to that net rail, for she rolls like a pig in shit, that she does.'

An apt description, Seth thought, grinning, for despite everything he was enjoying himself, and, besides, there was nothing left inside him to come up.

'If I were you I'd have a good slug of brandy and try

and sleep. There's a bucket under the bench if you need it, and if you wind the ropes over your body and loop them over the hooks it will stop you rolling off.'

'Later, Robbie. I'm quite enjoying the buffeting, you know. I'll try not to get in your way.'

'Mayhap you have the sea in your blood, sir.'

'I doubt it. Piss more likely, since my father always told me I was stubborn.'

'Having a streak of the mule in him don't do a man no harm, I reckon,' said Robbie, and he went off cackling with laughter.

The weather worsened and the rain began to pour down in cold slashing showers. The Dunn brothers went about their tasks. Water bounced off their sou'westers and sheeted off the sloping brim at the back. The sail shed spray with furious snaps and cracks.

The day lost its charm. Seth went into the cabin, though sleep eluded him as the boat butted and rolled its way along the coastline. But as it grew dark the wind eased off.

Jack Dunn came through the hatch, whistling tunelessly to himself. He faked surprise when he saw Seth. 'Ah, there you be, lad. We thought we'd lost you overboard.'

'I'm surprised you didn't turn back then.'

'No, sir. You paid us to go to London and back, and the Dunn brothers allus gives value for money.'

He took a swig of the brandy and gave a sigh of pleasure. 'That be a lovely drop, that do. It ferments the brain a real treat. If the gaberty men knew we had it, we'd be in trouble.'

'Gaberty men?'

'Revenue men to you landlubbers.'

'It's smuggled brandy then?'

'Whoever told 'ee that is a liar. 'Tis genuine plunder. As I recall, it came off the *Saggitario* back in eighteen forty. 'Tis said she was a pirate vessel out of Trieste.'

'Eighteen forty?' This had the flavour of a tall tale to Seth. 'It's a wonder it hasn't all been drunk since then.'

''Tis a wonder indeed, sir, but don't you go worrying your head about it.'

'Oh, I was just wondering where I could get hold of a keg.'

The man gave him a measured look, then smiled. ''Tis a rare drop, but it could be done, I suppose. Couldn't guarantee it was off the *Saggitario*, though, and it would cost a pretty penny.'

Seth took out a fold of notes from inside his waistcoat and money was transferred.

From a wooden crate nailed to the deck, Robbie removed a dish containing three mutton pies, which were covered in muslin and had been wrapped in an old copy of the *Dorset and Somerset Reporter* to soak up the grease. 'You fit your gums round that,' Robbie said, and poured a generous amount of scrumpy cider from a stone bottle into a metal mug for him to wash it down with.

Seth wondered if this pair ever drank anything but alcohol. He had to admit it was warming, though.

In the dark morning hours he was put ashore in London. The ground rose up to slap him in the stomach. 'What did I trip over?' he said, gazing down at it in surprise.

Jack Dunn hauled him upright and handed him his sou'wester. 'Don't forget this, sir.'

Seth staggered off towards the set of rooms he rented. His sou'wester seemed heavy, and he soon realized why. There was a small keg of brandy wrapped inside.

Letting himself in through the skylight, he set the brandy on the table. He needed a couple of hours' sleep before he went in search of Joanna. He was about to strike a Lucifer to light the lamp with when he realized it was already burning low. His wits had been too fugged with the brandy he'd consumed to notice before. They were fast clearing now, though.

There was something different about the place. A presence. Seth's eyes narrowed and he stood still, just listening, the hairs on his wrists pricking with alarm.

A floorboard cracked to his left, a mouse scratched. Perhaps his landlady had forgotten to turn off the lamp. There was a piece of paper next to it, probably an account for her services.

But no! There came a sigh from the other room and the bed creaked as someone turned over.

He picked up the piece of paper.

I've made Mrs Morcant comfortable. I'll see what I can find out about the child.

Geevers.

Good. If Joanna had turned up here, it would save him running around looking for her. Geevers had a network of informers, too. Seth put a light to the makings of a fire in the grate and heaped coals upon it before placing the guard around it to catch any sparks. Soon it was burning merrily.

Removing his shoes, he picked up the lamp and crept towards the bedroom. The cast of light revealed Joanna, her dark hair splayed across the pillow.

He gazed at her a long time. She slept on her back, the quilt pulled up to her chin. Her sleep-flushed face inclined to one side and was tracked with tears. One eye was puffy and bruised, her breathing an even rise and fall. On the chair her clothes were folded neatly.

Rage filled him at the thought of someone physically hurting her.

Seth's clothes were damp and he was cold – too cold to be the gentleman, since the bed was large and there was room for him on the other side of it.

Shedding his outer garments, he draped them over the chairs in the other room where the heat from the fire would dry them and went back to the bedroom, leaving the connecting door open. Carefully, he slid in beside her.

He'd just got settled when she turned again. Her arm slid around his waist and she murmured something incoherent as she snuggled against his back.

His smile was one of pure pleasure as the warmth of her moulded against him – as her breasts pushed soft and silky against his back, leaving very little to the imagination. There was an infinitesimal thinness of fabric between him and her, but it made sleep impossible for him now.

There was her hand too, resting warmly against his

stomach. It was a mere span away from his genitals, which reacted instantly, rearing up inside like a snake from a basket to perform for its charmer. 'Down, boy,' he whispered.

He adjusted his position slightly, trying not to wake her in the process. Forces were against him. Her nubs hardened against his back, then her palm closed gently around him and she murmured sleepily against his ear, 'Alex, my love.'

Seth's balls hardened and he suddenly wished his mother had named him Alex. It was tempting to allow her to believe he was her dead husband, but he knew she'd never forgive him if he did. He reached out and turned the lamp up. 'Joanna, it's me. It's Seth,' he whispered. 'For Christ's sake, unhand me, else I won't be responsible for what happens, and we'll both regret it in the morning.'

For a moment there was no response, then his words seemed to get through to her for her whole body stiffened. The hand was withdrawn. Her eyes flew open and she said with a false sort of menace, 'What the hell are you doing in my bed?'

'It's my bed, Joanna. We'll have to share it.'

At least she didn't scream for help, or try to kill him, both of which he'd half expected. She simply gazed at him and said casually, 'Mr Geevers told me you'd gone to Portland to see me, and he said I could wait here for you. How did you get back to London so quickly?'

'Jack and Robbie Dunn's boat.'

'Ah yes, no wonder you smell of fish and brandy.'

He felt ashamed. 'I'm sorry. Should I bathe?'

There came a gurgle of derisive laughter. 'You're not my bridegroom. Move over, would you, you're too close for your own comfort, and mine.'

'Now, that's interesting,' he said and moved closer.

'Believe me, there is nothing the least interesting about the smell of dead fish or the fumes of brandy on a man's breath.' She dragged the pillow from under his head and placed it between them. The small chuckle she gave sounded more like a purr. 'The brothers are a pair of rogues. You didn't buy any brandy from them, did you? They fill kegs with cheap stuff and sell it to strangers as rare smuggled brandy.'

He grimaced, saying loftily, 'Do you think I'm a man who can be so easily taken in?'

'Of course not.' Her voice sounded forlorn when she stated, 'I lost my boy, and I couldn't think of anyone else to help me to get him back. You will help me, won't you?'

He grimaced at the backhanded compliment. 'That's why I'm here.'

Her fingers touched his face. 'What if they kill him, Seth? What then?'

Taking her hand he pressed a kiss in the palm. 'Why would Durrington kill him when he wants him for his heir?'

'I'm scared . . . so scared.'

He put an arm around her and, discovering his need to protect her was greater than his need to ravish, eased her head against his shoulder. Tears dampened his skin. 'Hush, my dear,' he said. 'Try to sleep.'

'I'm sorry.'

'For what?'

'Mistaking you for Alex. I'm embarrassed, too. You could have taken advantage of me.'

'I was tempted to, believe me.'

'Poor Seth. You're too much the gentleman.'

'Circumstances are against seduction at the moment, but I'll keep your advice in mind for a later date.' He kissed the top of her head. 'I'm going to count to ten. For my own comfort I want you to turn on your side and go to sleep, while I turn the other way and do the same. One . . . two . . .'

Joanna left it until he reached nine, then kissed him goodnight for the next five seconds. Her lips were as smooth as silk, her kiss a warm and teasing promise that reached down to his toes and made them curl. She was all woman and her response boded well for the future of their relationship.

'. . . Ten,' he croaked, sighing with regret as she turned away from him. 'Goodnight, Joanna.'

There was laughter in her voice. 'Goodnight, Seth.'

I'll never sleep now, he thought, watching the shadows leap and dance on the walls as the fire crackled in the grate.

He remembered the brandy. He must get up before her and hide it, before she saw it.

12

The next morning Seth bought a breakfast from the street stalls, a slab of cheese, a loaf of crusty bread and some hard-boiled eggs. There was a jug of hot tea to follow, supplied by his landlady, who smiled at Seth and barely offered Joanna a glance until he said. 'This is Mrs Morcant, a client of mine. Joanna, my landlady, Mrs Spicer.'

The woman bobbed at the knee.

Ravenous, Joanna ate her breakfast with hasty pleasure, then sipped at the tea. She gazed at Seth with an apology in her eyes. 'I haven't eaten since Portland.'

'I had a mutton pie on the boat, washed down with cider and brandy.' A wry look came into his eyes. 'I can't remember much after that, though my head aches a bit.'

Her glance wandered to the spot where he'd hastily hidden the keg, behind the coal scuttle. She gave a faint grin. 'How much did you pay them for the brandy?'

'Too much, I imagine. They mentioned it was off a pirate ship.'

'The *Saggitario*? I'm surprised you were taken in by them.'

He shrugged and his mouth twisted wryly. 'Stop rubbing my nose in it, Joanna. I'll have you know that your cousin Leonard directed me to them.'

'I expect he gets a commission for every fool he sends their way.'

'I shouldn't be at all surprised. Tell me about Oliver.'

Startled, she spluttered out in surprise, 'How did you learn about Oliver?'

'Leonard told me the man was living with you.'

'He is . . . at least, he's living in the house with myself and his sisters.' She allowed him a small smile. 'It's Captain Oliver Morcant. He's my brother-in-law. Leonard must have given you the wrong idea.'

'Deliberately, I imagine. Leonard doesn't seem to like me.'

'He doesn't make friends easily, but he's honest, and once he's come to respect you he'll always be there when you need him. When he sent you to the Dunn brothers, he placed you in the hands of the most experienced of the islanders.'

'They were certainly that.' He gave a throaty chuckle. 'My head hasn't cleared yet.'

His eyes caught hers, cool grey in the morning light. He didn't look any the worse for drinking too much spirituous liquor the day before. In fact, Seth looked downright handsome with his hair still messy from sleep and his shirt open at the neck, so she wanted to run the tip of her tongue into the salty hollow at the base of his throat.

Instantly, Joanna recalled touching the hardness of him. There was an image of flesh pushing rampantly against a silky sheath of skin. The same desire she'd felt for him the night before rippled through her. She clenched her muscles as she experienced dampness, and a blush of heat attacked her cheeks at the thought of them together in that way. But her glance was speculative all the same as she wondered.

A grin slowly widened his mouth, as if he'd simultaneously read her thoughts and recalled the incident too. It startled her to realize she had that close a rapport with him.

'Say one word about last night and I'll strangle you with my bare hands,' she murmured.

'Like somebody tried to do to you?' He raised his own hand to her neck, his fingers gently caressing the bruises there. 'If I ever run into the man who did this to you I'll kill him.'

Joanna shivered, because Seth's eyes were so hard and his voice merciless. Obviously he was not the easy-going gentleman she'd imagined him to be. Hastily, she changed the subject by looking around her. 'This isn't your home, is it?'

'No. I keep this for business purposes, and use it as a hideaway. Very few people know where I live with Kate. It's better that way.'

'Someone would harm her?'

'It's possible. The circumstances of her birth embarrass my half-brothers. We don't get on and they would have me get rid of her.'

She paled. 'You mean they'd kill her?'

'I shouldn't think they'd go that far. They'd probably change her name and place her in a school somewhere, where she'd be conveniently forgotten.'

'You should take her abroad to live, where she can grow up without fear. Tell me about her circumstances, Seth.'

'She's the result of an assault on my sister when she was barely out of the schoolroom. Out of shame, Sarah fled, and she died giving birth to Kate in impoverished circumstances. The affair broke our father's heart and he died shortly after Sarah did.'

'And your mother?'

'Already gone. She's buried with her first husband.' He hesitated. 'He was an earl.'

Which explained why his half-brothers found the thought of Kate's existence distasteful. She leaned forward, covering Seth's hand with hers. 'Your sister was lucky to have you as a brother.'

'I feel blessed to have Kate to remember my sister by. She looks very much like her mother.'

'Thank you for trusting me with her story.' Guiltily, Joanna wished she'd been able to find it in her heart to tell Seth the whole truth about her first marriage – to tell him she was leaving. The *Joanna Rose* had been at her berth yesterday when she'd arrived in London. She was due to set sail in a few days and if Joanna found Toby she could still sail on her. But she needed to sell her jewellery. Perhaps James Stark would sell it for her.

'Do you have a hairbrush? There's someone I need to go and see and I need to tidy myself up first.'

He bristled with alarm. 'The last thing you must do is make your presence known to anyone. If Durrington gets wind of your presence he might take off abroad.'

'But I need to sell my jewellery.'

'I know someone who will give you a good price. Will you trust me with its disposal?'

She nodded, saying bitterly as she pushed the bag towards him, 'The man who waylaid me took the wedding ring from my finger.'

'He left you with something far more precious. Your life.' He rose, throwing her a cloak he picked up from the chair. 'Come on, let's go. Pull the cowl over your hair and face.'

'Where are we going?'

'To my home. There should be a hackney carriage waiting outside for us, since I ordered it earlier. You'll be able to see to your grooming once we're there. I'll find you something else to wear, too. No doubt Kate will be glad to see you. She hasn't stopped talking about you.'

'I don't want to be a nuisance, Seth. I just want my son back.'

'Much as I'd like it, I can't be with you all the time, Joanna. You'll be safer there.'

He pulled her to her feet and, gazing into her eyes for a moment, said, 'I'm humbled that you trust me enough to place this matter in my hands. I'll do all I can to find Toby for you.'

There was no doubting the sincerity in his voice. She felt a sudden stab of fear for his safety, for she'd remembered Bisley. 'Be careful then, Seth.'

'I'm always careful, and it's not often that someone can slip under my guard.' He kissed her on the forehead. 'You have.'

His caution was something he demonstrated as they left. 'Follow me out,' he told her and, after looking both ways, he slipped into the carriage and held the door open for her. Joanna headed swiftly after him.

Seth's luxuriously appointed house came as a surprise to her. Kate greeted her like a long lost friend, and the servants treated her like a revered guest, despite her unkempt appearance.

The room she was taken to was decorated with pretty wallpaper sprigged with cornflowers. Lace curtains hung at the windows, which had an outlook over the garden at the back of the house.

A fire was lit, a bath made ready. A maid called Dimity was appointed to look after her.

Immersed to her neck in the warm water, Joanna relaxed as best she could, considering her uneasiness over Toby.

Kate wandered in, distracting Joanna's mind from her troubles, chatting to her about everything and nothing in the uninhibited way children have. Then she said, 'Uncle Seth told me somebody has stolen Toby from you, but I'm not supposed to tell you I know, in case you get sad and start to cry.'

'You should be doing your lessons, Miss Kate,' the maid said, bustling in with fresh water with which to rinse Joanna's hair.

'Uncle Seth said I may talk to Joanna.'

'But not all day, and not about that.'

'It's all right, Dimity. I don't mind. Yes, I am sad, my dear. He's so small and I miss him. I love him so much.'

'So do I, even though I saw him only once.' Kate smiled at her with ingenuous charm. 'Can I spend all day with you?'

'Only if your uncle says so.'

'He will if *you* ask him. But he's not in.'

'Very convenient.' Joanna stifled a chuckle and emerged from the bath smelling sweetly of scented soap.

There was a gasp when the maid saw the purpled flesh on her side. 'Oh, my goodness. Did you have a fall, miss? Can I get something to put on that?'

Kate's eyes widened. 'I had a bruise once, on my arm.'

Dimity told her sharply, 'You shouldn't be in here with Mrs Morcant in her altogether. Turn your back, young lady.'

Kate did as she was told, but continued chatting. 'Poor Joanna. Does it hurt?'

Joanna wrapped the bath sheet around herself. 'Not any more. Where are my clothes, Dimity?'

'Mr Adams said they had to be laundered. He bought you some new ones, went out and got them himself.' Dimity tried to stifle a giggle when she picked up a froth of white lacy petticoats to wear under the sedate ankle-length blue skirt. The matching bodice was trimmed with lace and ribbon. There was a paler blue shawl fashioned from the softest wool, for warmth.

'Right, you can turn back now, Miss Kate.'

As her hair dried before the roaring fire Joanna

brushed it, using a silver-backed hairbrush she found on the dressing table. Afterwards, she quickly braided it. Then she realized she had nothing to secure the braid with.

'I have a blue ribbon you can have,' Kate told her. 'Shall I fetch it for you?'

Joanna kissed the girl's cheek. 'That's kind of you.'

'What shall we do after? Would you like to see the house? I can show you.'

Setting aside the niggle of guilt she felt at duping this friendly little soul, she whispered, 'I'd like that very much.' At least she'd be able to satisfy herself that Seth wasn't still working for Durrington, and he didn't have Toby hidden here.

Although Seth had kept the place under surveillance for a week, there was no sign of an infant having taken up residence in Charles Durrington's London home.

Nothing out of the ordinary had occurred. The peer came and went as usual, sometimes with Bisley in attendance, sometimes not. There was the normal number of domestic suppliers using the tradesman's entrance – including a couple of Seth's own. Questioning the house staff revealed nothing untoward. Seth reached the conclusion that the child wasn't there.

He questioned Joanna again. 'Is there anything you haven't told me, however unimportant you consider it to be?'

'It happened so quickly, and events were confused.' She shook her head from side to side in despair.

'Perhaps Toby's dead. Bisley might have killed him and thrown him into the sea.'

'You mustn't think that way. Bisley wouldn't harm Toby while Durrington is still alive. Let's go through it again.'

So they did, Joanna's forehead furrowed with anxiety while she tried to relive the moment when her child was snatched from her. Seth appreciated that she was doing her best to stay calm. But he sensed her emotions were on a knife edge, for there was a nuance of desperation in her voice.

Suddenly, she said, her eyes full of the horror she felt at the thought, 'There was no sign of Toby's carriage when I woke. It might have been thrown over the cliff.'

He kept his voice as calm as possible. 'Or it might have been kept for Toby to sleep in. A man wheeling a baby carriage is unusual, so somebody would have seen him. Durrington might have hired an accomplice in Portland. Can you think of anyone who would harm you?'

'On the island? No, why should they?' For a moment she hesitated, as if something had teased a thread from the edge of her memory. Then she shook her head – obviously the thought had slipped away again. She gazed at him. 'Has the *Joanna Rose* sailed yet?'

'That's the third time you've asked me that question this week. Do you think it's possible that Toby might be hidden aboard?'

'*God no!* Captain Staines was loyal to the Darsham and Morcant Shipping Company. He wouldn't do anything to harm Toby.'

'But he's working for Durrington now.'

Her chin lifted. 'Not for much longer, the clippers are to be sold and Edward Staines laid off. This next voyage is to be his last Australian run. I was going to—' Her lips pressed tightly over the remainder of the sentence.

'Going to what?'

Her eyes flickered away from his. 'Wish him a safe journey.'

She was lying, and that saddened him. 'Is that why you're so interested in whether the ship has departed or not?'

Placing her hands on her hips she gave him a look that could only be described as frustrated. 'Do you always talk so much? I'm not interested in whether the ship sails or not, I'm only interested in finding Toby.'

'Then you won't object if I go on board and question Staines?'

She gave a short laugh. 'Do what you like. If you accuse Edward of anything underhand, like as not you'll be thrown overboard.'

Seth raised an eyebrow. The man could only try.

'Why can't we just call in the constables and demand to search Durrington's house?'

'It would reveal our hand. Besides, I'm almost certain Toby isn't being kept there.'

'And I'm almost certain he wouldn't be on the *Joanna Rose*.'

'I just want to look at the passenger list to see if there are any children on it, in case Toby is one of them. All the better if he knows what Toby looks like. Has Captain Staines met him?'

'Yes, he came to the house not long ago, with Captain Scott and James Stark.'

Seth's nostrils narrowed as he drew in a deep breath. Why would the master of the *Joanna Rose* visit her in Portland? Why would James Stark, who'd been the legal representative for the Darsham and Morcant shipping company, visit with him. Seth smelled a conspiracy.

'What are you keeping from me, Joanna?'

Her shrug was too casual.

A remark she'd made was unleashed from the depths of his memory. *You should take her abroad, where she can grow up without fear*. Slowly, he said, 'You were going to sail on the *Joanna Rose*, weren't you?'

There was something bruised about the eyes that engaged his. She was nearly at the end of her tether.

'Yes . . . what of it?'

He turned away, trying to ignore the hollowness inside him at the thought of losing her. 'Why didn't you tell me?'

'I thought you were working for Lord Durrington.'

'And you didn't trust me?'

'How could I allow myself to trust you when Toby is so precious to me?'

She was entitled to think that, God knew; under the same circumstances he'd have thought the same. But even while he was able to rationalize it, it didn't lessen the size of the wound she'd inflicted on him. 'So why did you come to me?'

'I couldn't think of anyone else who was likely to know Lord Durrington's business better than you, and there was a possibility that you were involved and might lead me to Toby.'

Joanna Morcant could crush a man without even trying. More fool him for falling in love with her, Seth thought bitterly. He should walk away from this now, before he got in any deeper. But Seth knew his pride would keep him there, if nothing else. He'd find her son for her, then he'd watch her sail off and leave him broken-hearted. And he'd love her for ever.

A thought shot into his head, removing the self-pity that had tried to take root there. Like hell he would! He wasn't giving the woman up that easily.

'Please feel free to search my home in my absence.' He walked away, only to be arrested at the front door by her voice, as soft and regretful as a sigh. 'I've already searched it.'

He turned, saying without heat, 'Damn you, Joanna Morcant.'

Tears filled her eyes. 'I don't think you understand, Seth. Without Toby, I'm already damned.'

Halfway between his home and the *Joanna Rose* an idea suddenly hit Seth. No . . . it was too preposterous. But the more he thought about it the more feasible it became. He grinned, and his stride lengthened.

'Someone wishes to see you, sir.'

Edward Staines looked up from the passenger list he'd been checking. 'Who is it?'

'His name is Seth Adams.'

'What does he want?'

'The gentleman asked me to present his card and tell you he's a friend of Mrs Morcant.'

Seth Adams. Agent of enquiry. Edward's eyes sharpened as he remembered Joanna Morcant mentioning an investigator. 'Show him in, would you.'

When Seth presented himself, Edward waved him to the chair opposite. 'Are you here on Joanna's behalf? Where the devil is she? The passengers are coming on board in three days and I'll have to set sail, even though we're short of cargo. I'll be berthing at Portland before going on to Ireland. Will she be coming on board there?'

'Joanna's son was abducted over a week ago. I'm working on her behalf to find him. So far nothing of use has turned up and I wondered if I could look over your passenger list.'

'There's no child of Toby's age coming on board if that's what you're getting at.' The captain pushed a sheaf of paper towards him, then lifted a brandy decanter and raised an eyebrow.

Seth shook his head before allowing his glance to skim over the list of passengers. He wanted to keep his wits about him. 'Thanks, but too early in the day for me.'

'Likewise.' Staines placed it back on the tray. 'Mrs Morcant has been through enough of late, without losing her son. How's she taking it?'

'Badly, as you'd expect. I think she'd kill Durrington with her bare hands if she could.'

'She's a plucky young woman.'

'And too passionate for her own good. Sometimes she acts without thinking.' Seth gazed around the cabin, appreciating the brass fittings and wood panelling. 'Nice quarters. They do well by you.'

'She's a good ship, the best I've ever sailed in. Tobias Darsham of the Darsham and Morcant Shipping Line commissioned her.'

'Joanna's father? I imagine he'd have been pleased to see her after all those years.'

The captain's eyes washed over him for a few moments, then they suddenly narrowed. He frowned, changing tack. 'Aren't you Barnard Charsford's half-brother?'

'Something I'm reluctant to admit to.'

'I imagine it would be. And isn't Lord Durrington your client?'

'Past tense. Durrington *was* my client. What of it?'

'I'm surprised Mrs Morcant trusts you.'

Seth smiled mirthlessly. 'Joanna doesn't trust me yet, even though she wants to. But she will, eventually. She trusts you, though. She described you as being loyal to the Darsham and Morcant Shipping Company – yet you still work for Durrington.'

'A different thing altogether. The Darsham and Morcant families always treated me fairly. They were my friends. Durrington, on the other hand, is a scoundrel who conspired with Barnard Charsford to rob that young woman of everything she had, including the roof over her head. Not content with that, he's now stolen her son. And you expect people to trust you?'

'I'd be obliged if you didn't hold me accountable for my half-brother's actions, Captain Staines. What name does Tobias Darsham go under now?'

The man shot to his feet. 'I don't know what you're getting at, mister.'

'Of course you do. Tobias Darsham is still alive and kicking, and living in Australia, isn't he?'

Seth thought it prudent to rise to his feet too, but he didn't see the captain's fist coming. The next moment he found himself sprawling on his back, gasping for breath and hugging his stomach. 'That's for your trickery,' Staines said.

'You've demonstrated that you pack a mean punch, but don't try it again, because I'm capable of taking you apart,' Seth gasped, when Edward Staines bent over him.

The man grinned. 'You don't look it. I'm of a mind to drop you overboard.'

'A premature action, and one fraught with peril for me,' Seth drawled. 'I suggest you allow me to regain my feet so we can talk rationally. Believe it or not, we're on the same side.'

His jacket grabbed roughly in Edward's large fists, Seth was hauled unceremoniously to his feet and then let go. Calmly he straightened his jacket, satisfied that the man seemed to have finished flexing his muscles. 'You mentioned berthing at Portland, Captain. May I ask why? Do you have cargo to pick up?'

'Durrington has business there before going on to his estate in Ireland. From there I'll be picking up settlers and migrants heading for the Victorian goldfields.'

Everything fell into place for Seth then. 'Ah, yes . . . I see.' He smiled cautiously, when really he wanted to whoop with joy. 'It sounds to me as though the boy is still in Portland. My guess is that Durrington intends to pick Toby up there, then take him on to his Irish estate.'

Staines's eyes sharpened. 'Durrington has reserved the stateroom for himself, and two cabins for a manservant and maid.'

'How far does your loyalty to Joanna Morcant stretch, Captain Staines?'

'To the limit. But I'll need to consult with the lawyer, James Stark, on this before I set sail. Will you come with me?'

'Only if you feel you can trust me, and I'm told the whole story.'

'Mrs Morcant has advised us all of your involvement in this matter. She's not sure she can entirely trust you.'

'She can.' The thought that Joanna trusted him even a little made Seth's spirits soar. He held out his hand. After a brief moment of hesitation, the captain took it.

Constance Charsford heard voices coming from her husband's study. Nervously, she looked about her, then, observing that there were no servants hovering about, she crept to the study door and placed her ear against the panel.

'How was the couple, Charles?'

'They performed well. You should have come to watch the show, you would have enjoyed it.'

'I was breaking in my new little whore.'

'You should leave the younger ones alone, Barnard.

They're trouble, and they leave a man open to blackmail.'

Constance grimaced, for she remembered how brutally her husband had treated her on their wedding night.

'Have you got the boy yet?'

'Yes, it all went quite smoothly. Rushmore did his job, and I've come to pay . . .'

There came the sound of servants talking together and a rattle of china on a tray from the kitchen. They'd be bringing her husband his afternoon tea. The clock chimed four. Constance hadn't been outside for over a week. Red and suffocating, the house pressed in on her.

She backed away from the study door. Taking her warm cape from the hallstand she secured it about her shoulders. They shouldn't part a child from its mother and she wasn't going to allow them to get away with it. Letting herself out, Constance closed the front door quietly behind her.

The sky was beginning to darken, the air had a damp chill to it, yet it was invigorating after the atmosphere in the house. She decided not to go to Seth Adams's office, for the district it was situated in was unsafe for an unaccompanied woman, especially when darkness had fallen. Besides, he had given her his card and told her to call on him if she needed help, and his house was closer.

Constance hurried through the cold and damp streets, hoping she'd find him at home and could get her business over with quickly. A clammy fog was creeping in from the river. She must get back before her husband discovered she was missing, for she was not allowed out without his permission.

Joanna happened to be crossing the hall when Constance arrived on the doorstep. She waved the servant away and opened the door herself.

The woman standing there seemed agitated. 'I must see Mr Adams. I can't wait. If my husband discovers I'm not at home he'll be furious.'

'I'm afraid Mr Adams is out.' After satisfying herself that the woman looked respectable, Joanna allowed her into the hall. 'I'm Joanna Morcant. And you are . . .?'

'Constance Charsford. I'm married to Barnard Charsford, who is Mr Adams's brother.' Her eyes suddenly widened. 'You're her, aren't you . . . the boy's mother?'

Joanna only just stopped herself from grabbing the woman by the throat and shaking her. 'You know where my son is?'

'I overheard Lord Durrington talking to my husband. He said he had the boy.'

Joanna stared at her, her blood running cold. 'Your husband is involved in his disappearance? Does Mr Adams know?'

'Of course he does.' She jumped when a door closed upstairs. 'I must go. My husband will be incensed if he discovers I'm not home, especially since it's dark.'

The woman was as nervous as a cat, and Joanna could sympathize with her. 'I'll ask one of the manservants to accompany you. Thank you for coming. I'll make sure Mr Adams gets your message.'

Constance Charsford stepped forward and did something totally unexpected. She hugged her. 'I'm so sorry, my dear. I do hope your son is found safely. My husband sent mine away when they were very small, to be looked after by servants in the country. I rarely see them.'

A man appeared, seemingly out of the shadows. Powerful looking, he was dressed in street clothes. Joanna didn't know what his role in the household was.

'Are you going somewhere, Bart? Would you escort Mrs Charsford home?'

'I'd be pleased to, since it's on my way.' He gazed at her, a warning in his eyes. 'I advise you to stay indoors, Mrs Morcant. Make sure you lock the door after us. I'll be back before too long, most likely with Mr Adams.'

After the door closed behind them, Joanna pulled her shawl around her. She wasn't going to wait for Seth, since he'd only prevent her from doing what she was about to do – go to Durrington's house and demand her son back.

Yellow fog crept around her feet as she hurried through the dark streets, her anger keeping her warm. Seth had forgotten to tell her that his brother was involved in the kidnapping of her son. *Damn him to hell!* He'd deceived her.

She lost her way twice as the fog thickened, but eventually found herself standing outside Lord Durrington's imposing residence. That her own safety might be jeopardized didn't even occur to her.

Marching up the front steps she pounded her fists on the door. It was opened almost immediately. 'Where's

Lord Durrington?' she shouted at the hall servant, and pushed past him into the hallway. 'Tell him I'm here to collect my son.'

A hand closed around her arm. 'Hey, you can't come marching in here like this. Get out before I throw you down the steps.'

A door opened and somebody asked, 'What's all the fuss about?'

'There's a woman here, demanding to see Lord Durrington.'

'Is there, by God?' Bisley's head appeared and he smiled. 'Ah, it's Mrs Morcant. Lord Durrington is out at the moment. Would you like to wait? You can keep me company.'

'I'd prefer not to. I'm here for my son, and I'm not leaving without him.'

'You seem distraught, my dear. Is there anyone I can inform of your whereabouts?'

Remembering Seth telling her his address was to be kept secret, she bit down on her tongue. Not that he deserved any consideration, but there was dear little Kate to think of.

'Nobody knows I'm here.'

Bisley dismissed the servant and came towards her, his perfect features moulding his smooth, dark skin. It was somehow sinister, that fine-boned, cruelly feline face with its barbarian nose. He gazed down at her, unblinking. 'You really shouldn't have come here, Joanna.'

'I'm not frightened of you,' she lied, aware of the tremor in her voice.

'That's something I must rectify.' His hand gripped her elbow and he propelled her towards the room he'd just emerged from. 'Come, take a glass of absinthe with me and we'll discuss the situation. Tell me, is Seth Adams advising you in this matter?'

'I'm not telling you anything. I'll wait for Lord Durrington.'

'I think not, my dear.' He closed the door and locked it, coming towards her with a smile on his face. Then his hand whipped up and he backhanded her. The force of it sent Joanna staggering sideways to the floor.

13

Seth was furious. Just as everything was falling into place, Joanna Morcant had disappeared from his house.

'What did Mrs Charsford tell her?' he asked Bart Seager, a colleague whose services he used on occasions when he needed an extra pair of ears and hands.

'That Durrington has the boy. I tried to discover a little more as I was taking Mrs Charsford home, but she was too frightened of getting caught and she clammed up.'

'Constance is a brave woman. A pity she's married to Barnard, who is too grasping for his own good. He's always been a bully and a boor but I'm surprised to discover how dishonest he's become in his pursuit of money. If anything untoward happens to Joanna or her child he'll be brought to account, by hell he will.'

'I should have kept a better eye on her.'

'Neither of us can be in two places at once, Bart. My guess is she's gone to confront Durrington with all guns blazing. In this fog she could have walked straight into the river. I suppose I'll have to go looking for her.'

'You won't get very far, since you can't see your hand in front of your face out there.'

'I'll have to wait until morning, then. I swear, Bart. When I get her back I'm going to beat her backside until she can't sit on it for a week.'

'You wouldn't beat dust from a carpet, and I'm damned sure you could think of better things do with a backside like Joanna Morcant's,' Bart said, and grinned.

Constance had left her escort at the end of the road. Too frightened to go inside, she stood in the fog for a while. Relieved to find the hallway unoccupied when she finally ventured into her own home, she gave a sigh of relief as she shed her cape and bonnet. Thinking that her little escapade had gone undetected, she smiled to herself as she hurried upstairs to ready herself for dinner.

There she found Barnard waiting, his knees slightly apart, his bulging stomach resting on his thighs. There was an unpleasant smile on his face. 'Where have you been, Mrs Charsford?'

How she loathed him. The thought swelled up inside her, overriding her fright, and giving her courage. She'd never felt so powerful before and spoke without caution. 'I needed some fresh air.'

'You didn't seek my permission to leave the house.'

'I was going to but I heard you talking to someone in your study . . . Lord Durrington, I believe. Besides, I'm not a prisoner, am I?'

When his smile was replaced by an expression of

alarm, she experienced a little flare of triumph. Good, she'd rattled him

'Did you overhear the conversation between myself and Lord Durrington?'

Constance thought fast, then kept her voice deliberately vague. 'You were discussing a play, I believe . . . ah, yes, he said you would have enjoyed the performance.'

'Good. I wouldn't like to think my wife would eavesdrop on my business conversations, since I'm associated with powerful men who would expect – no, *demand* my discretion.'

How discreet was it to ruin young girls who were just emerging from childhood? Discretion would certainly be required by someone who held himself up to be a pillar of society – a man who deprived children of their mothers and mothers of their children. Men like her husband should be lined up against a wall and shot. How she despised him.

Just daring to think such a thought was so liberating that she wanted to laugh from the freedom she felt. Why not laugh? she thought, so she did, but it came out as a nervous titter. Afterwards, she stared at him in defiance. Then, from behind his back he brought out the cane he used to humiliate her with.

'From now on you will remember to ask my permission before leaving the house. Ready yourself for punishment, Mrs Charsford.'

Punishment usually consisted of stripping down to her drawers and bending over the back of the chair while he beat her repeatedly with the cane and called her insulting names. He raised welts and bruises and sometimes drew blood, but never where it was visible to others.

Sometimes, if he was in a particularly aggressive mood . . .? Constance tried not to think of that particular humiliation. The name calling of whore and slut while he expended himself on her like a dog was the most vile punishment for her. Since Constance had no choice but to obey her husband, she took pleasure from the fact that he lacked the self-discipline to control his disgusting urges.

What if she refused to accept punishment? Her unexpected rebellion against his treatment surprised even her, and her heart began to beat very fast. Surely it couldn't make matters any worse since she already lived like a prisoner in her own home – a home her dowry had brought to the marriage.

'If you cane me again I'll go to the police and tell them you assaulted me,' she said quite clearly, and her heart was pounding now.

'What, you dare to defy me!' he roared, and he thumped his fist on the table, setting the crystal beads on the lampshade tinkling, and making her jump.

Constance backed away from him as he advanced on her, so incensed that foam gathered at the corners of his mouth. She shouted, 'I'll tell the police you helped abduct a child, too.'

He stopped, his hand still raised, staring at her while colour ebbed from his face. 'What are you talking about?'

'Joanna Morcant's son.'

He threw the cane aside and thundered, 'What do you know of the matter?'

'That you arranged it. You're a fool, Barnard. That woman isn't like me – too frightened to demand that I be allowed to bring up my own sons. I hope Joanna Morcant pursues all those involved in his abduction, and I hope she exposes every one of you.'

As Barnard stepped closer the unpleasant smile returned. 'My, what a loyal wife I have. So, you're prepared to see your husband go to prison.'

'Yes, and hang by the neck until dead. I'd even travel to Newgate to watch the event myself, unless . . .' Giddy with the euphoria of being liberated from her fear of him, Constance scooped in a breath and completed her sentence. 'Unless I'm allowed to go and live with my sons.'

'*My* sons, Mrs Charsford. You were merely the vessel who carried them for me.'

Her husband turned away. Thinking he was about to leave she relaxed, and was unprepared when he snatched up the heavy brass poker and swung around again.

She raised her hands, heard the splat of metal against flesh as she tried to defend herself. Pain shot through one arm as it fell to her side. Her heart began to flutter and all strength suddenly left her when a second blow smashed against the side of her head.

When Barnard had expended his rage sufficiently, he stared down at Constance, lying so still on the floor. Panic rapidly set in. What the hell had he done? He'd killed her! The panic was replaced by animal cunning.

They'd hang him for this. But not if he made it resemble an accident, he told himself.

He wiped the blood from the poker, then threw his handkerchief into the centre of the fire. He then arranged his wife's body so that her head rested against the fender. As an afterthought, Barnard turned the edge of the carpet up so it looked as though she'd tripped over it and banged her head on the fender.

Creeping down to his study he poured himself a brandy with shaking hands. His teeth chattered against the rim of the glass, unnerving him even more and causing him to spill the brandy across his desk as he found himself making terrified snivelling noises.

Constance's maid would find her in a minute. She'd scream and raise the whole household. Barnard could almost feel the noose tightening around his neck. Falling to his hands and knees he crawled across the room, wedging himself in a corner between two bookcases, his knees pressed against his stomach, his head down, as he used to do as a child when hiding from his father's wrath. To his shame, he wet his trousers.

Barnard didn't know how long he huddled there, waiting for something to happen, but he was suddenly startled out of his funk by the dinner gong sounding in the hall.

Nobody had seen what had occurred between himself and his wife, he told himself. He must behave as if nothing untoward had happened. He'd go into dinner, as usual, then feign annoyance at her absence and send one of the servants to look for her.

Feeling a fool at having lost control, Barnard dusted himself down, mopped the sweat from his forehead and sucked in a few deep breaths to steady himself before going upstairs to change into dry trousers and linens.

He took his place at the dinner table and allowed the manservant to ladle soup into his bowl. He started to eat. The soup had no taste.

Bile rose to his throat and he threw his spoon into the bowl. Liquid splashed on to his clothing. He rubbed at it with his napkin and it came away red with her blood. He'd got some of it on him. 'Oh God!' he said out loud.

The servant stared at him, puzzled.

'What are you looking at? Where's Mrs Charsford? Go and find her.'

The door crashed open against the wall and she stood there, swaying. Ashen faced, her eyes were wide and accusing as she stared at him. Blood trickled from under her hair.

Barnard could have screamed with the relief he felt, and had the wits to say for the servant's benefit, 'Constance, my dear, what has happened to you?'

She passed a shaking hand over her brow. 'I don't know. I think I fell and hit my head.'

Jubilation filled him. She couldn't remember. He was on his feet in an instant, his arm around her. 'Help me get her upstairs, man, then fetch Dr Phelps. He lives five houses along, so you can't get lost in the fog.'

He helped his wife into bed, then rang for her maid and hovered – the embodiment of the solicitous husband – while Constance was undressed and put to bed.

He watched as the maid gently washed the blood away from the wound on her head. There was a purple bruise on his wife's arm, where she'd tried to defend herself from him, another on her shoulder. They could be explained by the fall, he just hoped the doctor wouldn't look at her buttocks, thighs and back.

He crossed to Constance when the maid went to empty the bloodied water from the bowl and, hearing the heavy tread of the doctor on the stairs, whispered, 'Are you sure you don't remember how you hurt yourself?'

She gazed at him directly then, her mouth twisted into a snarl. 'Of course I remember. I want to see my sons, Barnard.'

He recoiled from the hate in her eyes, saying to Phelps as he came in, 'Mrs Charsford has fallen and hurt herself. Her mind is wandering a little, I'm afraid. I was thinking of sending her to the country to make a full recovery.'

Constance smiled at him. 'I'll be pleased to reacquaint myself with our sons . . . unless they're being kept prisoner too.' Her words began to slur and tears rolled down her face. 'I doubt if I'll come back.'

Dr Phelps nodded. 'It does sound as though Mrs Charsford's mind is wandering a little. Her brain might be concussed. Now, perhaps you'd prefer to go outside while I examine my patient in private. Don't look so anxious, man. Things could be worse. At least your wife is alive and conscious.'

Now Barnard had got over his fright, he began to wish she wasn't, for she'd ruined a perfectly good dinner.

Seth's card was presented to Lord Durrington.

'His lordship is too busy to see you at present,' Bisley told him with an oily smile. 'But he's holding a small dinner party tomorrow evening in honour of his house guest, and has asked me to extend an invitation for you to attend.'

'Am I to take it that Mrs Morcant is that house guest?'

'Mrs Morcant came to us last night, looking for her lost son. She seemed to be under the impression he was here, and was quite beside herself. His lordship couldn't send her away in her distraught condition, especially since the fog was so thick. Fortunately I was able to calm her down and she has accepted the earl's invitation to remain here as his guest.'

'I'd be obliged if you would allow me to speak to Mrs Morcant, since up until yesterday she was my house guest, and I've received no instruction from her that she no longer wishes to take advantage of my hospitality.'

Bisley merely smiled. 'May I suggest it was a poor sort of hospitality, since Mrs Morcant arrived here in an exhausted and hysterical state. She's still asleep, and I'd prefer not to wake her. You may see her at dinner tomorrow.'

Inwardly, Seth gave a sigh. The man was playing games with him and he wasn't going to bite – not yet.

Nodding, he made his retreat and marched over to James Stark's office, then the pair headed towards the *Joanna Rose* to inform Edward Staines of the new development.

'Do you think you can get her out?' Edward asked him.

'They'll be using her son like a carrot under a donkey's nose. If there's the slightest whiff of them leading Joanna to Toby I doubt if she'll listen to anyone's counsel but her own.'

Edward rocked on his heels. 'If only we could get our hands on the boy first.'

'I'm sure he's still in Portland. I'm just as convinced that Durrington intends to pick the boy up before going on to Ireland.'

'D'you think he'll bring Joanna on board?'

'It's unlikely. There's a possibility that she'll just be made to disappear, or he'll simply leave her behind. I'll have to get her out of there and get her on board myself. If we use other means of travel it's unlikely that we'll reach Portland before you. Would you risk your employer's wrath by hiding us, though?'

Edward nodded, as though this sort of thing happened every day of the week. 'Easy enough. As for my employer, since the ship is up for sale, my position is already forfeit, along with my entitlements, I've been led to understand.' He gave a faint grin. 'I'm of a mind to break the man's balls. On a financial level, Durrington is sailing too close to the wind, I believe.'

And his half-brother had underwritten the man. Now, that was interesting to know. Seth laughed. 'I'm sure you could think of many ways to achieve that, especially while you have command of the ship. I understand you already have a cabin set aside for Mrs Morcant and her son.'

Edward's eyes flicked his way. 'Do you?'

Seth wouldn't like to play cards with this man. 'It took some persuading to get it out of Joanna, but she finally told me the truth. I'm under the impression there's a conspiracy between the whole lot of you, too.'

'Is it that obvious?' James said, exchanging a grin with Edward.

'Detection is my profession, gentlemen. I've also reached the conclusion as to why flight has become necessary.'

'Have you, by God? State it, then.'

'You're a cagey bugger, aren't you? Well, the fact is that I know Tobias Darsham is still alive. And in case you're wondering why I've taken such an interest, I'll tell you something else. I intend to pursue Joanna Morcant to the ends of the earth.'

'Makes sense,' Edward grunted, exchanging a glance with James, which made Seth wonder if he'd missed something.

'We understand each other, then. Can you delay the ship's departure after Durrington's party comes on board. Is that possible?'

Edward gave an incredulous chuckle. 'Not if they come on board at the last minute.'

'Ah yes, I see . . . the tide.'

'Unfortunately, we can't overlook it. But there are other considerations, like being in line for the towing services.' Edward sighed. 'I can always delay the ship in Portland until you get there and the matter is resolved. Why don't I just lock them in their cabins?'

Seth viewed the captain with some alarm. 'We don't want him to know you're involved. The person who's holding Toby prisoner in Portland might decide to dispose of him if there's a possibility that the sorry affair has been discovered.'

Brian Rushmore was going crazy. 'Shut that brat up, would you, Ma?'

Fanny glared at him. 'Ah . . . shut up yerself. The boy's hungry. He needs some food and we haven't got any.'

'Well, he'll have to wait until it's dark, since I can't go out in case somebody recognizes me. Then I'll go and pull up a few cabbages and turnips and wring the neck of a hen.'

Leaning on the sticks she used as crutches, Fanny Rushmore made her way rapidly across the floor. She was blind in one eye and her foot was twisted under her, the result of a severe beating inflicted on her years before by her late husband, after she tried to leave him.

'Get me a drop of gin while you're out, our Brian,' she whined. 'I'm running short.'

'I haven't got any money.'

'Yes you have. You could sell that ring you've got hidden to the Barnes brothers. And you took money from that Ada Cooper, who does for me. Where is she, anyway? The child's beginning to stink.'

'I sent the nosy old witch away, so you'll have to clean him yourself.' Brian had in fact strangled the Cooper woman and thrown her over the cliff into the sea after she'd threatened to fetch the constable. Her body would be halfway to Ireland by now.

'What did you send her away for? I can't remember things sometimes, and I need her to fetch and carry. I'm blind and crippled, thanks to your pa. I haven't got the strength to look after a young un.'

'You never looked after us when you *did* have the strength, you stupid old hag.'

'You show some respect when you speak to your mother, Brian Rushmore. You're just like your pa, bad through and through. I heard about that girl you forced yourself on. 'Tis said she walks around with a mazed look on her face, and cries and trembles when a man speaks to her. Her brothers have sworn to spill your guts if they set eyes on you in these parts again, so you better watch out.' Alarm suddenly filled her voice. 'I thought you were in prison. Did you escape?'

'They found out that somebody else hurt that girl, and they let me out.'

Brian adjusted his crotch, cupping his genitals in his palm. He could do with a woman. He closed his eyes and thought of Joanna. She owed him one, and she'd been widowed for over a year now, so he'd heard. She would be begging to have a man between her thighs, same as him. He should have stuck it into her, right there in the yard. But she'd been unconscious and, when he did stick it in, he wanted her to know it was punishment for scorning him all those years ago.

His tongue slid along his lips. There were women living in the Rushmore cottage, too – a ripe pair of uppity creatures, with skin soft and fair. Not that he cared what their skin was like, only what they had under their skirts. All women were the same in that regard, only some smelled sweeter.

There was money of his hidden in the cottage they occupied, too. While he'd been living there he'd made a hiding hole under the floorboards. There he'd stash any cash he managed to get his hands on, for he'd discovered that earning a living by stealing, was easier than fishing.

The brat was screaming now. 'For God's sake, shut your face,' he shouted. 'See to him, Ma, before I cut his flappin' tongue out. Give him the rest of the milk in the jug.'

'It's on the turn.'

'As if I care. Give him the bleddy milk when I tell you.'

Fanny poured the milk into a mug and took it through to the other room. The boy stopped screaming to stare sullenly at her. His nose was running, his face was flushed and he stank something rotten. Well, that couldn't be helped, and she wasn't going to clean up after him. Brian had brought the boy here, and Brian could look after him. Besides, he didn't have any clothes other than what he was wearing.

Fanny supposed she could take his reeking trousers off.

'Want Mama,' he said.

'You can't have her, you pest.' She held out the mug. 'Here, drink this.'

The boy gulped the sour milk down with barely a grimace at the taste. Rivers of it ran from the side of his mouth, over his chin and down his dirty smock. Vaguely, Fanny wondered whose child it was.

'Want more,' he said holding out the mug.

'Well, you bleddy well can't have more because there isn't any. Go to sleep.'

'*No!* Want Mama.' He threw the mug. It hit Fanny on the bridge of the nose and fell to the floor. She slapped his face, then spread a blanket over him and snarled, 'Another word out of you and I'll take a stick to your arse, you see if I don't.'

Brian had gone when she slammed the door on the screaming child. She fetched her bottle of comfort from its hiding place. There was barely a couple of mouthfuls left. Carefully, she sucked at it, making it last. Blood dripped from her nose and she staunched it with the hem of her skirt.

Fanny thought of her daughter, respectable now, and living with her husband in that big house. She was proud of Tilda. She'd given the girl a chance to better herself when she'd handed her over to Anna Rushmore to be company for that wilful little pest Joanna. That one had tried to queen it over all of them, she remembered bitterly.

Such a long time ago, that had been. Now Tilda was all growed up and married to a respectable man, and with a girl of her own to care for – a nice little thing who reminded her a bit of her stepdaughter, Mary.

Fleetingly, she wondered what had happened to Mary. Married a soldier most likely, since she was always chasing after a uniform.

The boy had stopped screaming, and was now giving long, shuddering sobs. Fanny suddenly felt sorry for him. Perhaps Tilda would give her something clean for the child to wear. And some fresh milk to drink. She might even offer to look after the child for her.

'I'm too old to have a babby foisted on to me,' she said self-pityingly as the bottle yielded nothing more than the faintest taste of juniper berries to her seeking tongue.

But Brian had told her not to go out, and it was a long way to Fortuneswell.

'Sod Brian, I need my comforts,' she said out loud, throwing the empty bottle on to a chair. She picked up the ring he'd left on the dresser and stared at it. Thick, solid gold, it was, by the look of it. And unusual, with two hands, fingers entwined. She could buy several bottles of mother's ruin with that.

The child had gone quiet. She closed the door gently so as not to wake him, then walked out into the raw night. Storm clouds were boiling in the sky and rain was flung in scattered handfuls against her body.

She made it to the nearest inn before her legs would take her no further. Leaning on her crutches she gazed through the window. There was a blazing fire in the parlour. The Barnes brothers, their faces as sly as sewer rats, were seated in their usual corner.

Pushing the door open, Fanny gave an ingratiating smile when one of them gazed up at her.

A few moments later Fanny was sipping a brandy they'd treated her to. One of them said, 'How did you come by this ring, Mother Rushmore?'

'It was a gift from my son Brian. He's a good boy to his mother. Not like Leonard, who never comes to see me.'

The pair exchanged a glance. 'Brian's out of prison then, is he?'

'He is that. They let him out because he didn't commit any crime. A good boy is my Brian. Now, about the ring. I know solid gold when I see it. How much are you offering?'

'Ten shilling,' the older one said.

Indignantly, Fanny stared from one to another. 'That's daylight robbery.'

'We'll throw in a bottle of gin,' the other said.

That was more like it. 'Two bottles,' she said.

'You drive a hard bargain, Mother.' The ring was replaced by a small pile of coins. Barnes the younger jerked his head towards the barman. 'Tom, find two bottles of the special gin for Mrs Rushmore. Good day to you, missus.'

When she got outside, Fanny quickly uncorked the bottle and took a long swallow. By Christ, it was potent stuff, especially after the brandy.

She started to walk, stopping every now and again to take a swig from the bottle. A cold and fitful wind sighed and moaned around the streets, carrying grit and dust before it.

Stopping in the shelter of a wall, she stared around her, disorientated. What was she doing here, when she lived in the fishermen's cottages down at Chiswell with her husband and children?

Fanny began to make her way down the hill, dragging her crippled leg behind her, singing quietly and tunelessly to herself.

Brian's need for a woman grew stronger as he watched the two girls bustling about. If he had the cash on him he could buy one of the women who hung around the soldiers – or he could take the pair in the Rushmore cottage for nothing. But there was an older man and woman living in the cottage, too, now. He couldn't risk going in, not even for the stash of cash he'd hidden there.

There was no sign of Joanna. For all he knew she could still be lying under the fishing nets, where he'd left her. But he hadn't hit her hard enough to kill her, and she'd still been breathing when he'd left. He reckoned she might have gone running off to London, as the man who was paying him to snatch her child had said she would. He'd be glad when he could shed the responsibility of the boy, collect his pay and take off. He'd decided to go to America after he was paid. He'd heard that gold could be picked up in the streets there.

Brian turned away. Going to the church he broke the lock to the back door and emptied the contents of the poor box into his pocket. Tilda lived nearby. She would have a kitchen garden where he could pull some vegetables.

He watched his sister through the kitchen window

for a while. She was better looking than he remembered. Dressed in a pretty pink gown with an apron over the top she ladled steaming stew and dumplings on to plates, watched by a little girl. Brian's mouth began to water and his stomach rumbled. Tilda had gained weight, he thought, and, as she turned away, he realized she had one in the oven.

He briefly wondered about the little girl. Something about her reminded him of his sister, Mary Rushmore. She'd been a good-looking girl who'd attracted all the soldiers. But Mary's head had been screwed on, and she'd never have given her favours away.

'Well, well,' he said out loud, and wondered if Tilda's husband knew that he and his dead brother had been under her skirt before him.

Tilda gazed up at the sound of his voice, as if she'd heard him. Her eyes narrowed to peer into the darkness beyond the window, and for a moment she seemed to look straight into his eyes. Holding his breath, Brian stood very still.

Then a man came through from the other room; his arms came round her from behind and he kissed the back of her neck.

Brian moved away now Tilda was distracted, and when he looked again a curtain had been drawn over the window. He pulled a cabbage and some carrots from her garden and placed them in his sack. Not too many, lest they be missed.

Tilda's chickens began an agitated clucking as he neared the pen. He moved away from them so the noise wouldn't alert her.

Instead, from a garden further up the road he plucked a rabbit from a hutch and bashed its head against a rock to kill it. Blood and brains splattered as it twitched in its death throes.

At Widow Hutton's house Brian thumped on the front door. When the old lady, who was afflicted with rheumatism, began to rise painfully from her chair to open it, he nipped round the back. The kitchen door was unlocked, so he helped himself to a jug of milk, half a loaf of bread and some eggs from her pantry.

Satisfied he had enough for their immediate needs, he started off back towards the cottage, keeping to the shadows. He hadn't got far when he almost stumbled across his mother, who was sprawled on her back in the shadow of a wall, snoring loudly.

'You drunken slut,' he snarled. 'You're supposed to be lookin' after the kid. I should've known better.' He picked up an empty gin bottle and flung it over the wall into the cemetery, where it smashed against a headstone. He couldn't carry her all the way back to the cottage. He'd have to come back for her with the wheelbarrow.

It was beginning to rain heavily. Putting his stolen goods down, Brian rolled his mother over the other side of the wall, where she was sheltered from the worst of it.

Twenty minutes later, he flung open the door to the cottage and set the jug of milk and the other fruits of his labours on the table.

The boy was asleep. His cheeks were flushed and he was breathing noisily through an open mouth. His hair was matted and wet with sweat. He stank something awful.

Brian hoped he wasn't sick. That was all he needed.

Down at the Fortuneswell cemetery, Fanny rolled over. She didn't feel or hear anything when she fell, not even her son calling her name.

She travelled six feet, landing in the mud at the bottom of the grave dug for the funeral of Jimmy Upton, who'd died at the ripe old age of seventy-two, leaving a goodly amount of cash and several nice properties to be distributed as his will dictated.

Jimmy had fathered nineteen children, ten on his wife and the other nine on his several mistresses.

Rivulets of water were eroding the piles of earth heaped each side of the yawning grave, and mud had begun to slide into the hole. Fanny's mouth automatically fell open when her nose became blocked. The mud quickly filled the space she made for it, preventing the passage of any more breath.

Fanny couldn't open her good eye, but she felt the wetness and wondered mildly where she was. She couldn't be bothered to struggle so she didn't wonder for long.

The next morning, Jimmy Upton's coffin was lowered into the hole, pressing Fanny further into the mud.

'He was good man and a good father,' one of his women muttered – a sentiment echoed by several of the other women and many of his children.

'May God accept him into heaven,' the Reverend David Lind said.

Jimmy's wife stared challengingly at the reverend and stated caustically, 'May the devil take him, for all I care, for the wicked auld bugger was only good for one thing, and that was lying on top of one woman or another.'

14

Seth wore an immaculate evening suit with a cutaway jacket over a waistcoat of blue silk that matched his cuffs and revers.

Because it had been drizzling and was wet underfoot, he tugged on a pair of boots, adjusting them around his calves under the narrow legs of his trousers. He wore a small pistol in a shoulder holster under his jacket.

Kate, in her nightgown and robe, and with her hair twisted into rags, an action which Seth had been led to understand would supply an abundance of feminine ringlets, inspected him critically before she smiled. 'You look pretty tonight.'

Seth grinned at the thought. 'Only ladies look pretty. Gentlemen look handsome.'

'Why?'

'I don't know why. They just do. Aren't you supposed to be in bed, my love?'

'I'm not tired yet. Where did Joanna go? Are you going to see her?'

'She was invited to stay with another family for a day or two. I hope to see her tonight.'

'She's pretty, isn't she?'

Kate had a smitten look on her face, and Seth took her hands in his. 'She certainly is. You like Joanna a lot, don't you, my love?'

'Oh yes. I love her and she loves me,' Kate said with a sudden enthusiasm.

He didn't want Kate to get hurt. 'Did she tell you that?'

'Nearly. She said if she ever had a daughter to love she'd want one just like me. Have you found Toby for her yet?'

'No, but I think I know where he is.'

'Joanna said if you wish for things hard enough, sometimes the wishes come true. Tell her I'm wishing hard for Toby to be found. Where do you think he is, Uncle Seth?'

'I think he's being held prisoner on the island where she lives. So if I go away again, that's where I'll be. Looking for Toby.'

'Will Joanna be with you?'

He intended to persuade Durrington to hand her over, one way or another. He gave a faint smile. 'I certainly hope so.'

Kate got to the point of the conversation then. 'If you married Joanna she could be my mother, then I'd have somebody to love when you're away, and Toby to play with, as well.'

Seth held Kate close for a few precious seconds. He hadn't thought that she might be lonely. 'You'd better put it on your wish list then, Kate. Now, off you go to bed before your governess comes looking for you and grumbles at me.'

Her eyelids began to droop as she slid her arms around his neck and laid her head on his shoulder. 'Tuck me into bed and tell me a story.'

A few minutes later Kate was fast asleep. He gently touched her cheek, marvelling at the flawless perfection of her skin. Love for her flowed through him in a way that robbed him of breath.

He'd seen children of Kate's age begging on the streets, as thin, nervous and pinch-faced as grey mice. Where did they end up? he wondered. Working as dips, or in brothels from an early age, perhaps. The boys would be sent down the sewers to clean the pipes, sometimes dying down there, their lungs filling with poisonous gas, if diseases such as cholera didn't kill them first.

Kate would never have to suffer like that, despite the unfortunate circumstances of her birth. Joanna was right. He should take her abroad to grow up, where nobody knew of her background.

The anger he'd felt over Joanna's hasty action dissipated, leaving the ashes of shame in its wake. He should have seen it straight away – should have understood how frantic she felt about losing her son. She'd be worried beyond reason – beyond thought of her own safety. Joanna would do anything to get Toby back. He wondered what humiliation Durrington was putting her through, and how the hell she was holding herself together.

Gently, he kissed Kate's cheek, then nodding to her governess made his way to the hall. He took an umbrella from the stand, one with a blade in the handle, hoping he wouldn't need to use it. He disliked violence, but he'd drive it through Durrington's heart to save Joanna from further grief.

Durrington's windows spilled light across the wet road. Opposite the house was a small park. Seth's glance searched the shadows of the foliage for signs of Bart Seager. The rustle of a branch brought a nod from him. Bart was well concealed.

Seth was shown into the drawing room, where a small party was assembled. There was his brother Barnard and Mrs Charsford, and Durrington. Constance looked pale, and a bruise disappeared under her hairline. Her wrist was supported by a bandage.

'A slight sprain, but I can still use it.' Constance answered his enquiry politely, but her eyes flickered towards Barnard.

His half-brother was showing signs of strain. He had a fixed smile on his face, as though he were there under sufferance, and he talked in a high-pitched voice. Could he be having second thoughts about the situation? Seth wondered.

Of Joanna and Bisley there was no sign, and Seth was sorely tempted to rattle Durrington's teeth from his head. But he couldn't do anything to place Joanna in danger, and would have to see the game through to the end if he was going to win it.

'I understood Joanna Morcant was to be present,' he said quietly to his host.

Durrington offered him an amused smile. 'An altogether charming and spirited young woman, who affords me hours of amusement. Joanna is resting, and will put in an appearance at dinner. She will be seated between myself and Bisley. But I've given instructions that you be placed opposite her, so you can converse in comfort. No doubt you and the Charsfords will provide an appreciative audience.'

Durrington had designed the evening to be play-acted, then, with Joanna in the lead role. Seth wondered what Durrington had planned for the ending. The hairs on the back of his neck prickled.

'I would prefer to speak to her privately, first.'

'No doubt you would, Mr Adams. Unfortunately, that's not Joanna's wish. You must wait until she makes her entrance.'

Not by the flicker of an eyelid did Seth divulge the frustration and fury he was feeling. He merely nodded and turned to examine a painting of a nude woman on the wall.

It was a long wait, but shortly after the four of them had seated themselves at the table Bisley came in, leading Joanna.

Constance Charsford's gasp was audible to everyone.

Joanna was wearing a scarlet gown, one cut so low over the bosom that it was almost indecent. Rouge splotched her cheeks and her mouth was smeared with it, giving her a clownish appearance. Under the thick layer of white cosmetic powdering, many bruises were visible, as though she'd been pinched and punched repeatedly. Her hair was hanging loose, covering burns from a rope which had been tied around her neck. Rope burns could also be seen on her wrists.

'Joanna,' Seth whispered, his heart going out to her, for she moved as if she were in a daze, sitting opposite him when she was told to.

When she lifted her eyes to gaze at him, he saw they were filled with misery and despair. But fire still smouldered in their depths, and a faint wry smile was offered to him. She had still got some fight left in her and that was a blessing, for she'd need it.

'What happened to her?' Constance said, her voice as hard as stone.

'Mrs Morcant has met with a little accident, rather like you did, Mrs Charsford. It gave your husband quite a fright, I understand. Very unfortunate when a woman is damaged, since they have such soft bodies compared to men. I'm sure the pain they experience is much worse as a result. Such delightful creatures, though.'

Constance bestowed on her husband an utterly disdainful glance. 'You will not intimidate me into keeping quiet. Nor you, Lord Durrington. That woman has been ill used. How can you treat her so badly?'

'Joanna Morcant is a slut, who deserves nothing less. Now she dresses like one.'

Joanna made a protesting sound and Bisley's hand tightened around her upper arm.

Seth's muscles tensed. 'I must insist that Mrs Morcant is allowed to leave with me, and now,' he said to Lord Durrington.

'She came here of her own free will, didn't she, Bisley, my dear?'

Bisley giggled. 'And she can leave with Mr Adams if she wishes. Aren't you helping her to find her son?' He gazed around at them all, his eyes half hooded. 'She accused Lord Durrington and myself of abducting him. We allowed her to search the house, of course. Then she said we had killed her little bastard. As if we'd wilfully hurt an infant.' He turned to smile at Joanna, his olive skin shining in the light 'Do you want to go with Mr Adams, Joanna dearest?'

As Joanna shook her head in a befuddled manner, tears slid down her cheek.

Durrington dabbed them away with his napkin. 'You've made our guest of honour cry, Mr Adams.'

Joanna's eyelids began to droop, and she slumped in her chair.

'What have you given her?' Seth demanded to know.

Durrington chuckled as he gazed at him through eyes sunk in a web of wrinkles. 'Just a little absinthe. She's taken quite a liking to it. To my mind it's a filthy brew. Wormwood oil is addictive and it rots the brain, I hear. Though I believe it's a strong aphrodisiac, as well. What do you say to that, Bisley?'

Bisley stroked Joanna's arm. 'A very strong aphrodisiac, My Lord. Isn't it, Joanna?'

Her hand slowly curled and her head came up. With great difficulty she focused on Bisley and whispered distinctly, '*Pig!*'

Durrington smiled expansively at them all. 'Such spirit our little island peasant possesses. Ah, here comes the soup. Perhaps you'd like to serve our guests, Joanna.' A silver tureen was set in front of her, a ladle placed in her hand. Joanna stared at it, as if she didn't know what it was for.

Constance Charsford stood up, a determined look on her face. 'Barnard, I don't like this. I want to go home and I think we should take that young woman with us.'

'Stop whining and sit down,' Barnard barked at her.

Instead, Constance remained standing. 'Do shut up, Barnard.' She strolled sedately around the table, saying, 'Mrs Morcant can't handle that ladle. Allow me to serve the soup.' When Bisley leaned across to stop her, she nodded towards Seth, then calmly picked up the vessel and upended it over Bisley's head before banging it down over his forehead. It was a tight fit. 'There's your serve, you odious creature.'

Bisley's scream became a gurgle as soup filled his nose and mouth.

Barnard's mouth fell open and so did Durrington's when Seth leaped across the table, scattering cutlery and flower arrangements. He dragged Joanna's chair backwards.

'Come along, my dear,' Constance said to Joanna. Joanna managed to stagger to her feet and ambled unsteadily towards the hall with Constance for support.

Durrington had just brought his weapon up when Seth kicked it from his hand. He flicked his own pistol from the holster and backed away from the three men.

Barnard had scrambled under the table for shelter and gazed at him from under it, wide-eyed with terror.

Durrington was red-faced with fury. Bisley was screaming curses as he tried to remove the tureen from his head. The servants watched, open-mouthed. One of them sniggered and opened the door for Seth and the two women.

They gained the hall where, at Seth's request, Constance hurriedly grabbed their outer garments and his umbrella.

'Run across to the park, Constance,' Seth whispered, grunting as he heaved Joanna over his shoulder. They made it out of the door and into the park unseen.

Bart greeted them. Taking half of the burden of Joanna, they carried her swiftly to a seat in the most densely foliaged part of the park.

'I'll keep watch while you sort yourselves out.'

'I don't think we'll be followed.' Thank God he hadn't had to shoot anyone, Seth thought, wrapping Joanna in his coat.

That done, he turned to Mrs Charsford and kissed her on the cheek. 'Thank you, Constance. You're a brave woman. Do you have anywhere safe to go?'

She shook her head, panting a little for she was out of breath as she whispered, 'I shall have to go home.'

'If you wish, I have some rooms you can use for now. Keep out of sight and we'll sort something out when I come back to London. I'll be seeing your husband shortly. Is there any message you want me to convey to him?'

'Tell him that if I never set eyes on him again, that will be soon enough.'

Joanna gave a slurred chuckle.

He grinned and called Bart over. 'Escort my sister-in-law to my accommodation address, would you, Bart? Perhaps you'd ask Mr Geevers to see to her needs until I get back. I don't know how long I'll be. Take my umbrella, my dear. It's quite a step and it'll keep you dry.'

Seth kissed Joanna when the others left. There was nothing sexual about it. He grimaced at the smell and taste of her breath. Apart from the bitter taste of the absinthe, she'd been fed a mixture of opium and brandy. Her head would feel like the inside of a tar barrel when she came out of it.

''S'nice kiss,' she said with a sigh. 'More.'

'Certainly not. It was a scientific test. If I held a flame to your breath you'd ignite like a bonfire. I'm taking you on board the *Joanna Rose* to sleep it off.'

Hope flared in her voice. ''S Toby there?'

'No, but I have a good idea where he is. I've just got to get it confirmed. Edward Staines will look after you for now.'

She gulped. 'I feel sick.'

'I'm not surprised.' The brew she'd been given was best out of her. To help the process along, Seth placed her on her hands and knees then thrust his fingers down her throat. After she'd finished he hauled her upright and wiped her mouth with his handkerchief. 'Is that better.'

She whimpered when she nodded. 'I was a fool.'

Sliding her arms into his overcoat he did the buttons up. 'We'll talk about that when you're more yourself. You're not thinking straight at the moment. Can you walk?'

'I'll try, but the ground keeps shifting sideways.'

He slipped his arm around her waist and they made their way across the park, looking for all the world like a man on the town with a drunken doxy. Rain began to fall from the sky in a steady deluge. 'Wait, I'm thirsty.' She turned her face up to the sky and hung her tongue out of her mouth, lapping at the rain as it came down.

Cold as he was, Seth smiled at the sight. 'I love you,' he said quietly, but she didn't seem to hear him, for the next moment she chuckled. 'Didn't Slisby look funny with the soup bowl on his head?' Her next chuckle turned into laughter, which then became a series of hysterical gulps and sobs. 'I hate myself,' she wailed.

He drew her into his arms. 'Joanna, my love, don't cry. Everything will be all right.'

'But I love Toby so much, and I miss him. What if he's dead?'

'He's not dead,' Seth said fiercely. He stood there, growing colder and wetter while Joanna sobbed her heart out in his arms. Then she stopped, blew her nose on the handkerchief she found in the pocket of his overcoat, and stuffed it back where she got it from. 'My head's a bit clearer now. Where did you say we were going?'

'On board the *Joanna Rose*.

'My legs feel all wobbly.'

'I'll carry you.'

She fell asleep against his shoulder and as her breath warmed his ear he prayed he wouldn't die from the fumes. He was lucky to pick up a Hackney carriage on the other side of the park.

It was a relief to deposit the sleeping woman with Edward Staines. After quickly explaining what had happened, Seth told him, 'I'll bring her something decent to wear. Whatever you do, don't sail without me. Tide or no tide.'

'What happened to her?'

'Apart from filling her to the gills with laudanum, absinthe and brandy, I don't know. Joanna wasn't in a state to answer questions, and neither did I want to ask. She'll tell me, if and when she wants to. I'm just happy to get her back in one piece.' He chuckled. 'The best thing for Joanna is to sleep it off, and I'm praying that takes as long as possible. Having a woman like her around is distracting to a man with a mission, especially when she does the opposite of what you tell her. Clap her in irons if she shows signs of rebellion.'

Edward grinned as Seth loped off.

Seth found James still at his desk and pounded on the door until he came to see who it was.

He filled him in on what had occurred, then said, 'I need a credible witness to all that is about to take place. Will you be it?'

'You could have picked a better night,' James grumbled, and fetched his overcoat. Taking a look at Seth's sodden clothes, he pulled a shabby coat belonging to his clerk from a hook. 'Here, wear this, it's better than nothing. Where are we going?'

'To visit Barnard Charsford. He's going to tell me where Toby is being held.'

The tone in Seth's voice told James that Barnard would do exactly that.

When they reached the Charsford residence, there were signs that Seth's brother was making a hurried departure. There was a carriage outside and the servants were piling luggage into it.

They found Barnard skulking in his study. Grabbing him by the lapels Seth dragged him to his feet. 'Where the hell do you think you're going?'

'Out of the country. I want nothing to do with what's going on.'

'It's too late for that, since you're part of it.' Seth shook him 'Where's the boy being kept?'

'I don't know.'

'You'd better remember, else I'm going to take Joanna Morcant to a magistrate and swear out a warrant for the arrest of all of you.'

Barnard looked terrified. 'The child is in Portland. Joanna Morcant's cousin has him.'

Seth couldn't believe his ears. 'Which cousin? Tilda or Leonard?'

'Someone called Brian Rushmore. Durrington bribed a guard to help him escape from Newgate.'

'So the plan is . . .?'

'Durrington will pick the boy up in Portland and take him on to Ireland.'

'As I suspected,' Seth said to James before turning back to his brother. 'What about Brian Rushmore? What does he get out of it?'

Barnard's eyes shifted. 'I imagine he'll be paid off.'

'To blab to the authorities when he's caught. I think

not, Barnard. You know, if Rushmore is murdered, that will make you an accessory.'

'A hanging offence,' James said casually.

Seth was just as casual. 'Have you thought that Durrington might send Bisley after *you* before they leave?'

Barnard's face turned to clay. Fear rose from him in waves and his eyes darted to the dark corners of his study. 'I don't know anything about plans to murder Rushmore, I swear.'

Seth felt no sympathy for him as he shoved him back into his chair. 'How much did you say you'd loaned Durrington?'

'Almost everything I have. But I have the ships as collateral.'

'No you don't. Two have already been sold to fund his purchase of the steamship company, and the proceeds have been used for progress payments of the new steamship under construction. The city is talking about the pair of you. They don't like the way you do business. Cargo and passenger bookings are drying up. When tonight's little affair becomes common knowledge, Durrington's business will be in ruins, and so will yours.'

Barnard was beginning to sweat. 'The *Joanna Rose* is worth a bit. She's mine, on lease back to Durrington. I have her papers in my safe.'

'Did you know there are plans to sell her off after her next voyage? I wouldn't be surprised if Durrington hasn't got a second set of papers naming him as owner. And the outward cargo won't cover the cost of the crew's wages.'

'Durrington can't do that. He promised me she'd pay me twice what she cost me within three years.'

James laughed. 'You're a fool if you think that. Steam is taking over, and once the Suez canal is completed shipping costs will drop. *Joanna Rose* was only just beginning to pay her way. Believe me, the vultures are already beginning to gather around the corpse.'

'Nobody will buy the *Joanna Rose*, since a claim is about to be lodged by Joanna Morcant, on the grounds that the *Joanna Rose* was a legacy, and you seized the ship illegally,' Seth announced. 'The ship will be laid up until the mess is sorted out and the dispute is resolved.'

James raised a surprised eyebrow and turned away to hide his grin.

'I'll lose everything,' Barnard whimpered.

'Including what remains of your reputation. I can't imagine what the Earl of Alsonbury will say. He'll be furious, I imagine, and will probably withdraw patronage of your sons. You know how vitriolic he can be.'

Barnard placed his head in his hands and whispered, 'Oh, God! Help me, Seth. What shall I do?'

Seth winked at James, and took a hasty step backwards when fear forced flatulence to gust from Barnard. He fanned a handkerchief under his nose. 'I'm willing to make you an offer for the ship. I had an arrangement with Joanna Morcant to buy it from her anyway, once she'd gained possession.'

Barnard looked slyly at him. 'Ah, you're as willing to bypass the widow as I was, then. Now, let me see.' Barnard did some quick calculations on a piece of paper, then looked up and named an extortionate sum.

Seth chuckled as he put in his counter offer, which was less than half of what Barnard demanded. 'That's a fair offer, and there will be no negotiations, Barnard. I have taken crew entitlements, provisioning and lack of profitable cargo into account.'

Barnard hesitated for just a moment. 'Cash?'

'I can get that amount in cash, if you wish.'

Barnard eyed the shabby coat he was wearing and sneered, 'From where?'

Seth spared his brother the finer details of his wealth, telling him briefly, 'A legacy from my aunt.'

Along with the greed, suspicion surfaced in his brother's eyes. 'I'll see the colour of your money first, then.'

An hour later, James Stark witnessed the signatures, and Seth became the owner of an ocean-going clipper with no cargo and hardly any crew to her name.

James punched him on the shoulder when they got outside. 'You certainly move when you have to. What are you going to do with the ship?'

'Leave it to the experts to run, but it seems I must swiftly learn how to operate a shipping company.'

Seth also had an idea forming in his brain, one he thought might suit everybody. But he had to think it through a bit more. So he grinned, and said nothing.

Joanna woke to pitch darkness, her head thumping relentlessly and her tongue stuck to the roof of her mouth. She must have died and been buried, she thought, and now she'd woken up. She was so thirsty, and desperate to relieve herself.

She gave a soft groan, indulging in a moment of panic before she thought to reach out and explore her immediate surrounds. At least she was thinking more clearly now. Her bed was too big for a coffin, and her fingers only encountered rough wood. Faintly she heard creaks and cracks, the slap of lines against the masts. She smiled, she must be on board the *Joanna Rose*. But how did she get here?

What's more, she wasn't in a passenger cabin, and she could sense space around her now. She was lying on a mattress. Feeling around it, she found a place where she could swing her feet down to wooden decking. Cautiously, she stood up, cursing when her head collided with what appeared to be a cubicle above her. She dislodged something soft, which fell and enveloped her. After she'd fought herself free of it, she said crossly, 'Where the hell am I?'

There was the scrape of a Lucifer and a flame was applied to a lamp swinging from a beam. Joanna nearly screamed when an odd, grinning face was illuminated by it. A demon! *She was dead!*

'You awake now, Missy Morcant?'

It was Thaddeus Scott's former cabin boy. Joanna breathed a huge sigh of relief. 'Mr Lee? How you startled me.'

He beamed a smile at her. 'You remember Chin Lee?'

'Of course I do. You looked after me so well. Where am I on the ship?'

'Women's quarters for the Irish passengers. Captain Staines had partitions built for sleeping in.'

Water slapped against the hull. 'Are we underway?'

'Too soon. We sail later tonight. The master said there are bad men aboard, and you must stay here, out of sight. All right, missy?'

Her head set up a drumbeat when she nodded. She felt stale and smelled worse, as she said with heartfelt pathos, 'Would it be possible to have something to drink and some water to wash in, Mr Lee?'

He passed her a metal jug filled with water and a bucket with a cake of soap in. 'Drink first, wash second, make pee-pee third. Clean clothes are on the next bunk. Chin Lee will bring you food soon. I go now, tell master you're awake.' He disappeared silently into the darkness.

The water was almost freezing, and it took all of Joanna's courage to apply it to the warm folds on her body, for her skin puckered in protest and her teeth began to chatter. She felt better afterwards, however, as if the removal of her painted mask had lessened the humiliation of the abuse she'd suffered – though the physical abuse was still all too apparent in the various bruises, aches and grazes that disfigured her flesh. They looked worse than they were.

She reached for a set of clean clothes and blessed Seth for taking the trouble to return to his house to fetch them. Her familiar skirt, bodice and shawl, washed and repaired by his housekeeper, felt comforting after the red gown, which stank of Bisley's sweat, his cloying lavender oil and liquorice.

Shuddering, she threw the garment to the floor, kicked it into the darkness and pulled Seth's coat around her shoulders. She snuggled into it for the warmth and comfort it brought her. It was almost like being in his arms.

She scowled at the thought of Bisley being on board, and curbed the almost irresistible urge to seek him out and plunge a knife into his heart. The tortures he'd inflicted on her had been humiliating and painful, but she'd earned them by not listening to Seth's advice in the first place.

Bisley had forced that foul drink down her throat, and he'd tied a rope around her neck and compelled her to crawl on her hands and knees after him, like a dog. He'd kicked and pinched her as the whim took him, and had bound her hand and foot and threatened to prick her eyes out with his knife point and blind her. The most frightening threat was when he said he'd cut Toby's feet and hands off as soon as he got hold of him.

It had occurred to her then that Toby wasn't being held in Lord Durrington's house. Joanna began to shake with the rage she felt. She should have listened to Seth.

Just then she heard footsteps coming down a ladder, followed by Edward Staines voicing a cautious, 'Are you decently dressed, Mrs Morcant?'

'Yes.'

He appeared a few seconds later with Chin Lee in tow, who was carrying a steaming jug and a plate with cheese, ham and some crusty bread. There was a bottle of wine, too.

Chin Lee set his offerings on a bench and, when she

thanked him, beamed a smile before leaving. Pouring herself a mug of the tea, Joanna warmed her hands on the outside of the mug while she sipped it.

Edward shuffled awkwardly from one foot to the other. 'I'm sorry I have to put you down here, but I can't risk Durrington setting eyes on you. It's only for a short time and you'll have company when Seth Adams comes aboard. You're not scared, are you?'

'On this ship, how could I be? She's an old friend.'

Edward offered her a faint smile. 'How are you feeling after your ordeal?'

'Battered, bruised and damned angry, as though someone is banging on my head with a hammer. My mouth is so dry and thirsty I could swallow the Thames in one gulp.'

'You must be desperate.' Edward's voice took on an authoritative note. 'I must point out, though, that you brought most of your troubles down on your own head. And as master of this vessel I'm obliged to inform you that you will be locked in. If you mutiny I shall use any means necessary to restrain you. Is that understood, Mrs Morcant?'

Her laugh had a hollow ring to it. 'Mutiny? How very dramatic. You're being horribly mean, you know, Edward. And don't tell me I'm a fool to have gone after Bisley and Durrington. I learned that the hard way. Lock me in if you wish, but restraint won't be necessary, and spare me the lecture. I bet this was Seth Adams's idea. He probably told you to clap me in irons,' she said darkly.

He chuckled. 'You sounded just like your father

then. It will be good to see him again. I'm looking forward to it.'

'Don't remind me of him, Edward,' she said with a catch in her voice. 'I can't afford to become emotional about anything else until this business is over and done with and my son is safely back in my keeping. I know I'll never stop weeping if I start. I feel so alone without Toby, and he must be frightened out of his wits.'

'You're not alone, Mrs Morcant,' the captain said gruffly. 'Alex had a network of friends and family, and we'll always be there for his son, believe me. You only have to ask.'

She gave him a watery smile. 'Why are you sea captains always so formal when you're aboard your ships? If you don't start calling me Joanna, I'll throw you overboard.'

Now he laughed. 'Joanna it is, then. Seth Adams temporarily came back on board, and asked me to inform you of what's going on regarding your son's whereabouts.'

'Does he know where Toby is?' she asked eagerly.

'Not exactly. But he's learned that a cousin of yours is holding Toby prisoner in a cottage on Portland.'

'A cousin?' There came a sudden, clear memory of a voice against her ear when Toby had been abducted. 'Bitch!' Then the netmaker's wife saying she'd seen . . . Fear leaped into her heart like a tiger, and dug its claws deep. 'Brian Rushmore? I thought he was in prison.'

'I imagine somebody would have bribed a guard to allow him to escape. Bisley or Durrington, I expect.'

Her eyes widened. 'Brian Rushmore is a man with no conscience.' She couldn't tell Edward that Brian had repeatedly forced himself on his own sister and had nearly starved Tilda to death. Indeed, he had tried to rape Joanna herself, and would have if Tobias Darsham hadn't intervened. And look what trouble that had brought them all.

But her precious son was another thing altogether. He was part of her heart as well as her body. Joanna would sacrifice everything she owned to save his life, which was exactly what her father had done for her when he'd decided to fake his own death.

'We must go to Portland as soon as possible and rescue Toby from him.' She gave a shiver as fear attacked her again. 'Brian would kill him without a second thought. Perhaps he already has.'

'Hardly likely. He'll wait for Durrington and Bisley to turn up so he can exchange the boy for payment, then go abroad.'

'Thank you for telling me, Edward. Will Seth be coming on board soon?'

'He had a couple of things to do first, but aye, he'd better, else the ship will be dragging her arse along the bottom. He'll have to sneak on board unobserved, though. Bisley is keeping an eye on the gangplank.'

She gazed at him in dismay.

'Don't worry, we'll provide a distraction when the time is right.'

A thought occurred to her and she laughed softly. 'I won't worry too much. Seth Adams is the sneakiest man I've ever met.'

Edward grinned at that. 'He's also a compassionate man who keeps a cool head under pressure. He's certainly earned my respect this night.' Reaching above him, Edward dimmed the light. 'Keep this low, if you would, Joanna.'

'Edward?' she said when he turned to leave.

'What is it?'

'With all of my heart, thank you.'

He gave a brief nod, then was gone. There was a click as the key turned in the lock. Edward had meant what he'd said.

Joanna ate a small amount of the food and drank half the tea, then she curled up inside the cubicle with Seth's coat over her, and rested her thumping head. In a little while she began to doze off.

15

Joanna was woken by a slight scuffling noise against the side of the ship. A pulse thumped inside her ears. She'd nearly drifted off to sleep again when there was a click. She listened for the sound again, but there was only the noisy rushing silence of herself straining to hear, and a creak or two, as if the ship's timbers strained against the ropes tying her to the shore.

As she listened she could make out the faint sounds of activity on deck. They were about to cast off. Fear took root in her. Where was Seth? What if Edward sailed without him on board?

But the fear suddenly fled for she could sense another heartbeat beneath her own. He was near, there was a darker shadow moving in the shadows beyond the light. How silent he was.

She scrambled to her feet. 'Seth?'

He stepped into the little patch of light, grinning at having his game discovered. 'Were you expecting anyone else, then?'

Knowing he was unharmed put pleasure in her beaming smile. 'I was worried about you.'

'Liar. You were snoring. How do you feel now?'

'Better by a mile. How did you manage to get on board without Bisley seeing you?'

'I was rowed to the other side of the ship and a Chinaman threw a rope ladder over the side.'

'Oh, Seth.' She shrugged, knowing she must say this to him, but finding it hard to admit it. 'I'm sorry I was so much trouble. I should have listened to you.'

He closed the space between them. 'Never mind that, I'm just relieved you're still in one piece. Has Edward told you what's been going on?'

She nodded.

'Then you'll know we can do nothing else until we reach Portland. We'll have to be very careful we're not seen. No sudden moves, Joanna. From now on you must listen to what I say.'

There was tension between them now, a new awareness on Joanna's part that Seth was more the man than he looked. She had a sudden run of memories, of Bisley with a silver soup tureen on his head. Seth holding her upright as they crossed the park and helping her when she heaved into the grass. Of him telling her so tenderly that he loved her. That particular memory pleased her the most, but she couldn't linger on it. What if she'd imagined it all?

'Did a woman help me escape?'

'My sister-in-law, Constance. She's married to Barnard Charsford, who is my half-brother and one of the architects of the plot against you.'

'Why did he do it?'

'Greed.' Seth was dispassionate, matter of fact. 'It

affords me great pleasure to know that Barnard and Durrington will soon be ruined.'

She gazed at him in some alarm. 'Don't expose them, not until my son is safely back in my keeping. Please, Seth, don't do anything that might cause Toby harm. I'll never forgive you if you do, and I don't want to place myself in that position – not now.'

He took a step closer, his eyes gleaming in the dim light. 'Believe me, Joanna, I know how precious he is. I'm going to get Toby back for you.'

If Toby was still alive. The thought hung unspoken between them.

Unexpectedly, the ship moved and Joanna lost her footing. He caught her in mid-stumble, swinging her against him before she could fall.

His reaction was immediate, unashamed and predatory. There was a sudden intake of breath as he edged her closer, savouring the contact between them. He had a good body, lean, taut and well-muscled. He stooped, his mouth brushing against hers, testing her vulnerability to his advance.

Her reaction was obvious, even to herself, for she allowed his exploration, fully understanding what it would lead to. She wanted him. She needed the comfort of experiencing love in his arms and the oblivion that the physicality of it would bring.

She placed her palms against his face, her thumbs gently caressing the sensitive sides of his mouth.

He stopped kissing her to say, 'Are you sure this is what you want, Joanna?'

'Yes, it's what I want. It seems so inevitable, somehow.'

'It was inevitable the moment I first set eyes on you.' He slid his hands down her back to gently cup under her buttocks, pressing her into him so she could feel his hard outline against her softness, and know the strength of him. It was a subtle salesmanship of his manliness, but it was one tempered by sensitivity when he said, his voice ragged in his throat, 'I want you naked, but it's so cold.'

'There's a warm blanket.'

She'd hardly finished speaking when his fingers were seeking the fastenings on her bodice.

She stilled his hands. 'It will be quicker if we undress ourselves,' and she began to divest herself of her clothing. When the task was done they stood there, naked to each other's feasting eyes for a second or two.

He reached out and brushed her hair away from her neck, gently touched the rope burns.

'Ignore the bruises.' Watching him frown, and the unspoken question gather in his eyes, she told him, 'Bisley is capable of inflicting cruelty, but he lacks any manly urges or qualities.'

Taking Seth's hands in hers she drew him down on to the mattress and pulled the blanket over them.

He gathered her gently against him and they lay there, thigh to thigh, belly to belly and breast to chest, while their bodies lost the shyness of first contact. His hands smoothed down over her buttocks, cupped them and pulled her closer. He grew harder against her belly before he turned her over on to her back. Propping himself up on one elbow he gazed down at her, his smile so faint as to hardly be there.

Joanna, who couldn't breathe properly with the anticipation of knowing him, felt his heat reach out to envelop her.

She ran her forefinger along the length of his lips, then took his silky hair in her fingers and gently pulled his face down to hers so she could kiss him. He took the initiative from her, making unmistakably suggestive and exciting little inroads into her mouth with his tongue, teasing her so she responded with her own.

From there, he slid downwards to apply a moist tongue to the rigid nubs of her breasts.

This was a man who was going to make a meal of her, who would make it his business to discover what pleased her, and who would coax her into enjoying what pleased him.

As the caress of his fingers against her skin brought her body to life she dared to taste and touch him in the same way. He seemed adept at finding something to exploit, so her sensual pleasures were layered one on top of the other and anticipating release.

There was a sense of purpose about Seth. Gradually, he made every inch of her willing flesh part of his own, leading her into delights she'd never experienced, so she was helpless and craving for more. Her mind and body were merged into one being, quivering with anticipation.

So when he straddled her hips, even if she'd wanted to, she was helpless to prevent his relentless slide into her body. He paused there, his eyes full of silvery light as he stroked the strands of hair from her face, and she was sure the expression of need she wore was very apparent.

'Seth,' she murmured, tasting his name on her tongue as she moved against him.

Whatever he was looking for in her face, he found. As he began to stroke inside her, she arched against each mounting thrust and her muscles tightened around each slow withdrawal. His breathing gradually quickened.

Joanna closed her eyes as the exquisite loving became too much to bear. Their bodies slid one into the other dewed by the moisture of desire. He sensed that moment when the pleasure peaked in her, to join her in a frenzied climax of loving that ended when they tumbled over the edge and he collapsed against her with a final shudder.

She laughed from sheer relief that the tension between them had relaxed, and snuggled against him, her head against his racing heart.

There was the sound of water hissing along the hull. 'Listen,' she said. 'We're moving. Do you think we untied the knots holding us to the shore?'

'You've untied my knots,' he whispered, gently nipping the lobe of her ear.

'It was my pleasure.'

There was laughter in his voice. 'I do hope so, but it wasn't entirely yours, I assure you.'

Seth was different to Alex, who had often been a selfish and impatient lover, as if his mind was somewhere else, and the pleasure his alone to savour. There was nothing rushed about Seth. He was aware of her every need, and some she wasn't aware she had. He exploited them, making her deliciously aware of them too,

As contented as a cat, Joanna stretched against him. Enjoying the freedom of their mutual nakedness. Despite the cold creeping under the blanket with them her body was glowing.

'I suppose we must dress.'

'Of course we must,' he said lazily. 'But not just yet, hmm?'

'No, not just yet.' Already eager for more of him, she tilted her face up to his and kissed him.

'The stupid old hag has run out on me,' Brian muttered. He'd just eaten the last of the rabbit, which he'd boiled in a pot with the vegetables. The meat was tough, the stew watery. He spat the bones on to the floor and gazed at the brat.

He'd been grizzling all night and was now asleep in a smelly patch of dampness. Brian thought he might be sickening for something. His face was flushed, his eyes were dull, his nose ran thickly, and he wouldn't eat or drink. He just turned his head away.

'Well, that's Durrington's problem, not mine,' he said to himself. 'And if he doesn't come and get him soon, I'm going to chuck the sulky little bastard over the cliff. That'll teach you for thinking you were too good for me, Joanna. We'll see if you like that.'

He shut the door on the boy and went through to the other room.

The thought of his mother being at large worried

him. If somebody fed her some gin and she opened her mouth he'd be done for.

He went out into the raw morning and piddled against the wall, sighing with relief. Something moved inside the mist.

'Is that you, Ma? Where the hell have you been?'

When a skinny dog came to cringe around his ankles, Brian kicked out viciously at it. 'Get away from me, you cur.' It ran off, tail between its legs, squealing loudly.

He wondered if the ship had docked yet. No good trying to see anything until the mist had lifted. He had a mind to go to Bill Point, see if there was anything to steal from the local fishing boats. And sometimes there was contraband to be found, stashed out of sight in the caves undercutting the cliffs.

He must take that ring to the Barnes brothers, too. They were the only people he knew he could trust, since both of them were as crooked as cripples. He should go now, before they went to open their market stall in Weymouth.

But the ring wasn't where he'd left it. He swore loudly. No wonder his mother hadn't come back. 'Solid gold that was, and the old sot has probably poured it down her gullet and pissed it out through the other end. You wait till you come home, Ma. I'm going to give you a beating you'll never forget.'

In the other room, the boy gave a cry as he woke up with a start.

Slamming the door back on its hinges, Brian gazed at him and shouted, 'Shuddup!'

Toby cringed away from him and began to sob quietly.

The next morning, Mrs Abernathy was at Weymouth market. She liked to get there early, to browse amongst the second-hand stalls in case she came across a bargain.

People sold all sorts of valuable items when they were hard up. The month before she'd bought a pretty gold locket for next to nothing, from a woman with several ragged children to feed. Mrs Abernathy had managed to haggle her down in price, though.

When she came across the gold ring she paused. It was unusual, with a pair of clasped hands, and heavy. She had the feeling she'd seen it somewhere before.

'How much?' she said to the stallholder.

He shrugged and named his price.

'That's ridiculous.'

'It's solid gold.' Barnes shrugged. 'Take it or leave it.'

As Mrs Abernathy walked off in high dudgeon, a man stepped forward. 'I hear you wanted to see me?'

'I have some information regarding Brian Rushmore.'

The man's eyes sharpened, and then Barnes showed him the ring and whispered what he knew in his ear. The man nodded and handed over some coins for the information.

Leaving it until the end of trading, Mrs Abernathy caught Barnes just as he was packing up his stall. Smirking a little, the offer she made was lower than the first one.

Barnes the younger stared at her. The woman was a Kimberlin from the island, one of the quarry owners' wives. She was a mean-natured woman, he'd heard, and could afford to pay more than that. He shook his head.

'How do I know it's not stolen?'

''Twas sold to us by Mother Rushmore . . . her who lives up at Southwell and is mother to the Reverend Lind's wife. We told you the price earlier. D'you want it or not, missus? We can't stand here all day.'

'It's daylight robbery,' she grumbled, thinking it a disgrace that the reverend's mother-in-law had to sell her jewellery to these thieves to survive. And she'd tell Tilda Lind so the next time she saw her. She fumbled in her bag and threw the money on the stall. Sliding the ring on her finger she stalked off to catch the cart back to Portland with her purchases.

'Yes, missus, it probably was,' Barnes the elder said, and grinned at his brother. 'But it's no business of ours where Fanny Rushmore got it from, is it, Bob?'

As Mrs Abernathy made her way back home, a ship was coming into harbour. She hardly gave it a glance. It was one among hundreds to her. Gazing at the ring as she opened her front door, she wished she'd stayed to haggle him down. She'd spent much too much on it.

But what was going on? She could hear one of the Misses Nash talking and the other one answering. Then the piano started and one of them began to sing.

It was irritating not being able to tell the two apart, and sometimes she thought the pair was laughing at her because of it. Well, that was all right, as long as the second one didn't expect to be paid as well.

Her husband's deeper voice joined in with the chorus. Her eyes narrowed. What was he doing home?

There was a momentary silence when she threw the sitting-room door open. One Miss Nash was seated on the piano stool, with Harriet standing next to her. The other was sitting on the sofa with Mr Abernathy.

'Mrs Abernathy,' the one on the sofa said. 'I trust you had a good day shopping. You're just in time for the concert. Mr Abernathy has just taken his turn with my sister. Now it's Harriet's turn.'

As if she were mistress of the house. Mrs Abernathy intercepted a smile between her husband and the girl siting next to him. There was barely twelve inches of space between them.

'Hussy!' she said, her voice as outraged as she felt.

Both Misses Nash looked startled and the one on the sofa said, 'Are you referring to me, Mrs Abernathy?'

'Who else could it be, carrying on with my husband in my own house, and behind my back.'

The Miss Nash on the piano stool stood up. 'How dare you make such a wild accusation against my sister. Singing together in the company of others cannot be classed as *carrying on*, a rather vulgar expression, don't you think, Lydia? I demand that you apologize to Lydia, and at once.'

'Well?' her husband said.

Mrs Abernathy's hand fluttered to her breast. 'I will not.' Oh, why did she feel so intimidated by these superior girls? 'May I remind you that we pay these people to work for us, not to sit around singing. And where is Joanna Morcant, when she's supposed to be cleaning my house today? That's what I want to know.'

'She was called urgently to London,' Lydia said. 'Today, in the absence of Mrs Morcant I have cleaned your house from top to bottom, so you will not be inconvenienced.'

Irene's glance narrowed in on the ring. 'You're wearing Mrs Morcant's wedding ring. Pray, where did you get it?'

'Joanna Morcant's ring?' she stammered, suddenly realizing why it had seemed familiar to her.

'Don't pretend you didn't know it was hers. I heard you admiring it a few weeks ago. She told you it was bought for her by her late husband when they were in Melbourne, Australia. She must have left it here the last time she cleaned. It's very precious to her. May I have it, please? I'll give it to her when she returns.'

Mrs Abernathy opened her mouth to refuse, then closed it again. 'I bought this from a stall in Weymouth.'

'And you didn't question where it came from?'

'Of course I did. The man told me that Tilda Lind's mother sold it to them. The dreadful woman drinks gin, I believe. She must have stolen the ring, for I certainly didn't.'

Her husband was observing her in a rather speculative manner now. He wouldn't approve of her spending all that money on a ring. She capitulated because she had no choice. 'You can have the ring back for the price I paid for it.'

'Exactly how much was that?' her husband asked silkily.

She hoped her lie sounded convincing as she hurriedly removed the ring from her finger. 'Only five shillings. I thought it was bargain.'

'Yes, no doubt it would have been,' her husband said dryly 'Perhaps you would hand it over to Miss Irene.'

'And which one of these women is Miss Irene, pray?'

'The one nearest the piano, of course.'

'Thank you,' Irene said when her employer handed over the ring with a hard look. 'Perhaps you'd care to deduct the money from what you owe us, Mrs Abernathy. We haven't yet decided whether we will return to work for you, have we, Lydia?'

Lydia shook her head. 'A favourable decision may be considered, if an apology is forthcoming.'

'But what about Harriet's music lessons and my cleaning?'

'We'll let you know if we can accommodate you in due course. At the moment we're offended by what has taken place here today. We'd be obliged if you'd now pay us for our services, and may we remind you that last week's is still owing.'

Irene gazed at the small amount of cash Mrs Abernathy pressed into her palm. The Saturday academy provided a much better return for their skills. But Joanna had said they must earn as much as they could and be thrifty in their spending, and finding ways and means of saving money had been turned into a game.

Joanna was saving up for a pair of sheep. First to

provide wool, then fertilizer for the garden. Afterwards, they would pay a shilling for the service of a ram to breed the next season's lambs. Cheese would be made from the milk, and finally the animals would provide mutton for their table. The sheep would cost several shillings apiece, but once they were purchased they'd save them money. Sheep were truly remarkable.

It was quite interesting to learn how one thing depended on another. Irene hadn't realized how complicated maintaining a kitchen garden was. Or, indeed, how essential such an animal was, when one had to live off the land. It was much easier to buy commodities from the market, but now they'd learned how to produce these goods they had a much better understanding of how they had got to the market in the first place.

Obviously being a business owner was better than working for an employer, though, Irene thought. She must discuss this with Lydia when Joanna was home and after little Toby had been restored to them. Women like Mrs Abernathy had too much power over ordinary women who worked to eat.

She sniffed as she slid the money into her pocket. 'Perhaps an increase in our hourly rate might convince us. Good day, Mrs Abernathy. Mr Abernathy.' After mischievously offering Mr Abernathy a dazzling smile apiece, they swept off.

They'd hardly closed the door when Harriet burst into copious tears and yelled at her mother. 'You spoiled our concert, you beastly woman, and I didn't even get to sing.'

'Whatever have those girls been teaching her? Fetch the cane, Mr Abernathy,' her mother shrieked.

The twins felt sorry for Harriet, but at least they'd been spared her singing. They hurried home, their strides lengthening as they saw the *Joanna Rose* furling her sails, in case there was news of Joanna.

Tilda was visiting with Grace, and Charlotte Scott had a pleased look to her.

'James asked Henry Wetherall to telegraph the harbour master, who told Thaddeus and Oliver that the *Joanna Rose* is on its way. We understand that Joanna and Seth Adams are aboard.'

Lydia and Irene exchanged a grin. 'The ship is in the harbour now.' They had high hopes regarding Joanna and Seth, and had discussed endlessly the likelihood of a match between them.

Lydia nodded and Irene said, 'We found Joanna's ring. Mrs Abernathy was wearing it.' She gazed apologetically at Tilda. 'I suppose I should tell you, because we wouldn't want you to find out accidentally. Mrs Abernathy bought it on a market stall in Weymouth, and was told by the stallholder that your mother sold it to them.'

'My mother? How on earth would she have got hold of it?'

'Mrs Abernathy said she must have stolen it. We thought your mother was crippled.'

'So did I,' Tilda said bitterly, 'but David found some crutches and an empty gin bottle in the churchyard, which could have been hers. And I could almost swear that someone was watching me through the kitchen window the other night. Vegetables were pulled from the garden the next morning, and a piece of clothing was stolen from the line. One of Grace's smocks. The same night somebody broke into the church and stole the contents of the poor box.'

'I doubt if your mother would have had the strength to do that.'

'She's not as feeble as she pretends, Mrs Scott, and is as crafty as a coot.'

'Perhaps your mother was hungry, my dear. She might have been desperate.'

Tilda looked doubtful. 'David has hired someone from Weymouth to look after my mother and she is provided with money for food. I do hope she's not going to start wandering into people's houses to steal things. She would do anything to get her hands on some gin, though. I must ask David to go up there and talk to the woman who looks after her.'

'Joanna could have lost the ring in your garden, and your mother might have found it,' Charlotte said kindly. 'And if she was looking through your window, I expect she just wanted to catch a glimpse of her daughter. She must be very lonely in that isolated cottage.'

'Perhaps.' Biting her lip, Tilda stopped to fuss with Grace's hair, regretting that she'd sounded so uncharitable towards her mother. Guilt attacked her. She should find out how her mother had got hold of Joanna's ring. If she left Grace with David she could be back before Leonard and his family arrived for dinner.

She was pleased Joanna was on the way back. She

intended to visit her friend in the morning to find out the details of Toby's abduction.

The two men were sitting on the top of the cliff.

'Look at her, Oliver. Isn't she a grand sight.'

Oliver had to clear the lump in his throat before he could answer. 'She is that, Thaddeus.'

Thaddeus pointed the stem of his pipe at the clipper. 'She's light in the water.'

'Aye. She can't be carrying much cargo and she was only half rigged when she came over the horizon.'

Thaddeus handed Oliver his telescope. 'Here, you've got better eyesight than me. What else do you see?'

'There's not much activity on board. She seems to have sailed short of crew.'

Edward won't sail her to Melbourne like that. Can you see Joanna?'

'I can't see much going on at all.' Oliver swung the telescope round. 'There's a bunch of men coming off a boat down at Chiswell. They're after trouble by the looks of them. They've gone into the inn.'

'And Tilda Lind is coming up the hill.' Oliver swung back to the *Joanna Rose*. 'A dinghy is going out to the ship.' A seagull flew into his vision and Oliver chuckled. 'Duck, Thaddeus, my father's flying overhead.'

Thaddeus's face cracked into a smile as he punched Oliver on the shoulder. Then he said with some seriousness, 'That young woman is more vulnerable than she seems. When she was young, her pa provided her with Lucian. When her life began to fall apart and she needed someone to cling to, she turned to him. She knows Lucian was responsible for saving her life and I reckon he'd be pleased to know she looks to him for guidance.'

Oliver nodded, then turned to gaze at him. 'Alex wasn't really the right man for Joanna, you know, although he loved her in his fashion.'

'In case your thoughts are wandering in that direction, neither are you, Oliver.'

'I know.' His glance went back to the *Joanna Rose.* 'I've had no thought of marrying again. All I want to do is to get back to sea, and it's not through want of trying.'

The afternoon light was beginning to dull, the air was drawing moisture into it and the sea was the colour of unpolished pewter. There was movement on the water.

'Two men are going ashore in the dinghy. And the Dunn brothers' fishing boat has just disappeared behind the *Joanna Rose.* It looks like things are moving.'

'Let's get on down then. I want to be at the house before they arrive. Seth Adams is a canny sod, I understand. He must've had it all worked out in advance.'

Oliver grinned. 'I believe he's got Joanna worked out in advance, too. I'm looking forward to meeting him.'

'Aye . . . she could do worse, I reckon. She needs a man who can out-fox her.'

Seth went over the side first, followed by Joanna, who was less nimble footed and had her skirt to contend with. Seth helped her as she neared the bottom, his hands spanning her waist to lift her down.

They exchanged a glance and an intimate smile with one other. Seth chuckled when she gave a faint blush, and planted a kiss against her hairline.

Having observed the exchange, Edward grinned and, sure footed, dropped down beside them. Immediately, Jack Dunn shipped the boat hook holding them to the side of the clipper and the fishing boat turned about and headed for a different part of the shore from where the dinghy was at.

The Dunn brothers nodded pleasantly to them. 'Captain . . . Joanna Rose . . . Mr Adams. It's nice to see you again, that it is.'

'I bet it is, you thieving varmints.' Seth turned to Edward. 'Never buy brandy from this pair, Captain Staines.'

'Off the pirate vessel *Saggitario*, was it?' Edward said with a grin. 'These gentlemen have been selling it for years, I believe. They're a legend.'

'A pity someone didn't warn me until after the event, then.'

'The *Saggitario* brandy was a good brew, indeed. It fetches a good price.' Dunn the elder said, nodding his head sagely. 'It might interest you gentlemen to know there's a group of Weymouth men getting themselves all liquored up at the inn. There's talk of revenge.'

'Are they after Brian Rushmore?' Joanna said directly.

'This be men's business, girlie.'

Joanna's hands went to her hips. 'He stole my son, so that makes it my business.'

The brothers exchanged a glance. 'There'll be no

arguing with you, Mother. That's a wicked thing, to steal a child from its mother's arms. That Brian Rushmore's a bad bugger, and no mistake.'

The younger brother advised, 'Now you let your man here handle it, dearie. He might be daft about some things, but he's a thinkin' man for all that. In some situations that's better than going in with a gut full of drink, blood in your eye and with fists flying willy-nilly all over the place. A woman could get hurt.'

'Can we do anything about the Weymouth men?' Edward asked them. 'We need to find where the child is and get him out before they get there.'

'Seems to me they've got right on their side for revenge, since the man wronged their sister, and she's been touched in the head ever since,' the older brother said.

To which the other answered, 'Could be they can be delayed, so Joanna Rose's lad can be found first. One thing's for certain, he's got grudges against him. Nay, if Brian Rushmore is on this island, he won't be gettin' off it without takin' punishment. The fishermen will see to that.'

They both nodded. 'As for his whereabouts, he ain't in the cottage he grew up in. That place has been as quiet as the grave since Peter Rushmore was shot by the revenue men. The fisher folk would have noticed any comin' and goin'. There be only one person who would take him in. His mother, Fanny Rushmore, sozzled auld crow that she be. Lives up Southwell beyond the village.'

When they reached the shore, the group saw that Durrington and Bisley hadn't made much progress.

'Not very good at rowing, that Abe Watson, on account of him having two left hands. He tends to go round in circles,' Dunn the younger remarked, as Seth helped Joanna on to the beach. 'I shouldn't be at all surprised if you didn't get to where you want to go faster than they do.'

'I do hope so,' Seth said as the three strode off across the beach. 'Is Fanny Rushmore's cottage hard to get to?'

Joanna told them how to get there as they neared her cottage, slightly surprised at how thoroughly he questioned her.

Edward said, 'I've got the feeling that the islanders know more of what's going on than we do.'

Joanna slid her hand into Seth's. 'It wouldn't surprise me in the least.'

16

Tilda was annoyed that she'd been placed in the position of visiting her mother. The woman had not only abandoned her when she'd been small, but she'd never made any attempt to prevent the abuse Tilda had been subjected to by her father and two of her brothers.

Tilda had never had wild, adventurous dreams for herself like her friend Joanna had. She'd never even possessed the courage to think like Joanna. If Tilda had imagined marriage, she'd never thought past a humble quarry labourer, and life in a modest cottage.

She hadn't expected anyone as nice as David Lind to come along and fall in love with her, nor imagined that her modest artistic endeavours would bring her an income. Indeed, she would never have known she had any talent if Joanna hadn't encouraged her to discover it.

Her hands covered the child growing in her womb and she quietly glowed with the contentment of the way her life had turned out. This child was her personal miracle. David said it was God's reward for bearing her past treatment so bravely.

He always said something sweet like that. But only Joanna and herself knew the truth. That she'd been as near death as anyone could come, and only hate had kept her hanging on to life until Joanna had rescued her and nursed her back to health.

Despite David's plea to her to turn the other cheek, she felt only disgust for her mother. There could be no true reconciliation between them. Not ever.

As for her father and his two younger sons, she still feared and despised them in a way that sometimes sickened her, even though two of them were dead. She often prayed that Brian would soon follow them into hell, for she would not be free of her past until he was gone from this earth.

Tilda had looked forward to coming back to the island. Now she regretted it, for the bad memories too often crowded in on her. At this moment it seemed as though Fanny Rushmore was setting out to destroy her happiness. And she was worried that her baby might inherit the bad streak that seemed to run through her family.

Hiram, who'd been talking non-stop all of the way, brought the donkey cart to a halt and broke into her black thoughts with a bit of a nudge from his elbow.

'Here we be, then, Mrs Lind. You mind those stones when you go across the field, with you being in the family way, and all. Not that I need to tell you mind, you being an islander born and bred. Accidents happen when you least expect them, though. I well remember my Hulda Jean, she was my first wife . . . or was she my second? Can't quite remember now.

Anyway, she fell flat on her belly, she did. The infant was stillborn the very next day. Are you sure you don't want Hiram to wait? 'Tis gettin' dark.'

'No, that's fine, Hiram. You get off home and have your dinner.'

'Folks be better off sitting safely by their firesides on a night like this, I reckon.'

'It's a clear night with a bright moon to show me the way. At least it's not raining.'

'There's danger abroad tonight, all the same. I feel it in my bones. Are you sure, now? Satan is after some souls tonight, I reckon.'

He was giving Tilda the willies. 'You've been working with the dead for too long. Don't worry about me, Hiram. I need the exercise and it's all downhill on the way back.'

''Tis true, the island has a way of either goin' up or goin' down. It makes the legs hardy, it do. Now you mind what I say, missus.' Hiram looked about him into the gathering gloom. 'I'll be off then,' he said, and he clicked his tongue at the donkey and moved away.

Tilda waved goodbye, then picked her way down the path, which was strewn with loose stones. Now she was left alone without Hiram's friendly chatter, she felt the danger in the air too, as if the island were full of spirits. It was lonely up here. Unease filled her, so she nearly turned back. The back of her neck prickled, as though she were being watched.

There was an odd sound coming from the cottage, like a cat mewing. Tilda wondered if her mother was ill. A shadow moved across the window; the woman who looked after her must still be there. The sound stopped.

Her nerves prickling, Tilda shook herself and said out loud, 'Goodness, you'll be seeing ghosts next.' She turned the doorknob and the door swung open, creaking as it went. Taking a reluctant step over the sill she sensed danger, and was about to turn and run when there was a scuffling noise. A hand closed around her wrist and she was jerked forward. The door slammed shut behind her and a key turned in the lock.

'Where the hell have you been, you stupid old hag? You deserve a thumping for worrying me like that. See to the brat, would you. There's something wrong with him.'

Tilda's mouth dried up and her body became paralysed with fear. For a moment she stood there, unable to move or talk, then her limbs began to tremble as if she had a fever.

'Well, what've you got to say for yourself?' Brian shouted. Picking up the lamp he thrust it close to her, his face looking devilish in the flickering light.

Tilda could only mew with terror.

A smile stretched his mouth when he realized it wasn't his mother. His voice soft with menace, he said, 'Well now, if it isn't our Tilda come a callin', and her looking like the queen herself in her finery. I was prayin' for a woman after all that time in prison, now the devil has provided me with one. How about giving your brother a nice welcome-home kiss, then? I can almost guarantee I'll find something to reward you with afterwards.'

'You *are* the devil,' Tilda managed to gasp out before she buckled at the knees.

'Then you won't mind me stickin' my fork into you, for I'm as randy as a dog,' Brian muttered. Falling to his knees beside her he fumbled open his trouser fastenings, then pulled open her bodice. He turned up her skirt and pulled her drawers apart, so he could take a look at her.

Tilda's belly was as round as an apple. Beneath it, her little beard hid what she had to offer. His mouth dried as he imagined sliding himself into it. As his genitals reared up, his trousers slid down, leaving his backside bare. He kicked them off. He had quite a load to get rid of.

Still, he couldn't take his eyes off his sister. Tilda had always had a nice body; now she had gained a bit of weight it was even better. He placed his hands over her breasts, fondling and kneading them. Now there was a nice couple of handfuls, soft and heavy. She smelled lovely, too, not like one of those pissy tarts who used to sell their wares to the soldiers.

His sister was wasted on the churchman. Taking advantage of her like this didn't bother Brian. Tilda was a woman, and good for only two things, keeping a man's house clean and easing his need. His father had taught him that. It didn't matter whether she was awake or asleep – or even dead come to that.

There was a clink as his knife fell to the floor.

Coming out of her faint, Tilda saw the weapon glinting in the lamplight. Her brother's smell almost made her gag. She recalled with great clarity the weeks she'd spent half starving while Brian and Peter humiliated her. They'd expended their filthy lust on her, when she hadn't had the strength to fight back. And their father had said not a word.

But she had the strength now, Joanna had made sure of that. And the devil wasn't getting her soul without a fight, no matter what Hiram had said.

Brian's knee was between her thighs now, nudging them apart. The baby inside her kicked in protest as his heavy weight was lowered on to her. No! she thought wildly, she wasn't going to allow him to harm the child she wanted so much. Using all her strength, she twisted away as he tried to thrust himself into her, dislodging him. In his hurry he couldn't hold himself and he bucked like the animal he was, against her bunched petticoats.

Tilda's hand closed around the handle of the knife. She brought it up, then with a terrified cry struck out.

Rolling sideways, Brian swore horribly and chopped her across the wrist. The knife slid off into the darkness.

Brian began to slap Tilda back and forth across her face, making her scream with the pain. The noise woke Toby from his sleep and he began to cry out. 'Mama . . . Mama.'

It must have alerted her brother to the fact that he might be discovered, for he suddenly got to his feet, hauling Tilda upright by her hair. Thrusting his face close to hers he spat out, 'Shuddup, woman, else I'll slit your throat for spoilin' my pleasure. Bandage my shoulder, then go and see to the brat.'

Tilda scrambled to cover her breasts, drawing her shawl over the torn bodice as she accused, 'It was you who took Toby, then. How could you steal Joanna's infant, you fiend?' Oh God! the boy had been here all this time. If only she'd visited earlier. She had to try to save him, she thought, taking a deep breath to calm herself.

She prayed Brian would bleed to death. 'I haven't got anything to bandage it with.'

'Use your damned petticoat, you useless lump.' Dragging it down over her hips he tore a wide strip from it and threw it at her. 'Wait while I get my trousers on, my arse is getting cold.'

Blood welled from the wound on his shoulder. It wasn't much of a cut because the blade had gone in sideways. She wished she'd plunged it straight into his heart instead of merely nicking the skin.

When she'd staunched the blood flow to Brian's satisfaction, he scowled at her. 'Go and shut that kid up. Give him some milk.'

The window had been boarded up, Tilda saw with dismay, for she'd intended to try to climb out through it with the child. A few moments later, she said, 'Toby's feverish. He's soiled and sore, and he needs to be cleaned up. He needs a doctor, as well.'

'He can't have one . . . least, not yet. Just get on with it.'

Toby drank a mouthful of the milk, refusing any more by turning his head away. Tilda did the best she could to clean him up, with a jug of cold water and the remains of her petticoat. She'd never wear it again, anyway, she thought with a shudder. Toby's teeth chattered in his head as he tried to push her away.

'I know it's cold, Toby love, but it will make you feel better.' She found some arnica in a drawer to help soothe the rash on his sore bottom, and spoke softly to him.

Toby was wearing Grace's smock. As she threw the badly soiled garment into a corner, she thought it must have been Brian looking at her through the kitchen window, not her mother. So where was Fanny Rushmore? Brian had obviously been expecting her back. And where was Ada Cooper, the woman who'd been hired to care for her mother? Tilda was frightened to even think about what had happened to her, since she knew her brother had nothing to lose.

'Hush, Toby,' she said. She fashioned him a garment from the pillowcase, making holes for his head and arms to go through, and knotting it around his waist with a strip from her petticoat. There was a shawl in a trunk at the foot of the bed to wrap him in. Afterwards, Tilda cuddled his shivering body close to her own.

He buried his head against her chest, bewildered and frightened, clinging to her for comfort. 'Want Mama,' he whispered, his voice painfully husky.

'I know, my darling,' she whispered against his ear. 'And we'll find her, I promise. But you be a good boy for Aunt Tilda now, so we don't make the nasty man angry.'

The introductions were over. Joanna's bruises had been examined and exclaimed over by the women.

She'd dismissed them as insignificant. 'Right at this

moment I don't care if I'm black and blue all over. I only care about getting my son back safely. Seth, perhaps you'd tell everyone what has happened.'

Outlining what had occurred, Seth then said, 'We need to get up to the cottage as swiftly as possible. Brian Rushmore is probably armed. Lord Durrington and Bisley most certainly will be.'

Edward had taken the precaution of bringing a firearm. He also had a cudgel tucked into the back of his trousers.

'We thought you looked a bit light on crew. Doing a bit of crimping while you're ashore, are you?' Oliver scoffed.

'Could be.' Edward grinned at Oliver and handed him the cudgel. 'I might make you my first victim.'

Oliver's smile faded. 'Durrington's blacklisted me.'

'Sod Durrington. From what I've gathered over the last couple of days, it won't be long before he's down to the bones of his arse.'

Seth had a sudden coughing fit. It was cured by a thump on the back from Thaddeus, who nearly knocked him flat.

'Thank you,' he said politely.

'My pleasure, lad.'

Joanna went into the kitchen and came back, brandishing a carving knife.

Seth gazed at it, then at her, his eyes glinting. 'What do you intend to do with that?'

'Defend myself, if I have to.'

'You're not coming, Joanna. Having a woman underfoot in the dark, especially one who's feeling emotional and waving a carving knife around, would be the height of stupidity.'

There were murmurs and nods of assent from the men.

Her hands went to her hips. 'Toby is my son.'

'We know he's your son. All the more reason to keep a cool head. There are three armed men to contend with, and another gang of men from Weymouth, all after your cousin with revenge in their hearts and skins full of liquor. We can't watch out for them if we have women to defend, as well. You're staying here, Joanna, and that's that.'

'Is it, indeed? Let me put you straight. Brian Rushmore isn't my cousin. He's stinking, dogeared prison scum. I intend to gouge his eyes out with their roots intact. So, in short, Seth Adams, I'll do as I damned well please.'

'Will you, now.' Seth twisted the knife from her hand and gave it to Irene. 'Put that back where it came from, would you, please?'

He then pushed Joanna into the room Oliver used, and turned the key in the lock. Joanna began to pound on the door.

Handing the key to Charlotte, Seth sighed. 'I'm sorry to leave you with this, Mrs Scott. If I were you, I wouldn't allow her out until she's calmed down and is able to listen to reason.'

'She'll rip your ears off when she gets out,' Thaddeus warned.

Seth shrugged. 'Hopefully, she'll have cooled down by then. Gentlemen, are we ready? Thaddeus, do you have a weapon?'

'I've got my hands. They'll do.'

Charlotte handed him the poker and scolded, 'You're not getting any younger, Thaddeus Scott, and I want you back in one piece. You take this.'

'Don't you start crawling out of your corsets, woman. Nothing's going to happen to me.' Placing a hand at either end of the poker, Thaddeus slowly bent it in half and handed it back to her.

The three master mariners grinned at each other when Charlotte snorted and suggested haughtily, 'Perhaps someone should hire you as a circus entertainer?'

'You're gettin' too saucy by far, Mrs Scott.'

Joanna shouted against the keyhole. 'Let me out this instant, Seth Adams, else I'll never speak to you again.'

Seth ignored her.

The short silence while she waited for his reaction was followed by a grudgingly muttered, 'Please, Seth.'

Seth's glance went to the door she was hidden behind, and he seemed to waver. Then he drew in a deep breath and opened the door to the street. The four men left.

As the door shut behind them, Joanna rattled the locked doorknob, saying mutinously, 'I'll kick that damned man in the seat of his fancy pants when he comes back – and he'd better have my son with him.'

Lydia exchanged a smile with Irene, who gazed at Charlotte. 'Joanna's as mad as a nest of red ants. Shouldn't we let her out now?'

'Not yet, dears. Mr Adams was right. He obviously cares for Joanna, since he's trying to keep her out of danger, you know. She'll soon come to her senses and realize she was acting childishly, and he locked her in for her own good.' She raised her voice a little. 'You think about that, Joanna Rose.

There was a disgusted 'Hah!' from the other room.

Charlotte tied her apron about her waist. 'Let's get on with the evening meal, my dears. The men will be hungry when they come back, and it will keep us occupied.'

In the other room, Joanna quietly crossed to the window and opened it.

The streets were almost deserted, the womenfolk and children safe behind closed doors. A few men loitered at strategic places, where news could be passed quickly along the line.

Having grown up on the island, Leonard knew when something was going on. There was an atmosphere of tension abroad.

He was surprised to find his sister wasn't at home, for she would have felt it, too.

'She went to visit your mother, earlier,' David told him.

'On foot?'

'Hiram took her on the donkey cart. Tilda was going to walk back. She said she needed the exercise.' David gazed at the clock and a frown wrinkled his brow. 'It's getting late and I thought she would be home by now. I'd better go and look for her, though she's probably stopped to talk.' David smiled, his expression one of innocent pleasure. 'I'm so pleased this reunion has happened. I've been trying to reunite them for a long time. Your mother has nobody, and Tilda needs a female to confide in. Who better than her mother.'

'Tilda has Joanna. I know you meant well, David, but you should have left things well alone. My mother brought her isolation on herself. She's a predator, always has been.' Leonard sighed as he pulled on his coat. 'I'll go to look for her. It's a long way from Southwell in the dark, and I know this island like the back of my hand.' He exchanged a glance with his wife. 'Kirsty, perhaps you'd start on the dinner.'

'Be careful, Lenny,' she said.

'Don't you fret, my love. I'll mind myself.'

'Mind yourself?' David gazed from one to the other, puzzled. 'I don't understand.'

'Neither do I yet, but the streets are much too quiet, so something's afoot. If I were you, I'd stay inside. The islanders don't take kindly to Kimberlins meddlin' in their business.'

Leonard was just in time to join the four men as they strode past. The only one he hadn't met before was Edward. He nodded when he was introduced. He'd seen the *Joanna Rose* in the harbour, and guessed this was her master. The four men had a sense of camaraderie and purpose about them.

'Is there any news of young Toby?'

Seth Adams did the speaking. 'You haven't heard?'

'Would I need to ask if I had? I've brought the family across to have dinner with the Linds, and I'm going to pick Tilda up from visiting our mother. What's going on? Something is. The boy's all right, isn't he?'

The quartet stopped to gather round him. Seth said, 'Did you say that Mrs Lind had gone to visit your mother?'

Leonard felt the menace in the men, and his blood ran cold. 'Is someone going to tell me what's going on?'

'Brian Rushmore . . . your brother has escaped from prison. We believe he abducted Joanna Morcant's child on behalf of Lord Durrington and is holding the boy at your mother's cottage.'

Edward Staines took Leonard by the lapels of his jacket and shook him. 'Tilda is Joanna's friend. Is she involved in the abduction, too?'

Thaddeus placed a restraining hand on his arm. 'Nay, let him be, Edward. Tilda has no liking for Brian Rushmore, and she wouldn't do anything to harm young Toby.'

Leonard spat out, 'If Tilda falls foul of Brian, it'll be the worst for her. That bleddy cleric is a fool. Of all the stupid ideas, sending Tilda out into danger.'

'He wouldn't have known your brother was there.'

Leonard shook himself free of Edward's grasp. 'Follow me. Harry Cullins's old sailing lerret is beached down at the bottom of the hill. She lets in the water a bit, but she'll take us up round the West Bay in a hurry if we hug the beach. Mr Adams, perhaps you'd tell me everything that's happened, on the way.

What Leonard heard only added to his unease.

Seth said, 'Tell me the layout of the cottage.'

''Tis small. The front door is reached by a path from the road. It opens straight into the living room, which is about four strides across. On the facing wall, two doors side by side lead into the bedrooms. To the right there's an alcove with shelves, it's used for cooking in. To the left is a coal shed and storage space.'

'Which room does your mother use?'

'The one on the left.'

'The back door is situated where?'

'Through the coal shed. The lock's loose and a well-placed boot should open it.'

'Good.' A few more questions and Seth knew how much furniture there was, and where it was positioned.

It was a risky business, sailing round the curving line of the shore, especially where the quarry spoil tumbled down over the cliffs into the water, but Leonard knew exactly what he was doing.

The five men were soon dragging the lerret up on to a small strip of beach. Leonard tied the boat to a rock by a long rope, so she wouldn't go under, or float away when the tide covered the strip of beach.

Not that it mattered, since Harry Cullins had died six months previously, and he wouldn't miss the boat. Leonard leaned the boat hook against a stone block at the top of the path, so he could pull the lerret in when needed.

The lower lighthouse had come into view. The thin tower had a pavilion-like lantern house on the top that gave it a slightly exotic appearance; in clear weather it was capable of sending a beam across the dark sea for eighteen miles.

Tonight, the beam disappeared into the horizon. It was fuelled by six Argand lamps, their light concentrated by lantern windows that had been specially designed by Thomas Rogers. Set in copper frames, they were separated by six glass panels.

Above them, the moon sailed in a clear sky, and was surrounded by a wide, incandescent ring.

'There's some frost on the way,' Thaddeus said knowledgeably as he followed Leonard up a winding path through the scrub to the top.

'Thaddeus's bunions must be aching,' Oliver whispered loudly to Edward, and he received an elbow in the ribs for his trouble.

Over a rise and slightly below them there was a cottage, its windows dimly lit by a low-burning lamp.

There was no sound, except the low eerie sough of the wind through the rock-strewn grass.

The five men stopped, and Seth took out his pistol. 'Perhaps you'd all spread out in case he tries to escape with the boy. I'm going to the window to have a look. Remember, the aim is to rescue Toby and Mrs Lind and get them to safety. That's all.'

'I'll back you up,' Leonard said. 'Brian might listen to reason from me.' But he sounded doubtful.

Nobody bothered to question the role of leadership Seth had taken upon himself. But just as they were about to move off, a horse and cart came into view, carrying Lord Durrington and Bisley. It was being driven at a reckless speed by Bisley, who brought it to a halt in a cloud of gravel dust. The horse gave a shrill whinny of complaint at its treatment, and the light in the cottage was dimmed.

Seth swore. 'I won't be able to reach the cottage before them, and Rushmore will be keeping watch at the window. As soon as they go inside I'm going to try and gain entrance through one of the bedrooms.'

The pair thumped on the door, then disappeared inside. The light flared again.

Oliver cracked his knuckles. 'I'll cause a diversion.'

There was a string of flares bobbing in the distance. So that's what the islanders had been up to, Leonard thought. They were going to run Brian into a corner and trap him like a rat.

'I don't think you'll need to. Look.'

Just then, Joanna came tearing up the path, her skirts tied to one side. Seth could almost hear the harshness of her breathing. She disappeared around the back of the cottage.

'Damn woman,' Seth said with heartfelt annoyance and, bending double, he set off at a trot.

When he caught up with Joanna she had her back to him. One ear was pressed against the boarded-up window. He grasped her around the waist with one arm while he pressed his hand over her mouth.

She froze for just a second, then heeled him in the shin and sank her teeth into the fleshy part of his palm.

'It's me,' he hissed, trying not to yell.

She released him, planted a kiss on the pain she'd caused him, then turned in his arms and hugged him tight. Her heart beat fast against his own.

'You fool, Seth Adams. You gave me such a damned fright. Tilda is on the other side of those boards. I think Toby's with her, I heard him.' Pain and longing filled her voice. 'I can't bear it that he's so near to me and I can't hold him. Can we pull the boards off the window and get them out?'

Setting her aside, Seth tested his strength against the boards and found that they held fast. 'It would take too long, and make too much noise.'

From the other side of the window, Tilda shouted, 'No, you can't take Toby—'

Joanna let out a sobbing breath at the sudden cry of pain Tilda gave, which was followed by silence. Her hand went to her mouth. 'Oh God! What have they done to her?'

'I'm going in.' Locating the back door, Seth threw caution to the winds and heeled it open. It smashed back against the wall. He leaped over the coal rattling underfoot, palming his pistol.

Inside, the light was suddenly extinguished. Seth flattened himself into the nearest shadow, hoping Joanna would have the sense to stay outside. He could make out the outline of Durrington, the child in his arms. Toby was screaming with fear. Of Bisley there was no sign.

Brian Rushmore was creeping across the floor towards the door. Seth put his pistol away, he couldn't risk hitting the child.

A commotion erupted outside, momentarily distracting Brian. But as Seth threw himself across the room to tackle him, Bisley rose up from the floor and hit him in the gut with something hard. Seth doubled up, badly winded. The next moment the three men were out of the door.

Seth staggered out after them. Outside the cottage, a fight was going on. Leonard and the three captains were exchanging blows and insults with the four drunks from Weymouth. The seamen seemed to be having the most success.

The line of flares was about a hundred yards away and closing in fast. They'd begun to chant. '*Brian Rushmore . . . Brian Rushmore . . .*'

Brian gave the line a panicky look.

Going in fast, Seth managed to snatch the child from Durrington's arms. Instinct made him leap back, just as Bisley slashed out with his knife. Blood flowed warmly under Seth's coat. Durrington produced a pistol, shooting over his shoulder as they left.

Crouching low, Seth zigzagged through the darkness, soothing the child, whose screams gradually quieted to a whimper. 'Papa,' he whispered, and clung tighter to him.

Seth coughed to clear the lump in his throat. 'That's right, Toby lad. You're safe now.' Returning to the cottage with his prize, Seth found Joanna in the bedroom.

He stood in the doorway, unnoticed, savouring the moment when she'd look up and discover what he'd brought her.

Tilda looked dazed; blood seeped from under her hair and trickled down her face. 'I tried to stop him from taking Toby, but he hit me on the head with his stick. I'm so sorry, Joanna.'

There were tears running down Joanna's cheeks. 'My poor little Toby. What he must be going through.'

At the sound of his mother's voice Toby shouted joyfully, 'Mama! Want Mama.'

'You've got her,' Seth said.

Joanna's head jerked up. 'Toby?' She plucked her

son from Seth's arms and held him tight, tears pouring down her face as she laughed and cried at the same time. 'My darling love. I've missed you so much. But how feverish you are.' She gazed up at her son's rescuer, her eyes shining despite the worry in them. 'Thank you so much, Seth. I'm truly indebted to you.'

To have her look at him with such adoration in her expression wasn't too hard to take. Seth knew he was full of reckless pride, pumped up with the successful outcome of what could easily have been a disaster. He should take Joanna to task for placing herself in danger, but he didn't have the heart. 'That you're not.' He gazed at Tilda. 'Are you badly injured, Mrs Lind?'

She managed to smile at him while Joanna fussed over her son, but the fright in this gentle young woman's eyes was still dark inside her. 'I've survived worse.'

He kissed her cheek. 'You're a brave woman, Tilda, and it's been a privilege to meet you. I'm going off now, to watch those three felons captured by the islanders. I might as well be in on the finish. Stay here and rest until I get back, then I'll escort you both home. We might have to make a statement if they're to be charged.'

The two women exchanged a glance, and a faint smile, as if they knew something he didn't.

17

Leonard had finished with his Weymouth trouble-maker, who was now staggering off back in the direction he'd come from. He was to one side of the line of islanders, who'd begun to pick up speed now their quarry had been spotted.

The flares curved around the hillside like the pincers of a crab, and were closing in on the fugitive. It was one of their own they were after, not the Kimberlins – the Rushmore who'd gone bad and who'd brought disgrace down on the heads of the islanders.

No Weymouth men, however just their cause, were going to come between them and their purpose, though it was rare for Portlanders to turn on one of their own.

Up ahead, Lord Durrington was beginning to tire. He was an old man, not used to such rough terrain. Bisley had him by the arm and was half pulling him along, swearing at his slowness. 'Get a move on, would you? Damn that poxy brat. I've pandered to your every wish. I've lied, cheated and killed for you. I'm your son. If you think you're going to change your will in favour of that by-blow and give him what I'm entitled to inherit, think again. I knew the brat would be more trouble than he was worth. If I ever see him again I'm going to cut his throat. Yours as well if you don't give me my due.'

Charles Durrington knew what Bisley was capable of. He believed him. He'd not expected the affair to turn out as badly as it had. As soon as he got back to the *Joanna Rose* he'd order the captain to set sail for Ireland, where he could lie low for a while.

Brian turned to see how much ground they'd made up. Spotting Leonard in hot pursuit, he shouted out in panic, 'You're my soddin' brother. Help me.'

Help Brian? Leonard thought. After what he'd done to Joanna and Tilda. Brian had brought down shame on the Rushmore name. The islanders had had enough of him, and were driving him into the sea because of it. Leonard wasn't about to get in their way when he had a wife and children to support. But the islanders seemed in no hurry to catch up with their prey.

The reason came to him suddenly. The tidal race! It was a feature of the island, the danger their fathers and grandfathers before them had made them all aware of – a place that should be avoided at all costs. He should have remembered it before and his blood ran cold. But then perhaps what was about to happen would be preferable to a life sentence in prison.

Leonard slowed to a halt, and said before he turned away, 'There's a sailing lerret at the bottom of the path. The sail's still rigged and the boat hook's leaning against the stone. Take that. Could be you can get yourself away to Weymouth in it.'

Releasing Durrington, Bisley grabbed Brian around the neck and pressed a pistol against his head. 'You're going nowhere without us, unless you want a bullet in your brain.' He pushed Brian before them down the path.

'Keep out of this if you know what's good for you, Len,' somebody shouted.

'I'm not in it. I was here to find my sister. Brian is heading for Cullins's boat.'

'That won't get him far.'

'D'you think I don't know that?'

It was passed along the line. '*Cullins's boat . . . Cullins's boat . . .*' Somebody gave a harsh laugh as the line of men overtook Leonard, their flares burning acrid black smoke. Their weather-worn faces were set and determined. Some had smeared soot on their faces so they couldn't be recognized.

The islanders didn't bother going down after their prey. They just stood at the top of the path, chanting Brian's name to single him out for the devil. The sound was unnerving. Leonard joined them, waiting to witness the inevitable result of his brother's bid to escape – the result he'd taken a hand in. Suddenly sickened by the thought, he turned and walked away.

Thank God for Leonard, Brian thought as he hooked the boat in and held it steady for his companions to board. He scowled at them, knowing he'd have left them behind if Bisley's pistol hadn't been trained on him.

Durrington said. 'Take us to the *Joanna Rose.*'

'I'll have to sail around Bill Point for that, and I'm not doin' it. 'Tis too dangerous. I'll drop you off on the pebbles at Chiswell. You can walk to Castletown and get the dinghy to the ship from there.'

Durrington said, his voice stronger and more authoritative now, 'Drop us at Chiswell, then. Put the pistol away, Bisley, unless you know how to sail a boat. In which case you can shoot him and throw him overboard.'

Brian's mouth dried. Instinct should have told him he couldn't trust these men. He should've left the kid with its mother and just taken off, since the two men obviously had no intention of paying him for his services.

After a moment of silence Bisley lowered the pistol, though he kept it handy.

Brian couldn't see his brother at the top of the cliff. He was surprised Leonard had come to his aid, since there was no love lost between them. But blood had proved to be thicker than water in the end, though you wouldn't think so, the way Tilda had carried on.

Tilda had got her fancy ideas from Joanna. Not that Joanna had anything to be fancy about, for everybody knew she wasn't a Rushmore by birth, only an orphan brought in by the storm from one of the wrecks. It was a pity his uncle hadn't left her to drown, considerin' the trouble she'd caused everyone.

Water slopped about in the bottom of the boat, covering his shoes. As if his feet weren't bleddy frozen already.

He pushed them away from shore and took his place

at the tiller. As he was about to turn the craft in order to take them to Chiswell, Durrington said, 'What are those lights in the distance?'

There was a string of them in a line. He swore. 'Damn. It's the fishermen. What the hell are they doing out at this time of night? We can't go through them, else we'll be caught in the nets.' That said, Brian guessed the answer to his own question. The fishermen were there to prevent his escape.

'Go round them,' Durrington ordered.

They headed out from the land. With no lights showing, there was a chance he might get past the fishermen undetected, even though the moon was bright.

Behind them, spaced along the hill, was a line of sputtering flares. The chanting had stopped, leaving an eerie silence in its wake. Cold vapours streaming from the men's mouths were lit by the flames. They resembled devils, breathing fire.

There was no wind. Even the water was silent, except for a gentle lapping, like a giant tongue licking at the shore. Wetness slopped into his boots. It was slack water and the silence was unnerving. What were they waiting for?

Fear suddenly churned in his stomach and his bowels turned to water. 'You bastard, Leonard,' he suddenly screamed out, as he remembered the tide.

The sea moved under them, as though it were suddenly waking from slumber. The small craft began to move rapidly away from the shore, being drawn inexorably into the race of water that came with the tidal change.

Brian began to laugh when Bisley gave a high-pitched scream and brought up his pistol, shouting, 'Take us back to shore.'

'I can't. We're going to drown in the race.' With nothing left to lose now, Brian backhanded Bisley. The shot Bisley let loose went straight through Brian's heart.

'You fool, now there's nobody to steer the boat.' Durrington pushed Brian's body aside and clung grimly to the tiller. His efforts had no effect on the course the boat took.

Bisley was cowering in the bottom of the boat, whimpering in fright.

'For God's sake, Bisley, die like a man,' Durrington said calmly.

The men on the clifftop watched as the waters beyond the lighthouse became a maddened maelstrom of white froth.

The moon shone serenely down on the drama as the tragedy unfolded – limelight on a stage of water. Sixty-five feet or more above it, the lighthouse beamed a friendly warning to shipping eighteen miles away.

Buffeted by the savage currents, the lerret was skewed this way and that. Then the leaky craft was gone, pulled under by the currents and torn apart. The sea chopped over the wreckage in a fury of cold, frothing water.

Somebody spoke. 'That was Harry Cullins's auld lerret, weren't it? He tried to sell it to me afore he died, but I heard it let the water in.'

'If it didn't then, it does now.'

One by one the islanders extinguished their flares and dispersed, walking off alone or in pairs. Some went to their homes, others to the inns, where not a word was spoken about the events of the night.

Down at Chiswell the fishermen pulled their boats up on to the pebbles, to find some of the revenue men waiting for them.

'Catch anything?' one of them asked the fisher folk.

'The moon was too bright. It frightened the bleddy fish off, that it did.'

'Mind if we search your boats?'

'Since when have you needed to ask? Help yourselves.'

When the revenue men shrugged and turned away, the fishermen went off towards the inn, laughing.

The four Weymouth men, eyes blackened, noses bleeding, supporting each other, staggered off down the road, hoping they had enough strength left to row over to Weymouth, and vowing never to return to the island.

The captains watched them go, grinning at each other, slightly shamefaced at the pummelling they'd given four complete strangers. Not that they'd got off altogether lightly. Thaddeus had a black eye, Edward had grazed his knuckles and Oliver was favouring his left side, where his ribs had taken a pounding.

'Charlotte will give me a tongue-lashing,' Thaddeus said, 'but, by hell, I enjoyed that little stoush, so it will be worth it.'

Edward pulled on his cap and straightened it. 'You

might as well be hung for a sheep as for a lamb then, Thaddeus. You're both invited back on board. I've got a keg of best brandy which needs the company of fine gentlemen to appreciate it, and I think we need to keep our heads down for a while in case the authorities start sniffing around.'

'Are you going to invite fancy pants back on board with us?' Thaddeus asked.

Edward began to laugh. 'Seth Adams can't tell good brandy from pony's piss. Would you believe he bought a keg of *Saggitario* from the Dunn brothers?'

There was a cackle of laughter from Thaddeus. 'What sort of idiot would do that?'

'The sort of idiot who knows a good ship when he sees it, though. He's bought the *Joanna Rose*.'

'I'll be buggered,' Thaddeus said.

Edward grinned. 'James Stark was signatory to the deal. Seth Adams is related to Barnard Charsford, and he got the ship for a song. Charsford is finished, and if by some quirk of fate Lord Durrington survives the tidal race, so is he.'

Dumbfounded, Thaddeus and Oliver stared at him, then Thaddeus said slowly, 'Seth Adams seems to be a wily sort of customer, despite the brandy. Heck, I bought a keg myself once, for my sins. I knocked the Dunn brothers' heads together and got myself a refund, of course.'

'Of course,' the other two said promptly.

Thaddeus ignored the sarcasm. 'What does the lad know about running a shipping company?'

'Nothing,' Edward said. 'But I'm sure it won't take

him long to find out. I think Joanna would like it fine if we were to assist him, gentlemen.'

Seth and Leonard had gone back to the cottage to collect the two women and the child, who was seated on his mother's lap, his head snuggled against her breast.

'Is everything over?' Tilda asked Leonard.

'Aye. Best we get you back home now, before the authorities come snooping.'

'Our mother and Ada Cooper are missing, Leonard. We'll have to report it.'

'It's likely that Brian killed them both,' Leonard said soberly. 'There'll be an enquiry. We'll go and see the authorities together in the morning. We'll tell them you went to visit Ma and found the pair of them were missing. Tell them that Brian took you as a hostage, then Lord Durrington and Bisley arrived. After they hit you over the head you became unconscious, and you can't remember anything else.'

'And what will you tell them?'

'That when I came to look for you, they set about me. Then they all ran off towards the shore, where a boat was waiting, and they got swept into the race. That will account for my bruises and your head injury.'

'I don't want to lie, Leonard.'

'It won't be a lie. We'll tell the law what they want to hear, within the bounds of truth . . . leave the others out of it, since the islanders won't say a bleddy word of what happened tonight. You know that. The authorities will think some contraband deal was going on. I'll come back later and bury a keg or two of *Saggitario* brandy in the cave. They won't entirely swallow the tale, since they're not fools. But they won't be able to prove anything different. Besides, there were several law officers among the islanders. I recognized a couple of them, including a magistrate.'

'What about me?' Joanna said, her blue eyes tender on her son as she attempted to gently untangle his matted curls.

'No need to mention you at all, since Toby's abduction has been kept from the authorities. Least said the soonest mended with that lot.'

Toby turned to gaze at Seth, his eyes half-hooded and sleepy from the caress of his mother's fingers against his scalp. Recalling how that caress felt, Seth envied him. The boy managed a half grin, flung out a hand towards him and murmured 'Papa' before his eyes closed.

Something inside Seth warmed, then melted, tears pricking his eyes. Joanna looked his way and gave a faint grin, even though she was exhausted and frantic with worry. 'Toby's not well, Seth. I've got to get him home and into his bed, where he'll feel safe.'

Assisting the women on to the cart Durrington and Bisley had arrived in, Leonard turned the horse's head around, then clicked his tongue. 'She'll make her own way home after she's dropped us off. Like as not she was taken from outside the inn. Bang on the bakery door on your way past, Seth, and the baker's missus will stable her.'

They overtook their seafaring companions on the way down. Seth was relieved to see the three men were still able to walk as the horse plodded placidly past them on the way downhill, for it seemed to know where it was going.

'We'll see you at the bottom,' Edward shouted out to him.

Seth's arm was beginning to hurt, but he was looking forward to meeting the captains after he'd settled the women.

Charlotte Scott and the Nash twins welcomed Joanna back with soft murmurs of concern, tears and hugs. How loving women were towards each other in times of trouble. It was beautiful to see. Toby was fussed over, and it was obvious Joanna was in good hands.

Charlotte gazed at him over Joanna's shoulder. 'Where's Thaddeus, Seth? Is he all right?'

'Perfectly, except for a bruised eye. Oliver has sore ribs, and Edward has collected a few grazes. Joanna will tell you what happened when she's got the boy sorted out. I'm off to join the others on the *Joanna Rose*. We need to talk things over.'

'No doubt you'll all have sore heads in the morning.'

'No doubt,' he said, his grin rueful in advance at the thought. 'But I don't know how I would have managed without their help.'

Charlotte's expression softened. 'They have a past together and are loyal to each other. You could be in worse company. Tell Thaddeus . . .' She shrugged and looked slightly sheepish. 'Well, just let him know I'm thinking of him, if you would.'

Seth's glance slid to Joanna. She was fully involved with the comfort of her child. But that was how it should be and he didn't resent the fact that she hadn't given him another thought since she'd got the lad back.

She proved him wrong. As if she'd read his thoughts, Joanna turned to gaze at him. Her eyes clung to his in a moment of intimacy, then her smile bathed him with radiance. 'Thank you, Seth. You've been wonderful.'

In all ways, he hoped, feeling himself grin all over. Seth let himself out feeling like a man with a new purpose in life after such a reward, leaving the women to their chatter.

How like her father Joanna was when she smiled, Charlotte thought. And she'd learned to put that smile of hers to good use. Seth Adams had been instantly smitten.

The four men were rowed back to the ship, and scrambled aboard.

The thought that this ship was his awed Seth. She was as beautiful as the woman she'd been named after. He wondered what to do with her as he stood on the deck and felt her gently move beneath his feet.

'Well, lad, what do you think of her?' Thaddeus asked him.

'That she's going to be quite a responsibility. I've only just realized how much organization must go into sailing and maintaining her.'

'You have a good manager to advise you. Henry Wetherall knows the business inside out and he'll do his job if he's left to it. Durrington kept undermining him.'

'I guess my first task will be to secure cargo and passengers.'

'We have Irish migrants waiting to board, and some other passengers already aboard. We were talking it over when we came down the hill. We could pool our money and supply our own cargo. We'll get a good return for it from the merchants in Melbourne if we auction it straight off the ship.'

'What type of goods?'

'Anything domestic. Clothing, fabrics, china, books, building materials, farming tools, tents, furniture, liquor.'

'*Saggitario* brandy?' Seth suggested wryly, and they all laughed. 'What about return cargo?'

'Mostly wool, some gold. Royal mail and passengers. There'll be a cargo waiting for us.'

'Provisioning?'

'Some provisions are already on board. We still owe for them, by the way.'

'I've only just bought the ship, but I'll honour the chandler's bills and crew wages, since we'll need both in the future.'

Although Seth didn't know it, his grasp of the situation and his single-mindedness were impressing his three companions.

'Provisions will depend on the number of passengers and the size of the crew. We're short of crew and a couple of officers. Since some of them heard Durrington was going under, they found berths elsewhere. But we can sail the ship short-handed if we don't take a full complement of passengers.'

'What about the Irish migrants? They would have paid their fares.'

'Aye, and most can't afford to forfeit them. But their fares are lost to you, so you won't have to honour them. The migrants would have brought most of their own provisions aboard, though.'

'I'm not about to rob the poor of their hard-earned cash, gentlemen. I'd rather lose money first up than lose the goodwill. If you explain the situation, can you pick crew up from amongst the Irish in exchange for their passage?'

'Aye. They'll also keep their quarters clean. Irish women seem to be able to fend for themselves, whatever environment they find themselves in. They're used to hardship and will help with menial work if needed, like taking a holystone to the deck.'

Excitement coursed through Seth, though he hesitated for a moment. 'What if I wanted to base the ship in Melbourne?'

The three gazed at each other and grinned.

'Good,' said Seth. 'I'm going back to London tomorrow. I'll have a cargo ready for you in one week, and I intend to stuff this ship to the gills. I take it you'll need a second in command, Edward?'

Consternation registered on Edward's face. 'You're not expecting to learn seamanship that fast, are you?'

Seth slid a wink towards the other two before he contemplated the captain. 'Not all at once, of course, but I thought that if I went to Melbourne with you, you could instruct me on the way. It shouldn't take long, and what better a way to learn a trade than taking a hands-on approach?'

'Did you now, mister?' Edward growled, looking

ready to throw him overboard. 'This is a profession for real men, not some fancy-pants weekend sailor, who doesn't look as though he can work up a sweat.'

'Perhaps you should teach me to dance the hornpipe, then?'

Oliver and Thaddeus exchanged a glance with Seth and the pair howled with laughter.

Seth chuckled. 'Don't fret, Captain. I wouldn't be foolhardy enough to come between a master and his ship. It just seemed to me that there's some skilled labour going to waste at the moment, so I thought Oliver might like to keep his feet wet, if you've got room for him.'

'Damn it, I'll take him and defer to him, for Oliver is a better master than I'll ever be.'

'No need for that, Edward,' Seth said with a smile. 'If I can make this venture pay, I might take on a partner, buy a second ship and expand.'

'And I might just know the perfect person,' Thaddeus murmured.

Seth nodded. 'I thought you might. Now, where's that brandy you promised us, Edward?'

When Thaddeus patted Seth on the shoulder, pain shot through him. Letting out a groan, he clapped his hand over his arm. Blood seeped through his fingers.

'Jesus, he's bleeding,' cried Oliver.

They helped him into Edward's cabin and uncovered his arm.

'There's the tip of a knife broken off in there, and it will need a stitch or two after it has been removed,' Thaddeus said. 'Fetch the surgeon's bag, would you please, Oliver.'

'Bring the surgeon with it,' Seth added hopefully, as an afterthought.

Thaddeus planted a hand on his stomach as he tried to rise. 'Don't panic, lad. I've done this hundreds of times before, and every one of my victims survived.' He turned to Edward. 'We'll clean the wound with that brandy, then pour a dram or two down his gullet. It will help calm him. Chin Lee, see if you can clean up his coat, and find him a clean shirt. We can't have the new owner looking like a ragamuffin.'

Thaddeus inspected the wound. 'It's a good sharp cut and should heal as clean as a whistle. How did you come by it, lad?'

'Bisley's knife. I got between it and Toby.'

'That's what comes of playing the hero to impress a lady.'

Seth said seriously, 'Do you think Joanna was impressed then?'

Thaddeus grinned. 'Aye, lad, she couldn't fail to be. Now, stop talking and take a slug of this. It's real brandy.'

The brandy was excellent when applied internally. On the surgery it hurt like hell, but Seth wasn't about to let them know it. Afterwards, he drank some more and listened to the seamen's tales with a warm glow of contentment. The adventure of it all fired him up. It was a good feeling. Later, Chin Lee took out a flute and Thaddeus taught him how to dance the hornpipe, to the guffaws of the other two. Eventually, they all collapsed on to chairs and opened another bottle.

'What name will you register the new shipping company as?' Edward asked.

Head buzzing, a brilliant idea occurred to Seth. He smiled expansively at them all. 'The Shegle Sipping Company. Jonah likes shegles.'

'No Jonahs are allowed aboard the *Joanna Rose.* That deserves a toast, gentlemen.' Grinning at the others, Edward refilled Seth's glass for him, then held up his own glass. 'To the Shegle Sipping Company, then.'

'The Shegle,' they said solemnly and clinked glasses.

Seth carefully placed his glass on the table, slumped sideways in his chair and began to snore gently.

There were grins all round. 'What's a shegle?' Oliver said.

Edward refilled the glasses. 'Beats me.'

Thaddeus shrugged as he examined the contents of his glass. ''Tis a female gull, I reckon.'

The twins had gone upstairs and were talking in low voices, making plans.

Charlotte and Joanna sat by the fireside. Toby had been bathed and his wounds properly cared for. Now he slept in his mother's arms.

'He should be in bed, dear.'

Joanna refused to part with her son. She gently kissed his curled palm. 'Not tonight, Grandmama. I want him to forget what happened and begin to feel safe again. And I can't bear to have him out of my sight yet.'

'It's been a bad two years for you, my love. First Alex, then this.'

'We have to go forward. I'm going to tell Tilda

everything tomorrow. She had to face her past tonight, and although she was trying to be brave, she was shattered. History nearly repeated itself. Her brother tried to force himself on her in that cottage.'

Horrified, Charlotte stared at her.

'Oh, he didn't succeed. Yet Tilda risked her own life and put my son first. It made me realize how very much I love her. I owe her too much to just go off to Melbourne without another word.'

'And what about Seth Adams? Don't you owe him something?'

Colour rose to her cheeks. 'Obligation doesn't come into our relationship. In the first place, he was working for Lord Durrington, so I could never quite bring myself to trust him until right at the end.'

Charlotte gasped.

'But even so, I allowed him . . . we became lovers.' Joanna closed her eyes, remembering the exquisite lovemaking that had occurred between them, something more passionate and gloriously intimate than she'd ever experienced before. Her eyes came up to Charlotte's. 'Seth has never mentioned marriage. What if he doesn't love me in the way that I want him to?'

'But, my dear—'

'He never told me so. I thought he did once, but I may have imagined it because I wanted him to so much, and I had been drugged. Oh, I'm so mixed up. He might not even respect me now, since mainlanders are different from the islanders in that respect. I've never loved anyone as much as I love Seth. Not even Alex, and I feel so guilty because I thought I would love

Alex for ever. But I rarely think of him now, my mind is filled with Seth.'

Charlotte smiled at that. 'You mustn't feel guilty. It's not healthy to grieve all your life, and you're too young to remain a widow.'

'Why aren't you shocked, now I've told you my secrets?'

'Oh, Thaddeus and I were lovers for years. It started not long after your grandfather died, and I felt as you do now. We're not meant to live life alone. Alex wouldn't have expected you to remain celibate, I'm sure he wouldn't have.'

Or even remain faithful, Joanna thought sadly.

'But as I was going to say earlier, anyone with half an eye can see that Seth Adams is totally besotted with you. He strikes me as being a man who likes to do things his way, but will listen to reason.'

'He certainly does like his own way,' Joanna said darkly. 'I didn't expect him to lock me in the back room.'

'He did it only to protect you from harm. I didn't think you'd be so foolish as to climb out of the window.'

'I'd climb the highest mountain to find my son.'

'And so would he. Be guided by that man, Joanna, my dear. In return he will nourish and protect you every day of your life, and he'll work only to ensure your happiness.'

'But what if he doesn't want me, now?'

Charlotte's smile was complacent. 'Don't be so ridiculous.'

*

The magistrate cleared his throat and began to read from a piece of paper.

'29th day of November 1859. Portland. Having heard the sworn testimony of Tilda Lind and Leonard Rushmore, it is the finding of this enquiry that Fanny Rushmore and her paid companion, Ada Cooper, were murdered by the escaped prisoner, Brian Rushmore, and, furthermore, that their bodies were disposed of by means unknown. It is further found that the said felon, Brian Rushmore, a person known to the courts for violent acts towards his fellow men, as his court record will attest to, and who was under the sentence of life imprisonment at the time of his escape from Newgate prison, perished along with Charles Durrington, peer of the realm with the esteemed title of Earl, and his servant, known only as Bisley, who were conducting business together with the said felon when their boat was swept into the tidal race off Bill Point, and was taken by God's hand into the deep. It is concluded that the conspiracy of the men involved an attempt to smuggle brandy without the payment of due duty. Kegs of illicit brandy marked *Saggitario* were found hidden in caves nearby.'

A ripple of laughter went through the people in the court.

The magistrate, who'd been on the clifftop two nights before and had caught a cold for his trouble, gazed severely around him and banged his gavel on the bench. 'Justice has now been done and the matter is closed. May God rest their souls. Amen.'

*

As they were heading back home a horrible suspicion came into David Lind's mind. He'd found Fanny Rushmore's crutches lying beside an open grave, which had been filled with mud, washed there by recent rainfalls. He wondered if he should dig up Jimmy Upton and take a look.

He decided against it. Tilda had been through too much already, and something else was worrying her.

His heart went out to her when she threaded her arm through his and said, 'Are you happy living here, David?'

He wasn't. The islanders were mostly methodists, and they were self-sufficient and insular. His congregation was too small and nobody needed his help. David was looking forward to the birth of their child as something that would make him feel slightly less redundant.

Sometimes he thought his nature wasn't suited to being a minister of the church. The routine of it bored him, and when he prayed for guidance he rarely received an answer. People were stiff with him, treating him with a deference he didn't deserve, so it set a distance between them. His retiring nature often made him awkward with people too, and he was happiest when he was studying, or helping someone less fortunate than himself. Often he thought he might like to do something else. Teach, perhaps.

'I'm happy to be where you are, Tilda. What's troubling you?'

'There are too many bad memories here. I still can't go near my father's cottage without feeling ill.' A rueful smile touched her mouth. 'I seem to have no connection with the island now my mother's gone.'

'What about Joanna?'

'Joanna and I love each other, but I've always needed her more than she needs me. Joanna follows her heart.'

'And you sense she's going to spread her wings and fly away from you?'

Tears in her eyes, Tilda nodded miserably.

David turned her round to face him. 'My love, Joanna has her own life to lead. You have to let her go.'

'I don't think I can bear living here without her. We've been through too much together. She's had something on her mind for some time. Now she wants to talk to us.'

'Then let's wait and see what she has to say.'

'There's another thing, David. It's about my ma.'

'What of her?'

'Can we put a headstone in the churchyard? Although we didn't get on, it doesn't seem right that there's no record of her passing. It's as if she never existed.' There was a moment of hesitation. 'I don't think Brian did away with her. He was expecting her home when I turned up at the cottage.'

Alarmed, David gazed at her. 'We could put a headstone in the corner of the churchyard, over where Jimmy Upton is buried.'

Tilda offered him a wry smile. 'You know, when you found her crutches I had the strangest thought that she might have fallen into Jimmy Upton's grave and he was buried on top of her.'

David began to perspire. 'So did I.'

Tilda chuckled and, after a while, so did he. As they continued walking, David relaxed.

Five minutes later, Tilda murmured, 'You don't suppose she did fall into Jimmy's grave, do you?'

18

Joanna had not expected Oliver to go sailing off on the *Joanna Rose*.

He came back that morning, a jubilant smile on his face, to pack his bag, and said, as he emptied his pockets into the money jug, 'There, I won that from Edward and Thaddeus at cards last night.'

'Sleight of hand,' Thaddeus grumbled.

'Where's Seth?' she asked them both.

'Aboard the Dunn brothers' fishing boat, on his way back to London. He should just about be waking up by the time they get him there.'

Exasperation filled her then. 'Didn't he even send a message?'

'Only to Tilda.'

'Tilda? What about?'

Oliver elbowed Thaddeus in the ribs and said vaguely, 'I couldn't rightly say, since I didn't read it. Besides, in the state he was in he couldn't even think coherently, let alone write, but he did mention you several times, didn't he, Thaddeus? He waxed poetic. How lovely your eyes are, your hair the colour of midnight.' His glance ran down her body, 'Your delightfully . . .'

Joanna had never seen Oliver in such an ebullient mood. 'That's enough from you, Oliver Morcant. You two are hiding something. What is it?'

'. . . sweet temper.' Oliver grinned and took her face in his hands to thoroughly kiss her.

'Oliver?' she said in surprise. 'Will you kindly behave yourself.'

He laughed. 'I've always wanted to do that, but don't worry, I won't do it again. Thanks for everything, Joanna. Say goodbye to my sisters for me, and tell them I love them and will be back for them.'

'Wait a minute,' she said as he headed for the door. 'We were all supposed to go to Melbourne together.'

'The ship has changed owner. We've decided to go later in the year. The weather will be better for sailing in early April, anyway, and it will give everyone time to properly decide about whether a move to Australia is what they want, and to prepare for it.'

'Who owns the *Joanna Rose* now?'

Oliver exchanged a glance with Thaddeus, who grinned before he said, 'The Seagull Shipping Company.'

'I've never heard of them.'

'It's new, but I'm sure you'll hear of it in the future.'

Leaving Toby with Charlotte to mind him, Joanna went up on the hill with Thaddeus to watch the ship leave.

Tears filled her eyes as the sails filled with wind and the *Joanna Rose* headed out of the harbour.

Thaddeus handed her his handkerchief. 'There's a sight to gladden the heart. She's in good hands with my two lads, and she knows it.'

'I'm going to miss Oliver. I enjoy his company.'

'You were there when he needed you, my dear. You lifted him up, gave him a place to rest his head and restored his faith in women. But his heart and soul belong to the sea, just like his father before him. I bet Lucian is the proudest seagull in the sky.'

'Oh you,' she said, and laughed, for the sky was full of seagulls, soaring, wheeling and diving. 'Come on,' she said, 'we'd better get you back home, otherwise you'll miss the steamer. I know Charlotte wants to get home.'

Later in the week, Joanna gazed down at her son. He'd recovered well from his ordeal except for some slight soreness where he hadn't been kept clean. Once he'd begun to drink he'd lost his fever, and although his nose was still a bit sticky he'd only been suffering from a slight cold. Her robust little son was recovering quickly.

Toby was so very precious to her. Joanna blew against the soft skin of his neck to make him giggle.

'More, Mama.'

Toby started laughing as soon as she pursed her lips again, all quivering anticipation. Joanna felt a momentary regret that Alex wasn't there to see him. But she must not look back, she reminded herself. There was no point.

After reducing Toby to a paroxysm of giggles again,

she wrapped him in a shawl, then took a rolled-up canvas from her wardrobe. 'We're going to see Aunt Tilda today, and you've got to behave yourself.'

But Toby had other ideas and began to leap energetically up and down on the bed. The bed thumped on the floorboards.

Downstairs, Irene and Lydia had just finished dusting. They grimaced as more dust floated down. Then something shiny dropped on to the couch.

Picking it up, Irene said in astonishment, 'It's a florin.'

Lydia stood on the couch for a closer look. 'There's a crack at the side of the beam where it goes into the wall. I think it came out of there.'

They took it up to Joanna. 'We think it fell through the ceiling, and we wondered if it came from under the floorboards, by the dividing wall.'

It was with great excitement that they found the loose floorboard, which had been sawn through. It came up easily. Underneath, hard against the beam, was a hessian bag. Mice had bitten through it and coins spilled through a hole in the rough material. There was a crack at the side of the beam, the width of a coin.

Joanna lifted the bag out carefully. 'It probably belonged to Brian Rushmore.'

'What will you do with it?'

'I doubt if Brian came by this money honestly, so I'll give it to David Lind to help the poor. Aren't you two going to the academy today?'

The twins gazed at each other and laughed. Irene said, 'It's Sunday, had you forgotten?'

'Her head is full of more important matters – the handsome Seth Adams for example.'

'Papa,' Toby yelled, and flopped on his back.

Tilda was painting a design on a piece of paper, a seagull with wings spread, flying against a blue background. She tried to cover it, but wasn't quick enough.

'That's pretty. Is it for a card?'

'No, it's a design for . . .'

Tilda gazed at David, who finished smoothly, '. . . a stained glass window. Come into the sitting room, Joanna, there's more room there for the children to play, and less mischief for Toby to get into. I didn't see you in church this morning.'

'Sorry. I forgot it was Sunday.'

'Easily done,' he said. 'What did you want to talk to us about?'

Joanna would have rather talked to Tilda alone, but the pair presented a united front, and she tried not to resent the fact that Tilda seemed to be growing away from her. She was genuinely glad that her friend was so happy and settled, though.

Toby was kept entertained by Grace while Joanna told the dumbfounded Tilda about the relationship she'd had with her first husband. 'That's why the marriage record was missing. When Richard Lind found out, he tore the page from the church ledger. On his death bed he asked Charlotte to destroy the evidence. So she did.'

David gave a disapproving shake of his head. 'My uncle tampered with parish records?'

But Tilda placed a hand on his arm. 'Hush, David. He was trying to protect Joanna. If this had happened to you, would you want records left as proof, when you know how condemning people can be? Why didn't you tell me this before, Joanna? I would have understood.'

'There's more, Tilda. My father faked his own death. He's still alive and is living in Australia under a different name. He's married again and has a family.'

'So that's why you went to Australia?'

'I went to Melbourne to find him, to let him know I was all right, and loved him for what he did to protect my good name. He gave up everything he had, for me. But the trouble was, others had begun to work the situation out too. Everyone on the island knew I was washed ashore in the storm and that Anna and Joseph Rushmore had taken me in as their own.'

'Nobody thought any the worse of you for it.'

'It was Charlotte who first noticed the resemblance I had to my real mother, and she who alerted Tobias to the fact that I was possibly her granddaughter.' Joanna unrolled the canvas. 'You remember Honor Darsham's grave over in the churchyard. This is her. My real mother.'

Tilda sucked in a deep breath when confronted by the blue-eyed, dark-haired replica of Joanna. 'There's no mistaking the resemblance, and she's wearing your rose brooch, the one your ma gave you.'

Joanna's fingers went to the brooch. 'No, I'm wearing *her* rose brooch. Didn't you ever stop to wonder where Ma got it from. She couldn't have afforded to buy it.

'Even Seth managed to piece the story together. It ended up that everybody but you knew. James Stark said we could be charged with conspiracy, and I could go to prison for committing bigamy, though how could I be charged with that when my shipboard marriage to Alex wasn't legal in the first place? It's all too complicated for words, and the lie has grown too big to handle, so we're all going to Australia to live.'

'All of you?' Tilda stared at her, wide eyed.

'Well, all those who want to. Me, the Nash twins, Thaddeus and my grandmother for a start. Seth doesn't know I'm going,' she said, miserable at the thought of losing him.

'Oh, I imagine he does. He's as thick as thieves with everyone now, even our Leonard. I'm surprised you haven't noticed.'

'Seth Adams is an enterprising young man,' David said. 'He seems to act positively when an opportunity presents itself.'

'What an incredible pickle you managed to get yourself into,' Tilda said, giving a little giggle.

'All of which could have been avoided if you'd simply got the marriage annulled,' David said sternly.

'Or had been allowed to drown in the first place. I wasn't offered a choice of either option, since others acted on my behalf. David, would you concede, perhaps, that God took a hand in deciding my future?'

He smiled. 'You have me there.'

Tilda collapsed on to a chair and doubled up with laughter, choking out, 'This could have only happened to you, Joanna. If you'd only stopped to think in the first place, instead of rushing headlong into marriage with a man you hardly knew.'

'Quite,' David said, which made Tilda laugh even harder.

'This is not funny, Tilda.'

'Oh, it is, it is, Joanna, my love. David sounds like a stuffed shirt, and you sound like a wounded donkey. Don't you realize that this story is so incredible that nobody in their right mind would ever believe you if you told them the truth?'

'I suppose it does sound a bit far-fetched.'

'Quite,' said David for the second time.

'Now I'll tell you our secret. David found a broken gin bottle and my mother's crutches in the cemetery. We think she got drunk, passed out, then rolled into Jimmy Upton's grave and was covered in mud. It's more than possible that he was buried on top of her.'

Although they shouldn't have, both women began to howl with laughter.

David rolled his eyes and grinned. 'How can I maintain any dignity with you two around?'

'You're much more lovable without any,' Tilda said.

'Quite,' Joanna said, and brought out the bag of coins. 'Irene and Lydia found this hidden in the cottage. We think it might be Brian's ill-gotten gains. With Christmas not far away, I thought you might be able to use it for the less fortunate, David.'

Tilda exchanged a glance with her. 'Since it might be the last Christmas we spend together, I hope you and the twins will celebrate it with us. We intend to invite your grandmother and Thaddeus. Mr Adams is invited as well.

Joanna's smile faded as she said quietly, 'I haven't heard from Seth. But my Christmas turkey is fattening up nicely, and I'll contribute it to the dinner.'

Seth had been working non-stop. He'd managed to obtain a cargo of mixed goods, and with a sense of satisfaction had watched the *Joanna Rose* sail over the horizon with a full payload.

He'd been busy ever since, dealing with the legalities and trying to learn certain aspects of running a shipping company. He'd also had a stroke of luck, with Bart Seager willing to buy into the detecting agency. The invaluable Geevers was happy with the arrangement.

But others were not so fortunate. Barnard's properties had been seized, leaving Constance very poorly off.

As Seth had suspected, the Earl of Alsonbury had disowned Barnard, and had named Constance's eldest son as his heir.

Constance told him, 'Albert is now thirteen, and he hardly knows me. But he's doing well at school, and so is Thomas, so I don't want to disrupt their education.'

'It would be unwise,' he agreed.

'The earl said he's prepared to continue being their benefactor as regards to their schooling. I'm invited to visit him and my sons for Christmas. He wants to discuss our future.'

'He will have it all decided, Constance.'

'I know, but I have little choice. The earl said he might

be prepared to make a cottage on the estate available to me, if I'd act as companion to the countess.'

'Who will run you off your feet. The boys are your sons, Constance. May I offer you an alternative? Compromise. Allow the earl to educate the two eldest, since one is to inherit the title. Thomas will provide companionship for him.'

'And my two youngest? They are only seven and eight years old.'

'I'm going away shortly, perhaps for good, since I think it better that Kate be brought up abroad, and also I'm thinking of taking a wife.'

'Joanna Morcant?'

He nodded. 'That's if she'll have me. My feelings for her are very profound.'

'She's an independent young woman, but a courageous one. I do hope she accepts your proposal.'

'Either way, I intend to keep my property in London. You and your sons are welcome to reside in my house, and there's a perfectly good church school nearby for the younger boys. I attended it myself. I shall make you an allowance, which you can use as you see fit, and all the household bills can be handed to my accountant. There will be no conditions attached to this offer, and in all household matters you can act on my behalf.'

A smile lit her face. 'I'll be for ever indebted to you.'

'As I will be to you for your help. Because of it, Joanna's son was restored safely to her.'

'Thank you. I accept.'

That arranged, Seth turned his mind to Joanna.

He'd received an invitation to spend a few days with Thaddeus and Charlotte Scott.

We're going to spend Christmas day with the Lind family, and Tilda has asked me to extend an invitation for yourself and your niece to do the same, Charlotte had written.

That he'd found approval with Joanna's grandmother and friends was not lost on Seth.

He and Kate travelled down the week before, spending the extra time doing some shopping. Seth consulted with Kate as he carefully selected gifts.

It was cold, and a few snowflakes drifted down from the sky. Her nose pressed against the glass of the shop window, Kate looked sweet in her warm blue coat and fur-trimmed bonnet. There was a permanent smile on her face, and she'd been the essence of good behaviour for her hosts.

He said, 'What do you think we should give Joanna for Christmas?'

'She said she needs some sheep.'

Seth smiled at the thought. 'That's not a very good idea, Kate. They'd stink the carriage out and their feet would go through the tissue paper they were wrapped in.'

Kate giggled.

'I'd prefer something more personal. What about that gold locket, there?'

'But Joanna has all those jewels she gave you to sell.'

'Those belonged to her mother and I intend to give them back at the appropriate time.'

She slid him a smile. 'I like that little brooch with pretty stones on. Uncle Seth . . .?'

He cocked an eyebrow. 'What is it, Kate, my love?'

'Will we marry Joanna?'

Kate had a strong romantic streak. 'I don't think this is something we should discuss now. What will you buy Joanna?'

'That little beaded bag with the butterflies on we saw in the other shop, I expect.' She gazed sideways at him, her face wearing a sweetly serious expression, refusing to be put off. 'If you marry Joanna, can I call her Mother?'

'With her permission.'

She scooped in a deep breath. 'So, can I call you Papa, instead of Uncle Seth? It will be the best Christmas present ever.'

Surprised, he gazed down at her, warmed by the simple request. 'If it pleases you, Kate, I'd be very proud to be known as your papa.'

'Thank you . . . *Papa*.'

'My pleasure, *Daughter*.'

As they exchanged a grin, Seth knew exactly what to inscribe on the brooch with the pretty stones he intended to buy for Kate.

Joanna had efficiently necked the turkey she'd been fattening up for Christmas.

It had met its fate without fuss the week before. Placing its neck under a broom handle with her feet at either side. Joanna had tucked its body under her arm and given it a quick jerk to break it. Its insides then drawn, Joanna plucked the bird of its feathers and hung it by its feet, allowing the blood to drain into a bucket. The procedure had left the meat white and deliciously tender.

Now it was in Tilda's oven, the skin turning a crispy brown while Joanna basted sizzling lard over it. The kitchen was warm, pots steamed on the range and the house smelled of Christmas pudding.

Irene and Lydia took turns minding the children, alternating their task with setting the dining-room table. Holly and mistletoe decorated the house, and gifts had been piled high on a table. Leonard had arrived with his family earlier.

Tilda was taking a rest. She was large and ungainly now. Joanna thought her friend had mistaken the date, and the baby might come earlier than expected. But they could only wait and see.

She closed the oven door and straightened up from her task, pushing a stray strand of hair back from her face as she did so. Her heart gave a leap as she heard David talking to someone. Then her grandmother and Thaddeus came through to greet her. They exchanged smiles, Christmas wishes and hugs.

Behind them came Seth, his hair ruffled by the wind. She hadn't really expected to see him, though she'd placed a present for him on the table, one of her most treasured possessions, a book of poetry Richard Lind had signed and presented her with on her eighteenth birthday. And for Kate there was a book and some paints.

The hubbub of other people around them faded. Her feelings for Seth crowded in on her. Was it obvious to everyone in the smile of pleasure she gave at seeing him? 'I didn't know you were coming.'

'I didn't know you'd be here, but I hoped.' Their glances joined, and they remembered being together.

Joanna smoothed her apron down over her skirt, then patted her hair. She was hot and flustered from the oven. Why couldn't he have arrived after she'd tidied herself up?

Her smile was uncertain as she murmured, 'Seth. I look so untidy.'

'So you do.' He gave a slow, intimate smile. 'I've missed you.'

'And I've missed you.'

Thaddeus looked from one to the other, grinned, then steered Charlotte into the other room.

Kate came in and was scooped up in Joanna's arms, where she received a kiss and a long cuddle before being set on her feet again. 'Hello, Miss Mischief.'

Self-importantly, Kate stated, 'My papa has something important he wishes to say to you.'

Seth pointed to the door. 'I'm not doing this with you looking on. Shoo!'

'Doing what?' she said when Kate skipped off, grinning from ear to ear.

Seth crossed to her in two strides, took her face between his palms and gazed into her eyes. 'Joanna, it would make me the happiest man alive if you would marry me.'

'Of all the times and places to propose,' she grumbled, staggered by the simplicity of his declaration and the deadly timing, just when she was rushed off her feet and was likely to accept, just to get him out from underfoot. She grinned, knowing she would have accepted wherever the proposal had taken place.

'I want you to know that I love you, and Toby. I'll be a good father to him.'

'Thank you, Seth. I believe you will.'

'You'll have me then?'

She remembered the plans she'd made for her future – that they'd all made.

'There's something I should tell you. First, I want to remain here on Portland until Tilda's baby is born. And . . .'

He placed a finger over her mouth. 'Shush, woman. I know, and there's something you need to know before you say anything else. I've bought the *Joanna Rose*, and I intend to run her from Melbourne, so if you decide to wed me, that's where we'll be living.'

So, Seth had known her plans all the time and he'd arranged this surprise for her. How thoughtful a man he was. She smiled and whispered, 'Damn you and your tricks, Seth Adams, I adore you.'

He kissed her then, a tender yet insidious caress that weakened her at the knees – a kiss that was abandoned only when they heard giggles and saw Grace and Kate gazing at them from the doorway.

At the end of January Tilda gave birth to her son. It had been a long, hard birth and Tilda was exhausted.

'Look how beautiful he is, Tilda,' Joanna said, taking the squalling infant from the midwife after the doctor had departed, and placing the child in Tilda's arms.

A tired smile lit Tilda's face as she cuddled him close. As she began talking soothingly to her son he settled against her breast, his complaints about his painful birth fading into a few protest noises before he fell asleep. By the time he woke up he would have forgotten all about it.

Then began the admiration ritual as the midwife made Tilda comfortable.

'Look at his tiny fingers. You can see the light through them.'

'He has your hair, Tilda.'

'David's ears.'

The boy was inspected from head to toe, exclaimed over while Tilda fell in love with her handsome son. Tears in her eyes, she suddenly said, 'He resembles my uncle, Joseph Rushmore. We could use his name, and David's uncle's name. Joseph Richard Lind. Do you think David will agree.'

'He will agree to anything you want. Joseph and Anna Rushmore will be so proud when I tell them.'

'You still visit their graves then, even knowing they stole you from your real folk?'

'They loved me and I loved them. They're always in my heart, so nothing will ever change that, Tilda. I must go and tell them I'm leaving soon.'

'I wish we were going to Melbourne with you, Joanna. I'm going to miss you. It would have been nice for our children to grow up supporting each other, as we did.'

Joanna kissed her cheek. 'I'll miss you too, my dearest friend. But it will be a few weeks before we leave, so you'll be well and truly over the birth by then.' Her glance went to the midwife, who'd bundled the soiled sheets together and was about to depart. 'Leave those in the outhouse, Mrs Scrivens. I'll soak and boil them, then hang them on the line to dry.'

'Thank you, Mrs Adams.'

Mrs Adams? A big grin appeared on Joanna's face at the contentment she felt. David had performed the ceremony just a week before. Seth, who still had loose ends to tie up, had gone back to London afterwards, gazing with awe at the shopping list she'd presented him with, and leaving Kate in her charge. Joanna wouldn't see him again until he returned with the ship to pick them up.

She found David downstairs in the sitting room. He was reading a letter and smiling to himself.

'You can go up and see your wife and son now, David. He's a fine boy. Congratulations.'

'I have some news for Tilda, but I'll tell you first, Joanna. I've been offered the appointment of headmaster at a new Anglican school in Melbourne. Not only that, but the Church has made me a good offer for this house. With Tilda's permission, I intend to accept it.'

Throwing her arms around him she hugged him tight. 'Oh, David. I'm so happy for you. Tilda married such a wonderful man and I'm so pleased that we won't live apart.'

'Thank you, Joanna, my dear.' She sensed the excitement in David when he kissed her cheek. 'You know, I was given no choice in the profession I trained for. On the whole, I've been contented, but I'm looking forward with eagerness to the adventure of pastures new.'

'You'll make a wonderful headmaster, and I shall send Toby to be educated by you. I'll try and teach him some manners before then, though.'

David looked gratified by the thought.

'Now, you must go and take a look at your new son before Tilda goes to sleep. She's totally exhausted. And don't you worry about anything. One of us will visit every day until Tilda decides she's well enough to kick us out. And Grace can come over to play with Kate and Toby every day. That will keep them all occupied and leave you free to go about your business, for you'll have plenty to do if you're coming to Melbourne.'

It was at the end of April when the *Joanna Rose* put into Portland. There was a soft breeze blowing showers across the sky, and the daffodils had turned the landscape to gold.

A steamer was waiting to take them and their luggage to the ship. Joanna could see Thaddeus and Charlotte, who had boarded in London.

Irene and Lydia talked in excited voices and waved furiously to Oliver, who looked totally at home pacing about the deck and issuing orders while he tried to hide his grin.

James Stark had decided not to join them, after all, but would stay in London and help Henry Wetherall conduct the business of the Seagull Shipping Company.

Leonard was there to see them off. Invited to go with them, he too had decided to stay behind, saying simply, 'Kirsty doesn't want to be parted from her folks.' Now,

Joanna handed him the key to the Rushmore cottage. 'This is for you, Leonard. The cottage will bring you in some rent. Or you can sell it.'

'But it's yours, Joanna.'

'I was never a Rushmore, you know that. But I loved Joseph and Anna, and they gave me a good, loving home. This time I'm not coming back, but I don't want to think of their hearth and home standing empty and neglected, so I'm placing it in your trust.'

She gazed at Seth. 'My heart lies elsewhere now. I must live my own life.'

Seth came forward with a smile on his face to help his family safely on board. Their eyes met, and clung. 'I've missed you,' he said and hugged her tight.

The only furniture Joanna had brought with her was the cradle she'd floated ashore in. She had a feeling she'd need it once Joseph Lind had grown too big for it.

A flag was run up the mast, and unfolded into the breeze. It was a silver-winged gull flying against a background of midnight blue. The last time Joanna had seen that design it had been on Tilda's work-bench.

Seth slipped an arm around her waist as they gazed up at it. He whispered. 'For you, Joanna, my love, the Seagull Shipping Company. Tilda designed the company flag for me, and I hope it will remind you of the people who made, shaped and loved you.'

How lucky she'd been to have such a man fall in love with her, and to love in return. 'Thank you, Seth. I know it always will.'

As the shadows lengthened, the ship became a hive of activity.

They sailed away into the soft golden haze of evening. Gradually, the sun dropped below the horizon and the mist rose to veil the isle of Portland.

Joanna stood alone at the railing, watching her past life retreat. She thought of the Rushmore cottage, the home of two loving people who'd raised their foundling child with a simple and honest dignity, the way they knew best. As long as it stood, that cottage would always retain the cherished memory of what had been before.

She was leaving behind four graves, too, people she'd meant something to. People she'd loved. Their graves would remain untended now. The stones had mellowed long ago, but the wind would blow the seeds, and the wildflowers would bloom in the cracks in the cemetery wall, season after season. The grass would grow long and they would be left to rest undisturbed.

Alex would rest alone in London, the place he'd loved with a passion. Such a waste of her first love's life, but he would live on in their son, and in his sons after that. Joanna would never forget any of them.

When a seagull came to perch on the railing she smiled through her tears and said simply, 'Thank you for giving me my life, Lucian.'

The bird made a noise in its throat, then rose on a current of air and circled the mast before soaring into the sky and back towards the island.

Joanna turned to find Seth behind her. 'I was saying goodbye to my past.'

'I know.' The smile he gave her was tender. 'But it's making you melancholy. Come here, my love. I've missed you.'

Joanna went into the arms of her future, and left her island ghosts to their rest.

POCKET
BOOKS

The Stonecutter's Daughter

Janet Woods

Dorset, 1838. The evening after a violent storm, a taciturn stonecutter prowling the Portland coast in search of plunder finds himself in possession of the most priceless treasure of all: a crying, hungry baby girl strapped securely in her cradle has miraculously survived the battering of waves. With no children of their own, Joseph Rushmore and his wife adopt the infant and bring her up as their daughter.

The child blossoms into a beautiful young woman, blissfully ignorant of the extraordinary truth about her origins. But Joanna Rushmore's happy childhood is about to come to a shattering end. For the past cannot be kept hidden forever, and the secret of Joanna's birth is destined to catapult her into a future she could never have dreamed of, causing untold heartache, an impossible dilemma, and – finally – a passionate love.

ISBN 0 7434 8400 2
PRICE £5.99

POCKET
BOOKS

Beyond the Plough

Janet Woods

Now a wealthy young widow, former peasant girl Siana Forbes has overcome her humble beginnings to become mistress of Cheverton Manor, the handsome estate which her infant son, Ashley, will one day inherit. When the man she has always loved, country doctor Francis Matheson, asks for her hand in marriage, it seems her happiness is complete.

But trouble lies ahead. An unexpected tragedy means Francis must leave for Australia – a land where danger and hardship await. Left behind to raise a growing family, Siana too has problems when a sinister figure from her past emerges, determined to cause havoc. And a terrible ordeal suffered by her stepdaughter on the night of the harvest supper leaves Siana with a heartbreaking choice. Will she be able to overcome the odds stacked against her and keep her family together? And will she ever be reunited with her beloved Francis?

ISBN 0 7434 6800 7
PRICE £6.99

POCKET
BOOKS

A Dorset Girl
Janet Woods

When her mother and stepfather perish in a fire, Siana Lewis finds herself destitute, with a younger brother and sister to support. Although her prospects seem bleak, Siana's beauty and intelligence will attract the attention of three men.

Daniel, her first love – the man who will betray her.

Francis Matheson, the village doctor, who admires Siana's determination and thirst for knowledge.

And Edward Forbes, the local squire. A sensual and devious man, Edward is used to getting what he wants. He desires the beautiful peasant girl from the moment he sets eyes on her – and he's determined to have her. Whatever it takes.

'A thoroughly enjoyable saga with a delightful heroine and vivid characters' Anna Jacobs

ISBN 0 7434 6799 X
PRICE £6.99

POCKET
BOOKS

A Handful of Ashes

Janet Woods

After an unhappy period apart, Francis and Siana Matheson have settled into a loving marital relationship in their comfortable Dorset home. Siana's only sorrow is that so far she had been unable to bear her husband another child. Francis, however, is content to be a father to his grown-up daughters and his young son, Bryn, born while he was overseas.

But Siana is hiding a secret. Although she hates keeping something from her husband, the need to protect all concerned has left her with no choice. She must keep quiet and live with the guilt of her deceit.

No one can keep the truth hidden forever – and when Siana's shocking secret bursts into the open, there will be tragic and far-reaching consequences for the close-knit Matheson family.

ISBN 0 7434 8401 0

PRICE £6.99